LADIES
IN
WAITING

ALSO BY
GWEN DAVIS

NOVELS

The Aristocrats

The Motherland

Kingdom Come

Touching

The Pretenders

Sweet William

The War Babies

Someone's in the Kitchen with Dinah

Naked in Babylon

POETRY

*How to Survive in Suburbia
When Your Heart's in the Himalayas*

Changes

LADIES IN WAITING

A NOVEL BY

GWEN DAVIS

Macmillan Publishing Co., Inc.

NEW YORK

Macmillan Publishing Co., Inc.

866 Third Avenue, New York, N.Y. 10022

Collier Macmillan Canada, Ltd.

Library of Congress Cataloging in Publication Data

Davis, Gwen.

Ladies in waiting.

I. Title.

PZ4.D2617Lad   [PS3554.A9346]   813'.5'4   78-26192

ISBN 0-02-529850-X

First Printing 1979

Printed in the United States of America

For Bob Gutwillig

Some take a lover, some take drams or prayers,

    Some mind their household, others dissipation,

Some run away, and but exchange their cares,

    Losing the advantage of a virtuous station;

Few changes e'er can better their affairs,

    Theirs being an unnatural situation,

From the dull palace to the dirty hovel;

    Some play the devil, and then write a novel.

—LORD BYRON, *Don Juan*

Acknowledgments

My deepest gratitude to Dr. Leroy Davidson and

his wife Martha, for an extraordinary education in Sri

Lanka and its art. My thanks to Tony Liebig and Kathy Hallberg

for involuntary illumination in the Law.

LADIES
IN
WAITING

1

¶ Rumor was Abby Cochran's party would be attended by
Gloria Stanley, movie star, victim, heroine, hysteric. So at first
there had been a crush for invitations. Abby's phone hadn't
stopped ringing with acceptances, even from those who hadn't
been invited. More people wanted to come than could be
accommodated by the Jeffersonian Club.

Movie stars made Washingtonians provincial, set them jumping to their feet, gaping like children, which even the presence
of Presidents and history couldn't do. Presidents merely made
them grow hushed, fitfully respectful, attentive, as if something
grave hung in the balance, like their jobs. In many instances
this was exactly the case.

But movie stars made them giddy, happy, especially as
Hollywood had taken the heat off Washington, finally, mercifully, generating juicier scandals, like in the good old days.
Once again greed and abuse of power were back where they
belonged, sort of: in the ranks of civilians, lustrous civilians,
most lustrous of whom was Gloria Stanley. People couldn't
wait to meet her.

The occasion for the party was the publication of a new

novel by Chris White, Mrs. Jess Betzer she was called in the social columns, but not too much lately. Abby's hostessing the party was an affirmation of their friendship. No one of importance in Washington could easily turn down an invitation from Abigail Cochran, whose pale, patrician good looks sat harmoniously on what was an obvious nobility of character.

If she had been any other woman in the world, she could not have carried so gracefully the name Abigail. Gentle of manner, generous of spirit, she could be rationally resented by no one: an impeccable woman in a city that breakfasted on flaws.

Naturally there were some who tried to despise her for her kindness. There was about her a glow of such honest affection for the human race that it gave rise to suspicion of hypocrisy in hypocrites, and searches for ulterior motives in those whose lives were riddled with them. Since her husband was in politics, it was assumed that she was subordinating her character to his, as was the wont of all well-behaved Washington wives.

The truth was Abigail Cochran was exactly what she seemed. She considered life a gift, sharing the better part of it with her husband, her children, her friends, and anyone else who needed it. Her warmth was such that people forgave her her obvious breeding and style, and servants would have dedicated themselves to her, could she have afforded them.

That she couldn't, that she and Larry Cochran struggled perilously close to the edge of financial disaster, was in an age of political corruption a tribute to him. He had long moved in the circles of power, where an opportunity for enormous gain was omnipresent, and did not always involve selling out the country. So it would have been understandable, considering the financial pressures they were under, if Larry had accepted some favors.

Everyone in Washington accepted favors; the city was founded on exchanges, just as countries had been bought, goodwill for beads. That the prices had escalated was only a sign of the times; on this particular day in November, a dark one.

Abigail had risen before dawn, her habit when she wanted

to get centered, so that the coming events, no matter what they were, would not throw her off balance. She walked in the woods along Chain Bridge Road, made breakfast for the family, got them off to school and office. Then she closed her eyes for a few minutes before reading the paper, as if she could draw from inside herself a healing balm that would make the news be better.

It didn't work. Above the usual disasters and man-made terrors and several grueling issues that excited Washington glared a headline proclaiming, "Hiro Takeda Eludes Justice." From the sound of it, Dillingerish. The facts were less exciting: Hiro Takeda, the Japanese businessman suspected of bribing various government officials, had not been present at his home when men from the Justice Department had come to question him. Nor had he been found at the Jeffersonian Club, of which he was owner, or at his office. There was a rumor that he might have left the country.

Normally, Abby would never have bothered to read past the first sentence of such a story. But Hiro Takeda was a man she knew and liked, and the party for Chris was that evening at the Jeffersonian. That Hiro had chosen that moment to make what the reporters were already describing as his getaway boded ill for the evening. If there were too many clouds over the club, people wouldn't come.

She sat with her hand over her mouth, numbly staring at the words, her pale blue eyes expressionless. Shadows played along the hollows of her cheek, darkened the ash of her hair, matched the parts of her mind where she wondered if Hiro was guilty. No one had ever really known where all his money came from; there had been no loud questions about it till recently. That he had been lavish in entertaining had seemed benign enough to those who accepted his hospitality, which had included half of Washington. Then the ugly part started, sinister allegations, rumors of his being a foreign agent. He had become highly suspect even in the few remaining places where a man was presumed innocent until proven guilty.

She had considered changing the locale of the party to a

country club, but the invitations had been sent out too long before: everything was more or less settled. Chris, for whom the party was being given, was also a friend of Hiro's and didn't want it to seem as though everyone was deserting him. Hiro had called and said he would be unable to attend.

Abby was grateful to him for sparing them all the embarrassment. It was a terrible way to feel, ungenerous, but she couldn't help it, she was relieved. Press receptions were difficult enough without scandals attached to them. As it was, the loftier crowd was likely to make its excuses simply because the party was at his club. She wasn't sure even her own husband could afford to come. Especially with the latest headline.

She called Chris several times to reassure her. But both of them were anxious about the evening ahead, in spite of the fact that there had been such a struggle for invitations.

Abby had deliberately trimmed the list of too heavy seekers, blatant strivers, a trick it had taken her many years to perfect, balancing a guest list. Invited were mainly those involved with the arts, some lobbyists, a few token ecologists, and a number of the Beautiful Famous, people so chic they had abandoned *Women's Wear Daily* for *W*.

The honoree, Chris Betzer, one of Abigail's closest friends, was a woman whose talent was matched only by her insecurity. Slender and dark, she viewed the world with chocolate eyes lightly coated with anxiety, fearing failure as children fear being abandoned. The party loomed for her as Dickensian, filled with cruel characters who would not even appear at the orphanage to refuse to adopt her.

"Nobody's going to come," Chris said to Abby on the phone.

"Everyone will," said Abigail, and wondered.

¶ By seven-thirty the downstairs of the Jeffersonian Club was actually crowded. Already on tap, caftan blossoming with sequins hand sewn, sent from Rome by a dear friend of Gore Vidal's, was Louise Felder, the most powerful agent in Hollywood. The honey of her hair had hardened to brass, as had the honey of her mouth, and she had given up the battle against weight waged twice yearly at the Golden Door. But behind her eyes were still some traces of battered innocence. As Chris's agent, she stood near Chris's side like the mother of the bride, not quite affectionate enough to hold her hand, not quite cold enough to let her be alone.

"Well, here we are in the new entertainment capital of America," Louise said. "Any minute MCA-Universal is going to run a tour through this party."

"Does it seem all right to you?" asked Chris.

"I don't know," said Louise. "It's hard to tell. I haven't seen this many dark suits in one place since I moved to California, except at funerals." Louise looked appraisingly around the room. "Or this many stiffs."

By the ten-foot-tall grandfather's clock next to the doorway a footman dressed in lace ascot and bib, burgundy velvet vest, coat, and knickers held out a silver tray on which those entering the party placed formal calling cards and inscribed invitations. The footman did not blink or acknowledge the presence of life by smiling or seeming to breathe. Only his left hand moved, passing the calling cards and invitations to the security guard who sat behind a table, checking them with a list. There were two more security guards stationed discreetly near the entranceway. They had been told to try to be inconspicuous, so both had dressed in tuxedos. They would have looked like waiters except that the waiters at the Jeffersonian wore the garb of the eighteenth century. So what the two looked like was overdressed security men.

It was not unusual for there to be private security forces at the better parties in Washington. A man who could afford to serve good food could also protect his guests. The presence of "security" always had implicit in it the hint that the President might be coming, or the First Lady, or someone of high political import. And if no one controversial showed, the guests at least would know their host thought highly enough of them to protect them from thugs, crashers, and ordinary press.

It was the capital of the world, Washington, no matter how the doomsayers ranted about its fall, its failures, its headlong descent into ignominy. Citizens who hungered for power still coveted being there, diplomats from other countries still maneuvered to be transferred to it for the comfort, the physical beauty, the comparative ease of life. And there were still, of course, Americans who believed what the country was supposed to be about and so aspired to political office to help the country be that way again. But nobody talked about them too loudly, especially at parties.

Pragmatism, not idealism, was the order of the day, pragmatism larded with lobbying, exchanging favors, secreting information. So it was all the more remarkable that Chris Betzer, living in the midst of it, had been able to write Washington novels in a romantic fashion, making them palatable and interesting to the public, not loading them with too much inside knowledge. She was a keen observer and understood as much of politics as politicians did. Perhaps a little more, bringing to the scene an intuition deeper than observation and a tolerance for being sent into the other room when the men had something "important" to talk about. At Washington dinner parties women were still ushered off by themselves after dinner while the men had brandy and cigars, as if there had been no movement in history for several hundred years.

Chris was a beautiful woman who had not been a pretty girl, unsure of her looks, grateful for men's attention. She was used to capturing women: they had always liked her for the warmth and the wit she'd overdeveloped to make up for not being pretty. But like her mother, she preferred the company of men and considered their chauvinism merely a symptom of knowing they had the edge. As a result, in spite of the fact that she was considered a triumph of women's liberation, a high earner, a self-starter, unencumbered by the prejudices against the softer sex, Chris had yet to be liberated from herself. The most foolish man could make her feel inadequate by seeming not to like her. A smart man could throw her completely off balance by seeming in love.

These were not things Chris discussed with her friends, least of all her agent, Louise. There stood Louise, as smart as she was overwhelming, ready and anxious as always to deal, to trade her way to the top. And it was no longer a sin. A woman could be aggressive, smart, and have a big mouth: people enjoyed it. As long as she was successful, of course. The world had turned a circle and a half, done a curtsy to the girls. But there was still no forgiveness for failure.

"Be careful of every word you say," Chris suddenly cautioned Louise, as she saw the blonde woman in black, jeweled pen extending over the little notebook she carried, coming toward them.

"Well, Madame Authoress," Charlotte Dean said, smile tightly serene. She was a tall woman, pencil slim, silver blonde hair coiled tightly into a chignon, one loose blonde lock escaping, like leaked information. "How does it feel having your party at the scene of the crime?"

"What crime?" asked Louise.

"Who's this?" Charlotte asked, smile disappearing, face cold, a little too perfectly chiseled for its place in time. She pointed at Louise with her jeweled pen.

"Louise Felder," Chris said, "this is Charlotte Dean, the *journalist*," she tried to warn Louise still again.

"Felder," mused Charlotte. "The *Hollywood* agent?" The adjective carried contempt. "Are you in town for business?"

"I'm representing Chris's novel for movies."

"Do tell," said Charlotte. "I thought she had a reputation for literacy that didn't go over too well on your shores."

"Fortunately I have someone working for me who translates books into two-page memos that give no hint of style or intelligence," said Louise. "That way they sell."

"Well?" Charlotte looked back at Chris. "What's your comment on your pal Hiro?"

"I don't know the facts," said Chris.

"I'll bet," said Charlotte. "And what about your best friend, the hostess herself, not showing up?"

"Abby'll be here," said Chris. "She went to pick up someone at the airport."

"Sure she did," said Charlotte. "Well, mustn't be *too* hard on her for not coming. After all, Caesar's wife must be above reproach. Especially when Caesar works for 'Jimmeh.' " She filled the southern pronunciation with her teeth and venom at the same time, smiled and walked away.

"What *is* she talking about? Who didn't show up?" asked Louise.

"Abigail Cochran. She'll be here," Chris said, nearly with conviction.

"Charlotte Dean," Louise mused. "The famous Charlotte Dean. God, if only Bette Davis were younger, I could sell her life to the movies. What a horrible woman. Why did you invite her?"

"I didn't. Hiro had her barred from the club. She wheedled an invitation out of the banker who sponsored the loan to build this place."

"And they talk about manipulation in Hollywood," said Louise.

The women at the party seemed to have dressed not so much for cocktails as for the Style section of the *Washington Post*. Most of them wore black, which photographed well. One or two besides Chris were in colors. Chris was wearing lavender crepe de chine, which softened the black of her eyes and warmed the olive tone of her skin, accenting her dark brown hair. It also made her look vulnerable. An artist friend of hers had told her once that pastels made her less intimidating to men than she might be in red, for instance. She had laughed because it had never occurred to her that she could intimidate any superior species. The laughter over, however, she began reappraising herself. Could she possibly intimidate Scott Tamplin?

Scott. As precise and crisp a name as the man himself. She could see him pressed against the wood-paneled wall, the cut of his jacket giving his wide shoulders perfect symmetry. He seemed set at a slight angle, as if avoiding himself, in subtle apology that a brain like his should be housed in an admirable body. Gauzy light from a coach lamp softened the white of his hair, warmed the icy grey of his eyes. He did not actually look at Chris, or she at him.

That he was married, that they both were, did not account for this curious nonmeeting of eyes. It was a game that had developed between them. Only when they played backgammon could they acknowledge their desire for each other, locking irises as other lovers.

They played twice a week at the club, Chris and her husband Jess, Scott and his wife Elise. When they played, Scott clicked his chips with fastidious rhythm. He moved his men on the board with the assurance of a general maneuvering an army. His eyes never darted around the room as did those of the anxious and ambitious but fixed themselves on Chris's face as if to memorize her between each move. They never touched except when they handed each other the dice, the tips of his fingers only grazing her palm. It was the most subtle, sophisticated lovemaking she'd ever experienced. Chris was mad about him.

Once years before they had been completely alone, in the anteroom of a private box at the Kennedy Center, attending a concert. Both were late getting back from intermission, and seeing they were unobserved, moved toward each other with a swiftness that surpassed thought. His lips on hers, gentle, seeking as a schoolboy's, radiating sweetness.

"When?" she whispered against his mouth.

"Oh, God, I hope it's soon," he said, and touched her breast.

It hadn't happened yet. She was almost crazy.

It added to the dismal horror of her husband's being out of work, his hanging around the house so she couldn't call Scott. It added to the unforgiving grudge she bore Richard Nixon, that Jess Betzer couldn't get a job. Such a good man. Such a generous man. So capable. Unable to make a single connection that led to employment since he'd left the White House in 1974. Even those who'd been in jail were making money, but Jess, who'd been above reproach except for his loyalty to Nixon, could not find work.

Miraculously he hadn't become a drunk, or impotent. There was no external sign of his anguish. Only in his eyes, his pale green eyes, where the laughter used to sit, was the terrible evidence. She pitied him. What had once been love was now pity, and irritation that he was so uncomplaining, so decent in his defeat.

Watergate had destroyed the lives of several men, but the untold tragedy, the really sad tale, was what it had done to the wives. Not the ones who loved their husbands and stood valiantly by, waiting in court, writing autobiographies, but the women who didn't want to be with the men they were married to, to whom history had granted a curious reprieve.

For the two years of crisis their husbands hardly ever came home. When they did they were too weary for conversation, much less sex. The phones would start ringing at six in the morning as day after day revelations in the *Washington Post* poured out. It was a drama that kept even the most boring marriage going, not knowing where it was leading, how it would end.

And then the President was gone. He was out. It was over. And all the husbands came home. Women who had not had to deal with loveless marriages for two years were suddenly sand-bagged by reality. A number started drinking heavily; those who already drank became alcoholics. The bravest saw lawyers—the few who were not busy defending conspirators.

Divorce in Washington was still something women didn't do, especially if they couldn't support a family. Chris was one who could but had never thought she would have to. That she had become the monetary head of the household stunned her. It didn't occur to her to divorce Jess, however. In the beginning of his obsessive, crisis-ridden career with Nixon, she had been left free to lunch with Scott. Lunch was all they had had, brilliant lunches that massaged her brain with his journalistic insights. Then the lunches had ended, abruptly. "I'm having fantasies about you," Scott said. "Elise is very intuitive. She knows." "Why do they have to be fantasies?" Chris asked. As if in cold answer, he was gone, transferred by the network to England.

Now he was back, and they weren't even free to pursue the heat of their attraction by phone. Jess was always home.

Divorce in Washington occurred when a woman had someplace else to go, which in Chris's case was nowhere. She had a daughter and a son; they needed a male figure in their lives. She still took solace in the strength of Jess's physical presence; he was an imposing man, barrel chested, long limbed. There were robberies and burglaries and rapes in the District; she was glad to have him around.

The District was flagged with women who thought they could make it on their own, never dreaming that that was how they'd really have to make it. Men were at a premium: the ratio was two women to one man. The thinking of the town was basically southern, and so was its view of love. Gloria Steinem was no heroine here. Gloria Stanley was. She was rich, desirable, sought after, the consummate movie star, an enviable woman who'd had the grace to stay dependent on men.

Chris knew for an unpublished fact that Gloria was miserable and lonely when not in the midst of a grand amour, that she was bored most days, at a loss about what to do with an ordinary moment. But those things were beside the point to the women of America. That was not the stuff that magazine stories were made of. Women who admired Gloria Stanley admired her mainly in gloss. They were not interested in the truth of Gloria Stanley's life any more than Gloria Stanley was.

There was a flurry of activity by the entranceway, the dazzle of flashbulbs popping. Mimsy Watkins, Penelope Calder, and Claire Wolsey Mackenzie, the three dowager duchesses of Washington arts and letters, looked up from laps that contained plates of canapés to whatever was causing the stir. Miss Watkins, the baby of the group, having not yet broken eighty, moved to her feet with a trace of the energy that had freed her from "Miriam" and made her "Mimsy."

"I think she's here," she said excitedly. "Gloria Stanley!"

The security men in their tuxedos moved swiftly past the waiters carrying trays of quiche lorraine and smoked salmon and stationed themselves on either side of the door to the main salon. They had about them a curious quiet that might have passed for serenity were it not for the constant restless movement of their eyes. It was one of the tricks of their trouble-some trade, in searching crowds for a hostile face, a nervous demeanor, a too-quick motion that might herald a gun. Not for a moment was it imagined that anyone would inflict bodily harm on a movie star. But both these men had protected Presidents and knew how to watch a gathering. Like football players in off-season, there was frustration in being unable to show off their prowess, so they liked to look vigilant at the least opportunity.

"Oh," said Mimsy dejectedly. "It isn't her."

"It isn't who?" asked Diane Trejinska, looking in Mimsy's direction. She was letting herself be known as the countess again, although it had been nine years and three marriages since she'd divorced the count. She flowed into the club, a flurry of rust pajamas, a rust satin turban wrapped around her thick red hair so only her widow's peak showed. Chains looped delicately around her throat. Little golden infinity signs twisted about her celebrated flat bosom. Her nails were dynasty length, lacquered in the same shade of rust as her costume. She held them poised in front of her, as if ready to do battle with Barbra Streisand.

"Those are the Three Graces," said Abigail Cochran, coming up beside her. She was wearing a street-length beige wool dress, a single strand of pearls transforming it into elegance. "They're waiting for the curator of the Smithsonian."

"Oh," said Diane. "For a minute I thought I wasn't good enough."

"You're more than good enough," said Abigail. "You were an angel to come."

"As if I could turn you down," said Diane. "As if anyone could."

Abigail moved through the crowd, greeting friends, extending her cheek to be kissed, squeezing hands. Composure sat like a light coat of makeup on the even features of her face, the wide-set blue eyes, the aristocratic forehead, the straight thin nose with its slightly flared nostrils. She was a woman in charge of herself, in charge of the life around her, which seemed to take on a sudden calm with her appearance.

Chris hugged her. "Charlotte Dean thought you might not be coming."

"Well, isn't she full of wrong information!" Abigail laughed. "I'm sorry we're late. The traffic from Dulles was impossible. I think it took Diane less time to come from Paris than from the airport. Of course you know each other. Christine White Betzer, our honoree . . ."

"We've met," said Chris, smiling warmly, extending her hand to Diane. "This is my friend Louise Felder, Abby Cochran, Diane Trejinska."

"Not the erstwhile countess!" Louise exclaimed.

"Lulu!" said Diane, and giggled. The two women embraced.

"I can't believe it," said Louise. "Everywhere I go I run into you. The Bistro. Elaine's. A whorehouse in Morocco."

"Excuse me," said Abby. "I have to powder my nose."

Louise looked after her. "I didn't even say it was a male whorehouse."

"Abigail is a *poquito* straight-laced," said Diane. "She's Quaker or something noble. She'll warm up to you after a while."

At the piano in the corner, a stockbroker noodled the score of *Anything Goes*. A busty, chocolate black woman resplendent in white leaned over and fed him scotch from a crystal glass, humming along with him. Every few bars she took a sip herself.

A group that had flown down from New York huddled at the side of the bar, exchanging publishing gossip, worrying glasses of white wine. They were instantly recognizable as distinct from the Washington crowd, less by the cut of their clothes than by their attitude. They seemed intent on each other instead of the whole room, so it was easy to tell they weren't in politics.

Jess Betzer watched them from his vantage point on the arm of the sofa that cradled the three dowager duchesses. "Is there anything more I can get you ladies?" he asked Claire Wolsey Mackenzie.

"How kind," she said. "I'm fine."

"And I," said Mimsy.

"Then if you'll excuse me," he said, angling his dark handsome head so that he seemed to be bowing away from them, backing out of their presence as though they were oriental potentates.

"What a pleasant young man," said Penelope Calder.

"What does he do?" asked Claire Wolsey Mackenzie.

"He works for Mr. Nixon," said Mimsy.

"Not any more," said Penelope. "He's given up politics."

"Mr. Nixon?" asked Claire.

"No," said Penelope. "The nice young man."

In the ladies' room Abby Cochran stood by the mirror repairing her makeup. Preening was a bother to her: she liked the shine of her skin, enjoyed feeling a glow, showing it. But she had respect for the people around her and knew how it rattled her particular society when anyone seemed too open, too free. So she combed her hair in a traditional pageboy, sprayed it stiff, Republican, and powdered and lipsticked according to the current modes, so her spirit wouldn't show.

"You mustn't mind about Louise," said Chris, standing next to her. "She just talks salty to shock."

"I don't mind," said Abby, lips stretched to receive red gloss. "I know they like colorful people in show business."

"You think the party's okay?"

"It's perfect." Abby reached over to squeeze Chris's hand. "You're perfect. You look like a million dollars."

"So do you," said Chris. "Thank you for getting Diane here."

"Oh, it wasn't me. It was the time of year. She was bored. She'd never flown on a Concorde. I hope Larry doesn't find out that's how she came in or we'll never hear the end of it." She waved her hand in the air, despairing about pollution. "Ozone. As if there weren't enough on the ground to keep him worried."

"That's what happens when your husband is a humanist."

"Please," Abby said. "You mustn't use words like that around Washington. Someone will think he's un-American." She smiled. "How's Jess?"

"Deeply depressed," said Chris. "But you'd never know it to see him at a party."

"I don't understand," said Abby. "Such a lovely man. So bright. Isn't there a sign of a job?"

"Nobody returns his calls anymore. They know why he's calling."

"It's so unfair," said Abby. "It's not as if he were involved with criminal charges."

"Guilt by association," said Chris. "They wonder why he was loyal."

"Maybe I could . . ." Abby bit her lip. "Maybe there's something with Sri Lanka."

"With what?"

"The arts council of Sri Lanka. They're trying to stimulate interest here in their painting and sculpture. There's some gorgeous work from there, you wouldn't believe the treasures. They've asked me to lend a hand, their cultural attaché has, introducing their work to Washington. Maybe I can get Jess a job with them."

"Doing what? Art isn't exactly his strong suit."

"He's an executive. A good executive can execute anything."

Chris kissed her. "Thank you. Thank you for even thinking about him. That's more than anyone else has done."

"I don't know how you manage to keep it afloat."

"Jess would do something if he could. He's the nicest man in the world."

Abby looked at Chris's reflection in the mirror. "But you still love Scott."

Chris looked away.

"You know it will never go anywhere."

"I understand that," said Chris. "But I can't stop loving him."

"You have two beautiful children and a fine man who adores you. I'd just hate to see you do anything foolish."

"I won't," said Chris. "Scott won't give me a chance to." She put fifty cents in the ashtray for the ladies' room attendant who sat dozing in the Regency chair in the corner. "Well, back to the battle."

"Is this all very hard on you?"

Chris pushed open the pink satin quilted door. "Where is it written it's supposed to be easy?"

¶ The way you could tell how badly Megan O'Flannagan had been beaten was by her posture. Her eyes continued to glisten bright blue, the way they always had. Her teeth were almost baby small, her smile baby bright. Her nose had an optimistic tilt—and her hair was orange. There was nothing red about it, no way one could use the euphemism. It was orange. She looked like a beautiful Orphan Annie, with eyes.

She had yet to speak to anyone at the party; she could barely muster a smile. Nor could she keep from slouching.

When she had come to Washington at twenty-three with her degree in economics and her experience writing copy, her posture was as good as her qualifications. She quickly emerged as a *wunderkind,* falling into a job at the Bureau of Consumer Affairs, becoming its spokeswoman to the media. The reporters were so taken with her they made her a hit, interviewing her, putting her on the evening news, quoting her whenever possible, sometimes unnecessarily. Within a few months she was at the same dinner party with Eric Sevareid, which meant she had really arrived. She fell deeply in love with him for ten minutes until he told her he didn't like bright women, they made him nervous.

She became a borderline celebrity. Hostesses invited her. Somebody told her Sally Quinn didn't like her.

With it all, she worked very hard and did her job well. She exercised religiously to keep herself slender, which she was not by nature. It was also a good way of wearing herself out, since the only men in Washington she found attractive were married.

When she was asked to work for the Ford White House, she had been flattered and shocked. Her interview seemed to her unsatisfactory—she was too awed at being inside the actual building to be at her best—but they hired her anyway. She became a special intermediary to the press, who handled her sympathetically, feeling, as they did, that they had created her.

In the White House, every minute was exciting. There was always a crisis, a slip, a reaction, something that had to be fielded, amended. She had never thought any job could be that consistently exciting. Except that after a while excitement was boring. What really seemed exciting was the idea of peace.

On the campaign trail there was no such thing as respite. There were reporters, backers, and voters every way you turned. The same speeches every night, only in a different place. The same roast beef, only on a different plate. She would close her eyes sometimes, at the banquets, and hear the speeches and chew: the taste in her mouth blurred with all the bland tastes she had ever experienced, the words of the candidates blended with all the words.

She was too tired to be lonely. All the energy she had felt when she first arrived in Washington seemed to have been eaten out of her. Power was a worm that corrupted from the inside.

To her horror, she found out she was addicted to it, along with a little booze. Politics was a constant upper: even the bad news stimulated you. So you needed a little something to come down at the end of the day, and you weren't even conscious of the moment the words began to slur. She made constant memos to herself so that she wouldn't forget conversations. In the morning most of them were undecipherable.

She was so drained from relating to people on a one-to-one-thousand basis, she was incapable of relating one to one. In that, her psychologist friend Howard Kummer told her, she was like professional politicians.

She was also like them in that she was constantly lobbying not only for her candidate, but for her own survival. What was once energized ambition had become egocentric drive, cloaked in the respectable guise of presidential campaigning. She hadn't known how deeply she wanted to win until election night.

When she awoke in a puddle of loss, and stale champagne, the whole election seemed a gross unreality. America was a test of character, and she had failed. There was nowhere she could go to get her power fix: the White House would be off limits after January 20, 1977. Her voice had an edge to it now, like her nerves.

Her friend Howard had gone to a retreat in New Mexico to learn how to meditate and sent her an ecstatic letter. She knew from some CIA research that meditation could be used for mind control, and mind control in Russia was used to shape events. It struck her that in the course of becoming peaceful she could also manipulate those around her. And maybe get off the booze.

So she went to the desert. She did not tell anyone where she was going, or why. The silence weighed so heavily on her soul that for a while she nearly forgot herself. But Washington reclaimed her: the minute she returned to the city she was all open sores of ambition.

Now she stood in the midst of the party with her arms crossed in front of her chest, her shoulders rounded. She tried to bring to the clatter around her the knowledge that everything passed, that nothing could be clung to, that expectations brought disappointment. It had all worked in the desert. But what she needed in the Jeffersonian was a drink.

The man at the piano had switched to a Jerome Kern medley. The black woman in white was sitting beside him now on the bench. Her expression was the same as it had been: a party smile was on her face, glistening, toothy, blinding. But twin trails of mascara were coursing down her face now, as if she had found, in the lyrics or scotch, the secret of sorrow.

Megan moved toward the bar, tried not to seem too intent in getting there, tried to sidestep Charlotte Dean, who swooped toward her like an elegant harpy. "Megan!" Charlotte said. "I heard you were out of town!"

"I was."

"I mean really 'out of town.' Out to lunch. Out to pasture." The jeweled pen was poised above her notebook, the only flashy accessory in a basic black ensemble. "I heard terrible rumors about you."

"Probably all of them true," said Megan.

"First I heard you'd had a breakdown. Then I heard you found God. I don't know which upset me more."

The black woman on the piano bench started to sing. Charlotte winced slightly. "Wouldn't you know Melissa Mae would be the only one of them without natural rhythm."

"Excuse me," said Megan, and continued toward the bar.

"But where were you? Silver Hill? Were you drying out?" The voice continued, mellifluously relentless.

Megan turned. "I was learning compassion."

"That's a hot one," said Charlotte. "Where?"

"In the desert," said Megan. "That's a hot one, too."

"I love it!" said Charlotte, and started to write. "Where do press secretaries go when their candidates die? To the desert to learn compassion."

"It's an interesting study," said Megan. "You ought to try it sometime."

"I don't want to go anyplace but *Washington*," Charlotte said, giving a musical turn to the name. "Certainly not to learn anything stupid like pity."

¶ Scott Tamplin lingered in the alcove at the foot of the stairs, icy grey eyes appraising the party as if it were a potential story, alert for headlines. He was not at ease at parties. He was at his best interviewing, and there was no one present he particularly cared to interrogate with the exception of Chris.

There were some old buddies there from Dartmouth, who still went to reunions and refused to slip gracefully into middle age. He himself had danced rather silently into it when he was thirty-one, having decided he had everything he needed, a profession that welcomed his incisive intellect, a wife who was independently wealthy, a son who would doubtless grow up and go to Dartmouth, and white hair. So there was nothing lacking in his life, certainly nothing to take a risk over. He programmed himself subtly to maintain a personal status quo.

It was this balance, his calm demeanor, that led politicians to think they could level with him, as much as politicians could level. It was also this seeming serenity that had drawn

Chris to him, all the time she was trying to convince herself that what she was seeking was information. There was no doubt the man had clarity of vision, at least where the news was concerned. People's motives were no puzzle to him. He saw why everyone behaved the way they did. The only thing that confused him somewhat was that Chris loved him.

He was a startlingly handsome man, very tall and angular; but as he did not judge by appearances, it surprised him that someone else would. He had watched her feeling for him grow, over lunch, during Nixon. He had seen the obsessive joy she had taken in the man's fall, and equated it with the disappointment she felt with Jess. He himself felt fond of Jess, admiration for his loyalty, no matter how misplaced. Scott was also fond of his own wife, so an affair was out of the question. The town was too small. There was no real discretion: there were only promises never to reveal, which were eventually broken. Ben Franklin had said three men could keep a secret if two of them were dead. Scott supposed Chris could have an affair and no one would know it if she had her eyes removed.

Her remarkable eyes, that peered into him as if she could see his soul, convincing him for flickering moments that he had one, and it was immortal. Their lunches had become ritualistic, touching as they did on politics, spiritual aspiration, and food, all of it camouflaging why they were there. He gave her the Associated Press *Almanac*. She gave him Carlos Castaneda. She touched a part of him he thought had died when he was twenty. The transfer to England had come just in time.

And now he was back; his son was at Dartmouth, Carter was in the White House, everything seemed to be in place, including Elise. She sat on a corner of the couch in the Jeffersonian surrounded by the women she went shopping with, miraculously uncomplicated, angered by nothing except perhaps that she could no longer count on the quality of Italian shoes. He had no wish to hurt her, ever. Nor did he wish to unsettle the equanimity of his life. It was enough to play with Chris over backgammon.

He could see her legs coming down the stairwell, the best

legs in Washington. Long, gently rounded, cloaked in nylon sheen. As she reentered the party, Abby Cochran behind her, he reached for Chris's arm with his fingertips, and let them brush her skin.

"You have never been more beautiful," he said in the tone that rounded up how the world was, what the truth was. Then he turned and walked away.

Chris stood staring after him, dry tongued.

"Come on," said Abby. "You have a party to handle."

A waiter was passing tiny steak teriyaki on wooden sticks, to be reheated in the flame that danced from the miniature hibachi in the center of the tray. By a potted palm in the entranceway a photographer readied his camera for the coming of Gloria Stanley. It was still not certain that she would arrive, but he'd already taken pictures of all those there who were in any way notable. The photographer was a fan of Gloria Stanley's. He was so excited at the prospect of her appearing that his hands were sweating and his Nikon kept slipping. He worried about moisture on the lens. He anguished about an unflattering angle.

Gloria Stanley. The ninth wonder of the world. A woman so heartbreakingly beautiful that women adored her as much as men did. Her very failure in love gave constant hope to ordinary women. Maybe their eyes were not the color of Kir, white wine slightly darkened with cassis, but when they awoke in the mornings their husbands were beside them. Snoring, perhaps, but there.

Gloria Stanley, a legendary figure, cast in a statue's mold, breasts high, swanlike neck carrying her gracefully through every erotic defeat, gold hair waving in the wind as she sailed around the world on other people's yachts, caught in the telephoto lenses of the paparazzi. Her unhappiness, the darkness of loss that played behind the light-colored eyes lent her a nobility that surpassed beauty. A woman like that should have left a trail of broken men. But men had left a trail of Gloria.

The photographer knelt, aiming the camera at the front door, got to his haunches, turned his Nikon sideways, resumed a standing position, pressed the button on his flash attachment, smiled as the light split the air. "Hey, Charley," said the man behind the desk. "What are you doing?"

"Making sure everything's operational," Charley said. "I want to get a perfect shot of Gloria Stanley."

¶ The limousine pulled a little too close to the curb outside the Jeffersonian Club. Whitewalls squeaked against cement, rubbed black. The driver had been sneaking a look in his rearview mirror at the woman who sat in the back, her head lolling like a rag doll's against the grey velvet upholstery. He'd been so entranced he hadn't judged the distance properly.

So many men had tripped, floundered, run their cars up on sidewalks, driven their ships aground, thrown their marriages into the toilet, distracted by her, that a chauffeur in Washington scraping his wheels made not the slightest dent on her consciousness. Gloria Stanley sighed, hugged her mink tighter around her celebrated body, and prepared for the martyrdom of adoration.

When too many people loved you it was the same as having no one. Everyone assumed you were busy all the time, knowing how sought after you were. The truth was that hours and days came up empty, telephones haunted by their stillness, roses died in their vases as no new would-be lover pursued, convinced he was one of many.

In fact, there were never many, unless you counted hairdressers, clothes designers, free-floating faggots, fans, and employees whose life you were. But lovers, friends, were a different story, most of them, in Gloria's case, short ones.

She had been brought up on movies. Like a lot of her generation she was more impressed by reality as manifested on the screen. Love, war, the essentials, had been better done by MGM than by life, Gloria felt. Life never offered conclusions: it ran longer than a couple of hours. So no matter how neat a package it presented at any one moment, it was deceptive, an Indian giver taking away what it had offered the moment before. Undying passion. Youth.

She started to sigh, but even as she felt the breath go out of her body, she caught a glimpse of herself in the same rearview mirror that had almost undone the driver. She was more exquisite now than she had been when she was eighteen. Years had taken the roundness from her cheeks, given them angles, a high arch beneath the eye that spoke of aristocracy or Hungarians. She was one of those blessed creatures who grow more beautiful with age.

Age. The very word was an insult. Death had a breathy, mystical sound, as if there were something at the end of it, the hint of a hope, aspiration. Death did not sound as final as age.

Well, here she was, aging. Beautifully maybe, but for how long? She was one of the most sought-after women in the world (she'd read that enough times in countless papers and magazines). What puzzled her was how few people caught up with her, seized her, carried her off, made sure she lived happily ever after. Knocked her unconscious.

She believed it all, the myths, the movies, the fairy tales. She had come into life with a perfect face and a perfect attitude for being a star. She resented no one, never got angry unless she thought of good dialogue, enjoyed being pampered, pedicured, fussed over, celebrated, hugged. What surprised her was how easily those who spoiled her abandoned her. Apparently not everyone in the world had seen the same movies.

She had first become a star when she was nineteen years old, when females still mattered on the screen. There had been about her a tremulous innocence which made everyone want to protect her, especially women. She herself hadn't much liked women once. They were hard to relate to, because she didn't know what they wanted, whereas men very obviously wanted her. She had never been in a room where a man had his eyes on anyone else.

So she wasn't used to friendship. But now she coveted it, had gone two cities out of her way to appear at this party, because she admired Chris. Chris and Washington both. Each seemed to have a purpose unconnected to romance. Without romance, Gloria had always considered suicide, running away, overeating. That a woman and a city could function not on that level seemed inspirational, if terribly baffling.

"How long will you be, ma'am?" the driver said, opening the door.

"I haven't the least idea," she said. "How late do these things usually run?" She expected the driver to have the social knowledge of a hairdresser at least.

"Party was called for cocktails?"

"And dinner," she said. "How's the food here?"

He offered his arm as a brace to her. "The finest in Washington."

She accepted his verdict completely. If, on the road, the place to eat was where the truck drivers stopped, the *Guide Michelin* to private clubs was chauffeurs. She eased herself out onto the sidewalk. "Come back around nine-thirty," she said. "You won't mind waiting?" It was of course a rhetorical question. Nobody had ever minded waiting except her last husband.

"Will we be going to the hotel or back to the airport?"

"I'm not sure," said Gloria Stanley, saying it like a refrain that had run through her life, which it was. Had she ever been sure about anything, people would not have been so quick to inflict their opinions on her, their wishes, their ambitions, their pricks.

She saw herself as a tragic heroine in a drama of love unfulfilled: men had used her, and badly. She had trusted and been betrayed. In spite of quick intelligence and a degree of literacy amazing in an actress, she missed the true center of her drama. She was as capable a woman as walked: funny, direct, and honest. But she could not be in a room by herself without going mad.

She walked up the winding stone steps that led to the iron door, transported from an English church, majestic, as good as a movie set. She clung to the railing because it was pretty, and she liked to have something to hold on to, which also applied to her last husband.

The man at the door did not wait for her knock. He had looked through the peephole and instantly recognized her. All of the style and dash he'd learned in fifteen years of service melded into one great door opening. He bowed from the waist, smiled, saluted, and clicked his heels.

She smiled, very sweetly, and directly at him. She knew the moment would make his life memorable; it passed so quickly in hers that she could afford to be generous. That was also her attitude toward sex.

She entered the party. Flashbulbs popped. A diplomat, warming his steak teriyaki over the miniature hibachi, stared so hard he set his cuff on fire. His wife put him out with her champagne.

"You're here!" cried Chris, running to greet her, hugging her. "What a darling you are!"

"Hardly," said Gloria, easing her arms out of the mink, handing it to the cloakroom attendant. Rising out of the swirls of red chiffon like Venus from the half-shell, Gloria stood, shoulders naked and tanned to a gold a shade deeper than her hair. Little rubies hung like red teardrops from her earlobes. A heart-shaped ruby sat in the hollow of her throat. Several women gasped and suppressed the impulse to applaud.

Press scrambled toward the entranceway, trying to give the appearance of calm, vying for the position closest to the star.

"How long will you be staying in Washington?" a reporter asked.

"What designer is that?" asked a woman from *W*.

"Is it true you've been looking at real estate here?" asked someone else. "Are you thinking of moving?"

"Please," Chris said. "This is a party. Give her a chance." The security men in tuxedos made a wedge through the crowd and got Gloria and Chris to the bar.

"What are you drinking?" asked Chris.

"Tequila sunrise," Gloria said. The bartender eagerly snapped into action, colorful fluids at the ready.

"I apologize for their manners, or lack of them," said Chris, smiling at her luminous friend.

"That's all right," Gloria murmured. The frenzy of the

press, like the love of the multitudes, was a regular part of her life. She worried less about its presence than she worried about its disappearing.

"Gloria, this is my dear friend Abby Cochran."

Gloria took Abby's hand, just as someone jostled her from behind. "Oh, Abby," she said. "I'm afraid I've stepped on your foot."

"That's perfectly all right," said Abby, surprised at the innocent directness in Gloria's eyes, the childlike handshake. She had, like everyone else, expected a sophisticated woman.

"Tequila sunrise," proclaimed the bartender, flourishing the drink.

"Thank you," said Gloria.

"Tequila!" The voice of Charlotte Dean rumbled behind them as she pushed her way toward the bar. "You must be serious."

"I beg your pardon?" asked Gloria.

"That's a drink that means business. Are you still depressed over the divorce?"

"Do we know each other?" asked Gloria.

"Charlotte's a reporter," said Chris unhappily.

"Is it true your latest picture had to be cancelled because you were too depressed to work?"

"No, it isn't true," said Gloria. "And tequila happens to be organic. It's made from the mescal plant."

"Well, well," said Charlotte, making a note.

"Well, what you writing down now, Charlotte, honey," said the big-bosomed black woman who'd been sitting at the piano, singing. There were still traces of tears running down her cheeks, but she was grinning. "The names of the next group to be guillotined?"

"Go to the ladies' room or something," Charlotte said tolerantly. "You're a mess, Melissa Mae."

"You're a mess, Melissa Mae," the black woman sang, waving her arm in an arc so wide her right breast seemed about to jump from its white satin moorings. "And there ain't nobody going to straighten you out now that Hiro been driven out of town."

"Stop wallowing," said Charlotte, then moved to the black woman, lowering her voice. "You know he never *really* cared for you."

"Right," said Melissa Mae, the irony as heavy as her lids. She bobbed like a balloon. "Thank God I have you for a friend to set me straight."

Charlotte paused, studied the tired but still beautiful face. "Hiro was an adventurer. He was using you like everyone else. We know now he was simply a profiteer."

"Excuse me," said Melissa Mae. "*We* don't know now nothing. All *you* know is he gave some presents to members of Congress. People do that all the time."

"Not cash gifts of five and ten thousand."

"Hiro is a very generous man," Melissa said, and started to weep. "Oh, shit, why did you have to go after him?"

"Somebody better take her home," said Charlotte, turning away.

"Yeah," Melissa Mae agreed, finishing her drink. "Somebody."

"You'll see," said Charlotte. "You'll thank me one day."

"I hope I can find the words," said Melissa, moving unsteadily toward the door. A security man helped her into her coat and took her outside.

"This has got to be the finest publishing party in years," said one of the blue-suited men from New York. "Splendid hors d'oeuvres, excellent drinks, and an incident. What more could anyone ask?"

"I'm glad you could be here," Jess said.

"I wouldn't miss it, at these prices."

"Now, Ellis, don't be stingy." Jess grinned. "You're going to make a lot of money from this book."

"We're going to have to, with the advance we paid."

"Stop complaining," Jess said, good-naturedly. "It's a privilege to be in a position to pay good money for quality."

"You're right," said Ellis, and smiled. He looked hard at Jess, and his eyes clouded with concern. "What's happening with you?"

"I'm enjoying my life. I'm enjoying my family. But if by

what's happening you mean what's happening, the answer is nothing."

"Nothing at all?"

"I got an offer from Plowright but it would mean moving to Philadelphia. The kids wouldn't like that. And Chris would go crazy. This is her town. This is her career. You wouldn't like it either. There's not much of a market for Philadelphia novels."

"I don't know why you haven't found something," said Ellis, shaking his head.

"Oh, it isn't that tough to figure. I worked for Nixon, and my wife is more successful than I am. Those are equal sins in America."

"You really feel people look down on you because Chris is successful?"

"I know they do." Jess paused. "It's strange to condemn a man because his wife is a hit. You'd think the country would stand up and cheer for a man who gave a woman that kind of faith in herself." He took a long swallow of his drink.

¶ There was only one picture left in Charley's camera. He had two more rolls of film in his camera case, but he didn't intend to use them. To have taken pictures of the rest of the evening, after photographing Gloria Stanley, would have been like shooting marbles after making love. He was spent, exhausted, totally happy, eager to go home and not tell his wife about Gloria.

The man who now stood in the doorway looked familiar to Charley. He was clearly a government type, taller than some, better-looking than most, more amiable seeming. The smile with which he greeted the doorman was genuine, as if he really appreciated having a door opened for him, being told "Good evening, sir."

The suit he wore was dark blue, rubbed to a sheen by several years of wear, and the collar of his striped shirt was slightly frayed in the back. But there was, in his bearing, something that spoke of better things, even to Charley.

He snapped his picture.

The man turned to see who was behind him who warranted that attention. Seeing no one, he nodded at Charley and made his way into the party.

"Who was that?" Charley asked the doorman.

"Mr. Lawrence Cochran," George said.

¶ In a world where politics had lost its luster while acquiring a stench, Larry Cochran was of a breed apart. An old breed, some said: that rarity, an honest politician. Forthright, humorous, so clear in his thinking, so fair in his opinions, that many even called him statesman. There hadn't been a statesman in Washington for longer than anyone cared to remember: a man who thought in terms of the common good, a phrase that had shriveled from neglect, and so well liked he had a high appointed position in an administration not controlled by his party—as close as Washington had come to the millennium.

He made his way through the crowd, greeting people, smiling at those he knew and some he didn't, stopping to shake hands, to pat a few shoulders, to hug Megan O'Flannagan. "You two certainly seem to be old friends," Charlotte Dean said to him.

"She almost makes it sound dirty," Megan whispered in his ear.

Larry laughed. "See you later," he said to Megan, and walked past Charlotte Dean without looking at her.

"May I pay my respects to the honoree," Larry said, making his way to Chris.

"You may do more than that," she said, and kissed him. "I wasn't sure you'd come. Abby said you had business in the Oval Office. And I was afraid with what had happened with Hiro, you wouldn't want to be . . . associated."

"Poor Hiro," Abby said.

"He shouldn't have left the country," said Larry.

"Do you think he's guilty?" asked Chris.

"He isn't being tried for anything yet except in the press.

But it looks bad that he left," said Larry. Tiny webs of wrinkles played around his eyes, counterpointing the boyish look of them. "I couldn't stay away, Chris, not if I wanted to keep my marriage together. Abigail would never have forgiven me if I missed this evening."

Abby hugged him. "Thank you for showing up."

"There was a songwriter once named Bud Henderson," said Larry, "who said, 'It was not given to all men to be geniuses. It was not even given to all men to be talented. But it was given to all men to show up.' "

"Not my last husband," said Gloria.

"Oh," said Abby, drawing Gloria to her side. "You haven't met. My husband, Larry Cochran."

"I'll bet you're a movie star," said Larry, smiling.

"This can't be the first time you've met a movie star," said Charlotte Dean, who was there again. "Didn't Henry introduce you to Jill?"

"I need a drink," said Larry, and went to the bar.

"Your husband's deliberately ignoring me," Charlotte said angrily.

"Is he?" Abby asked quietly. She moved after him, pulling Chris by the hand, Gloria following.

"Charlotte Dean says you're ignoring her, Larry," Abby said.

"She's smarter than she looks," said Larry.

The bartender put a drink in front of him, and Larry lifted the glass. "I'd like to propose a toast to the fairest author in the land, and to her hostess, the loveliest patron of the arts in history."

"At any rate the poorest," Abby said, smiling.

"Thank you," said Chris. "I know how far all this is from what really interests you, so I really appreciate your being here."

"Not at all," said Larry. "Art and political aspiration in this country have always been closely allied. Why, right before the Constitutional Convention Madison wrote a criticism of . . ." His high forehead furrowed in concentration and he quoted: " 'The law concerning naturalization and literary property.' He asked for a congressional rule to 'secure to literary authors their copyrights.' "

"How thoughtful," said Chris.

"Well, not all lawyers are insensitive," said Larry.

"You should have seen my husband's," said Gloria. "We'd no sooner left the courtroom after the judge granted the divorce than he asked for a date."

"You can hardly blame him," Larry said.

"Oh, he didn't ask me," she said. "He asked my husband."

They were still laughing when Charlotte Dean finished pushing her way to them. "Mr. Cochran," she said to Larry. "I want to talk to you."

"Miss Dean, this is a party. If you want an interview you can call my office."

"I've called your office a number of times. They say you're busy."

"I am busy. And now I'm relaxing." He turned his back on her. Just as swiftly she had moved around and was facing him again. "Well, now, what's this?" Larry said. "I was going to say excuse my back, but you didn't give me the chance."

"Why are you avoiding me?" said Charlotte.

"I'm not. You won't let me."

"Every big politician talks to Charlotte Dean."

"I guess I'm not a big politician," said Larry.

"Don't start with that humility bullshit. You're as ambitious as any man in this town."

Larry raised an eyebrow. "Really? If you know so much about me, why do we need to talk?"

"I like to get my facts right."

"That's not what I heard," said Larry.

Charlotte narrowed her eyes, as if she were trying to read him by an inadequate light. "What are you afraid of, Cochran? I thought you led a fastidious life. Not a hint of scandal. What are you really afraid of?"

Larry paused for a moment. "Well, that I can tell you. Greed. Ignorance. Deceit. Delusion. Old age. And reporters who care more about a sensational headline than the security of their country." He stared at her with wide-open blue white eyes, so fixed in their innocence she could hardly tell if he was laughing at her.

"A monitored press," she sneered. "You want a monitored press."

"Just standards," he said. "Morality."

"What a sanctimonious man you are. What a privileged, pious prick." She poised on the edge of the words, and ascended them like stairs.

He stared at her for a long moment. "Your father climbs trees," he said.

¶ In the ladies' room, Charlotte lay on the chaise, trying not to bite her lips. She did not have skin she could afford to chew off anymore. A woman of her accomplishment, who had wrested power from a city that surrendered nothing, pitted against a Boy Scout. What smooth snobbism Larry Cochran had, what unctuous privilege. She despised his smugness, understood the background that had given rise to it, envied it. It was one of Charlotte's peripheral pains that she had not grown up among people with inherited money. Not that Cochran seemed to have a lot. She would have to look into it, look into everything about him.

Not that she really wanted revenge.

She opened her eyes. "Well," she said to the ladies' room attendant. "What do you have for me, Lurleen. Give me something spicy to cheer me up."

"The lady who the party was for?" said Lurleen.

"Chris Betzer?"

"She's in love with someone named Scott."

"Scott Tamplin?"

"I don't know. She only said Scott."

"Are they having an affair?"

"Not from how she was talking to the blonde lady."

"What else did they say? What did the blonde say?"

"Mainly they was talking about Miz Betzer's husband being out of work, and some country I can't pronounce. Something about art."

"Not enough. Not good enough. Get something more vicious." Charlotte got up rockily and went toward the pink quilted door. "Call me in the morning with the rest of what you hear."

¶ From the top of the stairs Charlotte could hear the harmonies of the Starland Vocal Band, a local group who had made it big and still stayed in Washington. She could see the sweet faces of the group as they sang their song. Chris standing to the side, smiling, applauding them. Chris Betzer and Scott Tamplin. What a scoop it might have been if all Charlotte were interested in was innuendo and rich people's sexual scandal.

But that was behind her now. Politics was her new arena. She didn't have informers only in ladies' rooms. She had them all over, in Bethesda Naval Hospital so that she could know when announced heart attacks were in fact cirrhosis of the liver, in the records room of the Justice Department, in the Bureau of Vital Statistics. There was no aspect of anyone's life that could remain secret to her, if she wanted to know. She would know everything there was to know about Larry Cochran, and more.

Not that she wanted revenge. Charlotte smiled. She wondered why people belittled revenge, when it tasted so delicious.

2

¶ Pieces of the past were scattered through Washington, besides the relics, documents, and buildings. There were woods so deep that, walking through them, a sensitive soul could forget the network of wires and ambitions that strung the city together and find the crackle of peace.

The woods seemed ordered without logic, without plan. A residential street in Wesley Heights would slope suddenly into forest, majestic spruce and eucalyptus, berry bushes and streams. The graves at Arlington stopped on one side of the road that twisted through the cemetery; on the other, steep embankments rushed toward a richness of trees. They had run out of level burial ground, Larry Cochran noted once. "Maybe that's how you put an end to war," he said to Abby. "You tell everybody there's no more room in the cemetery."

Autumn was the best time for the woods, the best time for Washington, in Abby's opinion, overlaying it with a crisp quiet, giving it the air of a country village, which she suspected it really was. Mornings she would awaken at dawn and go tramping through the forest that ran alongside the Palisades near Chain Bridge Road. It was a miracle to her, every time she walked in it, that such perennial majesty existed in the midst of a society with a life span of four years.

Men struggled all their lives to make their way to a city that gave them no lasting guarantees, no welcome that endured beyond one term of office. Mr. Olifierri, a congressman from California who lived in the house next door to the Cochrans, had sold his small paper factory in Buellton to finance his congressional campaign, and won by a narrow margin in 1972. He'd come to Washington, only to be defeated in 1976. Right after the election they'd discovered he had cancer. Surgery and medical care ate away at the family's finances. Mrs. Olifierri wanted to get him home to die; but there wasn't money enough to relocate with dignity, and the Olifierris were too proud to borrow.

Money. You needed it to live, you needed it to die. It was the center of politics. If you were a public servant and had it you were born with it, or probably corrupt. If you didn't have it, you were considered less honest than stupid.

Abby rankled herself with her cynicism, but she'd seen how impossible it was for even the best-intentioned man to survive in politics without a private source of income. The country cried for honesty in government; the newspapers scratched for scandal. The 1976 Federal Election Campaign Act provided funds for presidential candidates, but those who ran for Congress were still forced to raise their own funds. New laws limited individual contributions to a thousand dollars per campaign, organizational contributions to five thousand, to guard against special interests. So an honest man, competing in a field flushed with television lighting, newspaper advertising, would have to disappear or come up with his own money.

It was no time for a true man of the people, no matter how the climate demanded one, no matter how the media screamed for integrity. A low-born man with political ambition had hardly a hope, the American way notwithstanding. That Larry Cochran was alive and well and living in Washington was nothing less than a miracle. Especially since patriotism, along with plainspeaking, seemed to have gone out of style.

The dreamer who's grown up on Mr. Smith going to Washington and bucking the system, the believer who saw the Constitution as a great human document and not merely dated prose, once officially in government was weighted down with so many game plans he found it difficult to function. A dream needed air. Most longtime inhabitants of the District had forgotten there even was a dream, so pressured were their days. Few saw the physical majesty of the city around them, the brilliance of nature asserting itself between the formidable white buildings: the softness of its leaves, the clarity of color in the sky. It was a lyric city, Washington, D.C., but only for those with time for beauty. Lately that looked to be limited to those passing through.

A tourist could marvel at the structure: those who visited Paris could knowledgeably cite the architect who had designed both cities, point out as the plane descended toward National Airport how Washington radiated starlike from its center, as Paris did from the Etoile. A visitor could inhale the beauty of the Tidal Basin, blossoms falling, dome reflecting, without the added reflection that here fell Wilbur Mills. An ordinary pedestrian could walk along the red-bricked sidewalks of Georgetown and see the nation as it had been when it was young and free and innocent, two or three stories high, bright with gardens and geraniumed window boxes, no hint of corruption trailing from its eaves, no mossy webs of intrigue.

But nowadays the average Washingtonian drank dismay with his morning coffee, scoured the papers for what would be the stomach wrencher of the day. Soul-dissolving detail was heaped on the citizenry daily. A constant barrage of information emanated even from television shows classified as "entertainment." Cabs that drove weakened congressmen home from the Hill had their radios fixed on the news. It was, as Larry Cochran had said on "Face the Nation," "A city that couldn't see the truth, for the facts."

But Abby could still see the truth, the beauty. She tramped through the woods across the road from her house, inhaling the physical wonder, centering herself on the aroma of damp earth and fallen leaves. Smells were her way of connecting with life, the essence of it. When she'd been a child, she was constantly afflicted with head colds. Her mother confused refinement in girls with not being exposed to coarseness, by which she meant winds as well as harsh language, bad manners. So Abby had been constantly bundled up against the cold winds that seldom blew in Florida. She had not known what it was to breathe normally until she was eleven.

Then smells had assaulted her nose: lilac, jasmine outside the kitchen window, nutmeg inside the kitchen door. She had reacted with pure joy, loving even the odors that repelled other people. Perspiration. Horses. She would wake in the morning savoring her sheets, inhaling the warmth of her own body. She breathed so deeply her mother was frightened she had birthed a sensual child. But that passed quickly.

It was clear from her posture and the thin, firm set of her lips that Abigail would never yield, and certainly not to passion. She was as rigid as her mother, everywhere but her nose.

In school her conduct was exemplary. She was bright but not aggressive about it, which was seemly in a girl. That she was brighter than she showed, and with aggression might have developed rare brilliance, was beside the point, especially in Florida. Girls were allowed to be special but not so special as to frighten anyone. It was, after all, the South, and it had had enough of war.

When she rode on Wednesday afternoons, she trotted, according to custom. According to custom she also wore a peaked riding cap, a red coat, jodhpurs, black boots, and a piece of lace around her throat. A groom rode beside her. If ever the horse seemed to deviate from the path, the groom reached over and took the reins and righted him.

When she was twelve, she seized the reins away from the hovering groom, hit the horse with her riding crop, and galloped off into the woods. She spent the whole day weeping with laughter, and riding. They were still looking for her at midnight, when she brought the horse back to the stable. It was not until that time that she knew how much she resented being controlled.

Passion was not supposed to be the province of women. Lust

was the domain of men and whores, according to her mother, although she referred to the latter as "evenin' women." Abby had started feeling what she did not recognize as sexual stirrings from the time she was eleven. The mystery between her legs was something she did not ask questions about, knowing instinctively it would be a sin in her mother's catechism.

When she met Larry Cochran, she had decided never to marry. Larry was a scholarship student at Harvard Law School when she met him in New York in 1958. He was visiting his roommate, a nephew of Clifton Sanger, the financier. Harvard had ways of putting impoverished Protestants together with well-adorned Jews. The Jews felt flattered to be rooming with a gentile, no matter how poor, especially if he was bright. And Larry was the brightest.

He made Law Review his first year, and by his second he was spending Christmas Day with the Clifton Sangers in their annual celebration of being able to pass. Those who had known Clifton Sanger when he was still being benefactor to Jewish causes and had watched his transition to patron of the arts, saviour of the museums, cast no recriminations. There was tacit understanding. The family fortune, under his guidance, had quintupled in size. He was so rich he could no longer afford to be Jewish.

So it was any Wasp in a storm, especially on Christmas Day in Manhattan. The Sanger mansion on Sutton Place South was decked with boughs of holly, in between the Renoirs. Larry Cochran didn't speak too much at the party. He had never seen such a display of wealth, even subtle, as part of it was. It struck no chord of covetousness in him, he was simply intimidated.

But he did covet the girl in the corner. She was one of those slightly cool blondes that looked like champagne, and he couldn't afford champagne. But they got together anyway.

He asked her to marry him the second time they dated, because he wanted to make love to her, and he was a leftover from another time, a courtly gentleman. She told him she intended to be a very important woman, and very important women weren't wives. She'd majored in history of art and was leaving for Italy in February to learn how to be a curator of museums. She had made up her mind never to marry.

They were married in January.

Her father had a stroke the summer the twins were born, and the manager of the bank he owned embezzled the cash assets and disappeared. From a great deal of money there was suddenly almost none. Larry had always been poor. His father had died when Larry was eleven, and had left inadequate insurance. His mother had no talent except for despair. Larry understood that struggle was exciting, the positive center of life. Survival had never been a question for Abby. She had always had money. She'd never thought about it. Now she knew what it meant when you didn't have it: more than it should have.

All of Larry's jobs were prestigious, but none of them paid very well. His mother was invalided; so was hers, now. They had three cripples between them, and four children. Men like Clifton Sanger offered to help Larry out from time to time, but he accepted no favors from anyone, not even friends, for fear that he might be called on one day to return them.

Abby loved him with her heart, her head, and her body. So it didn't matter that her clothes were not this season's, or the one before's, that she had to be frugal, nor that the sofa in the living room still wasn't re-covered after twelve years of service. The finest men in Washington seemed not to notice the upholstery shredding. An invitation to the Cochran home was regarded as a flattering one, because they were such pleasant people. And he was one of the few in Washington who didn't see politics as a form of exchange.

In the Palisades, in the woods, she felt the branches fallen to earth snap beneath her boots, the crunch of acorns under her soles. She smelled the freshness of an uncomplicated day, a Friday with no obligations except for a meeting at the Kirkeby Museum, where she was now a trustee. She would be free to lunch with Chris at the Sans Souci, a treat she allowed herself from time to time, even though Larry warned her she might get spoiled and not want American cheese sandwiches, their usual lunchtime fare.

She raised her arms and allowed herself a joyous stretch, reaching up to the naked branches above her head. The sky was bell clear, she could see all the way to heaven.

On the way back to the house, she found a newspaper, a soggy, leaf-laden copy of the *D.C. Courier*. The date was September, two months before, the headline a screaming accusation against Hiro, the story bylined Charlotte Dean. Abby carried it back with her to their kitchen to throw it in the trash. "It's the end of paradise," she said. "I found this cluttering up my woods."

"Word pollution." Larry sipped his coffee. "The worst kind."

"Bye, Mom," the twins roared through the kitchen. "Bye, Mom."

It was always surprising to Abby how tall they were, Elizabeth and Sara, how sure of themselves they seemed, sporting their burgeoning breasts like prizes they had won.

"Did you take your vitamins?"

"Really, Abigail, you sound like their mother," Larry said, smiling.

Then they were gone, like noisy yellow-haired fantasies, trailed by Laddie, who was hiking his pants up, and J.J., who was hiking his own in imitation, as he imitated every gesture of Laddie's. They were so beautiful she was afraid to look at them sometimes, afraid to hug them too hard, lest they vanish from her arms and her life. Sometimes she would awaken in the night and wonder if she had imagined being happy and wasn't still alone, and loveless. At those moments, she would stretch out her hand and move it above Larry's face, feeling his breath on her palm. It was exactly what she had done with her babies, creeping silently into the nursery, listening for the sound of their breathing, her mind filled with newspaper horrors, crib deaths, haunting, unexplained.

It was not that she expected the worst. It was simply that she couldn't believe her luck. Almost every woman she knew was frustrated, discontent, silently angry at some dark trick the universe had dealt her, looking for men, or salvation. That Abby had found both in one skin dazzled her soul.

She reached over and touched his hair. It was a little too short to suit her taste. She loved the feel of it, thick, slightly coarse, smelling like a Virginia afternoon, clean but slightly musky. When it was longer it curled slightly, framing his open square face with a cherub's softness. But he kept it closely cropped, conservative. In spite of the moral upheaval the country had experienced, in spite of the growth, people still judged a man's character in Washington by the length of his hair.

"I wish you'd let it grow," she said.

"Hippie." He drew her down into his lap and kissed her.

His tongue was lightly laced with the taste of coffee. His fingers were gentle around her face, cupping her chin. She opened her mouth slightly, drinking his affection, trying not to tremble at his touch. It embarrassed her sometimes, the extent of her feeling for him. She had early gotten over the idea that sex was unwholesome, knew that the endurance contest her mother had run with the physical side of life was pitiful, a folly. But she had not become sufficiently free to exult in passion whenever she felt it, especially with the sun shining.

"We shouldn't be doing this," she whispered against his mouth. "Not at this hour. It seems indecent."

"Good," Larry said, and kissed her again.

"What would they say on the Hill?" she murmured. "A man making love to his wife."

"They'd say I'd lost touch with the mainstream of America." He kissed her throat. "And they'd be right."

"I don't think so," she said. "I think the country's just about ready for you."

¶ The morgue at the *D.C. Courier* was Charlotte's favorite place. There she could read the obituaries of her enemies in perfect peace, even before they were actually dead.

A newspaper of the size and importance of the *Courier* had death notices prepared for any citizen of prominence, starting with early accomplishments and kept up to the minute, so when they died all that remained was to set them in print. The tone of the notices was respectful, peremptory, but Charlotte didn't study them for style. The way they were written, the lives were over, the victories in the past. So Charlotte was free to visualize the world without the people she disliked, to dance merrily on their coffins before they were even in them. It was a benignly vicious universe, there in the obit file, where a God sympathetic to Charlotte had taken care of everyone.

She pulled the notice on Cochran, Lawrence, and chewed her lips as she perused it.

LAWRENCE COCHRAN, PRESIDENTIAL ADVISOR, DEAD

Lawrence Seton Cochran, a leading political figure in Washington for many years, died (insert day) at (insert place).

He was (insert age).

Mr. Cochran was also a lawyer and had practiced law in New York from 1968 to 1972, when he was appointed special counsel to the Environmental Protection Agency in Washington. Previous to that time he had been with the Justice Department. In 1973 he became special liaison between Congress and the State Department. In 1977 he was appointed special advisor to the President.

On his forty-fourth birthday in August 1978, Mr. Cochran received a citation from associates in Washington. It said that his associates had "had their lives enriched by his high standards, a code of ethics, and excellence."

Mr. Cochran was born at Holloway Farm in Elizabeth, New Jersey, the son of Dudley and Emma Seton Cochran. The late Anderson Porter Cochran who died in October 1978 and represented New Jersey's Fifth Congressional District in the House for many years was an uncle.

Mr. Cochran went to the George School in Pennsylvania and was a 1956 graduate of Yale University. He was awarded a Rhodes Scholarship to Kings College at Cambridge University in England and received a degree from the Harvard Law School in 1960.

His studies in Yale were interrupted when he left to join the army. In Korea he was a lieutenant in Army Intelligence.

Mr. Cochran shunned publicity. His chief philanthropic interests were the Boys Club of America and the Friends Service Committee, and he was a director of both. He was a member of the board of the Fischer Library in Detroit. His clubs were the Metropolitan in Washington and the University Club in New York.

He is survived by his wife, the former Abigail Trelawney of Florida, whom he married in 1959, four children, and his mother.

His children are Elizabeth, Sara, Lawrence, Jr., and John. A sister, Catherine Slate of Reno, also survives.

A funeral service will be held (insert date, time and place).

On the face of it, an exemplary life, slightly leaning to privilege, balanced by striving. If she didn't dislike him so, she might have admired him.

She hurried across the fifth floor of the *Courier,* her mind clacking as noisily as the typewriters all around her. Wall-to-wall distraction, that was what a career on a paper really meant—a vast sea of desks with no waves of silence between them. It was a wonder to her that journalists didn't go mad from the racket, with no doors to close, not even a partition separating them from the rest. The one advantage that newspaper reporters had over every other breed of writer was that they didn't have to have thoughts. Thinking would have been impossible in a newsroom.

It had come to her, through style and a certain clout, which some would have called blackmail, to have a room with a door—the only woman on the paper who did. She had told her boss that since so much of her work involved telephoning of a confidential nature, privacy was essential to her continuing ability to get a story. When he hadn't moved fast enough to improve her situation, she mentioned his high school roommate, whom he'd imagined nobody knew about. She got the closed office, and comfortable furnishings, within days.

The way Charlotte saw it, the world was divided into two

parts, victims and victors. Bluebirds and cats. Bluebirds looked pretty enough, they sang and spread their wings and joy, all that Walt Disney shit that went over so well with the tender-hearted. But cats had a better chance in life, being insensitive to needs other than their own. And if in the course of survival they ate a bluebird or two, that was the nature of things, especially in Washington.

She did not consider herself callous. She had feelings. Her job was a tough one where scoops were what were important, not feelings. It was her task to give the public what they wanted, revelations, pointing out the emperor's lack of clothes.

She closed the door to her office, leaned back in her swivel chair, and turned to face the wall, contemplating the Seurat she'd been given by an aspiring Virginia politician. Pointillism. A series of innumerable dots which, viewed from a slight distance, became a painting. The exact same technique as making a story, really. An infinite patience for detail.

Her eyes moved to the coffee table, inlaid with mother of pearl, oriental palaces stretching between exquisitely wrought trees, gardens. It was as fine a piece of furniture as she'd ever seen, an exact duplicate of one she had seen in Hiro's house in the old days, when he entertained royally at the drop of a hat, or a name. An advice-to-the-lovelorn columnist had come to town, and Hiro had thrown her a dinner party at the Jeffersonian. It was a meal so fine that Charlotte had actually tasted it, savored the caviar sitting in a soft bed of sour cream, on Scotch salmon. True Scotch salmon. Not Nova Scotia, or the Jew kind. Hearts of palm. Chicken Kiev, butter bursting from its plump little breast. Hiro really knew how to throw a party, where to steal a chef.

The evening was nearly a pleasure for Charlotte, tasting fine food, seated with a sparkling array of local celebrities, one congressman who was actually amusing, another not as drunk as usual, a fallen attorney general from the Nixon administration who could still think. After the dessert—flaming cherries jubilee—the party had adjourned to Hiro's house, where there were endless bottles of Dom Perignon. There would never be such a thing in the world as too much money, Charlotte could not help thinking, wondering all the while where Hiro had really gotten his.

There were tales of tie-ins with oil, lies about family wealth (she had run down his family, and they were merchants, successful, but not related to royalty, as the rumors had it, and which Hiro did not deny). He had come to Washington as a student in the late fifties, and had studied Americans from the better families for style, grace, elegance, all things he openly admitted to Charlotte he wanted. What he didn't tell her was where the money really came from, as he never told any of the press. When she questioned him, he smiled. "It is not discreet," he said, "to talk about where you get your money or your sex. Those are American obsessions."

"You seem to have done pretty well with both," Charlotte said, indicating the monumentally endowed Melissa Mae. "For a foreigner."

It was the only appellation that seemed to affront him. "I have lived here since I was sixteen," he said. "I have worked very hard to be worthy of our way of life." His attitude toward America was proprietary, almost jingoistic.

"We are a country of dreamers, basically," he told her once. "That is why there are so many people who drink, have breakdowns, take tranquilizers. It is the conflict of materialism versus spirituality. We would all like to be idealists, but the life-style argues against it. The pressure is all for success, and to be a success quickly, we must be self-centered. It is a terrible duality."

It amused her, a social climber who talked of philosophy. That he was less climber than climbed upon was beside the point to Charlotte. If a man offered hospitality, fine food, fine drinks, fine accommodations, it was incumbent on people to accept, especially if they couldn't afford it themselves, as Charlotte certainly couldn't. It was disgusting how little she made, considering she had the power to topple the mighty, a power that had blistered into atomic radiance since Woodward and Bernstein.

She had had a kind of affection for Hiro, finding his seeming innocence appealing. There was such an obviously shrewd intelligence operating, it made for intriguing counterpoint to the boyish charm. Everything he had learned of America had been translated into excess: he was excessively neat, the immaculate stiffness of his shirts parading a starch that had long ago left everyone else's laundry.

He conducted himself at the dinner party as though it were an evening in court. She studied his elegance, the careful way he chewed, the manner in which he used his napkin, as if he did not wish to do anything so indelicate as soil it. And, in the manner of exceptional hosts, he seemed able to participate in conversations in all parts of the room.

"Peripheral hearing," Charlotte commented. "That must be part of your oriental heritage. Ears in the back of your head."

"On the contrary," Hiro said. "That is my training from the United States. When I studied diplomacy in college, one of our final exams was to have to listen to four different conversations at once and still be able to tell what everyone really wanted."

What Charlotte really wanted the night of the party for the lovelorn lady was an inlaid table like the one Hiro had in front of the overstuffed couch in his living room. The house was embassy size, opulent, overwhelming. As with everything else he emulated of America, he had become excessively rich.

"That's the most beautiful table I've ever seen in my life," she said for the third time that evening. In spite of his ability to listen to four conversations at once and determine what everyone really wanted, he seemed not to have heard her the first two times. Always in Washington she had seen demonstrations of oriental generosity. You had only to admire a thing and they gave it to you. Perhaps she was being too direct. Perhaps what she should have done was stand in the corner and whisper her longing in Russian.

"You like it?" asked Hiro.

"Love it," said Charlotte.

"I'll have one made for you," he said, and did, sending it to her along with a bill for three thousand dollars.

She almost died.

She was too proud to return it. Too proud to admit she was poor and didn't really need an inlaid table. She had it moved to her office and didn't tip the movers as the beginning of economizing to pay him.

No one realized how little newspaper people made. You could write a story that took a year to research and pin down for facts, and they still only paid by the week, a paltry sum even if you were a "star" reporter (so much for Brenda). Sometimes when you got a personal big one going and wrote departures from the regular news—a hunch you followed that led to a bonanza—they gave you a bonus for the story: a hundred dollars if you were lucky. It was hardly a career for a decent woman when a hooker got that for one throw.

She looked with contempt on whores, except for their earning capacity. Sex had never been that heavy a lure for her, except when combined with power. Adlai Stevenson had once looked at her with what she was sure was longing.

It was one of the peripheral pains of Charlotte's life, in spite of her indifference to sex, that not many men had hungered for her. From time to time she would wonder about herself, appraise the tall, slim body in the mirror, study her sharp, regular features (not too closely now that she was fifty), and wonder why such an attractive woman was not more of a lure to men. She knew her brain was a little too big for them, her breasts a little too small, but if she had been a man (oh, the injustice!) she would have made a play for herself.

She supposed when it came down to it, it was her fault for being too selective. There were plenty of animals out on the road who didn't know who she was, and her power, who would have been happy to punk her, if she liked being with animals. Or on the road. But my God, why would anyone leave Washington?

Her own husband, that fourth-rate politician, that creep from *Loosyana*, he'd left Washington. Of course not under his own steam. She'd found out he was slipping it to his secretary, a cliché redeemed only by the fact that his secretary was a man. The Bull of the Bayou, they'd called him in *Loosyana*. Ha!

But she didn't report that in the papers, as his mother was still alive. What she did report was a minor swindle in which her husband was involved, and for which he was subsequently sentenced to between four and ten years in the federal penitentiary. She had not done it out of revenge. She had a responsibility as a reporter, to the free press. She baked him cookies once a month for the first six months of his sentence, remembering how much he disliked her cooking.

Now she had become a force in Washington, a journalist to reckon with. She didn't mean to drink so much. But there were so many parties, receptions, and she couldn't skip them or she might not pick up the scent of a story. She could smell it a mile away, a man being nervous because he had something to hide.

But she had never intended to go after Hiro. The first story had simply dropped into her lap. Congressman Ellerbe had gotten pissed at a reception for a judge and put down Hiro to Charlotte, saying he was not as immaculate in his business dealings as he was in his attire.

"How so?" asked Charlotte, who couldn't help herself, it was a possible story.

"Shorting me fifty big ones," Ellerbe mumbled drunkenly.

"Well, Charlotte!" Hiro was upon them, arm extended, smile on his face, strangely boyish above the starched shirt of his tuxedo. "I haven't had a chance to talk to you all night."

"The party seems a great success," said Charlotte. "Chalk up another big shot. What are you going to do with them when you've got enough of them in your corner?"

"I don't know," Hiro said, grinning. "Maybe run for President."

She hadn't asked him about Ellerbe then, or sniffed at possible illegal dealings, because it was, after all, a party and there was caviar. One of the peripheral pains in Charlotte's life was that she could only have caviar when it was other people's.

But the next morning she had started checking. She started with Ellerbe's bank account, his clothes, where he bought them, how much he spent. Getting the license number of his car, finding out from registration where he'd bought it, and from the place of purchase, the amount he'd paid. A congressman with a Mercedes, and not even married to a rich man's daughter. It didn't require too much effort to establish that he was on the take.

From there it had been relatively simple to find out financial facts about others in the Congress who'd spent time with Hiro. All of them were living just a touch beyond their means. The scandal had exploded like a witch's brew, from its own pressure, and the fact that Washington had had nothing else major and juicy on its mind at the time.

Timing. Everything was timing. If Hiro had been caught during Watergate, he wouldn't have been able to get any space in the papers at all. As it was, he got several top front-page stories.

He barred Charlotte from the club. "Don't be childish," she said to him on the phone. "There's nothing personal in this."

"You are so used to corruption that you see it everywhere," Hiro said.

"Well, have you or have you not given money to several congressmen?"

"I do not want to talk to you," Hiro said. "Please excuse me, I must hang up the phone."

"Why are you collecting these people if you're not lobbying for something?" Charlotte persisted.

"Everybody in the world is lobbying for something," Hiro said.

"And you? What is it you want in exchange?"

"Happiness," Hiro said.

"Don't make me laugh," said Charlotte.

"Why," said Hiro. "Isn't that the American dream?"

Well, sure it was, but so was money. And bribery was a BIG story. She had a responsibility as a journalist.

The newspaper business was in trouble—*The New York Times* was down 112,000 readers from 1970 to 1975, and even that staid paper sponsored and promoted a search for the Loch Ness monster to improve its circulation. At the *Detroit News*, where 65,000 readers had been lost, an internal memo circulated by the editors said: "I want at least one, preferably two or three, stories on page 1A that will jolt, shock, or at least wake up our readers. Go through the last few weeks of the early edition, and you'll see what I want. 'Nun Charged With Killing Her Baby.' 'Prison Horrors Revealed.' "

She had a responsibility. Not that she had any axe to grind. As a matter of fact, she'd felt nearly sad when it turned out Hiro was in real trouble. When he'd fled the country she'd felt an actual moment of loss—no one else gave such parties.

But she had no sense of connection with Larry Cochran. Imagine his nerve, snubbing her like that. So whatever she turned up on him wouldn't affect her in the least.

¶ It hurt Chris's eyes to go into Jess's den. They had had it built on especially, an annex to Chris's workroom, so the two careers could function free of each others' space. At the time it was constructed it was a great luxury, because they both knew Jess would hardly ever be at home.

Now he seldom moved inside it. Most of his time was spent in the bedroom on bad-weather days, in the garden pruning and fussing when the sun was in evidence. On those rare occasions when he got up the courage to telephone the "friends" who had become so silent since the fall, he would wait until the children had gone to school and use the phone in the kitchen. Yellow made him cheerful, he told Chris once: it was not the color of cowardice at all. It was bright and spoke of life and optimism. So he liked being in the kitchen.

But the den was paneled in wood, dark walnut, mandatory good taste, expense implicit. It deepened the feeling of terrible gloom, personal history shot through the heart: the career of Jess Betzer, nailed to the wall like a dead butterfly.

To the left of the doorway was a framed certificate of Jess's presidential appointment, in elaborate calligraphy on parchment. Next to it was the presidential seal, above it a portrait in bronze, below it the name Richard M. Nixon. "I ask you to join in a high adventure—one as rich as humanity itself. And as exciting as the times we live in," was the quote beneath, dated January 20, 1970. A gallery of the men who had worked with Jess were on the walls, their autographs beneath their dark-suited, stiff figures: Bud Krogh, Pat Buchanan, Ken Cole. A tribute from the *Cincinnati Post,* the paper of Jess's hometown, thanked him for outstanding community service on behalf of the present and future citizens.

On the top of the TV, which was seldom used—he watched the news in the bedroom upstairs—was a 1973 Christmas card, a painting of James Monroe, outsized, with a gold leaf oak paper overlay, signed by the President and Mrs. Nixon. A 1974 Christmas card, gigantic as its predecessor, less elaborate, more folksy, a New England country scene, was beside it, signed by President and Mrs. Ford. It was as if they had taken Nixon's Christmas list, in a gesture of kindness, and let Jess have the illusion that he was still alive.

The shelves were laden with books for, against, and by Richard Nixon. In the corner lay a waist-high pile of old newspapers. On top was *The New York Times* of August 4, 1974, a lead story marked with dark pencil: *Report Links Watergate, Hughes-Rebozo Funds.*

It was as if time had been suspended inside that gloomy chamber. The trees that grew outside the French windows blocked the sun. The maid was not allowed inside to straighten or dust. Once every few months Jess would permit her to vacuum the carpet and fluff up the cushions of the sofa, behind the red, white, and blue needlepointed pillow with an elephant and Nixon's name. But he permitted her to touch nothing. Nor did he seem inclined to straighten the room himself, in spite of his having become so helpful around the house Chris thought she would go crazy.

She did not mean to be intolerant. She knew she should thank God every day of her life that she was married to a man who had none of the ordinary hang-ups about men-women roles. But every time he got up to put the dishes in the sink, it startled her. Each time he washed a pot or a pan, she felt uneasy. The truth of it was he was better at those things than she, tidier even than the maid. The maid was off two days a week, so Chris should have been grateful. But she was a male chauvinist and knew it. Men didn't have to perform services the way women did to be accepted, unless of course they were four years out of work.

Her heart ached for him when she wasn't gritting her teeth at his presence. She could not understand the cruelty of a world that judged a man by his employment. Jess was warm and kind, handsome, with a loving sense of humor. The children would have stepped on her to get into his arms.

But people didn't care about what a man was, they cared about what he did. It was cruel and unfair, and stupid, but it was the way of the world. She hated everyone who had ever snubbed him. She hated herself for being less than patient, less than compassionate, just because he was always home.

It was unseemly in a man to be trapped in a house. It was sad and degrading for women, but at least it was traditional.

That was all he did now, take care of her needs, the children, and the house. And not allow anyone to mess with his mini-museum of Richard Nixon.

She had thought of setting fire to the room, like a political Mrs. Rochester, of running mad, screaming, in the middle of the night and ridding them of that past. But the past was all he had. Even disgrace was more memorable than nothing. And it was history. He told her that all the time. You couldn't despise history. You just had to see it for what it was. But he didn't see the present for what it was: empty of meaning for him.

She looked over at his back, tried to feel some affection for the sleeping man, tried to feel the pitiful waste instead of contempt.

He stirred, turned slightly, made a light grunting sound. "Hi, there," he said, opening his eyes. "You pretty thing." She patted his hand, sisterlike, and slipped out of bed. They had not made love the night before. She had pretended exhaustion when what she was feeling was longing for Scott.

Jess watched her move toward the bathroom, a sleepy look on his face, the corners of his mouth curving slightly upward, as if he were suppressing a smile. She did not wonder at the true emotion behind it. It was too early in the morning to become insightful about pain, or longing.

He actually wanted her. All the time. It had been a part

of her life that she considered a miracle, having a man who looked like that and felt like that be crazy about her. But it was an intrusion now, an assault on her sensibilities, having him make love to her when she yearned for Scott. It disgusted her, Jess's passion. Her disgust made her despise herself, for being like everyone else and condemning the man for his circumstances.

She was still caught in ambivalent feelings not only about Jess, but about herself. Her mother had told her no one would ever love her; she really loved her mother. So she had no choice but to believe, and implement the dark prophecy, masquerading behind overweight and a tart, too quick tongue. No man had ever been tender to her because she had seemed to be tough. Then Jess had come and seen how fragile she really was.

Now her body was slender, and her hopes blazed clear. Men still did not fall at her feet: she was an accomplished woman, intimidating. But their eyes followed her, and sometimes so did little notes, secret invitations. She ignored them. She had never had any intention of being unfaithful, until it came to Scott.

That she couldn't reach him, couldn't get to him, that all they had were moments playing backgammon, whispered exchanges on the telephone, and not enough of those because Jess was always home and might pick up the extension, made her furious. She wondered if he didn't really know. He was too smart to want a confrontation. If he accused her of anything, there might be a showdown. He was without an orthodox career. He didn't need to lose his unofficial one, the marriage that had become the center of his life.

Besides, what could he accuse her of? Nothing, damn it. She washed and powdered herself, avoiding her own eyes, the discontent in them, the perfidy. Where did fidelity end and the wish for adultery begin?

She would call Scott at the office at lunchtime. He never went out for lunch. He said it was because he was preparing his stories. She suspected it was easier for him not to lunch anymore than to reject her invitations. She had grown very bold of late, pressing him for a time, a meeting, speaking her feelings shamelessly.

"There's a place in Puerto Vallarta," she said to him once on the phone. "Individual cottages with waterfalls running into private pools, sunken, hidden. And lush tropical fruit and flowers, everything blazing scarlet. It's so beautiful there. I want to go with you. It's called the Garza Blanca."

"Write it down," he said softly.

"Can we go there? Can we hide in our cottage and make love in our pool, and no one will ever see us?"

"Write down the name," he said, with deliberate urgency.

"Can we run away?"

"Not right now," he said. "We have responsibilities. But put the name away somewhere so you don't forget it."

"I won't forget it. Can we go there?"

"Maybe someday," he said. There was a sharp intake of breath on the other end of the telephone. "Oh, God, I hope we get together before I'm too old."

"You'll never be old," she had whispered.

The phone calls kept her alive, like the backgammon games, but there weren't enough of either. Backgammon was only twice a week or on special occasions. And the phone calls couldn't be made from home because Jess was there, always there, pathetically, sickeningly there.

Jess was waiting outside the bathroom when she came out, his grin set like a jack-o'-lantern's, caving in from a too long ago Halloween. "What's the itinerary for today?" he asked her.

"Lunch at the Sans Souci," she said. "Want to come? It's just the girls." She saw the expression in his eyes. "I didn't mean that the way it sounded. You're really welcome."

"No," he said. "Thanks. I don't think so. I have. . . ." He averted his eyes. "I'm expecting some calls."

She smiled, as if she were convinced. He put his arm around her. She resisted the impulse to pull away. She tried to remember how lonely she had been, how empty she had felt before he rescued her. She touched against the warmth of his naked chest, felt the strangely babylike texture of his skin against her face.

"Oh, Jess," she sighed.

"Well, at least you're a hit," he said, and held her.

"You'll have your turn again."

"Sure I will," he said, unconvincingly.

She wondered why there was not more passion in sorrow.

¶ Gloria Stanley paused on the threshold of her suite at the Hay-Adams, and a new life. She was forever thus tremulously poised. There was no day she approached without the hope sewn into it that everything would change, any moment. Maybe even during lunch at the Sans Souci.

The terrible part of being a movie star was that people confused you with the roles you played, and nobody knew who you really were, including yourself. With the climate of revelation that pervaded Washington, she expected some blaze of understanding might emerge about herself. Then she could confront her own reality at last, provided she had some.

She remembered the blur of her childhood, which now seemed lamentable, especially during interviews. If her father really loved her, he wouldn't have thrown her so cruelly into the world of show business, she reasoned. She forgot that he had been hagridden, that it was her mother and her aunt who had pressed her career, that her father had actually died before her first screen test. She remembered only the sense of abandonment that had worked so well for Marilyn Monroe, envying her vulnerability, her pathos.

If only Marilyn had lived, people said all the time, so wistfully. Even in death she'd upstaged all other movie stars. Gloria herself had toyed with the idea of suicide from time to time, usually late at night when there wasn't anything on TV or anybody in the bed beside her. She believed very strongly in an afterlife, where she'd be able to hang out with Gary Cooper and Clark Gable, men who could appreciate her, deal with her monumental femininity, because they were men enough, big enough, had had enough of the world's approval and probably, by this time, God's. Not that she considered that the only men worth having were movie stars—she knew them all and knew better. But the options open to a woman with everything were limited, limited, limited.

When she read a script, for example, her reality became perfectly clear. Either it had good words or it didn't, especially her part. When she read a book, which she actually did on more than a few occasions, she could see the scope of a story. When it touched on heaven (love) and hell (loneliness) she knew it was major and recommended it to all her friends, sending copies to those who could actually read. But her own life stretched out before her without the guidelines of a movie or a book, and as she had no idea where the plot was going, it frightened her. Especially as she was so clearly the star and didn't know if she would be memorable in the role.

Life was like getting a tan: you no sooner had it than it faded. Love was elusive, orgasm was transient. Money certainly wasn't it. All money did was wrap you in furs and dab you with jewels and transport you to your next adventure, which most of the time didn't happen. Both Howard Hughes and J. Paul Getty had died the same year, the only billionaires she knew. Money was no protection even against looking bad in the coffin. She had already paid her hairdresser and her makeup man to lay her out, preferably in something wonderful by Edith Head.

But alive? Where would she spend the rest of it? Hollywood was dead, a myth of the used to be. The nature of the industry had changed completely: now it was the province of banks and conglomerates. No more great studio heads to bounce her on their knee, not that they'd meant anything by it. But her whole life had been a search for a father, as she saw it in retrospect. There were no more father figures in the movie business. With that loss, the rest of the society had gradually vanished. Parties were funereal, manufactured, peppered with hustlers and gossip columnists dedicated to keeping the image alive, if only by becoming scandalous themselves.

Nor could she easily run with the international set. They'd been much better done in *The Barefoot Contessa* than in real life. Weeks, sometimes months would pass without anyone saying anything witty, or giving a masked ball.

She'd thought of moving to some country where they'd never heard of her. She'd asked her agent if there was any such place, and heard to her horror there were several. She'd never thought about moving to them again.

Always at the center of her hope, her dreams, her unconfirmed plans, was romance. Romance all-consuming, all-devouring, elevating, sanctifying, operatic. A hero so fine and so bold that reality would disappear and they would find that life was just like in the movies.

To that end she dedicated her daydreams, and several mattresses. Not that she had started out easy. She had been a virgin till her nineteenth year, to the wonder of all her friends, including Hedda and Louella, whom her mother promised would be the first to know. At that time she had gone on location for her first film, costarring with Bart Adams, a dark-eyed method actor with whom all the world and she were in love. When he did not respond to her, terrible doubts were driven into her sexual psyche. She had no idea what a woman was supposed to be, besides irresistible. That she reached for him with loving hands he avoided gave her hives.

Hives were not a good thing to have on a first picture. An allergist from Beverly Hills was flown to the location, and seeing through to her fluttering heart, he offered himself as solution, besides pyribenzamine. On the verge of hysteria from the pressure of her first great opportunity and her first great rejection, she accepted him with gratitude.

Her mother routed him as a suitor, rejecting him as unsuitable. She told him she would take him to the Board of Ethics, if doctors had any, and find out what the penalty was for seducing a minor while under the influence of antihistamine.

From then on, Gloria had been intermittently a willing victim of passion. The rest of the time she'd spent becoming interested in literature.

She was astounded by Chris's productivity. The creative act was beyond Gloria. She'd spent all her adult life being dependent on others for dialogue, even for life-style. The occasional bon mot that shot from her lips she considered the gift of a benign God who'd forgiven her for sleeping around and understood that that was how it was with movie stars.

She wished it weren't like that. As much as she longed for romance, she would have preferred its not entailing so much sexual foraging. She longed for a way she could project a relationship to its bottom line before jumping in, to see if she and the latest love would be together in the final frame.

It was hard being a fallen woman and a prude at the same time. She'd had a terrible battle after Chris's party the evening before, with a congressman who'd gone mad for her at the party, followed her back to her hotel, called her from the lobby, and said he wouldn't leave until she talked to him. He'd been fairly attractive, and eligible, and was, after all, a representative of the people. There was very little she could do to put him off without showing contempt of Congress. Besides, she'd been lonely and cold, and a little bit horny.

"I want to suck your pussy," he had murmured by her lower belly. "Your beautiful pussy," he said, moving his head downward. "Your sweet pussy."

It was Gloria's opinion that her female equipment was the least attractive part of her, one which she could not turn over to an expert for improvement. Nothing romantic about that area. The word "pubic" said it all.

Still, she tried to accept praise of it from lovers. She hadn't meant to have so many. If it had been up to her she would have abided by the fairy tale and found Prince Charming right away and lived happily ever after somewhere she could sun. But the same world that had created her belief in eternal love had offered her a reality of fags and aging executives. So when she found someone even vaguely acceptable, she tumbled a little precipitously into bed, scarcely able to believe her luck. But it was not that she was a loose woman, except around the nether lips.

"I love your cunt," the congressman had said, licking at her, nipping at her with gentle teeth. "Your juicy cunt."

One thing to which Gloria had a genuine aversion was dirty

language. Her second husband had been a film revolutionary, who could hardly make it through a sentence without saying "fuck."

"Your beautiful clitty," he whispered, and wiggled it. "Your shiny pretty clitty," he murmured.

"Shut up and suck," said Gloria.

The worst of it was she loved it, really enjoyed sex while it lasted. But if love didn't last, sex didn't last twice as much. You couldn't look at a man and think, I sexed him once, and feel anything inside but a vague sense of poverty.

Today, though, she'd decided to forgive herself, pretend that it had never happened, which indeed it hardly had. She would not permit the congressman intercourse and had sent him on his way about half past one. So what had resulted was a fine night's sleep, and a sense of being vaginally, if not spiritually, cleansed.

Now she stood on the threshold of the Hay-Adams, ready to lunch at the Sans Souci, a bird of paradise transplanted. Ready for her life to begin anew. Again.

¶ A famous philosopher once wrote that the rare exception was not that one was in despair, but that one wasn't. It was hard to tell that at lunchtime at the Sans Souci.

Familiar faces of politicians, ex-White House staffers who still had clout, socialites and stars of the media, television journalists, filled the restaurant, tilted it noisily away from its traditionally French, slightly soiled old world decor to the bustle of America doing its most important business over lunch. The food was less than the quality of Maxime's, but so were the prices. And the service was first rate, spurred by a maitre d' who combined Gallic charm with political savvy, seating the leading attractions where others could comfortably gawk without interfering with the observed one's public privacy.

There was a comfortable snobbism at lunchtime. Not just anyone could come. Unless reservations were made well in advance, the man on the street would find no sanctuary. The general ambiance was one of a club.

At the height of the Watergate scandal, it had looked like

a criminal *Who's Who*, with five or six tables featuring conspirators, or their attorneys, at lunch. It had lent the room a
cosmic immediacy: You've seen them on TV, ladies and gentlemen, now see them as they are in real life, eating crabmeat
farci, on their way to jail.

In the two years of the Ford administration the place lost
none of its lunchtime luster. But a few days after Jimmy
Carter won the election, uncertainty set in about the social future of Washington. During that time a woman in Spring Val-
ley, who gave cooking classes to the socially elite, introduced
an emergency recipe for baked grits, and it was possible to
find an empty table at the Sans Souci.

Gradually, however, men had appeared with slightly longer
hair and golden peanuts in their lapels; crisp diction had given
way to soft southern tones. Although White House people no
longer came, lobbyists, diplomats, foreign service members,
and the rich did. The restaurant was filled once again, albeit
with a different breed, who deferred to the maitre d' as if he
knew what real power was.

As accustomed as even that gentleman was to celebrity, he
was slightly unstrung by the entrance of Gloria Stanley. Megan
O'Flannagan watched him conducting her toward a table almost directly at the front of the room, where everyone could
see, including the hatcheck girl.

"I've never seen Paul visibly impressed before," Megan said
to her companion. A heavyset man in his early forties, with a
brain of which Megan was fond, he was head of a company
that lobbied for magazines, and tried to keep the postal rates
down. His expense account lunches were usually with the staffs
of congressmen who drew up legislation. But he still considered
Megan political, and therefore deductible.

"She's not as tall as I thought she'd be," he noted.

"Well, maybe the top of the world isn't as high as we imagined it was," Megan said.

In the dim-lit luster of the Sans Souci, Gloria stepped with
dainty feet toward the table where Christ waited for her. The
whole restaurant appeared to be smiling, attentive, as if she were
about to make a presentation at the Academy Awards. From the

benign expression on the maitre d's face as he turned and smiled and nodded, Gloria supposed he was up for something humanitarian.

The only one not looking at her was Louise Felder, seated at Chris's right, gouging the soft insides from the crusty French bread. Louise was wearing the same shade of dark green velvet as lined the walls of the restaurant; her hair was the gilded brass of the fixtures. It was as if she had studied the decor of the place and decided to match it, rather than blaze against it as Gloria was doing, in orange. Not that Gloria ever dressed to make an impression, she simply couldn't help herself.

She would have enjoyed being more like Chris, the esteemed local matron, talented, in muted blue, a lighter blue silk shirtwaist tastefully tucked beneath the Givenchy suit, loved by her husband, beloved by her children, successful writer, called honoree. It made Gloria squirm inside how some women had it all, while for girls like her it was struggle, struggle, struggle.

But she didn't resent her friend's happiness. She merely intended to study her for style. And maybe get her to write a novel about a noble soul in a slut's body, set in Washington, to be a major motion picture, starring Academy Award nominee (six times, and never the prize!) Gloria Stanley.

"Chris! Louise!" She kissed the air beside both their cheeks and angled her bottom toward the seat the maitre d' held out for her. "You both look like you've been to Elizabeth Arden. I'm a wreck!"

"Contradict her," said Louise, eating.

"You look beautiful," said Chris.

"Do I?" asked Gloria.

"She still doesn't know," said Louise. "I have to phone my analyst."

"Would you like a telephone?" asked the maitre d'.

"It was a joke," said Louise. *"Une petite plaisanterie."*

"I see," said Paul. "Would you like a drink?"

"A margarita on the rocks, no salt," said Gloria. He was gone. "Well," she said, and sighed, settling back in her chair. "Are you elated from your triumph, Chris?"

"I don't know if it was a triumph," said Chris.

"I can't handle all this humility," said Louise. "I'm from Beverly Hills."

"Of course it was a triumph," said Gloria. "It was a beautiful party and the whole town adores you, and the book is wonderful."

"You read it?" asked Chris.

"Why do people always sound surprised?" said Gloria.

A short, dark, white-jacketed busboy started removing the fourth place setting. "No, leave it, please," said Chris. "We're expecting someone else."

"Who?" asked Louise.

"Abby."

"Does that mean I can't talk dirty?" asked Louise.

"You can do what you want," said Chris. "Be yourself."

"In front of her? That's like spitting on the *Reader's Digest.*"

Gloria laughed. The waiter brought her drink. She did not lift it to her lips too quickly, for fear someone might think she really needed it.

"Excuse me a minute," said Chris, and left the table.

"I envy her her life," said Gloria, looking after her.

"Oh, my God," said Louise. "There is no Santa Claus."

"She's a really together woman. And a fine writer. Why don't you get her to write a book that would make a movie for me?"

Louise buttered another hunk of crust and averted her eyes, and her words. Gloria was one of her favorite clients, and favorite people, a bright gutsy woman with personal style she had no idea she had. But her view of the motion picture industry was deluded, outdated. There was nobody rushing to put up money for a Gloria Stanley film. Pictures went forward only with important men committed to them, with few exceptions. Gloria Stanley was alive and gorgeous in a world that belonged to Al Pacino.

"Why don't you get married again?" said Louise, pushing the bread in her mouth.

"Nasty, nasty," said Gloria. But she smiled.

¶ There was no one in the ladies' room, as Chris had known

there would be. She had been lunching in the Sans Souci for five years, and no one had ever gone to the bathroom before two-thirty, when Art Buchwald and anyone else who might do or say or be something memorable had left the restaurant. She sat down on the small leather chair in front of the pay phone, took the fifteen cents she had held clutched in her hand all morning, deposited it, and dialed his private number.

"Yes?" Scott answered, his voice deep, so soft she could feel it.

"It's me." Her voice was shaking.

"You beautiful creature. You sweet, sexy woman," he murmured.

"What are you having for lunch?"

"Chicken salad," he said. "I wish it were you."

"It could be, Scott. Anytime you say."

"We can't, we have to be careful."

"Why?"

"Because we have obligations. People who love us. You have young children. You have a responsibility to them."

"What about me? Don't I owe something to me?"

"We can wait," Scott said. "We have to."

"How long?"

"Not too long," he said. "Just till it's safe."

"I don't want to be safe. I want to be with you."

"I feel the same way," said Scott. "But it's got to be right. It can't be some tacky motel."

"Then where?"

"What was that place, in Mexico?"

"I've forgotten," said Chris.

"No, you haven't. You wrote it down."

"I love you, Scott."

"My producer," he said, and hung up.

She sat for a moment with her head in her hands, shaking. Then she went to the sink and washed her face, as if cool water could rinse away the guilt that she felt nearly as strongly as the fear that she might never be really guilty. He had to open himself to her. They loved each other, there was no question.

There was desperation in her need for the affair, as if it could restore the balance, reaffirm her conviction that men were superior to women.

When she got back upstairs, Abby had joined them at the table. She was talking animatedly about an exhibition that was due at the Kirkeby Museum in spring.

"You must come back for it," she was telling Gloria. "It's going to be the art event of the year. And you too, of course," she said to Louise.

Chris leaned over and kissed Abby's pale cheek. "Thank you for my beautiful party."

"I did nothing," said Abby. "It was a joy to be there." The grey blue eyes seemed to darken slightly as she looked past Chris. "Don't look now, but here comes Charlotte Dean."

"Well, well, it's a reunion," said Charlotte, stopping at their table. "A beautiful gala last night, Mrs. Cochran. Quite spectacular to be sponsored by an underpaid presidential aide. And I didn't know you and your husband were members of the Jeffersonian."

Abby's face reddened.

"Perhaps Hiro Takeda helped out with the bill?"

"He did no such thing," said Abby softly.

"Who is Hiro Takeda?" asked Gloria.

"Forget it, he's in big trouble," said Louise. "You can't marry him."

"I don't even know him," said Gloria.

"That never stopped you before," said Louise.

"Who really paid for the party, Mrs. Cochran?"

"My publisher," said Chris hotly.

Charlotte smiled knowingly.

"What a horrible woman," Gloria murmured to Louise. "Another margarita, waiter, please," she sang into the air. Four waiters bumped into each other hurrying toward the bar.

"Let's order," said Chris. She signaled for menus. "The fish here is always excellent."

But Charlotte was not through with Abby. She sidled into an empty chair next to their table. "How does a man like Larry

Cochran live so well on such a mean little salary?" Her tone was insulting.

"He's writing a book exposing the journalists in Washington," said Louise. "I've sold the movie rights to Bert Lance."

"Stop it," said Chris, laughing.

The whole restaurant had grown silent. All that could be heard was the whirring of the blender at the bar.

"I'll find out, you know," Charlotte wheezed. "There's no way you can hide things from me."

"Oh, really," said Gloria. "You are overdoing it."

"Stay out of this, you . . . movie star," said Charlotte. She turned back to Abby. "There won't be an inch of your life that you can keep secret, Mrs. Cochran. Don't think you can."

"You know, I think she's seen more movies than I have," Gloria said with open amazement.

"I told you to stay out of this."

"But it was such a poor reading," said Gloria.

"Don't mess with me, sister," Charlotte murmured.

"Ida Lupino in *Roadhouse,* right?" asked Gloria. The waiter set a margarita in front of her.

"I'm not old enough to have seen that movie," said Charlotte. "Weren't you in it?"

"Ah," said Gloria and picked up her glass. "You just went too far." She stood, and let go of the contents of the glass, jettisoning them toward Charlotte's face. Ice and fluid connected with cheekbone.

Charlotte screamed and covered her face. "You bitch," Charlotte yelped, holding her hand over her left eye. "I'll see you in jail. I'll sue you for assault."

"I drink my margaritas without assault," said Gloria.

"I'll ruin your career!" said Charlotte.

Gloria laughed, a short quick peal. "What career?" she said. Then she laughed so long and hard it was as if she understood what the joke was, finally.

Charlotte choked with rage, and left the restaurant. There was a moment of stunned silence. Then a man at the side banquette began to applaud. The clapping spread through the room. Gloria seemed a little startled at first, but warmed to it, and smiled before sitting down.

"You were wonderful," said Chris.

"You shouldn't have taken my part," said Abby, "but I appreciate it."

"Oh, I enjoyed it," said Gloria. "I haven't had a scene like that since my last divorce."

"Excuse me," said a tall dark man in a grey business suit coming over to the table. "Chris, would you introduce me to the ladies?"

"This is Louise Felder, Abby you know, and Gloria Stanley. Robert Green, the director of the Kennedy Center."

"Miss Stanley," he said, not quite kissing her hand, bowing over it in the European manner. "It's delightful to have you in Washington. I was wondering if you'd ever thought about doing a play."

"She thinks about it all the time," said Louise quickly. "What dates are we talking?"

"Spring," he said. "The beginning of May. We have an opening."

"It's our loveliest season," said Chris.

"She'd love it," said Louise. "I'll be in your office at three o'clock this afternoon to firm up the deal. Do you have a card?"

"Of course," he said, and took one from a Gucci card case. "You have a play in mind?"

"It's a play by Mrs. Betzer," said Louise.

"But . . ." Chris started to say.

Louise held up her hand like a conductor, silencing the words. "I know Chris is probably reluctant to let you produce it at the Kennedy Center when I've promised it to Broadway, but I'm sure we can work out a guarantee of a first-rate production, plus director approval." She looked at him intently.

"Certainly," he said, handing the card to her.

"Three o'clock," said Louise, and waved him goodbye.

"I couldn't do a play," Gloria said, her eyes suddenly twice their normal size. "They'd kill me, the critics would kill me."

"The toughest audience in the world is in this restaurant at lunchtime," said Abby. "You seem to have captured them."

"Really?" asked Gloria.

"You captured me," said Abby. "I'll bring the whole Junior League to your opening."

"The who?"

"Do it," said Louise.

Gloria heaved a great sigh. "All right, I will." She turned to Chris and squeezed her hand. "Tell me about the play."

"There is no play," said Chris.

"There will be," said Louise. "You know how quickly you work when you're inspired. Aren't you a Gloria Stanley fan?"

"Of course," said Chris. "Who isn't?"

"Well, that ought to inspire you. Gloria Stanley is going to do your play. And she's going to be sensational in it!"

"You think?" asked Gloria.

"Oh, my God, you'll be a smash. This town will never have seen anything like it. Whatever it is."

"Telephone," said the maitre d', setting a portable white phone, its antenna pointed skyward, on the table next to Gloria.

"Who could possibly know I was here?" asked Gloria.

"How about the whole of Washington?" said Chris.

"Hello? Oh, hello, Congressman," Gloria said. "No, I can't. Not tonight. I'm flying back to Rome. . . . Oh, don't say that, your life isn't over. Besides, I'm not leaving forever. As a matter of fact, I'm coming back to do a play."

"It's a gift from God," murmured Louise. "She finally threw something at the right person. This play is going to save her life, move her right back where she should be, get her the Tony instead of that mangy Oscar they never gave her."

"But the play isn't written yet," said Chris.

"That never stopped the theatre," said Louise.

3

¶ A lone bird sat on the terrace of a sixth-floor apartment in the Foxhall. Across the vast complex sunlight filtered, striping the cold grey concrete with a slightly warmer hue. In the courtyard below, leaves whirled toward an empty swimming pool, umbrellas closed and roped around it like ships harbored for the winter. Surrounding were the windows of those who had learned to keep their curtains drawn.

The bird emitted a joyous chirp, as if mindless of the passing of summer, the coming of the chill. The sound seemed to offer its own inspiration and became song, feeding on itself, a frenzy of happy notes. From inside the apartment came a sickly moan. Melissa Mae August had a hangover.

"Shut up," she groaned into her pillow, pulling the sides of it up around her ears to blot out the noise. "Fucking happy bird."

Blindly, she reached for the high-heeled slippers she had just managed to slip out of before passing out and hurled one of them toward the window. It clunked against the drapes and fell to the floor. The bird kept singing.

She rolled over on her side and eased herself to a sitting position, feeling her body, noting with disgust she was still in white satin, crumpled beyond repair. Her hair had pulled free of the diamond clips and was fuzzy, an unintentional Afro. Her lips had a sticky little line inside them the consistency of glue.

"Oh, shit," she said, and held onto the top of the mattress, weaving. "Shut your mouth, you son of a bitch, or I'll get my gun."

The singing stopped. Melissa Mae grinned, delighted with herself. Then she thought about the feeling inside her head and fell back on the black satin pillow.

Brown satin on black satin, that was what Hiro had called her, that was how he had touched her, treated her, when he wasn't too busy improving his place in society. He loved her best when her clothes were textured, seductive. But sometimes even black velvet slit to the hip hadn't done anything for him, he was so occupied succeeding.

It made her laugh to see who the biggest victim was of the great American dream: a little Japanese boy. The son of two who had believed the emperor immortal. Born in 1941, to give the irony perfection. A young man who thought the United States was heaven, and to be among the angels one had only to bribe the gods.

He had seen it himself. In the palaces of the rich who had sometimes invited him, he noted that the guests were always elegant, perfectly dressed, and grateful for the invitation. He himself had felt joyous to be so welcomed. Only his natural oriental calm had kept him from showing his elation. It was good for the spirit to be wined and dined on occasion, especially in a regal place.

At each of the parties he attended, only a few in the beginning, he had carefully cultivated the dowdiest-looking person there. They were generally old ladies who proved to be very rich, very influential, whose husbands were dead, whose sons had deserted them or never been born. Because they fancied themselves liberal, it gave them satisfaction to be kind to a foreigner, especially one of a different tint. And because they were lonely they appreciated his gentle good manners, his attentiveness.

So they invited him to other parties, ones where he would meet still other people who would be charmed by him. He was not merely trying for their friendship: he genuinely liked old American people. The base of his life was respect for elders, it was habit engrained in him. It was a pleasure to meet those who did not think it their due.

He found especially amusing the little old ladies with big mouths. He thought it probably fortunate, though it seemed sad, that their husbands were not alive. He wondered how the best of them would have lasted through the constant barrage of chatter. Himself, he didn't mind. He was studying the language of Americans, and the more trivial words he could pick up and use, the more the community would respect him as an American.

He had no intention of going back, except to say goodbye to his parents. They would weep, and his uncle would be angry for having invested in his education. He would say America had spoiled Hiro. And he would be right.

Showers. Everybody had showers. For Hiro, splashing in liquid heat was an orgy. But the average boy at his university here thought nothing about them at all, or toilets that flushed. It was one big miracle of plumbing, the United States of America.

He had no intention of living in Japan, not ever again. He would stay in Washington and seek his fortune, and become a leader of society.

He had told Melissa Mae all of it, the yearning, the young man's hope for style and position, transmitted to her the whole of his long-ago dream, the afternoon they met in Washington. It was a rush of honesty that had taken place rarely since, in all the years she was his mistress. And he had left out the part about ambition, and where the money came from.

When she met Hiro she was twenty-five years old. Her mother had only recently stopped asking her when she was going to get married. She thought graduating with a degree in higher mathematics and a job on Wall Street was accomplishment enough for a black woman.

Hiro and Melissa became lovers the first afternoon they met. She had come to Washington with the head of her firm, who was consulting with Hiro's lawyer. All through the luncheon she had been very still, watching Hiro from beneath heavy lids, as he watched her.

"Do you know why Orientals are considered inscrutable?" he had asked her, over dessert, a marron glacé so sweet she thought her teeth would melt.

"No," she answered.

"We are taught respect," he said. "To look directly at someone is a sign of arrogance. It means I consider myself your equal. So I avert my eyes." He was not looking at her. His lawyer had gone to answer a phone call, and her boss was in the men's room. They were alone at the table.

"In your case, of course, I also cannot look because you are too beautiful."

Men had flattered her, cajoled her. A few had made noteworthy love. But no one had touched the part of her that believed in poetry.

Around them were pewter plates and crystal goblets and linen so fine she could smell the richness of it, crisp, fresh flowers on every table of the dining room, gorgeously arranged. She had eaten in a few private clubs of the Knickerbocker sort, membership limited to those so wealthy they never touched capital, money so old it had lineage. So the subtle luxuries of the Jeffersonian Club were new to her. He was a man who enjoyed spending money, and it showed.

She had never seen anything like the cut of his shirt, impeccable, cotton of a sheen that seemed to be silk, tailored to the exact curve of his rather bullish neck. His suit was black gabardine with a light grey stripe running through it, fit to his exact measure, unusually broad in the chest for an Oriental. His hands were manicured, nails buffed pink, the half-moons of his cuticles exaggerated beneath a coat of natural polish. She suspected that his toenails would be pedicured.

"What are you thinking?" he asked her.

"I've never seen anyone as clean as you."

"Cleanliness is next to godliness," he said. "And American."
She laughed.

"Have I said something amusing?"

"You're so . . . sincere," she said.

"Is that wrong?"

"It's . . . unusual."

"You consider it foolish." He was looking at her now, directly,
an abject expression on his very full face.

"I consider it very appealing."

"Really?" He smiled, and reached across the table, almost
touching her long brown fingers, circling the air above her
ring. "Is that for betrothal?"

"No."

"Who gave that ring to you?"

"I did. I have a tendency to wish I were spoiled."

"I would like to spoil you." He wasn't looking at her again.

"That's very generous of you, but we've only just met."

"I don't think so," he said, very softly. "I have the feeling
we are very old friends."

"From another life?" she asked him, smiling.

"From several."

By the time they left the club, she knew she would not be
going back to New York. They went in Hiro's black limousine
to the airport and saw her boss onto the shuttle.

"I have a few things I'd like to see in Washington," she said.

"I understand. When will you be back in the office?"

"I'll call you in the morning."

In the morning she was still drunk from wine and making
love, and the improbability of it all. He had ushered her
through marble halls, the royal museum that was his home,
gentled her across carpets woven for majesty, past tapestries
that would have embarrassed Hearst with their opulence, into
a bedroom stolen from an Arabian night.

He sat her down in a mountain of cushions, silks, brilliantly
printed, a fountain of color: they flashed at her eyes. He kissed
her once, very gently, lifting her chin in the cup of his hand,

drinking her mouth. Then he let her go, as much tenderness in the release as the holding.

He lay down on the pillows a few feet away from her. "I want to know how you feel about life. How you feel about love. I want you to tell me what makes you happy."

"Okay." She started to warm to it. It wasn't the usual first date for a token black on Wall Street. "If you'll do the same thing."

"I will," he said. "And while you're talking, let me look at your beautiful body. Will you grant me the privilege?"

Nobody had ever told her aloud that she had a beautiful body. Men had said she had dynamite tits and a foxy ass, and one word freak from Harvard told her she had the finest steatopygia he had ever seen—she found out in the dictionary later that it meant deposits of fat on the buttocks of black women, especially Hottentots—but no one had ever told her she had a beautiful body. She had never been more excited in her life.

She unbuttoned her jacket, slowly, giving him a quick resumé as if it were a business interview. Then she opened her blouse. She wore no brassiere, not out of any militant conviction, but because she didn't have to. Her breasts were huge, firm, pointing jauntily at the world, like her spirit.

"Magnificent!" he whispered, as if she had unveiled a work of art. "May I kiss them?"

"First tell me about you," she said. "And take your clothes off."

He told her about coming to Washington, and the old ladies, and the hope of becoming important, while he undressed. His diction was as meticulous as his clothes, and the way he folded them. His chest was the color of bronze, and looked as strong. She couldn't wait to touch him.

He told her about Charlotte Dean, and how she had befriended him at one of the dowager's parties. He told her of everyone who had been kind to him, some very influential names in Washington.

"Is your family influential?" she asked him.

"There is a rumor in town that I am related to the royal family of Japan. I do nothing to discourage the rumor. It opens doors."

"But you're not related?"

"My parents lived in a village without plumbing."

What she had liked most about him at lunch was his total lack of contempt. There was no one or nothing mentioned about which he didn't have something kind to say. She had not been with anyone like that since she entered the business world. So it surprised her to hear the disparaging tone of his voice as he spoke of a home without plumbing and leaving it and going to live with his uncle to be educated.

"May I come near you?" he said, very softly.

"In me would be better." She instantly despised herself for having made a joke. Fortunately he didn't get it. It amazed her how humorless he was, and that she still enjoyed him.

He was as direct and innocent as a child, kissing her, plunging his hands into her breasts as though they were mud pies. Laughing at his joy at having them to play with, testing their resiliency with his fingers, his tongue. There was so much happiness in his eyes at the prospect of having her that the tenderest part of her soul was touched.

And he was on top of her, pulling her legs apart, plunging into her. Giving her no time at all, and she was coming anyway. He was grinning down at her, grinning and kissing her face in between, and she was groaning into his mouth and convulsing around him. She felt him shudder. He collapsed on top of her, filling her with warmth inside, and gentle rhythms.

"You beautiful woman," he whispered against her throat.

She had loved him as passionately as if they had indeed been together in many lives. He told her his religious philosophy, he told her his view of America. But he never told her where the money came from.

"As I see it," he said, some years later, "this is a society based on the exchanging of favors. Fortunately I am in a position to give some favors to friends, and thus reinforce our friendship." They had just come from a birthday party Hiro had thrown for a popular senator, and nearly every important politician in Washington had attended. He was looking particularly puffed up, his background in humility temporarily forgotten in the triumph of who had graced his club. "Come," he said. "Let's go to bed." He reached for her, touched her breast.

"You must be feeling good," she said. "I thought that part of our relationship was over."

"I've been tired," he said.

"If I wanted to hear middle-class complaints I could have found an American."

"In the village where I come from," said Hiro, "they made a woman eat human excrement for talking back to her husband."

"Is that a proposal?"

"Would you like it to be?"

She shrugged. "If I can't have a sex life, I might as well be married."

"Socrates said, 'The beautiful body of a pretty woman is nothing but a living chamber of voluptuousness.' " He kissed her belly. "What would he have thought about your mouth?"

When he didn't touch her for days at a time, sometimes weeks, she would think he had another woman. She would follow him around town, hiding in doorways, skulking, studying him at dinner parties, despising the women he seemed too cordial to, going to their hotels, waiting in the lobbies to see if Hiro showed up. It was crazy and childish, but she loved him with such a passion she could not imagine why they didn't spend more time in bed. He seemed strangely unaware of her jealousy.

"Have you got someone else?" she asked him, finally.

"You know," he said, "sometimes when you follow me I am tempted to ask you out to lunch, except I am so busy."

When the trouble started, in between her fear and anxiety for him, she felt strangely satisfied, as if the scandal were repaying him, exacting revenge for his caring more about men and business than he did about her. It was primitive, outdated, petulant, the most real emotion she had ever felt. She wondered why anger and hurt went so much deeper than love.

"What have you done?" she asked him. "How many of the allegations against you are true?"

"I have only done what everyone else in this country does to get ahead," said Hiro. "What I am is an American success story."

¶ The buzzer rang from downstairs. For a moment her heart suspended beating. He hadn't left the country after all. He'd only had that story passed around, but he couldn't have left. Not forever. Not without her.

Hope vanquished even her hangover. She made it to the speaker without staggering, without stumbling. She leaned on the button. "Yes?"

"Two gentlemen, Miss August," said the man in security.

"Two gentlemen?"

"Reggo and Simpson," said an unfamiliar voice. "FBI."

"Oh, shit," said Melissa Mae, releasing the button. She thought about running. She thought about throwing up. In the end, she brushed her teeth.

The doorbell rang. She wiped her face and slipped into a Halston. "Yes?" she said, opening the door.

"Miss August?"

"That's me."

"May we come in? FBI."

"What would happen if I said no?"

They closed the door behind them. "Do you know the whereabouts of Hiro Takeda?"

"Hold it a second," she said, hurrying toward the phone. She dialed a number. "Mr. McShane? Melissa Mae August. I'm sorry to disturb you, but you remember you told me if I ever needed any legal help, to memorize your private number? Well, I did. And I do. There are two men here from the FBI.

"Thank you." She hung up the phone. "He'll be right over. Till then, I'm not to say anything."

"You can tell me, Melissa Mae," one of them said. "I won't

tell anybody except the Justice Department." He grinned at her. "What was a cute girl like you doing with a bad guy like Takeda?"

"I was just a token," she said softly, sitting down on the white sofa, holding her head in her hands.

"A token black?" said Reggo.

"A token mistress," she said. "Nobody in this town really has time for sex."

¶ Chris did. Chris had a great deal of time for sex and an erotic imagination as grand as the great outdoors. She had had to develop it for her novels as a coloratura did her high notes. It helped make up for the lack of sexual adventures in her own life. All through her youth her friends had been busy defending their virtue, losing it, having dangerous alliances, erotic mishaps. Chris, however, had projected an aura of innocence, which in conjunction with overweight had drawn to her a series of brotherly men who protected her. She had not wanted protection. She had wanted lust and exciting times. Her inexperience appalled her. The admirable women of the world had been in sexual sail since they were fourteen, and she had been a virgin at twenty-one. It had been the central embarrassment of her life, her involuntary purity.

By the time she met Jess, she had managed a number of affairs with men who had as little affection for her as she felt for herself. Those qualities for which other women yearned, intelligence, talent, creative energy, all came effortlessly to her. What Chris regarded as true accomplishment was being wanted by a man.

Jess wanted her, and badly, and all the time. She had considered it weakness in him that he found her so appealing.

Louise Felder, her agent and friend, told her to marry Jess. "You can't fake a hard-on," Louise said, which Chris supposed was her way of describing sincere love.

Chris could not dismiss Jess. He was too loving, too funny, strong in bed, gentle late at night when her personal demons kept her from sleeping. He scratched Chris's back, and soothed her ego, and wondered aloud why she felt unloved when he loved her.

She had no choice but to marry him. Her mother said he wasn't good enough, which clinched Chris's decision.

In the first few years of their marriage it had been hard not to consider him a miracle. Besides his strong good looks and his gently humorous manner, he had a quality that made him unique in a pressured world: he didn't mind losing.

But once in the Nixon White House, he became as driven as any man, as fearful, as anxious, as secretive. Chris felt suspended, detached, as if the warmth between them had been imagined. At night she never asked what had happened that day for fear he would lie to her. When the telephone jangled into their dawn, she pretended to be asleep, while the latest revelation was communicated to him. She felt herself an observer to their marriage, a viewer of the times, not related to any of it by reality.

Only Scott seemed reality. Intellect, spine. Handsome, fatherly, irresistible. That she waited for him for years, that they were to be separated by oceans, and marriages to people that weren't good enough for either of them, added poignance to her lust. In the early days of their relationship, before he was transferred to England, her passion had been more simply passion, a need for his fingers to touch her as his mind had, a longing for the penetration to be complete.

They had seen each other at receptions and at the club, where they didn't speak much, surrounded as they were by friends who knew both of them and might pick up on what was going on. But on the day following the Saturday Night Massacre in October 1973, the talk at the club was more intense than usual. It was so unaccustomedly noisy around them, Chris had dared to speak to Scott directly.

"I want to be with you in private," she said.

"I want to be with you in public," he said, a little sharply, the crisp edge of his diction holding the words back slightly, as though they were tears. "I want to show everybody how proud I am to be with you."

"When?" she said.

"Tuesday morning," he said. "House of Representatives. Word is they're going to introduce a resolution of impeachment. I think it would be appropriate if we were there."

"So do I," said Chris.

They met on the steps of the Capitol. She'd called a congressman friend and he'd gotten her a pass.

Scott was wearing an overcoat of black-and-white tweed that set him like newsprint against the white of the building. "I'm sorry," he said to her, smiling apologetically. "I tried to head you off, but you'd already left your house. I couldn't get a pass for you."

"I've got one," said Chris.

"Good for you!" Scott said. "But I don't think we should go in together."

"Nobody we know will be there."

Nobody was. The corridors on the third floor of the House of Representatives were crowded with long lines of out-of-towners and the fresh-faced young. Some of them looked at Scott with a vague sense of recognition which seemed to draw him tighter into himself.

"I'm excited to be here," Chris said, her breasts lightly pressed against Scott's back.

"Nothing will happen," he said, moving forward in the line. "It'll be just another futile exercise."

"You think so? You really think so?"

"He's the President," said Scott. "They won't want to move against him. It'll be symbolic outrage, is all."

"I don't believe you," she said. "This is America."

He turned and smiled at her as if she were a child, bright, but deplorably innocent.

"Besides, it's cosmic." Chris ventured. "I think the Founding Fathers, instead of turning over in their graves at what's happening to this country, are back among us trying to shape us up for the Bicentennial."

"There you are," he said, fondly. "Dreamer."

A guard searched Chris's bag. They were admitted to the

gallery for the start of the proceedings at noon. Scott held her fingertips as they descended the sharply angled stairs, helped her into a chair. He leaned all the way back as she strained against the railing to see down to the floor. "There seem to be more congressmen than usual," she said. "It's over half full."

"Anyone we know?" he said, taking out a notebook. "Can they see us?"

Rabbi Sally Preisand offered the invocation, hoping that Congress would uphold the law of righteousness in America. Chris reached over for Scott's hand, but he was busy writing. On the floor Bella Abzug, in a wide-brimmed dark felt hat, addressed the Congress, saying that the presence of Rabbi Sally made the occasion historic in more ways than one.

Members of Congress began introducing resolutions of impeachment. Chris was amazed at how low key and disorganized it all seemed to be. A landmark day in American political history, and the members of Congress appeared lassitudinous, sociable. When they were not themselves addressing their colleagues, they chatted, milled around their desks, gathered in the aisles. None of them seemed to be paying strict attention to the proceedings, except Gerald Ford.

Carl Albert dozed off briefly. It never failed to surprise Chris that the nation was in the hands of a number of men who could not stay awake after lunch.

Mr. Kuykendall, a short, chubby man in a rumpled grey suit, accused the House of behaving like a lynch mob. In case they had missed his point, he drew from a brown paper bag a thick, white, well-knotted noose and waved it at everybody. There were some boos from the gallery.

Congressman Passman got to his feet, and in an accent redolent of magnolia, the sweet luscious anger of the South, allowed that history would declare Richard Nixon the greatest President the nation had ever had. He suggested that Congress commend the President, rather than condemn him.

There was clapping from the floor of the House. "His troubles began," Passman orated brokenly, "when he went after that Communist, Alger Hiss."

"Let's get out of here," Scott said disgustedly.

On the wall to the left in the corridor was a huge mural of the signers of the Declaration of Independence. "Look," Chris said. "The Founders. Don't you think they'd be excited about this day?"

"They were pragmatists," Scott said dryly. "They knew better than to get excited too easily."

"Do you?" she asked. She looked at him with unmistakeable longing.

"I don't like to start anything I can't finish," he said.

They walked in silence across the District, sometimes close enough that their shoulders brushed. Fingertips trailed designs across palms. They made their way to Lafayette Park, across from the White House. Demonstrators on Pennsylvania Avenue held up signs that said, "Honk if you're for impeachment." Almost every car passing sounded its horn.

She took a breath of the crisp autumn air, and stretched herself inside her coat. Her hands were deep down in her pockets, anchored, so she wouldn't try to reach for him. The front of the White House was not like the galleries of Congress, where none of their crowd went. Any minute any number of people they knew might go charging by them on their way to the Sans Souci. Including Jess.

Jess. He hadn't slept for more than four hours a night since the Watergate explosion began. She felt so much pity it almost balanced the hunger she felt for Scott.

She looked across at the main portico of the White House, wondering if Jess could see out, wondering if the men inside that august, spectacular edifice ever looked beyond the room and the situation they were in.

She wondered at the affection she still felt for the country, the fiercely protective, maternal bias that at a better time she might have called patriotism. She marveled that with the glut of information she had suffered, along with everyone else with eyes and ears in the town, she continued to hold the naive conviction that everything would sort itself out, that the great republic would continue to stand. It occurred to her that love of country had grown in direct proportion to the waning of her love for Jess. Anger that fed on the infrequency of lovemaking, the tincture of Richard Nixon around the edges of their marriage, like iodine, marshaled itself into a ferocious concern for history, future.

Had Scott taken her to bed, she suspected she would be less concerned with politics. Had she been fulfilled as a woman she doubted she would have been so American. If Scott would take her that very minute in the middle of Lafayette Park, she knew the country could probably go up in smoke for all she cared. But as it was, she loved it deeply, defensively. For her it still seemed inspired, comic, spiritually uplifting, a Baron Münchhausen of a country, continually falling into quicksand and, lacking a rescuer, pulling itself to safety by its own hair.

On the roof, between the flag of the country, waving, and the television aerial stood a statue of a man, his leg poised, like a sentinel. The statue moved. "But it's a man," Chris said. "There's an armed guard on the roof of the White House."

"Well, this is not exactly what I'd call a friendly crowd," said Scott.

A few feet from where they stood, young people sold straw boaters and bumper stickers with "Impeach Nixon" emblazoned across them, white on royal blue. A woman handed Chris an open letter to the President, telling him she was in direct touch with Jesus, and if Nixon would get in touch with her, she would get in touch with Jesus for him. The atmosphere seemed to Chris one of a demented holiday.

"I've got to go," said Scott. "I want to do a piece on this."

"What about me?" Chris said. "Don't you want to do a piece on me?"

"Oh God, you know I do."

"We'll never have a better opportunity," she said. "The city's in upheaval. Nobody's going to pay attention to two ordinary people going into a hotel. The Hay-Adams is right across the street."

"And nobody knows us there except the thirty people we'd meet in the lobby, and the desk clerk who watches me on television."

"We could go make love in the Justice Department," Chris said. "Nobody's there anymore."

A smile pulled at the corner of his mouth. "Let's just walk."

"Why don't we get in a car and go somewhere?"

"Elise is using mine. Her Rolls is being fixed."

"We could rent one," said Chris.

"And have to give identification."

"And of course," said Chris despairingly, "if we're in a fatal accident, they'll know we were together."

"Look," he said, "do you think I don't want to be with you?"

"It certainly seems that way."

He walked faster. "Don't you understand the way it is now, I can live with it. We both can. But if we make love, really make love, I won't be able to let you go. I won't be able to let you go back to him, to a life empty of me."

"It wouldn't have to be," she pleaded.

"I'm no good at deception," he said. "Neither are you. I see how you feel about me. I see the beautiful crystal of your face, shining, open. It's a miracle everybody doesn't see it. If we became lovers in fact, there would be no way that I could hide it. And I doubt that you could. You have too much to lose. You're a gifted, beautiful woman with children. You're responsible to them. You're responsible to society. And you're responsible to Jess."

"He doesn't need me," she said. "He has Nixon."

"You can't condemn a man for doing his job."

"Why are you taking his part?"

"I feel sorry for Jess. He's a good man, trying to earn a living the best way he can. Maybe he really believes in what he's working for."

"He does," she said. "That's the part that makes me sick."

"It should make you compassionate," Scott said. "Haven't you ever felt something blindly? Haven't you ever refused to give something up because it would mean you'd invested your time and energy for nothing?"

"Most of the things in my life," she said.

"Then be more forgiving."

"I am forgiving. I forgive Jess. But I love you." She touched the sleeve of his tweed coat, pulled on a loose strand of wool with so much tenderness it might have been connected to his heart.

¶ Of the signers, the one whose handwriting is biggest is John Hancock. He was wanted by the law in England and, if the United States had not come into independent existence, probably would have been hanged. What emerged was the only country in the world where criminals become so successful that tax men have to catch them.

So an aura of light scandal is salt on the morning eggs of Washington. Nobody is terribly shocked at anything. In general, the Washingtonian wakes up steeled, set for his small daily charge of gossip.

The news about Hiro, therefore, came as no big surprise. Everyone had known all along he was very conspicuous with his generosity. They looked at each other over orange juice and toast, the people who had known him, and realized that Hiro had been playing for power. Still, they acted stunned that what Hiro had wanted was influence, like nearly everyone else.

He had seen it from the moment he arrived in Washington. He had marked that those at all the best parties seemed to be able to deliver action: their names were always in the news, as having been somewhere or done something of consequence. To be mentioned in the papers at all seemed to Hiro to denote importance.

Like most Americans, he began to confuse celebrity with accomplishment. He determined to become a man of influence himself by entertaining those who knew where the bodies were buried, a macabre little American expression he found amusing until he found out how true it was.

He had easily started the Jeffersonian Club. He had opened it, after graduating from college, with the aid of the dowager ladies. They had helped him raise the money, as they would have aided any other worthy charity, especially one which would have given them comfort in return. A gallant young man, they considered him courageous enough to be kind, strong enough to take care of a patron who drank a tiny bit too much.

Drinking was a big problem in Washington. Everyone was under pressure all the time, those in positions of power, real or imagined. There were a lot of parties, and at every party there was someone lobbying, pulling for a favor, looking for a break. Even those hoping for sexual favors politicked for them, maneuvering their targets rather than wooing.

The town had more psychiatrists, tranquilizers, and bars than any other in America. Any one of the three would have been indicative of desperation. In addition, there was Savitri, who gave instruction in Yoga for social Washington. And for those who could afford a primrosier path, there was the Jeffersonian.

The more astute members of the press assumed that anything so posh had to be a money loser, and syndicate backed. A red velvet way of washing money. Mafia maybe, or something insidious from the East.

There was about the place the soft sanctity of a vanished time, of an innocent nation where, as Jefferson said, there was a natural aristocracy among men, the grounds of which were virtue and talent. Few of the club's members were more than moderately talented, and none of them counted themselves virtuous if they could help it. But there was a quality there that those who aspired to breeding would have described as "genteel." And there was silence. People spoke quietly, as if their conversation might be overheard, which it usually was.

"You better not admit you knew Hiro," Melissa Mae said to Megan O'Flannagan as softly as she could. They sat on a cushioned banquette in a corner of the club, lunching. "The FBI's taken to questioning everyone who was his friend, although they're getting very hard to find, Hiro's friends. I mean, even the people who were really his friends are getting cute. You know what I mean. Saying all they were were 'drinking buddies,' 'acquaintances.' Saying they kept their distance because they knew he was up to something. Did you ever know?"

"I still don't know," Megan said. "He hasn't been officially charged with anything yet."

"There you go again, being fair. You and Larry Cochran."

Melissa leaned her big full body back against the red velvet and started arranging the shrimps on her plate in parallel lines. "He actually called me and asked if there was anything he could do. Imagine. With my phone probably tapped. And the White House phones monitored."

"He's a very good man," said Megan.

"The best," said Melissa Mae. "If he wasn't so pale, I could fall in love with him."

"Me too," said Megan, with no expression at all in her light blue eyes. The worst of being a redhead was that emotions showed on the skin: excitement, embarrassment, flushed all her freckles together into a patchy blush. If she practiced a concentration exercise, focusing on her breath, she could detach herself from her feelings about Larry Cochran.

But it was hard to release longing, especially in Washington at lunchtime. The city bubbled with business anxieties, sexual hopes, although there were little of either at the Jeffersonian this particular day. Members were staying away in droves. The second floor, with its formal banquettes and informal low-cushioned sofas for luxuriant dining, was practically empty. Only Megan and Melissa were lunching. A man in the corner was downing gin gibsons, but the room was otherwise deserted, except for two hovering waiters and a busboy with a peruke at the back of his neck.

Megan tried to be interested in all of it, to observe the room and her place in it, and life passing through her, and the scent of the flowers in the little crystal bowl on the table. But still she felt the heat in her cheeks, and asked about Larry.

"I didn't realize Larry was that close to Hiro," Megan said.

"He isn't. That's what makes it all the more remarkable. He and Abby had dinner here once or twice was all. She's lovely, too."

"Lovely," said Megan hollowly. The world being filled with bounders and lushes with greedy wives, she would have to be interested in a noble man who belonged to an admirable woman. She had watched the way he touched Abby in public, taking her arm so gently there was seduction in the courtesy.

"He said I should try and get Hiro to come back, to fight it from here, that it'll look better for him. He has to come back. He loves this place. He couldn't live anywhere else." Melissa's dark eyes clouded. Her lush lower lip curled back on itself as she plucked a wilted daisy from the crystal bowl. "He's not even gone a week and they're letting the flowers die." She pulled the browning petals, and sat up sharply. "George!" she called to the waiter. "Where's Mr. Carlos?"

"I'll get him," the waiter said, and went toward the stairs.

"Are you going to try and persuade Hiro to come back?" Megan asked.

"If I hear from him," Melissa shrugged unhappily. "But how can he listen? Who would have dealings with him now? Hiro couldn't survive without dealings. But where will he go?"

"What does he really do?" Megan said. "Where did he get the money?"

"As far as I know he was in import and export, just the way he said. He never gave me any details. He mentioned his uncle a lot, a tycoon in steel and shipping in Japan."

"Was he involved with some big corporation?"

"Not as far as I know. It's terrible to have to get a lawyer and be questioned by the Justice Department, and tell them it was all innocent when you're not really sure it was innocent at all."

"Why did he give money to those congressmen?"

"He treated money as a form of affectionate respect, like flowers. He'd seen what goes on in this town. He was imitating the American way, the way he saw it." Melissa crumbled the depetalled daisy in the palm of her long-fingered hand. "Hell. It wasn't illegal when he did it. All his big donations were sort of campaign contributions when it was still all right to make campaign contributions. I admit it seems a little lavish, five thousand at a clip." She smiled wryly, her bright red lipstick an illuminated slash against the brilliance of her teeth. "But then he gave me that in one afternoon, and wanted nothing in return, more's the pity."

"You didn't make much love?" Megan had terrible fears

about her femininity, wondering if her private places were turning to flab, to stone. They were muscles like everything else. If she didn't use them, they would wither. But she couldn't just make love to anyone. She wanted someone fine, like Larry Cochran. She wanted someone touching her breast the way he touched Abby's arm.

"We made a lot of love in the beginning," Melissa Mae said. "Hiro was as courtly and mannerly as he was in the club, only not so controlled. Not nearly. Then he got a big hard-on for doing business." She spoke the word as if it were a plague.

The manager of the Jeffersonian, in Wall Street readiness, vested, pinstriped, ready to make a tycoon feel underdressed, moved toward their banquette. "Did you ask to see me, Miss August?" he asked.

"I did indeed, Carlos." She gave him the crushed remainder of the daisy. "Mr. Takeda would be unhappy to see that the flowers here are not very fresh."

"I'll see to them," he said, and bowed.

"I'm sure you will."

"It would not have happened, of course, had I been able to check the club myself this morning. But I was detained. I had some unexpected visitors."

"You, too?" Melissa Mae said.

"I told them, of course, what they suspected was impossible. It is, isn't it, Miss August?"

"As far as I know, George."

"Thank you," he said, and bowed. "I will see to the flowers."

Melissa leaned her arms on the table, put her head in her hands. "Where is it going to end, Megan? A whole circle of this city is getting in touch with its lawyers, including the lawyers."

"Did he ask them for anything in return, the people he gave money to?" Megan asked.

"I don't know. No one's admitted anything. But I can't believe there was anything insidious about Hiro. If he was an agent for a foreign government, if he was influence peddling for anyone but himself, how could he have been so visible? The houses. The limousines. How could he have lived so high? Doesn't a spy have to be subtle?"

"I would have thought so," Megan said.

Melissa Mae studied her friend. "You've got such an eager face, such an open heart. People would tell you anything. Look at me, I'm running off at the mouth, and you're not even CIA." She picked up a shrimp and dipped it in the dill sauce. "Are you?"

Megan smiled. "If I were, would I be looking for work?"

"I don't know," said Melissa. "It's a pretty good cover, an unemployed Republican."

Melissa's head was bound in a grey-and-black print scarf that matched a blouse cut so severely her breasts looked square. When Hiro was out of town, she did her best to glut on the current fashions, crushing herself into tailored clothes, the way the tall lean blonde society beauties did. Fashion-wise she yearned to be a honky, one of those cool ladies nicknamed Slim, who never seemed to be in the clutches of a passion other than for clothes.

Hiro hadn't particularly liked her dressing like that. He liked her soft, flowing, décolleté. But not too décolleté. Enough to remind him of the glories that were there, but not enough to show the full possibilities to other men.

"What would you ever do if you found me with another man?" she had asked him once.

"I don't know. My instinct, I'm afraid, would be to kill you both."

"Then I better not let you catch me," she said, and smiled at him. "I don't want to die for love."

"It's the only thing worth dying for," he said. "Except country."

Melissa looked at Megan now, a mass of curls haloing her freckled country face, and realized with sadness they were both the same age. She felt old. She felt empty. She wondered how he could have been so cold as to go without her, abandoning her.

But she was being ridiculous. Any minute now there would

be a message on her exchange, telling her where to meet him.

"Why doesn't Larry help you get a job?" Melissa asked.

"I wouldn't ask him." Megan speared a slice of pear with her fork.

"Why not?"

"Because I've worked in the White House, I know what happens. Everybody's pulling at you all the time for something. He doesn't need any extra pressure, least of all from me."

Melissa studied her friend with special care, noted the flush of red like a warning signal moving up Megan's throat. "Hey," she said very softly. "You love him, don't you?"

"Don't be crazy," Megan said, and clutched for her purse, getting up from her seat. "Excuse me." She fled to the ladies' room.

Melissa stared after her for a moment. Then she lit a cigarette and signaled for the waiter. "A stinger, please, George. Double. On the rock."

"A stinger on the rocks," George said, and started to move away.

"On the rock," said Melissa. "One."

He looked at her, and made a confused little grimace, part smile, part perplexity as if he had understood what she said, but not really. It was a look Melissa Mae encountered quite often, usually on the faces of those in loftier places. Congressmen, senators, even attorney generals often demonstrated the same bafflement. It was as if a woman, certainly a black one who looked like she did, was not supposed to have a mind, especially one that made theirs struggle to understand.

She finished the last of her martini, and reached over and finished Megan's. She got up and went to the ladies' room.

"Are you in there, Megan?" she called inside the partitioned toilets, but not too loudly. She didn't want to wake the maid, who was dozing in the chair in the corner.

"Yes," said Megan.

Melissa went to the marble-topped dressing table and tried to restore her makeup. Her eyes were smaller than normal, swollen from too much booze and too little sleep. If she didn't start going a little easier on herself, she was going to look her age. Twenty-eight. Fairly young to be washed up, but not for a woman in Washington.

The door from the other room opened. Megan went to the sink and started washing her hands. She washed them for a long time.

"Who are you doing?" asked Melissa Mae. "Lady Macbeth?"

Megan didn't answer. She splashed water on her face.

"Listen," Melissa said, coming close to the sink, "I don't care if you love him. I'm not going to tell anybody."

Megan was splashing cold water on her cheeks. "I don't love him. I don't know him well enough to love him."

"Okay, then you've got the hots for him. Nothing wrong with that."

"It can't happen. That's what's wrong with it."

"Men have been known to cheat on their wives."

"Not Larry. Not on Abby." She toweled off her face. "I would have to pick the one man in Washington who loves his wife as much as power." Megan left a quarter in the ashtray, and Melissa Mae left a dollar.

The ladies' room attendant waited a half hour, making sure they were no longer at lunch, before calling Charlotte.

¶ The Executive Office Building, cold, grey, imposing, runs the length of the block on East Executive Avenue. It is separated from the White House by a private street where White House employees with priority park their cars.

The halls inside the EOB are barren, echoing footsteps, sneezes. It is the most unfriendly building in official Washington, high-ceilinged, dark. The offices themselves, especially those on the second floor, have some majesty, and windows. Larry Cochran's office, however, was not particularly large, consisting of a small anteroom where a secretary sat surrounded by law books and plants (the last from Abby) and an inner office where Larry sat at a leather-topped desk with a picture of his family on it. His secretary had framed it in the midst of the Wayne Hays scandal because she was so proud of her boss being a family man, and the family being so beautiful. Also on his desk were a globe of the world, the *Dictionary of Thoughts,* some unanswered correspondence, and a framed copy of a poem by Chris:

> *Some you win*
> *And some you win by default*
> *Simply by being around*
> *When the battle is over.*

There were standard White House portraits and paintings hung on the wall. In the corner, stacked, were the things Larry intended to hang eventually, when he decided where to put them: some credentials, his presidential appointment, a letter from his youngest son.

On the back of the door to Larry's inner office was an excerpt from Washington's Farewell Address. Underlined was: 'The habits of thinking in a free country should inspire caution in those entrusted with its administration." It pleased Larry to think that Washington, a revolutionary, was conservative.

In spite of being among the most admired men in his party, Larry's politics were more universal than partisan. He was an admitted conservative, believing that much of what was good in the past should be preserved for balance, sanity. He loved his country and believed in it.

That he was in the Executive Office Building made him believe more than ever in America. That he was there in a Democratic administration reinforced his faith in God.

His secretary buzzed him on the intercom. "Mr. Cochran? Charlotte Dean is on the telephone again."

"Tell her I'm not in my office."

"I did, sir. She said I'd better find you, or her next call is to the President."

"Tell her when I come back I'm going to call her mommy," Larry said, and released the button.

He was studying the Congressional Record, checking to see if anyone had yet introduced a resolution to investigate Hiro and his activities with members of the Congress. He supposed there would have been headlines if they did. But sometimes the press didn't catch important issues at the time they really began moving the government machinery: on the floor of Congress.

The buzzer went off again. "The President's office," his secretary said.

It was one of the press assistants. "I think you better take Charlotte Dean's call," the voice drawled softly. "She says she has material which could be embarrassing to the President, but she will not make it public if she can talk to you first."

"Okay," Larry said. "Switch her here." He put the phone on amplifier, tilted his chair back, and waited.

"Am I through?" the amplifier squawked, spraying the room with Charlotte's voice.

"It's certainly a pleasure to hear your voice," Larry said.

"Am I on a box? Get me off that box. I hate those damned things. I can't hear myself think."

"You should count yourself lucky," said Larry, and shut off the amplifier.

"Why have you been ducking my calls?" Charlotte said.

He put the receiver to his ear. "You shouldn't say that about yourself, Miss Dean. You didn't really sound like a duck call."

"What's your relationship with Hiro Takeda?" Charlotte asked, undaunted. "You might as well tell me the truth."

"He gave me hearts of palm salad once, and veal Oscar."

"And for dessert a teeny-weeny check for a couple of thou?"

"I will not even dignify that with a denial."

"If you only had dinner with him, why did you call Melissa Mae August to try and help?"

"Are you tapping phones now in your quest for freedom of information?"

"Don't worry about what I'm doing. Worry about what you're doing. Why would you try to help him?"

"He's a human being. He's never been anything but kind to me."

"How many dollars worth of kind? I'll find out, you know. And *print* it."

"You're scaring me to death," Larry said.

"And don't think you'll be able to keep it a secret about you and Megan O'Flannagan."

"Now you have gone mad, Charlotte. Whom the gods would destroy, they first make mad."

"Very lofty talk," Charlotte intoned.

"Listen," he said. "If you have anything concrete to say, say it. Otherwise I have work to do."

"You may be interested to know," Charlotte said, "that a shipping firm, Tokushima Takeda, Ltd., has asked for court protection under Japan's bankruptcy law. The firm is based in Kobe and is owned by Hiro's uncle. They are claiming forty million dollars in debts."

"So?"

"They were counting on America granting aid to shipping companies hurt by the Arab oil embargo and the recession. Apparently in the last few days it's become evident that they might not get the help they wanted. So they're going out of business."

"I'm sorry to hear it," said Larry.

"What you might be sorrier to hear is that the company has admitted that Hiro was acting as their agent, and agent for a great many shipping firms in Japan. He should have registered as an agent for a foreign government."

"It hasn't been proved yet he was an agent," Larry said. "He hasn't even been officially charged. Maybe he was trying to help his uncle."

"With all that money? Of course he was an agent. I have it on very good authority."

"From whom?"

She didn't answer. "Did he ever ask your help in getting American intercession?"

"He did not," said Larry.

"If you've got money hidden somewhere, I'll find it, you know," Charlotte said.

"God, I hope so," said Larry. "I can always use a little extra cash."

"Did you tell Hiro that?"

He hung up the phone.

¶ "Hello?" Charlotte said into the phone. She shook the receiver a few times, as if it would bring back his voice. She clenched her teeth and slammed down the receiver. He had dared to hang up on her. Well, he might not be as invulnerable as he believed.

The phone rang. The switchboard operator said there was a collect call from Stanley Mink, in London. He was legman for an American gossip columnist and had called Charlotte collect when Hiro landed at Heathrow, figuring she'd be interested. Charlotte had put him on a retainer to watch Hiro's movements and promised him a bonus for every detail. So far it had all been boring stuff. Hiro hadn't left his hotel because of all the press waiting in the lobby. The three networks had sent cameramen in the hope of getting some footage, as they were doing specials on him, even though no one knew what he really did, or for that matter, what he'd really done. But hard news with a mysterious ring was hard to come by.

"I'll accept," Charlotte said. It was a terrible connection, filled with echo waves and what sounded strangely like sirens. "Hello?" she said. "Speak up, Stanley. I can hardly hear you. . . . What are you saying?"

"I'm saying he's dead," said Stanley. "Threw himself off his balcony onto Park Lane."

"Oh, come on," said Charlotte. "It's a hoax. He wouldn't do anything like that." Hiro wasn't just a party giver, Charlotte knew, he was a partygoer. He loved being with people. He loved being alive. He'd prided himself on his American outlook. He'd never have done anything as oriental as suicide. He was so shrewd he'd probably thrown some other gook out the window. "It probably wasn't him."

"It's him, all right," said Stanley.

"Oh," said Charlotte. "Oh."

Mink gave her the details. He'd been wearing pajamas. How unsplendid of him, Charlotte thought. How untypically inelegant. And he hadn't left a note. How unsporting and sullen. She was so stunned by his cowardice she nearly wept. A shudder of something that might have been remorse, had she been foolish enough to let herself feel remorse about anything, washed over her. It was a pitiless world, a pitiless universe. You couldn't let yourself be touched by much or you'd go crazy.

She sat down to write his obituary. To her surprise, a tear fell on the typewriter key. But she was a journalist, she had a job to do. She started writing the obit, in front-page fashion, citing the accusations against him a little more freely now because he couldn't sue, he was dead. Dead. It sent a chill through her on the way to the newspaper morgue. She doubted there would be much of a file on him. His life had not been nearly as important as scandal had made it.

Poor Hiro. How he had loved celebrity. She couldn't help thinking how fitting it was, in a truly American way, that he should have become the town's biggest headline for Thanksgiving.

4

¶ To be a Quaker and a warrior put a man between a rock and a hard place. Larry Cochran was not a warrior in the traditional sense. He agreed with Franklin that there had never been and would never be a good war, or a bad peace.

He had been in conflict about the army when he left college to enlist in 1951. There were Quakers throughout history who, in spite of the doctrine of passive resistance, had taken part in wars. When William Penn was thinking of converting to Quakerism, he'd asked an elder how long he should wear his sword. "As long as you can stand it," the man had answered.

Larry had joined before being drafted, in the hope of moderating the warlike thought around him. Jefferson had said that error of opinion could be tolerated when reason was left free to combat it; Larry reasoned that a good place to combat error was a battle zone.

He felt the same way about Washington.

He did not imagine that government harbored too many idealists. There were hard, fast facts like ignorance, greed, and delusion.

In Meeting, surrounded by those who knew what aspiration was and held it more fondly than ambition, he nourished the peace within himself, and hoped it would spread to the world.

It was a tenuous peace he harbored, based on convictions about his God but none about himself. In spite of everyone's seeming assurance about him, the love of his friends and family, the confidence of those in government, he had grave doubts about his own adequacy. From time to time a wave of uncertainty would wash over him, and he would be convinced he was putting something over on the world. The more people praised him, the more frightened he became. And the harder he strove for the perfection he was sure would always elude him.

Most of his doubts stemmed from money. He was ambivalent in his approach to the material world. Although he knew it was all a test for the soul, a challenge for the spirit not to take money seriously, he had terrible fears that he would be without it, and fail. The role of public servant, underpaid, zealously devoted, was in fact a safe refuge for him, so that he would not have to undergo the pressure of the marketplace. These were not feelings he shared with anyone, including his wife. He confessed them to himself only at Meeting.

The meeting house where Larry worshipped lay across the Potomac past Chain Bridge, in the rich countryside of McLean, Virginia. Wylhallen House was old, simple, unlike a church. No altar rose, no chancel, no organ, no choir loft. There were four rows of wooden facing benches, the ones in back slightly elevated so that older Friends and those who had insights to share could sit directly facing the meeting. There were usually between sixty and eighty present on Sunday morning, congregating for an hour of silent prayer. Larry would come a few minutes early, take his place on the facing bench, close his eyes, and still his body, preparing to still his mind.

Usually Abby and the children came with him and sat on the benches opposite. The girls would subdue their restless natures, becoming almost serene, pridefully maternal as they tended to their younger brothers. Laddie with great effort had learned to sit quietly, J.J. would try to imitate Laddie's silence, only occasionally scratching himself or shuffling baseball cards.

Today, however, Abby had gone to fix Sunday breakfast for the Olifierris. Mr. Olifierri had been taken to the hospital during the night, and the doctor had sent Mrs. Olifierri home to rest. The sad aroma of death seeped through their neighborhood. Larry had told the children they could stay home and watch television—a greater distraction than God. Be still, and know I am television.

He thanked God for the health of his family, the joy they brought each other. He held up Albert Olifierri to God for intercession.

There was a rustle as someone entered late. Larry marshalled his concentration, tried not to hear the noise of the cars on the George Washington Parkway, tried not to dwell on the whispers of wind rattling the glass in the window sashes. Tried to move his mind to the place where the Light was, and let it rest there.

A Quaker's theology was his own, filled with respect for the better part of man, the God in him. The conviction that every man had this better part carried with it an obligation to relate to the finer aspect. Sometimes it grew a little hard to see; but always Larry looked for it. Always he clung to the certainty that God was immediate and available, streaking the hidden recesses of the soul like a rich vein of gold.

In those terrible days of Watergate, Larry had tried to quiet the churning inside himself with Nixon's religious origins. Something of truth and eternity had to counsel the man, if he looked to his Inner Light. In the history that unravelled, Larry thought perhaps Nixon had found an Inner Dark.

Politics. As serious as it was, everyone in it knew politics was a game, filled with adversaries, challenges, official and unofficial rules.

For Larry, it was less a game than a way to serve his God, and what he still believed with total conviction was God's country. The fact that the United States had been founded by men of spiritual faith, in addition to the crooks, gave him happy certainty that there was a blessing on the nation, that healing arms rocked the Cradle of Liberty.

These, too, were thoughts he did not speak aloud, except at Meeting.

An elder leaned forward on the bench behind and spoke of compassion for all creatures nourishing peace. A restive sigh escaped his lips, and the silence resumed.

A woman spoke from the bench opposite. "I was thinking," she said, "that perhaps a good way to feel compassion for other people is to realize that we are other people."

The voice was familiar, but Larry did not connect it with the Meeting. He had been coming to Wylhallen for nearly fifteen years; he knew everyone there like family. He opened his eyes to see who was speaking, and saw Megan O'Flannagan. Her bright orange hair wisped around her face, freckles danced on her cheeks. Her eyes were closed, and she was smiling.

"What made you come to our meeting?" he asked her, after the worship was concluded and they were drinking coffee with some others in the back room. "How did you find us?"

"I saw the notice in the *Washington Post*." She sipped from a paper cup set inside brown plastic, holding it with both hands, as if it could ground her, still the trembling. She had spent the evening before determined to practice moderation, and instead had put away half a bottle of gin. Now her hands were shaking, like society lushes who just managed to get the first lunch martini to their lips without spilling.

She had awakened very early in the morning, struggling to remember the night before, recapturing the mood of boredom and loneliness. The television was still on. There was a bottle on the table by her bed, and a half-filled glass. She'd been too drunk to finish drinking, a terrible sign. There was nothing for it but prayer and fasting, and maybe an affair.

She picked Larry Cochran's place of worship for her spiritual repair. She admired him, felt enormous attraction. To her he exemplified the Shavian ideal, from the days when she'd still had thoughts, of the modern political statesman as the only way out of the world's misery, provided he worked on the highest level of spiritual will. The worshipful sense of mankind Shaw had besought men to draw on in the service of progress was evident in Larry. He seemed to sport like a shield those qualities the playwright had found in truly religious men: dignity, conviction, and force. She wondered what he looked like naked.

In the small anteroom, crowded with simple souls conversing about coming picnics and vigils against bombers, she felt strangely serene, protected by his presence. Icicles hung outside the windows. Frost invaded the room. A potbellied stove burned wood that various Friends had brought to combat the chill. In summer, Larry told her, everyone had agreed they wouldn't waste gas trying to heat Wylhallen, with its old, uninsulated pre-Revolutionary walls. In fall their conviction had lifted them but now in the bone-chilling cold of January, the number of those attending had diminished, and those who came wore several sweaters underneath their coats.

Larry himself had a light blue turtleneck peeking above the collar of his overcoat and an old striped scarf twisted several times around his throat. His ears glowed red at their slightly pointed tips, his cheeks were bright with color, and his nose shone vermillion, like a child's, just come inside from sledding. She suppressed the impulse to touch it.

"Ciao, hello," said a perky young blonde in a raccoon coat, coming over to them. "I really enjoyed what you said before about our being other people. I'm Alana Perkins," she said, extending her hand.

"Megan O'Flannagan."

"Ciao, hello." She smiled. Her two front teeth were slightly overlapped, so her smile seemed to be dancing with itself. Her eyes moved to Larry Cochran's as did her wool-gloved hand. "Happy Sunday," she said.

"It's nice you came back," said Larry. "I thought maybe you'd been driven away by the cold."

"No, I just had something else to do last Sunday." She smiled even wider, teeth prettily bucked. "Well, ciao, goodbye," Alana said, and moved toward the door.

Larry looked after her. "I really enjoy it when young people who aren't regular members of the Meeting join us. It gives us energy. Will you be coming back?"

"I don't know," said Megan.

"O'Flannagan," he said. "Are you Catholic?"

"I was."

"The good in one religion is consistent with the good in all religions."

"I guess I believe in disorganized religion," she said.

Larry smiled. "How come some clever man hasn't pinned you down?"

"That's a long story."

"Will you tell it to me sometime?"

"I doubt it," Megan said. "But it's nice to know you're interested."

¶ Charlotte Dean had not been to church on Sunday since she was eleven and a half, except for a brief bout with the Baptists, which had taken place shortly after the Inaugural. She had cloaked herself in the guise of religion in order to better observe Jimmy Carter. Not even the Secret Service could keep her out when she wanted to see.

But Sundays as a tired rule she spent in bed, exhausted, reading newspapers. Every once in a while, in between the news stories, her eyes would fall on a tale of love, or devotion, or tenderness, and she'd experience a twinge of pain and loss, wondering why the universe had so cruelly abandoned her for a share of those things. But fortunately the papers she read did not carry too many human interest stories. The title of the category alone made her queasy.

So she stuck to the facts in the *Washington Post, The New York Times,* and the *D.C. Courier,* which heralded her in a banner atop the comics when she had a story inside. That she was missing from this Sunday's issue gave her the slightest turn, especially as the *Times* and the *Post* both featured a possible cabinet shake-up about which Charlotte hadn't heard. The fact that she hadn't heard anything made her fairly certain there was nothing to it. She had too many sources for her to miss a potential tempest. There was nothing bad, rumored, imagined, or real in the past six years that someone hadn't tipped to Charlotte. Still it made her uneasy that someone had something upsetting to say and it wasn't she.

The telephone rang on the Lucite table beside the flower-sheeted bed. The flower motif was carried up through the headboard, across the walls, and down to the drapes that opened on either side of the windows.

"Hello?" Charlotte said, with an edge to her voice. The call was on her private unlisted number, which informers called collect, station to station.

"Ciao, hello," said the voice on the phone. "It's me, Alana Perkins."

Charlotte smiled, lit a cigarette, and lay back against the flowered pillows. How clever she was the world could not imagine. She even had a spy posing as a Quaker. What God hadn't wrought, she had. "So?"

"Larry Cochran was with a woman at Meeting today. Megan O'Flannagan."

"At church," Charlotte said. "What an amusing rendezvous." She tried to subdue the excitement in her breast, the flutter of enthusiasm that always heralded the onset of an exposé. "How did the lovely Mrs. Cochran react?"

"She wasn't there. But O'Flannagan didn't come with him, and they didn't leave together."

"Spare me the unsordid details," said Charlotte. "How did she look at him. With longing?"

"I guess you could say that," said Alana.

"Well, then, I will," said Charlotte. She pressed the button, clearing the line, and dialed Amelia Gomez.

Once Amelia had been her greatest friend. They were starting reporters together on the *Courier,* and by the time they reached their thirties Charlotte loved her dearly. She regarded Amelia as beautiful, intelligent, and lovely in manner. The three in combination were extravagant, admirable, enough to make Charlotte forget that Amelia was having a visible breakdown.

It took no untoward perception to perceive the latter. They

had lunch together at least twice a month, and with the entree Amelia would burst into tears. At first Charlotte would wonder if Amelia would cry again this lunchtime. After a few noons she wondered only if the woman would do it over fish, chicken, or salad.

Amelia was unhappily married, wasn't everyone. But her marriage was a special brand of sour. She loved a man who had been terribly vital, who'd been crippled in a bizarre accident. Now he was sick and unemployed. It was horrible, simply horrible, especially if you hadn't eaten anything. It would have seemed less than compassionate if Charlotte had consumed her meal, what with the sobbing, and the fact that Amelia hardly touched her food. Charlotte made it a point to get as many mouthfuls in as she could before it started. But as time went on, Amelia fell apart the minute the waiter's hand left the plate.

It was hard to be greedy in the face of such suffering, especially as, hysteria aside, Amelia was truly affecting. Her mind, free of its personal obsessions, was razor sharp and humorous. Her body was stunning: Charlotte had never seen flesh tied on so tight to a body that never exercised. A natural beauty. She admired Amelia in a way she usually reserved for men in authority. It never failed to amaze Charlotte that there were such things as natural beauties. That they were unhappy in spite of it gave her jolts of self-confidence, if only because no one else had any either.

"It's all about money," Amelia had wept, over sole amandine. "I thought life had a spiritual base to it, or sexual, or psychological, but it turns out it's all about money. It's such a damned struggle. No one will give him a job, and my salary doesn't carry us. How can you work for a better world when you're worried about the material one?"

To see those flashing green eyes with their oversized whites reddened with sorrow and pain almost made Charlotte a socialist. It didn't seem fair to her either that a woman like that, so brilliant and funny when she wasn't sobbing, should have to be preoccupied with rent and food. And she looked so divine all the time. Charlotte had never concerned herself too much with clothes. Pale blondes looked good in basic black, so she wore it like a good-taste uniform, popping in a little white blouse now and then when she wanted to seem ingenuous. But Amelia was like an earth-colored rainbow, luxuriously auburn against browns and greens and tans and yellows, always fresh, crisp, new. How could she afford her clothes? How could she afford the dry cleaning?

"Why don't you take a lover?" Charlotte asked.

"Oh, I've thought about it," Amelia said, and blew her nose into a Kleenex. "There are men who have chased me for years. But it seems so degrading to George, and he's already suffered so."

"It wouldn't be degrading if he didn't know."

"Really?" Amelia said, her green eyes brimming with fresh tears, new hope. "I feel so out of tune sexually. I tried my diaphragm on last week just out of nostalgia."

"Take a lover," Charlotte said.

"You don't think it would be callous?"

"Not if he were rich," said Charlotte.

That night Charlotte had dinner with the editor of the *Courier* and asked him to try and throw some heavyweight assignments to Amelia. It was a generosity of character that was not very typical, but she could afford to be gracious, since her position at the paper was strong. Bigger stories did not carry with them bigger wages, but the more conspicuous Amelia became the better able she would be to threaten the paper with leaving if she didn't get a raise.

About a week later, Charlotte got a call from a professional agitator who was at Kent State, tipping her to the rumor that there was going to be a militant protest. College campuses bored her, whether or not they were inflamed, and she had really grown apathetic about Vietnam. Still, it was a slow time in the news, and there was always the possibility that something dramatic might occur. She had started packing a bag when she remembered Amelia.

"I've got a hot one for you," Charlotte said into the phone.

"They're expecting big trouble—antiwar riots at Kent State University. I've made travel arrangements, and Jimmy Gillim's set to go along to take pictures. I'll send him over to your place with tickets."

"Tonight?" Amelia said.

"Well, of course tonight. Time, tide, and riots wait for no man."

"But I've got a date," Amelia whispered into the phone.

"I'm excited for you," said Charlotte. "But this is a story."

"You know how long I've waited," said Amelia. "Hold on a second." There was the sound of a door closing, the phone being picked back up. "I mean, it was you who gave me the courage, Charlotte."

"But this is a story," Charlotte said again, a litany strung on ambition.

"Another student protest," Amelia said. "What difference will it make?"

"It could make a difference to you at the paper," Charlotte answered. "You get hot enough, you can squeeze them for a bonus, or a raise."

"I can't," Amelia said. "It took me too long to work up the strength. I'm meeting him at eight."

So Charlotte went to Kent State herself. The story was so big Charlotte received a permanent by-line and a promotion to senior staffer. Amelia passed her in the hall and did not stop to speak.

That July, Charlotte received a congratulatory basket of flowers from Amelia, with a subpoena in it. Amelia was suing her for unfair competition, claiming the Kent State story should have been hers.

"But it's a joke," Charlotte said to her lawyer. "That's silly. No court would ever accept it."

"Unfortunately you don't know the courts," said her lawyer.

They did not go to court. Charlotte's attorney took Amelia's deposition, which contained statements of how badly she had been used, how Charlotte had manipulated her for information and had maneuvered to have Amelia unavailable so she couldn't write the story, which would have doubtless earned her the Pulitzer.

"Crazy," Charlotte said, shaking her head, when she read the deposition.

"I know," said her attorney. "She's a very angry woman."

"But why at me?"

"You're successful."

"She was my best friend. We loved each other."

"She sued you," said the attorney. For him it was simple.

In the end, he advised her to settle, just to avoid the court costs. "It costs fifty-one dollars to sue," he said. "So any flake can come out of the wall and sue anybody. And what it costs to defend it. . . . Well. . . . She has a look of fierce determination on her face, like my ex-wife. She won't let go without your paying something."

"It's all about money," Charlotte said, fighting back tears. "That's what Amelia told me."

It cost Charlotte twenty-four hundred dollars including lawyer's fees. And it helped diminish her love for anybody.

Amelia had moved to another paper. Once in a while they would see each other at a party, and Charlotte would walk away. They had not spoken for nine years.

"Hello, Amelia," Charlotte said into the telephone.

"Who is this?"

"Charlotte. Charlotte Dean."

There was a deep breath on the other end of the line. "What do you want?"

"I have a story for you."

"Another one?" asked Amelia.

Charlotte visualized Amelia on a spit above an open fire, barbecuing slowly. "This is perfect for your column. You are still doing a gossip column?"

"Society features," said Amelia coldly.

"Well, this should fit right in. Lawrence Cochran has been secretly seeing former White House aide Megan O'Flannagan. This morning they were observed together at Wylhallen House, the Quaker Meeting in McLean."

"That sounds pretty innocent," said Amelia.

"Well, it isn't. They're using the church as a cover."

"And Jesus Christ as the beard?"

"Laugh if you want to," said Charlotte. "But it's a hell of a scoop."

There was a pause. Heavy silence. "Why are you giving it to me? Why aren't you writing it yourself?"

"I don't do that kind of story anymore," said Charlotte.

"I couldn't possibly print it. It's libelous."

"Not if you run it blind. Just don't use their names, cloud it, make it a puzzle."

"Well," Amelia said. "I'll see."

"Let me know now if you want it. If not I'll call Jack."

"He wouldn't print it either."

"Somebody will," said Charlotte. "Do you want it or not?"

"All right, and . . ." the words seemed to stick in her throat, "thank you."

"Oh, you're more than welcome," said Charlotte, and hung up the phone. For a moment, she was suffused with feelings so vulnerable, so human, she thought she was going to fall apart. She wanted to call Amelia back, and ask what she had done, why she'd been so betrayed when she'd loved her. But to expose herself again to that fury would be a mistake, and she knew it. It was best just to keep herself cold, untouchable, protected. Still, for a moment it did flash through her brain that perhaps much of the scorn she had for others had at its base a rejection she really hadn't earned. But the insight left her quickly, vanished, bubbled down into the cauldron inside her.

¶ For those who lamented the fall of Hollywood as the orgiastic playground of the world, the rise of scandal in Washington was a godsend. Major film studios having scattered, pictures being shot mainly on location, movie stars in general having passed as a breed, Fanne Foxe's hysterical plunge into the Tidal Basin had come just in time to restore America's faith in debauch in high places.

According to psychologists, sex in the capital was a release from the overwhelming pressure of knowing a job could disappear with the next election. According to Megan O'Flannagan's psychologist friend, Howard, a politician was a man who could not relate on a one-to-one level, and could only manage on a one to one thousand.

"But Larry isn't like that," she said to Howard, lying on his velvet upholstered window seat, sipping the cocoa he had made her. Outside the bay window, its panes frosted like a Christmas card, she could see the brave citizens of Georgetown carefully making their way along the icy red-bricked streets. "He isn't an elected official. He can relate one to one."

"They're all the same. He hasn't run for public office, that's all. But the psyches are uniform. He'd probably be very blunt in bed, selfish." Howard sat cross-legged on the carpet at her feet, sipping cocoa. He was a slight man in his early thirties, fair, with an extremely high forehead, as if his genes had gone along with the myth that a higher forehead housed a bigger brain. "And that would be affectionate by comparison. A lot of politicians see sex as power, reward, and punishment, so they prefer it kinky. Sadomasochistic. Tying women up, beating them, being tied up themselves."

"Why?" asked Megan.

Howard shrugged. "If you can live through one kind of beating, you can live through another and still go back for more in the next election." He broke a sugared donut and popped some into his mouth. "It's a way of keeping in shape."

"Are you generalizing, Howard, or do you know what you're talking about?"

"Both," he said. He grinned at her, and reached for her foot, dangling over the edge of the window seat.

"What are you doing?" she said.

"Fighting your frostbite," he said, rubbing her toes. "I wouldn't want you to go to him with stumpy feet."

"He's not like the others," said Megan. "I know he isn't. How many patients do you have who are politicians?"

"A number," said Howard.

"Please don't get professional with me, Howard. You're my

closest friend. You can tell me things without breaching confidence."

"No, I can't," he said.

"I would never tell anybody."

"Neither would I," said Howard, and grinned again, a little wider. "Anyway, you should give him up. It wouldn't be good in the kip, or anywhere else."

"I have to find that out for myself," Megan said. She looked down and saw that he had removed her sock. "What are you doing?"

"Acupressure massage," he said. "All your nerve endings are in your feet. It'll relax you."

She slipped off her other sock, extended her foot to him. He kneaded her insteps, pressed between her toes. His hands were powerful, amazing in a man so slender. She sighed and gave herself over to the pleasure of it, closing her eyes. "Why are you so good to me?" she sighed.

"Because you deserve it," he said. "Because I love you."

"I love you, too," she said.

"Then why don't we do something about it?"

She opened her eyes, and smiled at him. "How funny you are."

"Really?" he said. "Maybe I'm in the wrong business. Maybe I should give up psychology and become a comedian."

"I didn't mean 'ha ha' funny," she said. "I meant droll." She had known Howard for nearly four years, and had spotted him for the academic type, devotedly intellectual, his sensual fires unlit. All through her university life she had bubbled around campus making friends with just such men, avoiding athletes and all those whose blood obviously flowed. At the time her innocence was strengthened by religious conviction, a commitment to purity, and her hope of becoming a nun.

Now, in Washington, Howard seemed a safe, familiar harbor, a man consumed with the things of the mind, and so, disinterested in the body. She was secure in her conviction he was not a sexual being, being so brilliant, and thin.

Howard was a gift to her, a balance in the craziness that had been her life since coming to the capital. A gentle mind that fluttered above the pragmatic pressures around it and saw the truth.

It had been he who had first learned meditation in the desert and had sent her there to do the same when she feared that her sanity would go. She was afraid that there was no such thing as peace in the world, there could never be peace as long as it was in the hands of politicians. Politicians could deal with peace only in a crisis. They didn't understand what real peace was: not having to win.

It troubled her sometimes that the grasp of life she had attained in the desert eluded her so often in Washington. The pressure of the city, its politics, its politics posing as parties, sucked the serenity out of any situation. Even church was a political trip. Catholics went to Trinity in Georgetown, where the best political Catholics went. Baptists crowded in to be around Jimmy Carter on Sunday. And she had become a Quaker for the week for a glimpse of Larry Cochran.

Sometimes, when she relaxed the dogmatic, rational part of her brain, she could accept the idea of reincarnation as making a great deal of sense. If there were an Intelligence behind the universe, which she firmly believed there was, the purpose of life had to be spiritual evolution. Man had an obligation to improve. A lifetime was simply not time enough to repair a wrong attitude. So a spirit probably had to return until it achieved human perfection. When she accepted this idea, it occurred to her that Larry Cochran had probably been Thomas Jefferson.

They did not look unalike. There were the same light eyes, pale complexion, the bold nose, the stance, upright, a little leaning to one side, as if always preparing for oratory.

"I think Larry Cochran was Thomas Jefferson in a previous life," said Megan aloud, lying back in full relaxed comfort on the window seat.

"Okay," said Howard, rubbing her toes.

"Only I wonder what he did last time that he's being given such a hard time this time."

"What makes you think he's having a hard time?"

"He's poor," said Megan. "I mean he earns a nice amount of money but he hasn't been able to save a bean."

"How do you know that?"

"Oh, I see his clothes. I see his car. I see the way his wife dresses. I mean, she's a society leader. They're proper clothes, but they're not expensive, and most of them aren't new. Their house is an ordinary house. It's big, but it isn't fixed up. My God, what a comedown from Monticello."

"Have you been in it?"

"No. I've just seen it from the outside."

"Driving by it?" Howard said. "Late at night?"

She looked at him. "I get lonely," she said. "I start wondering what he's doing."

"You better start coming here when you're lonely," Howard said. "You're asking for a whole mess of trouble."

¶ The outside of Larry Cochran's home was brick in not very good repair. The wood that trimmed it was painted white, but not very recently. Larry kept meaning to get to it one day, when he had the time.

In front, on an unruly lawn, stretching from the flagstone walk to the sycamore trees lining the edge of the Olifierri property, was a sliding pond, a ring of ice, trimmed with rocks and soggy leaves, fashioned by Laddie and J.J. As Larry pulled up to his driveway, he could see his children playing on it: Sara, the dark twin, cheering encouragement to J.J., balanced in the center, holding on to a rope being pulled by Elizabeth, the fair one; Laddie, jeering. They were so beautiful, it was difficult for him not to feel proud. But pride would assume he had himself to thank, and he knew better.

God had given him radiant gifts. The only way to feel was humble. His humility was a source of contention between Larry and Abby. She wanted him to demand more for himself, to adjust his priorities and not be so self-effacing. He was not without ambition, being American, but ambition was a very tough word. He preferred aspiration, a prettier sound, pulling man skyward.

He did not apologize for his innocence. There were enough people in the world who had contempt for it to more than balance his joy. And he had sufficient doubts about himself in other areas. Innocence, he felt, was a boon.

He pulled into the garage and reminded himself he would have to clean it out when he had the time. He bounded up the back steps and into the kitchen.

Abby stood by the sink, the slender line of her back slightly curved as she hunched over, washing a plate with trancelike slowness. It nagged at him sometimes that a woman with her vast capacity for organization—museums, educational facilities, charities depended on her fund-raising capabilities—should be undone by household chores. Not that they were beneath her, or beyond her. She went at the most menial task with her usual goodwill. But their house had none of the conveniences that helped the average housewife. There was no dishwasher, no garbage disposal, nothing to lighten the boring burden. That he could not afford to give her the simple gifts of convenience saddened him, especially as she never complained.

He moved behind her, bent to kiss the back of her neck. Her skin tasted salty beneath his lips. She felt cold.

"Did you make them a beautiful breakfast?" he asked her.

"Mr. Olifierri's dead," she said in a monotone.

"There goes a human life," he sighed. "Far from the orchards of his childhood."

"It isn't right," she said, and her voice was shaking. She turned and looked at him with red-rimmed eyes, her lips trembling, a sponge clutched tight in her hand. "It isn't right that a man who served in Congress didn't have enough money to move his family home so he could die there."

"I agree."

"Then why don't you do something about it?"

"There's nothing I can do," said Larry. "Men go bankrupt running for office."

"There's something terribly wrong with a system where a man's finished just because he loses." She started to sob. He pulled her gently to him. Her eyes were pressed to the soft wool scarf around his neck. "Terribly wrong," she wept.

"It's the nature of the beast," he said, stroking her back.

"It is a beast," she said. "Politics is a beast that consumes everybody. Why don't you get out? Get out now, while you can still breathe, while you're still alive."

"But politics is part of my life."

"More important than us? More important than me?"

"Are you asking me to make a choice?".

"Of course not." She reached for the handkerchief in his pocket and blew her nose. "I just hate it so much that he died like that. I feel so awful for her. I feel so awful for everybody."

"I know." He lifted her chin, looked into the pale blue, red-streaked eyes. "I wish there was something I could do."

"You could go into private practice," she said. "There are a million law firms in this country that would jump to have you. You could make a hundred thousand a year without turning a hair. And we wouldn't feel so pressed, so continually strapped —we could afford good schools for the kids, and take a real vacation sometime, and I could get a rug, and re-cover the sofa, like every other woman in America."

"But you're not every other woman in America," he said. "You're Abby. You're unique." He took her by the shoulders. "I know how hard this is on you. I know how beautiful you'd look in fine clothes. I know how nice it would be to have money in the bank. If you really mean it, if you're that un-happy, I'll do it. I'll go into private practice."

"Don't you dare," she said, and stopped crying. "When the country fell apart I'd have only myself to blame, for taking you away from it."

He smiled and hugged her. "You're the best of breed, Abi-gail Cochran."

"No, I'm not," she said. "I'm like everybody else. I'm afraid about money. I hate being the kind of woman who's afraid about money. Money was never important to me." She took a deep breath. "Until I didn't have enough."

"I'm sorry."

"It's not your fault you're incorruptible," she said, and kissed him lightly. "What do you want for lunch?"

"I'll make myself something," he said. "Why don't you go to the museum?"

"I love you." She kissed him in earnest. "I really do."

"I intend to hold you to that," he said.

¶ Once Chris had loved Jess with every fibre of her being. Once she had looked on love with the hunger of the little match girl, her nose pressed against the window, doomed to stay outside, only catching the fragrance of acceptance. Jess had opened the door for her and asked her in. Childishly grateful, she clung to him.

Like all good masochists who had studied at the feet of women with no opinion of themselves except in terms of the men they associated with, married, worshipped from afar, Chris took her identity from the males who liked her, an erratic showing. As a child she had struggled for the approval of her father, who read poetry to her. She had answered him in poems, capturing him with the Gettysburg Address, which she recited at the age of two years and three months. It made her an admired freak in her neighborhood, got her the reward of Beech-Nut gum. But they got divorced anyway, her mother and father. He disappeared from her life. In her grief, she turned to sweets. Love vanished, people spoke words they didn't mean, like "I'll never leave you." Nothing could be counted on but frozen Milky Ways.

She turned to food with disappointed moroseness, revenging herself on herself for not being more of a lure. She ballooned past puberty. Although the world looked empty of one who might offer her love, it seemed to spawn a surfeit of those ready with rejection.

She did not limit her vista of those who could hurt her to actual lovers. She formed emotional attachments with agents who wanted only ten percent of her success, not, as she was willing to offer, a hundred percent of her vulnerability, her need, her dependence. As she began to marshal her scattered gifts into the discipline of a writer, she sought affectionate regard from her publishers, who were prepared to give authors lunch, encouragement, royalty checks when earned, and an occasional cocktail party if the budget were big enough. Professional men were terrified by her eagerness to place her life in their hands. All they had hoped for was a novel.

The more she was betrayed, the greater the conviction became that he was out there somewhere, Prince Charming who didn't mind fat girls, the man who would embrace her once and for all, shelter her from the pain of the world, the insensitivity of those who didn't understand her soul. Coupled with her certainty that such a man existed was her sureness that she didn't deserve him. So she submitted to the blandishments of fortune and an occasional rude affair, where the love she gave increased in direct proportion to the cruelty shown her.

When she met Jess, he had been so kind she hadn't been able to deal with him. He took her arm when they crossed the street, he held her hand in a movie. He was too considerate, too attentive. He made her nervous.

She couldn't understand why he wanted her, this straight-forward handsome man, athletic, strong in bed, brutalizing her slightly. But then which one of them hadn't. It was all a ravishing one way or another, the body or the spirit. Even the ones who had seemed sensitive were most sensitive to themselves. No one had ever thought of her feelings before their own.

Until Jess. As powerful as he was physically, there had to be some terrible weakness in him, that he cared for her. The confidence that he gave her with his company was matched only by her mistrust of his motive at being there.

She married him anyway. The pressures of society, her friend Louise, and her mother's not liking him were overwhelming. Besides, he asked her.

Still, in the corner of her heart that nurtured unworthiness, she knew there was a flaw in him for loving her. With the fall of Nixon, it seemed to emerge clearly: misplaced loyalty.

Dependence on a less-than-admirable cause to her seemed flaccid, spineless. She had leaned for strength on a weak man, and now he wasn't even around. By November 1973, the day the impeachment proceedings began, there was nothing to keep her bouyant in the world but Scott.

That the affair was unconsummated, that they had spent that historic day walking through Washington without really touching, was maddening but endurable. He was keeping her alive.

When Chris got home that evening, there was a message on the service that Jess would not be home for dinner. More surprising would have been the news that he would be. They had not eaten together except for weekends and an occasional lunch since Watergate exploded.

She fixed a lackluster dinner for herself and the children, ate without tasting, a smile frozen on her face as if she were really perceiving how charming her children were. She drank wine with her dinner, a little too quickly and a little too much, and took a large goblet upstairs with her to watch the news.

The news had become addictive. Crisis was her daily fix, as it was to everyone in Washington. For her it was slightly more personal, tinged with sexuality. The state of the union, in turmoil, was the state of her union with Jess.

She turned on the TV, sat on the bed, and drank the wine. Most of the time, in her own home, she moved like a slumberer, only half aware. At night she would try to be asleep by the time Jess came home, so that there'd be no argument over sex. It amazed her that as drained as he was, as overworked and put upon, he still had the energy, still had the capacity to make love.

From the TV came the stunning announcement that Nixon had agreed to turn over the White House tapes. John Chancellor shook his head as he told the news, unable to believe it even as he reported it.

She did not know what time Jess came home, she was either asleep or unconscious. He was gone before she awakened. They missed each other again on Wednesday, but his secretary called to apologize for him. "Things are just a little crazy here," she said.

On Thursday Kissinger held a press conference that dealt with the crisis in the Middle East. Democratic scuttlebutt was that the crisis was invented to get the heat off. The truth of that rumor was nothing Chris could check. Jess didn't come home again till after she was sleeping.

She found a note pinned on her pillow in the morning. "My God, you looked lovely," he had written. "I had to control myself."

A rush of remorse passed over her. She had had too much wine again the night before. She smelled sour to herself, as if she had turned to vinegar inside. As long as he wasn't going to touch her, the private part of his life, the tiny corner that didn't belong to Nixon should have been sweet for him.

Jess. He was the nicest man in the world, she didn't doubt it for a minute. She was so covered with guilt, she called to invite him to lunch, knowing he wouldn't be able to accept.

"He said he'd be delighted," his secretary said. "He's in a meeting until one, so could you come here?"

There was always some feeling of martial grandeur in going to the White House. To pass through iron gates and show identification to special police made Chris feel terribly special, lifted her spirits in spite of her feelings about the President, gave her an automatic upper. But on that November noon there was such a deadly quiet about the building, and all that surrounded it, she was filled with a curious sense of apprehension.

On the ground floor of the Executive Office Building she passed the Searching and Central Files Section. A number of doors were marked Central Files, Referral Section. The custodian of those, according to the legend beside the door, was Miss Evalena Leake.

It was Restoration Comedy, Chris thought, more unbelievable in its mad reality. She climbed the cold, grey, stone balustraded stairs to the first floor. There were two Secret Service men outside the President's office. That meant the President was inside working.

She opened the door to Jess's office. She had always meant to redecorate for him. It looked so cold to her, the chalk grey walls strung with standard White House portraits; she had always intended to send plants. She would do it this afternoon, right after she called Scott.

"Oh, Mrs. Betzer," Jess's secretary said, getting out from behind the mahogany desk. "They were supposed to tell you at the gate. You're to meet Mr. Betzer in the West Wing. He's in the Oval Office. I'll take you over."

"Thank you, Ellen," Chris said. They started down the hall. "What's he doing in the Oval Office when the President's here?" she asked.

"Some visiting dignitary from someplace. Mr. Betzer's receiving him."

"The President's a little busy, I guess," said Chris.

"I suppose so," said Ellen very quietly.

"What's it like here now?" Chris asked. It was not a fair question to ask a secretary, especially within hearing of the Secret Service. Everyone in the place lived in fear of their jobs, of the next swift turn of the President's mind, of being bugged. Conversations among the White House staffers in which opinions were expressed were restricted to the aisles of Safeway.

"It's quiet," Ellen said, very deliberately. "What little action there is is on this floor. There used to be a lot of action on the floor upstairs. That was when we had a Vice President."

They exited the building, crossed the parking lot, and entered the West Wing. Chris moved up the tiny steps that always seemed more suited to a small Georgetown house than to an executive mansion.

They were outside the Oval Office. There was a small bronze statue of George Washington mounted on a pedestal in the curve of the alcove. On the head of the statue rested a red delicious apple.

"Mrs. Betzer is just waiting for her husband," Ellen told the guard.

"Okay," he answered.

"What's the apple doing on Washington's head?" Chris asked him, after a moment.

His face split into a grin. "I've had it there for five hours, and no one's noticed till you."

"Chris?" Jess was standing in the doorway.

She always forgot how tall he was, how imposing. She reached for him with warm tender hands. He looked so tired and drawn she was suffused with affection for him, especially as he could do nothing about it in the White House.

"The Galley all right?" he asked her, moving his arm behind her, gliding her gently through the door. His fingers were firm on her back, assuring. She wanted Scott's.

They hardly spoke through lunch. She wanted to ask him what was really going on, but she was afraid he might be evasive. The atmosphere and design were those of a small naval officer's mess. The kitchen was run by the navy. It was like being married to a man who was secretly at war. There were only eight other people, scattered, at the round wooden tables. But they too were quiet.

She told him an anecdote about the children. She told him about the apple on the statue's head. He didn't laugh. She realized with horror they had nothing to say to each other.

Somehow, she lived through the weekend. On Monday she went to the Cox hearing.

Across from her, the press gathered. Ethel Kennedy joined their line, leaned against the wall, a small, intermittent pout of devastation on her otherwise smiling face. Her eyes were as brightly brown as the zippered vinyl coat she wore, and her matching patent leather Gucci shoes. She seemed a little nervous, about her country and the possible presence of *Women's Wear Daily,* Chris supposed. She kept touching her yellow hair, gone a little frizzy in the rain. But her face was open and cheerful, the skin around her eyes remarkably unlined for the children, the years, and the pain. And once, only once, when George McGovern strode by the packed corridor and the students and internists in line broke into spontaneous applause, was there a sign on her face, when she realized who and what they applauded, of how much, exactly, had been lost.

Just before ten, a guard collapsed a few feet away from Chris.

The rescue squad didn't come. A janitor went by pulling a yellow painted dolly which for a moment was thought to be rescue equipment. Forty-five minutes passed. Another guard announced that the hearings were postponed until two that afternoon. The corridor slowly cleared.

The guard died at eleven-thirty, on the press table.

Chris walked numbly in the light falling rain, trying not to be intimidated by death. It had all been a drama, Watergate, an automatic rescue squad for the bored, the angrily restless, the people who ate chocolates and delivered homilies. Those who would have been suicides had they foundered in their own morbid desperation had suddenly found something to live for. Marriages were saved as it took husbands' and wives' minds off each other. All had a common fascination.

But as involving as it was, it seemed hardly the proper background for anything so real as death. It showed how vulnerable everybody was. How temporary.

She went to a nearby restaurant and stood at the bar drinking wine, not even attempting to make it seem pleasurable, downing just enough to make her stupid, to dull the pain.

Then she found a bench in the middle of a park and started to weep: about death, about life, for the guard whose story was over, for herself and Scott, whose story had scarcely begun, might not ever begin, really. She thought of her children and cried for them, that they, too, were mortal and had a mother who'd abandon them if Scott demanded it. She remembered how lovely they were, how funny, how desperately she'd wanted them, how much she'd feared she would be unwed, childless. Something greater than guilt washed over her, but not thoroughly enough to cleanse her of longing.

When she got back to the hearing she was empty, spent. There was a large basket of flowers in the front of the room, sent by the senators on the committee in memory of the dead sergeant. Senator Ervin reminded the onlookers how much everyone owed law enforcement officers. Behind Chris, three of his neighbors from Morgantown told those around them that yes, indeed, that was the way Senator Sam was around home, same as on television. In front of Chris, Ethel Kennedy took off her vinyl coat. Cox began his testimony about being fired. Several people fell asleep.

It was all so brief. Life. Death. Nothing continuous except testimony. Flowers as part of a scene for something else, that was all that was left of a man.

She got up and left the hearing room. Outside, the rain had

stopped falling. There was a stir of seedpods on the air, flutter-ing to earth like yellow beige butterflies, caught on the gentle wind. The sight of autumn lightly asserting itself brought sol-ace to her eyes. The promise of spring, and seedpods reborn, brought the hope of continuity to her soul.

Maybe there were brighter possibilities. Maybe life re-generated like seedpods fallen to earth. Maybe it was all a dance for the spirit. Maybe there was justice, and love, and God, and Nixon would be out, and she would be together with Scott.

5

¶ Gloria Stanley was all at sea. Literally. Contemplating her stage debut excited and terrified her. Contemplating her personal life, or lack of one, did the same.

The love of the world was transient, hypocritical, the love of men was cocky. She intended no pun, they were arrogant simply because they had one. So in the winter of her thirty-seventh year, there was nowhere to turn, except possibly God. Instead, she took a cruise.

Women were vessels, poured into, drunk out of, they had to bear; she understood that. So she set sail toward a new beginning, her own metaphor. She had decided to simplify her life, selling her villa in France, leasing the one in Majorca. She'd given away all her clothes, except for the ones she would need on the cruise, and for rehearsal time in Washington. At first she had considered sending them to Princess Grace, for Monacan relief, if there was any. Instead she had distributed them among the poor of Palma and thrown herself a farewell gala so that the women would have an occasion to wear the gowns.

It had been a glorious event, radiant with the impoverished. She had seen herself coming and going, as she would have been if her life were not enchanted, had she been born an ordinary woman, in a civilization not brightened with dreams. She had witnessed herself young and old, fat and thin, short and tall, wrinkled and innocent. It was like watching herself pass through many incarnations at the end of *Siddhartha*.

Having thus cut away excess, she squeezed her remaining worldly belongings into two steamer trunks and several hatboxes. She no longer wore hats—hardly anyone did but the Methodists. The boxes contained wigs, various lengths and styles, to make living possible. Having decided to change her life into one of basics, she thought it would not be seemly to take Sergei, her hairdresser.

That had been a harder farewell than to any of her husbands. He, less than she, understood what had happened to the movies. It was beyond Sergei how glamor could have been so cruelly banished, as if it were an old hairpiece. Gloria could not bear to look at the sadness in his eyes as, comb in hand, he waited for her next movie, like a faithful dachshund, age encroaching, ass dragging ever closer to the ground.

"There will be no next movie, Sir Gay," she told him over champagne at their farewell.

Theirs had been as loving a relationship as any in Hollywood. He had always helped her with what to wear, who to marry. But the days of entourages were vanished, like big budget extravaganzas.

So, bravely alone, she set sail on the *Halcyon*, from Barcelona eastward to the other side of the world, on her way to Washington. The steamer accommodated twenty passengers, the fare was exorbitant, assuring her there would be no one on board from the scandal papers, or any country that couldn't afford her as a houseguest.

Not that she was looking for friendship. What she sought was solitude, to prepare for her debut on the stage, she told Bunyan Reis, in the hope he'd tell everyone. Bunyan had come to her farewell party at the villa in Palma to give her a portrait he'd done from a nude of her shot through a telephoto lens and printed in *Hustler*. In spite of the fact that Bunyan's art had gone through an evolution (in the wrong direction, critics said) his personal popularity was at an all-time high. He had just been released from jail where he had been sent for the murder of his chauffeur-lover, was once again welcome at the best dinner parties, had been interviewed on "60 Minutes." That he flew all the way to Majorca simply to say goodbye to her moved her deeply.

"Oh, but it isn't goodbye, sweet princess," he said, donning his pearl grey gloves the morning after the party. Everything about him glittered greyly, his eyes, his straight Dutch-boy bob. Only his bright pink tongue, measuring his words, flicked color against his shiny pallor. "I'm seeing you off on your ship."

"How good you are to me," she said, wondering why the homosexuals of the world were the ones who were so attentive, so considerate. It was some hormonal imbalance in the cosmos, she was sure.

As he was going with her to the boat, she had no choice but to take along the portrait he had painted. She did not like it very much: the paparazzo who had taken the photo had caught her with her appetite up, and so lumpy around the hips. She had planned to leave the painting in the cellar of her villa, turned to the wall. But as Bunyan was with her, she had to take it to Barcelona. She covered it with a sheet and ropes. She looked at it sadly, a spectre it appeared to her, the ghost of her past. There was something horribly philosophic about it all. No matter how much you wanted to leave yourself behind, you always carried yourself with you, especially when the painter was watching.

"Well, it's good you're looking for solitude," Bunyan said when he saw the passengers gathered in the salon. "They're all so old." His face wrinkled with distaste. He took Gloria's arm and steered her toward her cabin. "Maybe you'll get some action from the crew."

"Bunyan!" she said. "This is a voyage for contemplation."

"Ah, yes, of course," he said, smiling slyly.

¶ "Well, you'd be safe," he said after the handsome young steward had gone. "The crew is Dutch, and the Dutch are the most fastidious people in the world. They'll be very busy preening the ship and polishing their dicks." He sat down in one of the blue upholstered chairs, nailed to the floor of the cabin. "Cleanliness next to godliness comes from them, you know. When the Pilgrims were held over in Holland on their way to religious freedom, it was the Dutch who made them anally compulsive."

"I didn't know that," said Gloria, reading the card attached to a big basket of flowers. It was from her lawyer. She tried not to be disappointed. Once, just once, she wanted to set sail on a voyage, a marriage, something, that didn't involve well-wishers in her employ.

"Hence the origin of Old Dutch cleanser." Bunyan settled back and put his feet on the nailed-down coffee table, nearly knocking over a basket of fruit from her business manager.

Her bank in Majorca had sent a case of sparkling wine. Her bank in Switzerland had sent champagne. Her bank in New York had sent nothing, either because she had forgotten to notify them or because she didn't matter any more, the account having been wiped out by her last ex-husband.

There was really a sense of relief in this voyage. For once she had no intention of looking for a man. What she'd told Bunyan was true: she wanted to prepare for the play. The PLAY. It already sounded more important than anything she'd ever done. The MOVIE. The WEDDING. It wasn't the same. The ghosts of Shakespeare and Sheridan danced around her stateroom. She felt nearly happy.

"I'm not on this trip for romance," she said to Bunyan. "I want to clear my head."

"It's your tubes I'm concerned about. I have something for you." Bunyan opened his zippered purse, from Louis Vuitton. All through his jail sentence he'd tried to sneak into Guccis so that his feet at least would retain a sense of proportion. That the guards kept making him change into regulation shoes showed the extremes of their cruelty. That, and that they didn't intercede when men were raped, or he wasn't. "Here." He handed her a small package, tied with a little pink bow.

"Why, thank you." As many presents as she had received in her lifetime, it always excited her to get a gift from a man.

Not that she would have admitted it. Not for a minute did her life depend on material things, as she had told Andy Warhol's *Interview*. Still, when precious little could be measured of how much the universe cared about you, it was reassuring to get a scarf by messenger.

She unwrapped the small package. Inside was a tiny gold square the size of a cigarette lighter. "But you shouldn't have," she said, not knowing what it was.

"It's a transistorized vibrator," said Bunyan. "For the girl who has everything. Aren't the Japanese clever?"

She withered him with a glance she had not been able to use since the one time they let her do Brontë, and handed it back to him, cheeks flaming.

"I only wanted you to have a relaxed voyage," he said. "I thought it was funny."

"Your sense of humor could use some work," said Gloria, rubbing lip gloss furiously on her lower lip.

"I've been in the slammer, belleza," he murmured. "All those Rough Trade Ralphs. I've lost my subtlety."

He looked so forlorn she remembered he had killed for love, and forgave him. It was not his fault that she was practically an innocent in his terms.

When the ship sailed, Bunyan was standing on the dock waving a pearl grey handkerchief. In the last glimpse she had of him, he was blowing kisses at her and several sailors.

¶ The skies above the Mediterranean were sprinkled with stars. Each night Gloria ate dinner in her cabin to avoid the wizened stares of the other passengers, and afterward she would walk on the deck, trying to spot the constellations, and to not want dessert. She was being very careful with herself, keeping her diet down to a thousand calories a day, drinking only Perrier water. In the morning she sunned to bring her complexion to a radiant gold, and in the afternoons she smoked hashish. Not enough to obliterate herself but sufficient to deaden the boredom, to make her believe she would be a success in the play.

By the time she reached the Gulf of Aden, she regretted having returned Bunyan's gift. There was no one among the passengers she had any wish to talk to: there was only one other woman under fifty, a German widow. Gloria had read everything in the ship's library and reviewed *The Complete Works of Shakespeare,* which she'd brought along. She was bored. There seemed to be nothing for it but to fall in love.

His name was Ahnie. He'd been following her around the deck every night since the ship left Barcelona. He was tall, extremely fair, and extremely slim in his white uniform, which was cut wide through the shoulders, accentuated with gold braid, and very narrow through the hips so she could see very clearly what Bunyan would have called his basket.

It was as fine a basket as she'd ever observed without seeming to be looking. Whenever she'd gone to gym class or sea or the beach in a bikini, she'd watched the eyes of men move directly from her breasts to her vulva, scanning her like a radar screen for important weapons. She had always felt a vague sense of distaste, a visual assault, insulted. As if she had no soul, no sense of poetry or of art. As if the celebrated champagne eyes, the classical features, the thick golden hair were incidental, and what really mattered was her hole. It practically made her a feminist.

In self-defense, or perhaps revenge, she began checking out men in the same manner. Offhandedly, of course; she was never blunt enough to stare. But she had become somewhat expert in judging how men were hung, especially if they were thoughtful enough to wear tight pants, which Ahnie certainly was.

She knew his name was Ahnie because he had come to her one dusk as she stood looking out at the sea, and whispered, "I am Ahnie." She hadn't said anything to him, merely turned and not really smiled, just moved her lips a little, and locked eyes with him. His eyes were very bright, wide set and clear, his nose was straight and slightly wide, his mouth was not very full, and his dong was enormous.

She did not tell him who she was; he would have to know that. There was a buzz on the ship whenever she moved around. Little Dutch sailors brought her bouillion as she sunned in the deck chair. Some of them spilled, they were so nervous at her presence. But Ahnie seemed very cool.

She judged him to be about twenty-six, which meant he was not as experienced as she, so his lovemaking would probably be crude. But the air was warm in the Gulf of Aden, the night was heavy with stars, more constellations than she'd ever seen in Western climes. The Southern Cross. She could actually see it, brilliantly. The climate of Arabs, sheiks, men who had no tenderness for women. She could hardly wait.

The hot night winds trailed her long chiffon scarf. She heard his footsteps and turned, and saw him illuminated against the starry night. She walked toward him and let the scarf blow across his face. He smiled. He looked so handsome she was tempted to kiss him, there on the deck, in the moonlight, in the presence of God and possible paparazzi. But instead she whispered, "Cabin twenty."

She nearly flew down the metal steps. Lightness of foot was not one of her salient characteristics, but there were moments when she was nearly graceful, when her ebullience lifted her above her natural clumsiness. It was a terrible thing to be a beauty, admired, adored, with a tendency to trip. A woman that looked like she did should have floated above the vicissitudes of life, should have wafted through it all like Isadora Duncan.

The mere thought of that tragic creature made Gloria slow her step, check her scarf. She had no intention of reaching an unhappy end, no matter what the fan mags said.

In her cabin, she undressed quickly and slipped into a diaphanous robe she always travelled with, in case. She never had intentions of being easy. At the age of thirty-six she still considered herself a girl who didn't put out, as they had categorized it in high school. But this was the ocean, this was a warm and balmy night in a place she'd never been, and she'd never had a Dutchman, and she hadn't gone off her diet.

There was a light knock at the door. To her surprise, she found her knees were shaking. She wondered if it was excitement, or if she wasn't really afraid, if the truth of her life was that men had hurt her, and this one might too. She gave a merry little laugh at the foolishness of such a thought, and opened the door.

He looked at her with the most direct look she had ever experienced. He started with her eyes, and then he viewed her body, measured it. He locked the door behind him and opened his jacket, unzipped his pants.

"Now just a minute," said Gloria. "You could at least say hello, or kiss me."

His erection sprung free of his trousers, targetting her. He slipped off his shoes, got out of the pants, and pushed her back on the berth.

"Hey . . ." she started to say, but his penis glowered at her, thickly purple, heavily veined, bobbing like an obscene buoy on a lily white ocean. For a moment she was afraid he was going to stick it in her mouth. Not that she minded when she knew who it was, but this was . . . my God, this was a sailor. And her mouth wasn't big enough.

Instead, he stuck it into her left breast, drilled against her nipple, then straddled her and rubbed up and down her belly, squeezing her breasts together and pressing himself between. His penis was hard and hot. She could feel his testicles gently bouncing against her ribs, the warm line of his scrotum straining on her skin.

His face swooped downward. For a moment she thought he was going to kiss her, and her lips softened, as did her heart, preparing for adventure that surpassed eroticism. But his face stopped inches from hers. He fixed her with a steely blue-eyed gaze, and pressed her legs together, hard. He began rubbing himself against her lower belly, stroking her mons with his penis, rhythmically rubbing himself through the tangle of her hair. Then he pressed her legs more tightly together, and insinuated himself between her clasped thighs. He moved himself slowly against the outside of her labia.

She could feel her own heat rising. Her nipples were burning. She wanted to beg him to touch her breasts at least, to cool them with his tongue, but he was moving with such grim efficiency she was fearful of interfering. A circle of warmth moved down through her pelvis, blazed across the inside of her thighs, fired the friction between them. All of her being jettisoned toward the place where he touched her.

And she was exploding. Relief washed over her like a balm. She moaned softly. He grinned, and thrust himself inside her. Her own releasing tremors broke around his hardness. He was moving like a sudden strong tide, ripping at her insides, carrying her away. He put his forearms under her buttocks and lifted her with powerful hands. He made slow revolutions with his pelvis, drew circles with his penis against the lips of her vagina. And then he was battering with hot, angry rhythm, poking so deep she could feel him in her womb. Her whole body was inflamed.

She pulled at him, tried to reach for his face so that she could angle him toward her, to kiss him. But he was speeding past her now, whipping them both into frenzy. His face contorted, the pummeling softened. He groaned, an animal groan. And she was coming again, feeling the warm, coursing wetness inside her. He eased her down and fell against her, sweat like a light veneer of dew between them. They were silent, breathing in each other's arms. He'd never even kissed her. Two orgasms, and there hadn't been romance. She had read every smart writer on sex from Marya Mannes to Masters and Johnson. She knew from Mannes the tyranny of the orgasm, from Masters the myth of the vaginal one. That she had accomplished two without benefit of foreplay stunned her. She was so nonplussed she didn't try to hold him when he climbed off her and went to the basin to wash it, just the way Bunyan said he would.

"Goodbye," he said, when he was dressed. "Tomorrow, yes?"

"What time?" asked Gloria.

"Ten o'clock. After dinner."

"Come at nine," she said. "I'll have your dinner here."

It was just the way Bunyan said, prophylactic, a cleansing of the tubes. A way to stay healthy. A release. In her whole life she'd never felt anything so uncomplicated.

She giggled through most of the next day, wrote brief, affecting postcards to everyone she liked. "Hi, miss you, love you," most of them said. It was a wonderful secret, loving a sailor. Not that she loved him, of course. She didn't even know if he had hair on his chest. He hadn't even taken off his jacket.

She walked on the deck around dusk, watched the sun sizzle in the sea, radiantly purple at its final sighting. She felt the hot winds against her face, stood aft on the topmost deck and studied the ship's rudder churning the green blue water white. The Arabian climes. In all her life she had never been kidnapped. And now fate had brought her an officer in the Arabian Sea.

It did not occur to her there was some subtle masochism in her nature. She considered herself a typical woman, more celebrated than most, but just as yielding, certainly as feminine. That that particular feminine principle at times wanted not only to yield, but to be victimized, eluded her.

The breeze was a myriad of warm, gentle fingers toying with her face, curling her hair, whipping her clothes around her skin like soft caresses. There was wind at her back, like a hug. The soft pink line in the sky receded, sank with the trumpeting sun below the horizon. For a moment the ocean glowed red.

Above her, a pocket of light opened in the grey blue dusk. A star appeared, tentatively, moving like a shy child into the panoply of sky.

The blue tent of night ballooned around her. Planets and stars began to present themselves in royal array. For a moment she perceived the universe in all its magnificence, all its generosity. A wave of something quite like joy washed over her. She assumed it was because she was going to get laid.

She had ordered two bottles of champagne, chilled, and several trays of hors d'oeuvres. That way the steward would think she was having several people in for drinks, and not a lover to dine. Discretion had never been in Gloria's erotic vocabulary: either a girl went to bed with men or she didn't. But discreet, discreet was something she understood perfectly. He was so silent and sullen he would doubtless keep quiet about her. If not, nobody would believe him anyway. There was no way the world could learn about their affair.

Affair. It sounded so important, already. She checked the hors d'oeuvres. They were splendidly aligned, like little fattening armies.

At eleven o'clock, Ahnie still hadn't come. She dressed, put on flat shoes so that she wouldn't go sliding into the sea, and went looking for him. She found him coming out of the cabin of the German widow.

"You . . ." slut, she wanted to say, but that wasn't the right word for a man. Besides, the ignorant son of a bitch probably only knew ten words in English: I am Ahnie, goodbye, tomorrow, yes, ten o'clock, after dinner. He hadn't even said "Hello," and now he wasn't even saying "I'm sorry." He just stood there grinning, like the ape he was. It was so insensitive she almost considered taking him seriously.

Instead, she went back to her cabin and started eating hors d'oeuvres. She looked down from the pinnacle of her rage and saw that an entire tray was empty, and she hadn't even tasted them. She realized with horror that a man who didn't understand who she was, what she was, was making her eat. She piled the remaining hors d'oeuvres onto one tray, went up to the deck, and threw them, a canapé at a time, into a soundless sea.

In the morning the ship was being followed by a school of sharks. "The story of my life," Gloria couldn't help thinking.

¶ Museums bathed Abby's spirit. They were shrines commemorating beauty, a yoga stretch for the eyes. No matter how dour her mood was, how complex the activity of her day, she had only to hear her footsteps echo against a cool terrazzo floor, to move through the quiet shadows, to gaze at a painting, a sculpture, a remnant of another time, another civilization, to feel cooled, to feel cleansed.

That she had been asked to serve as a trustee for one of Washington's finest museums was a tribute to Abby. Unlike most women who worked on the service council of museums, staffed membership desks, hostessed events, or assisted in curatorial departments, Abby was not wealthy.

To become a trustee was a great honor, one that held implicit in it wealth and connection. In Abby's case the connection was correct. She was an expert and graceful fund raiser. But money raising was not the only talent required of a trustee. There was as much politics in the successful conduct of a museum as there was in government. Each department bubbled with ego, each ego had to be assuaged. The man who sold postcard reproductions in the bookshop of the Kirkeby considered himself as important to art as the director of the museum. Abby treated him accordingly.

Setting up an exhibition, however, required more than a good political hand. Politics involved manipulation, trades and exchanges, an overall game plan. An exhibition at a museum was on a higher level, requiring the machinations of a Metternich. That the Kirkeby Museum had decided to sponsor an exhibition of the art of Sri Lanka had been the result of masterful diplomacy on Abby's part.

The importance of such a show to the Sri Lankans was inestimable to that small nation, eager to attract the attention of a large Western ally. Private representatives of Singhalese art had come to Washington to speak to the State Department about exhibiting their country's art. It was to be the first major exhibition of the art of what was once Ceylon.

The country's art was mainly in its temples. Sculptures fifty feet high stood tribute to man's admiration of serenity, but were impossible to transport.

But with the digging out of a recently discovered *stupa*, a monument containing priceless relics and bronzes, it became conceivable, and highly desirable, Sri Lanka had decided, to bring an exhibition to Washington. It had been noted that those who made inroads into art in America made inroads into politics. There had been a sudden swift turn of governmental mind, to want to cultivate the United States. The advantages of cultural exchange seemed inestimable.

After several attempts to interest the Smithsonian (booked for several years for such exhibitions), the Sri Lankan diplomats turned elsewhere. As a trustee of the Kirkeby Museum, Abby Cochran's warm presence and popularity at art events soon became known to the Sri Lankans. In their innocence they assumed the Kirkeby, being in Washington, was a government museum, and a suitable arena.

At a black tie dinner before the opening of an exhibition at the National Gallery, Mr. Nadapura, a member of Sri Lanka's Arts Council, had introduced himself to Abby. He seemed to know a great deal about her. She was embarrassed that she knew nothing of Sri Lanka or its art.

The next morning she received a basket of roses along with an invitation to a reception at the Sri Lankan embassy and a privately printed catalogue incorporating descriptions, sketches, and pictures of Singhalese art. Abby attended the reception, where she found herself gloriously wooed, the object of subtle oriental flattery. In the ensuing months she met with members of the Arts Council. Eventually she agreed to try for an exhibition at the Kirkeby.

Abby knew there was an opening for a show at the museum in spring. She took Dr. Sam, the museum's curator, to a champagne lunch at the Madison Hotel. By dessert, a chocolate souffle blazing with Armagnac, he considered the exhibition of Sri Lankan treasures to be his inspiration.

Dr. Sam presented the idea to Roger Hammermill, the director, who in turn brought it up before the board. All twenty-two trustees approved it with nothing less than the enthusiasm with which Abby had mentioned it to them at a cocktail party at the Sri Lankan embassy the evening before.

She did not have to be subtle, because she was so sincere. That it involved some minor intrigue, that there was promise of financial reward—not much, but enough to allow the Cochran's some small luxuries they couldn't otherwise afford, like a maid once a week—was, although slightly worrisome to her, beside the point. The art was good, her efforts in the end would benefit many people. There was no need even to mention the remuneration to Larry. It was all part of the Washington scene, doing favors, bringing people together. It would be a feather in the cap of the Kirkeby, the first large showing of the art of

Sri Lanka in the United States. A show in the spring, the loveliest season in Washington, a time of newness, of promise, for
the Sri Lankans, and for Abby herself.

She walked up the stone steps of the museum, clinging to the
railing, paying attention to each of her movements as she would
have to do with her words. One more favor for a friend—Jess
Betzer—was all there remained to do. She could not risk offend-
ing anyone by seeming to intrude her own choice of public relations man to handle the exhibit, however. The museum had its
own public information officer, a bright young woman named
Adrienne Harvey, who was efficient, and the tiniest bit imperious. She would resent having a co-worker thrust on her, no matter how amiable, no matter how helpful. Abby would have to
walk on eggs, employing more tact than she had ever shown, to
make Adrienne think that Jess was an asset and treat him as one.

Poor Jess. Abby wondered how he still walked around, how
he slept at night, *if* he slept. Once Larry had been out of work
for six weeks and had nearly gone crazy with worry. It didn't
matter what credentials you had in politics, how gifted you
might be, how experienced. Everything depended on who won,
and whose friend you were.

She wondered what she would have done in Chris's place,
how she would have survived. She could not imagine being
able to support a family. That her own great talent for helping
other people might be turned into an occupation never occurred to her. That the Sri Lankans had offered a gift was not
what inspired her efforts. There was joy in service. In having
to earn a living there was pressure, apprehension. She preferred
joy to being afraid of the future. As far as she was concerned
the future didn't have to take care of itself, Larry Cochran
would take care of it. Larry would take care of everything.

She knew the extent of his gifts, his compassion, his caution,
his vision, his love of country. She was not as passionate about
the country as he, but she was passionate about him, so she
chose to ignore the imposition on her life that government
service presented.

His salary was the same as that of a congressman, prior to
Congress's recessing in February 1977, $42,500. Once that had

seemed a great deal of money. Now it was all she could do to stay even. There were medical bills for her parents, nurses for his mother. If there hadn't been social security and medical benefits, things her parents had not believed in, there would have been no way to manage. As it was she could not even think in terms of saving a penny. The college she had attended was now $7000 a year, without pencils, without a peanut butter sandwich. And they had four children.

So she gritted her soul when she entered the houses of women with inherited money and drapes that matched the decor of the room. She had never in her life envied any other woman, because none of them had Larry. And she had her own remarkable talent for making things happen.

She felt about the Sri Lanka show as if it were a creative effort. The intricacies involved were tremendous, the care, and often the agonies, in arranging for a show. There were loan agreements for each single piece of art, insurance and shipping that had to be arranged, cataloguing and publicity for each entry. Cataloguing alone required incredible expertise, to describe, trace, and authenticate, all of it taking place months before the scheduled exhibition. The exhibition had to be designed, carpenters had to construct platforms and pedestals for sculptures which, in this case, no one had seen except in color transparencies accompanied by descriptions. Mountings had to be planned, as did the look of the whole exhibition. All of it to show off an art with which no one was terribly familiar. To think about it in detail made Abby dizzy, as she tried to imagine what could go wrong. The answer of course was everything, so she chose not to worry at all, leaving the details to people whose job it was to deal with details, like Dr. Sam, the curator. She had done her part, and brilliantly.

Dr. Sam was a European in his late fifties, nattily dressed, with an Oxford accent that seemed to deepen with each passing year in Washington. Abby enjoyed his affectations. They were harmless, and a great deal like his clothes. His flair for color was usually restricted to the linings of the suits he wore, the bright handkerchiefs tucked deeply into the pocket of his vest.

He greeted her now at the door to his office, sketches of the projected exhibition thumbtacked to corkboards on the wall. "Ah, the lovely Madame Trustee." He smiled a bent-toothed smile, and half-bowed. With a sweep of his hand he indicated the sketches behind him. "It's beginning to jell. Little by little. We will make you a poem."

"I'm so grateful you've taken such an interest, Dr. Sam," Abby said, looking at his sketches. The colors were flamboyant, crimson, saffron, turquoise, flung like shocking tapestries on the page. Against them were pencilled tiny statuettes.

"As the art is largely religious statuary," Dr. Sam said, "pieces of carved stone excavated from ancient Buddhist temples, bronzes, and jewels that turned up in the last dig, I thought the most important visual aspect should be spectacular colors in the background. That way the simplicity of the art becomes the exhibition."

"It looks absolutely inspired," Abby said.

Beaming, he took her arm and guided her down the hall past unopened crates marked with the international language of caution to stevedores: a champagne glass shattering, an open umbrella dripping, reminders that the contents were fragile, not to be left in the rain. "We had a most successful meeting of the Acquisitions Committee," he said. "It was noted how little actual Singhalese art there is in this country. So the exhibition from Sri Lanka should be especially exciting."

Outside the director's office, a secretary sat at a large black lacquered Chinese desk, its surface softened with plants tastefully arranged between the memos. "Mrs. Cochran," she said, smiling. "Mr. Hammermill's expecting you. Go right in."

"Thank you, Margaret." Abby smiled, as Dr. Sam opened the door to the inner office for her.

"Stop by when you're done, if you can," Dr. Sam said, and half-bowed again.

Roger Hammermill was seated in a Victorian wing chair behind a Sheraton desk piled high with art books, his glasses set forward on his nose as he leafed through a textbook on Sassanian antiquities. He was a sharp-featured man in his early sixties, who had about him an air of great reserve, which was strengthened by his formal manner of dress. He might as easily have been the father of the bride as the director of the museum.

"Abby," he said, moving to his feet with surprising agility, coming forward to take both her hands in his. "The prettiest part of my day." He kissed her cheek. "To what do I owe the honor?"

"May I shut the door?" Abby asked.

"Permit me," he said, and closed it, indicating the wing chair opposite his.

She sat down and straightened the folds of her skirt. "I appreciate your seeing me so promptly, Roger."

"It's always a joy," he said. "What can I do for you?" He made a church and steeple with his hands, and rested his fingertips on his sharply pointed nose.

"The exhibition seems to be coming along very well, according to Dr. Sam."

"Yes," he said, dipping the word into a question, preparing for what might be coming next.

"I've spoken to some of the members of the Arts Council of Sri Lanka, and they'd appreciate bringing in their own PR man to help with the exhibition."

"But that's foolish," said Roger. "Adrienne Harvey is the best public information officer in Washington. She knows every major art critic, all the art editors of the magazines . . ."

"I'm not disputing her qualifications. It's just that they have someone in mind they're particularly keen on handling this event. Naturally he'd work together with her."

"Who is it?"

"Jess Betzer," Abby said.

Roger pushed his glasses further down his nose, and stared at her hard. "You know, when Philip Morris gives a grant that supports an exhibition, you expect them to bring in Ruder and Finn. But I'm astonished that a country with the inexperience, art-wise, of Sri Lanka should come up with such an idea. Especially Jess Betzer."

"You don't really know him, Roger. He's as energetic and creative a man as any I've ever known. Devoted. He'll make this exhibition a rousing success, I know he will."

"Jess Betzer," he said again. "This isn't politics, it's art."

"Jess was a public relations man before he went to the White House. He knows everyone in the media."

"But from what vantage point? Hiding under a chair?"

"Please, Roger. You're a tolerant man. Don't make this an occasion to judge too harshly. Don't judge at all. He'll be wonderful."

"With you on his side I doubt he could be anything else," he said, and slapped his long-fingered hand on the desk top. "All right, subject closed. What else can I do for you?"

She sprang to her feet, moved around the desk, and kissed his forehead. "Thank you. You won't be sorry."

He pressed the button on his intercom. "Margaret. Please ask Adrienne to come into my office."

"Yes, sir," Margaret said through the intercom.

He released the button. "She's not going to like it, you know," he said. "She's an extremely competent woman, and she's very high on this exhibition. Any other time we've had outside PR help they've only gotten in her way."

"He'll make it easier for her, I know he will. And you'll make it easier for him with her, I know that too."

"How come you're not the politician in the family?" Roger looked at her admiringly.

"Oh, but I am," she said. "That's my job, convincing Larry he's the one changing the world."

"I wish I could believe you were joking," said Roger, and smiled. There was a knock on the door. "Come in," he called.

If Adrienne Harvey had not been so formidable, Abby could not help thinking when she saw her, she might have seemed a classic beauty. She stood very tall and straight. Her legs were extremely long and shapely, her hair was dark, almost blue black, and she wore it pulled extremely tight over her ears, twisted in a coil at the back of her neck. Her eyes were wide set and bluish grey, fringed with heavy black. Her nose was thin, flared at the nostrils, and her color was high, as if someone had just said something to offend her.

"Ah, Adrienne," Roger said, and got to his feet. "I have wonderful news for you. You know Mrs. Cochran?"

"Of course."

"How are you, Adrienne?" said Abby, and smiled at her.

"We're going to be . . ." Roger cleared his throat, apprehensively. "Lucky enough to have a top PR man working with us on Sri Lanka."

Two circles of red blazed in Adrienne's cheeks, as if she had suddenly rouged. "But I thought everything was going very well as it was. The catalogues are being prepared, and I was planning a press preview and a black tie opening . . ."

"My dear, it has nothing to do with you. No one could doubt for a minute you're doing a masterful job." Roger sat down behind his desk and indicated a chair for her. "It's just we've been graced with a bonanza, their Arts Council wishes to engage someone privately."

"I see," said Adrienne grimly, sitting down. "Who?"

"Jess Betzer," said Roger.

"What firm is he with?" Adrienne asked.

"His own," said Abby.

"I'm not familiar with the name."

"I'm sure you'll like him." Roger moved *A Survey of Persian Art* from one side of his desk to the other, as if his hands needed something to do, and his eyes needed someplace to look besides at the expression on Adrienne's face. "He'll be extremely helpful."

"Will he be in charge of the exhibition, or will I?" The rigidity of her spine seemed to transfer itself to her voice.

"You both will," said Roger. "I'm sure he'll be grateful for all the help you can give him."

"I see," said Adrienne.

"I should be running along," said Abby. "It was lovely seeing you, Roger."

"And for me," he said, getting to his feet, reaching for the hand she extended, shaking it.

"Adrienne. . . ." Abby held out her hand. "We must have lunch one day soon."

"That would be nice," Adrienne said. She gripped Abby's hand very hard, very firmly, according to the fashion of women's colleges that had until recently refused coeducation and so taught their girls to face life like a man, starting with a handshake.

¶ When Abby got home there was a long list of messages by the phone in the kitchen. Tuesday was her luxury day: the dayworker came, filling her morning with air, running the vacuum, washing the kitchen floor. Slowly, but washing it. The gratitude Abby felt in her heart was only matched by the feeling in her back. That Bessie was less than efficient did not bother her. The laundry got done more times than not—most of the time Bessie remembered to fold it.

And, in the meantime, there were messages by the phone. Not that Abby wanted or needed them. There were more people than she had time for trying to get in touch with her. But there was something tidily reassuring about knowing what you otherwise might have missed. It made her feel almost spoiled, like not having to rush home for J.J.'s arrival from school.

"I didn't have a chance to vacuum your bedroom," said Bessie. "The phone kept on ringing."

"I understand," said Abby. "Just finish up the best you can."

"Ringing and ringing and ringing," said Bessie. "One lady kept calling and asking for you and when I said you wasn't here she just hanged up. I kept asking who it was but she keeped on hanging up."

"If the phone is too much for you, Bessie, you don't have to answer it." Abby took her checkbook out of her purse. "They'll call back if it's important."

"But what if it's for me?" Bessie asked. She smiled. "Pot roast's in the oven. It'll be ready at six."

"Did Mr. Cochran say when he'd be coming home?"

"No, ma'am." She stood by as Abby made out a check. "Can you use me an extra day this week? My Thursday's out of town."

Abby sighed and handed her her check. "I wish we could afford it, Bessie. I'd love to have you every day if I could."

The phone rang. Abby reached for it. "Hello?"

"Mrs. Cochran?" The voice was muffled.

"Who is this?" Abby asked.

"Have you seen this evening's *Washington Journal*?"

"Who *is* this?"

"Specifically, Amelia Gomez's column?"

"Who is this?" Abby was getting angry now. She had been on top of herself all day, making sure every word, every gesture, could not possibly be considered offensive. She was ready to lose her temper, and she considered it might be just as well to do it with a rude stranger as with the children or Bessie.

"A friend," said the voice on the phone. There was a click.

Abby held the phone, stunned. What had whoever it was been saying? What could possibly be in the *Journal*? She never read the *Journal*. It was too flashy for her sensibilities. She would not read it now, because of some crank, no matter what was in it. What could possibly be in it? She tried not to look troubled.

"Was that the same lady hanged up on me?" asked Bessie.

"I suppose so," Abby said. "What kind of voice did she have?"

"I couldn't really tell. Sounded to me all muffled. Like she was talking in a tunnel," Bessie said.

"Or through a handkerchief," said Abby, hanging up the phone.

She would not dignify the caller by getting the paper. Although there was a newspaper rack at Safeway on MacArthur: She could be there and back in ten minutes. She shook the foolishness from her brain and dialed Jess Betzer.

She tried not to let the strain of the anonymous phone call sound in her voice. "Hello, Jess? It's Abby Cochran. I have wonderful news. At least it's wonderful news for me. I hope it's wonderful for you. The Arts Council of Sri Lanka, you know, the group sponsoring the exhibition I'm working on? They need a good public relations man to stir up excitement. I told them about you, and if you're agreeable, they'd appreciate your helping."

There was a pause on the other end of the line. "My helping?"

"They know what a crack PR man you are," Abby said. "And the public information officer of the museum will fill you in on the art. Will you do it? I'm afraid they're not very rich, so they can't pay you more than five thousand. I know it's not a lot, but would you do it as a kindness to me?"

"Of course, Abby. Of course. Thank you." His words seemed to catch on themselves.

"Thanks, Jess," she said. "That's a load off my mind. Can you come around tomorrow morning, and we'll go to the museum?"

"What time?" Jess said.

"Eleven."

"I'll be there," Jess said. "That's wonderful, Abby. You're terrific."

"I like you, too," Abby said, and hung up the phone. She smiled, happily. Then she remembered the earlier caller. Anxiety ran untender fingers across her face. Dialing the phone again, she asked Larry's secretary to have him bring home that evening's *Journal*. She tried to make it sound unimportant.

¶ In his kitchen, Jess Betzer sat down. The yellow walls he claimed lifted his spirits usually in truth blackened them. For the first time in four years the color did not hurt his eyes.

It had been like being dead, only worse. When you were dead, people told old stories about you occasionally, and remarked it would be nice if you were still around. When you were unemployed, they acted as if your not being around would be nicer.

Not everybody, of course. There were still friends like the Cochrans, who were close enough to care about Jess apart from the position he held. But it seemed a prejudice deeper than racial mistrust, the way people looked at a man out of work in Washington.

A job. It was life for Americans, no matter what was touted about Family, God, or Country. All his life he had busily established priorities. First, he had thought, came love. His childhood, like Chris's, had been lacking in affection. Before he was born, his parents had had enough of each other, so his father was seldom home. As a boy, Jess had imagined that heaven was a family with the father always there. As a man, and a father, he now knew that could be closer to hell.

He loved his family. He adored the openness of Chris, the innocent hunger, the yearning. That the many years of marriage had failed to assure her that someone really cared, and passionately, did not disturb him. He thought perhaps in their twenty-fifth year together she would finally realize there was permanence in him, permanence in them.

In the meantime, the children were gifted, funny, delicious. He enjoyed the whole package, cradles and all. Even a presidential appointment could not make his job more important than his home. Until the job began to disappear.

It was a horror show, being without a career identity. Sometimes in the beginning of the dole, Jess had believed the call might come. He got an answering service on the phone so he wouldn't miss it, the call that would change his life. Make him alive again, back the way he was, a man with a future, and a present, not just a past.

After a year, they had to cut back on expenses. "We might as well cancel the answering service," Chris said. "Somebody's always at home."

She didn't look at him. It ripped his heart. Whenever the talk was of money, or spending, she averted her eyes.

She couldn't bear the look in his eyes. He was afraid. He was a great, strong man, handsome, intelligent, and he was afraid. What hope was there for women?

To discover herself as the earner in the household threw Chris into a tailspin. She had had her career before they married, but it had never crossed her mind that her family's welfare would hinge on it. It was no longer possible to write for glory, inspiration, love. Now she had to write because her children's lives depended on it. It sent terror through her, paralyzed her mind, chilled her fingers. She sat at the typewriter unable to think.

Jess knew it, understood how his troubles had affected Chris, her writing, their marriage. He could see the shock, the pain, the contempt for him in her eyes.

And now he was going back to work. A job. At least for a few months. He had not known how deep was his sense of failure until he hung up the phone. He stood with his face against the cold of the refrigerator, weeping, for how long he didn't know. The telephone rang. It was Gloria Stanley for Chris.

"Hey," he shouted up the stairs. "It's Gloria Stanley. She's calling from the moon or somewhere."

"Hello?" Chris picked up the extension.

"Chris!" Gloria's voice was cracking. "Is that you?"

"It's me. Where are you?"

"I'm on a ship in the Indian Ocean. You'll never believe what happened!" Gloria said.

"What?" asked Chris.

"Nothing!" said Gloria and laughed. "I'm so bored I'm going out of my bird. Have you finished the play?"

"Not yet," said Chris. The truth was, she hadn't been able to start it.

"Will you be done by the end of the month?" asked Gloria.

"I don't know," said Chris, biting her lip.

"Because I'm thinking of flying back from Bombay. Do you think Washington's ready for me?"

"No," said Chris. "Enjoy your trip. There's no rush."

"Don't you want me?" asked Gloria.

"Everybody wants you," said Chris.

"Ha, ha, do I have a story to tell," said Gloria. "Maybe you can use it in the play. How about a woman throwing herself away on a man who doesn't have a thing to offer except his dong?"

"It's been done," said Chris.

"Not by you," said Gloria. "How many lines do I have?"

"I don't know yet," said Chris.

"It is coming along, isn't it?"

"You're worse than my agent," said Chris.

"Your agent is my agent," said Gloria. "I know how desperate we both are. Anyway, can you put me up? I'm trying to simplify my life, so I'd rather not stay in a hotel when I get there."

"I don't think that's a good idea, Gloria. Much as I love you. I have a lot of trouble writing when there's someone else around." She tried not to look at Jess, who had just entered the room. It aggravated her when he listened to her on the phone. Their lives had begun to merge so completely, it was as if he sustained himself on her conversations, not having any of his own. She knew it was wretched of her to begrudge him that vicarious pleasure, but it made her uneasy.

"Well, is there anyone else you know that has room for me?" Gloria's voice was pleading through the shouting. "I don't want to impose. But I'd love to stay with a family."

"I'll ask around if you're serious," said Chris.

"Oh, I'm serious," said Gloria. "I've never been more serious. I even let my hairdresser go. I'm ready to be a humble artist."

"That's some news," said Chris.

"I can't wait to read the play," Gloria said. "Love you, luv." There was a buzz on the line.

Chris hung up the phone. "She's coming," she said to Jess. "She's flying here from Bombay."

"And she wants to play Indira Gandhi, right?"

"Something like that," said Chris. She sat on the bed, dejected. "She wants to be a humble artist."

"How's the play coming?"

"I haven't started it." She rubbed her fingers in her eyes.

"That's only because you have a lot of trouble writing when there's someone else around," Jess said.

"I didn't mean you."

"Yes, you did," said Jess. "It's okay. I don't blame you. I'm a pain in my own ass."

He came over to her and raised her to her feet. "But it's okay now." He took both her hands in his, turned them over, and kissed her fingertips. "You've been so wonderful, I don't know how I'll ever repay you."

"This isn't a business arrangement, Jess. I don't want to be repaid."

"Too bad," he said, and kissed her palms. "I'm going to cover you with furs and jewels."

"Storybook stuff," she said. "Props for Gloria Stanley. I don't need them."

"I need them," he said. "I need them for you. And if I need you to have them, you'll have them." He looked at her squarely. There was light back in his eyes. "I've got a job. I'm going to handle the Sri Lanka exhibition for the Kirkeby Museum."

"Oh, Jess," she said, and threw her arms around him. They kissed.

He moved his hand inside her blouse. She wanted to tell him to stop, that it was the middle of the day, that the children might come home from school, that she had to work. She opened her mouth wide to receive his tongue, as if, could he plunge deep enough, he could wipe out the words she had thought though never spoken. How disappointed she was in him. How disappointed in herself. That she hadn't been woman enough to find a man who made her unafraid.

Well, it was America. The land of the big second chance. Maybe it would all begin again for him. At least he would be out of the house and she would be free to call Scott.

A rush of shame came over her. Even with Jess's fingertips fluttering her nipples, even with his lips on hers, she was thinking about Scott.

Subtly, slowly, she squinted her eyes and relaxed them, blurring her vision slightly. It was Scott's face that pressed close to hers, his tongue probing her mouth. His touch, a little harsh, on her nipples. Softening. The stroking of his palms against her. His hands undressing her. Moving down her belly. In between her legs, fingertips fluttering upward like tiny birds' beaks, open, plucking at her.

She moaned softly, collapsed against him. And he was strong, powerful, just the way she'd dreamed he'd be. He was lifting her in his arms, carrying her to bed. "Don't move," he said softly in the wrong voice, setting her on her feet. "I'll be right back."

She could hear him locking the door. It wasn't Scott, it was Jess, and they were in their own home, hiding from the children.

Her body stiffened. She stood by the edge of the bed and tried not to wince at the sound of his hurried undressing. She pressed her eyes tighter together, pressed her brain into fantasy—so hard she could smell Scott, his light aftershave lotion, slightly lemony.

Her lips were wet when he touched her again. He pressed his swollen nakedness into her hand. He lay down with her, easing her backward, lifted her over himself, and mounted her.

She felt him between her legs, entering her. It was only at the last that she managed to keep herself from crying out Scott's name aloud. As she felt how he loved her, how he loved her, how he loved her.

6

¶ (From Amelia Gomez's column in the *Washington Journal,* January 22, 1979)

At least twenty-two congressmen are under investigation for allegedly having received money or gifts from Japanese businessman *Hiro Takeda.* Takeda's suicide last November seemed the period to an influence-peddling scandal that rocked D.C. But apparently it wasn't *sayonara,* it was only the beginning. Claims against Takeda's estate now total in excess of twenty million dollars, including one from *Congressman Ellerbe* for breach of contract. Ellerbe is the gentleman for whom Hiro gave a fund-raising party that Ellerbe told a House Ethics Committee raised only $7400. (Shucks, I bet the party cost more than that.)

* * *

Speaking of Takeda, which hardly anyone does anymore, his own Madame Butterfly

Melissa Mae August seems to be emerging from her cocoon. Looking rested after her release from Payne Whitney, she was seen Sunday brunching at Clyde's.

• • •

"Politicians neither love nor hate. Interest, not sentiment, directs them," wrote Lord Chesterfield, only wouldn't he be surprised to see *That Very Trusted Man at the White House,* a Republican, holding hands in church, but not with his wife. Who SHE is is that *Cute Redhead* from the last administration. Well, as Publilius Syrus said: "In love, beauty counts for more than reputation."

¶ "How can she do this?" Abby said, stunned, looking at Larry. She put the paper down on the kitchen table, hands shaking. "It's a lie." She sat down next to him. A spasm of doubt marred the evenness of her features. Her mouth sagged slightly at the corners. For a moment she knew exactly how it would feel to be old. "Isn't it?"

"Of course." Larry reached across the table and rested his hand on her shoulder, touched his fingers to the side of her neck, rustled her hair. "Megan O'Flannagan came to Meeting on Sunday, and we talked afterward. That's all."

"Then how can she do this?" She picked the paper up and slammed it down on the table, as though she could smash the words. "Can't we sue?"

"The biggest mistake of all would be to dignify it with a lawsuit. That makes it seem important, not just garbage."

"It's the principle, Larry! You could sue them for a million dollars, and you'd be teaching them a lesson at the same time. We'd win, you know we would." She looked practically gleeful. "It would serve them right."

"But she didn't use my name."

"It's obviously you," said Abby.

"I'd have to prove that a large segment of the population

understood it to be me. That's a hard thing to do. And then I'd have to prove what damage it did me."

"Something like that could ruin your career!" Abby said.

"But it's not going to." He leaned across the table, took her face in both his hands, and drew her mouth to his.

"But you're not going to just leave it at this," Abby said, pulling gently away. She picked up the paper, pointed to the column. "You can't just ignore it."

"That's the best thing to do."

"You must let people know it isn't true."

"My friends will know that."

"This is Washington. It isn't just made up of those who wish you well. You have to do something."

"What?" asked Larry.

She thought for a moment. "Take her to lunch at the Sans Souci."

"Megan O'Flannagan?"

"Yes, of course. Take her to lunch tomorrow and let everyone see there's nothing to it."

"Come with us." Larry said.

"No. That will look like I'm chaperoning. The point is, the whole town must know it's a lie."

"But I've never taken *you* to lunch at the Sans Souci. We can't afford that kind of thing."

"We can't afford *not* to do it, now." She got up and went to the refrigerator, took out a head of lettuce, opened the sideboard, found a bowl, and started making salad, a little too busily, controlled anger in the tearing of the leaves. There was the din of laughter from the hallway. A shriek. Sara and Elizabeth entered the room in pursuit of each other.

"Please," Abby said hotly. "We don't need this noise."

"I'm sorry." "I'm sorry." They echoed each other.

Abby turned and saw the expression on their faces. "So am I. It's been a long day."

"Why don't you and Daddy go out to dinner?" Sara said.

"We'll take care of everything," added Elizabeth.

"Me, too," said J.J. from the doorway.

She felt a rush of love for them, all of them, but especially the little boy. It was a terrible source of guilt in her that she loved all her children, but J.J. pulled at her insides. She went to him and took him in her arms. "You're very kind to volunteer to help."

"I wasn't volunteering to help," said J.J. "I was volunteering to go out to dinner."

She laughed and kissed him, got to her feet, and hugged the girls. "You are almost as beautiful as you are smart," she said. "Well . . ." She turned to Larry. "Since they have such good ideas, shall we listen to them?"

"I don't think we should," Larry said. "The middle of the week."

"Stop being so cautious," said Abby. "I got a dividend check from a stock I didn't know we had. It's my treat."

"Well, in that case," said Larry. "I am eminently available."

"But first you have a telephone call to make," Abby said.

"Where's the telephone book?" asked Larry.

"Where it usually is," said Abby. "Don't you know her number?"

"No," said Larry, opening a kitchen drawer, taking out the directory.

"That's good," said Abby.

He looked through the district directory and dialed. Abby took the pot roast out of the oven and began carving it with exaggerated concentration, as if she cared not at all about what might be being said.

"Hello, Megan? This is Larry Cochran. . . . Megan? . . . Yes, that's who it is. How are you? . . . Can you have lunch with me tomorrow? . . . Fine. Twelve-thirty at the Sans Souci. I'll look forward to it." He hung up the phone. "She sounded very startled to hear from me."

"What's she like?" Abby asked. "I've only seen her around, chatted a little. I don't really know her."

"She's extremely intelligent and quite sensitive."

"Really," said Abby, carving.

"It comes as kind of a surprise. When a girl is as cute as she is it's always amazing that there's so much equipment inside."

"Really," said Abby.

"Not that it astonishes me when beauty houses knowledge. Not since knowing you." He put his arms around her, hugging against her back as she carved.

"Don't be too affectionate," she said. "For someone who isn't interested, you sound interested."

"Of course I'm interested. She's an interesting girl. But I happen to be married to a fascinating woman."

"You're so smart," she said and turned and kissed him. "Maybe I'll join you tomorrow just for coffee."

He smiled. "Good. That'll make it a celebration." They kissed again.

"Woo woo!" said J.J.

"I think we should do our celebrating tonight," Abby said.

¶ It had been a long time since they'd been in a hotel together. And where they were was a lifetime away from the Plaza, where they'd spent a brief but exquisite honeymoon. The place Abby had brought him to tonight, over his laughing protest, was a motel on the outskirts of Washington.

"But why here?" he said, as she pulled the car up.

"It's *notorious*," she said. "They have champagne in your room, and red lights in the lamps, and mirrors on the ceiling. As J.J. would say," she raised her eyebrows at him, "woo woo."

"I'm surprised at you."

"I know," said Abby, smiling. "Isn't it wonderful?" She switched off the ignition, touched his hand. "I want to be wanton with you, Larry Cochran. I want to make you moan with pleasure and not worry that the children will hear. I want to make you forget that you ever even thought about another woman."

"I didn't."

She kissed him. "I want to make it so you never will."

¶ In the soft red light of their rented motel room she stroked his belly, lightly tongued his thighs, watched the glowing tribute to her caresses, saw it rising, growing, kissed it, ran the tip of her tongue along the length of it, plunged her mouth around it. He moaned and reached for her.

"My turn," he whispered, and lay her gently on her back, kissed her lips, her throat, her nipples, tasting them with his tongue. Then his head was by the darkest part of her, his tongue was sweetly urging her open, as his fingers stroked the soft inside of her thighs.

In the mirror above them, she could see the back of his head moving along the secret parts of her body, all the while she was feeling him. It made it seem like there were two of her, one of them a stranger. It was so exquisitely erotic, she was ashamed and closed her eyes.

His tongue moved up her belly, across her breasts, and he was tasting her mouth. She could feel the hard, hot length of him moving inside her.

"Open your eyes," he said hoarsely. She did, and saw him raising her, lifting her legs, setting them on his shoulders as he started thrusting forward, insistent, tenderly unrelenting. She broke into pieces around him, screamed, reached for the soft underside of his testicles, stroked their middle strand, reached behind them, scraped gently. He cried aloud, and burst inside her.

When they were quiet, when they were gentle in each other's arms, she with her head on his chest, she asked him if he wanted champagne.

"Maybe later," he said.

"Can we stay all night?"

"You don't want to sleep here?" he said.

"Who said anything about sleeping?" Abby said, and kissed him. "You want to watch a dirty movie? For ten dollars extra they give you a dirty movie on TV."

"You're all the dirty movie I'll ever need." He smiled. "Besides, it's expensive enough already. Not that it isn't worth it, but . . ."

"I told you it was my treat." Abby said. "Let's just enjoy it and forget about the cost."

They lay for a while in each other's arms, quietly. Then she lifted her head and looked at him. "I bet we're the only couple who ever came here and signed their right names."

"Unquestionably," said Larry.

She lay her head back on his chest, smiled against the silky warmth of him. "I'm tempted to send a copy of the room receipt to Amelia Gomez."

¶ Melissa Mae August awoke that January morning and remembered she had a lunch date. There had been only one man, besides Larry Cochran, who'd admitted at the height of the scandal that he was a friend of Hiro Takeda's. Everyone else was so busy disappearing when the FBI began investigating about who his friends were that Melissa Mae had begun to imagine she'd dreamed it, all the parties he gave, the important people who accepted his generosity, all those whose welfare had become more important than her sex life.

She had always known it was a spoils system, Washington. Government jobs fell to the victors. It was a city controlled by those who had eaten at the right tables. The power gourmets. Influence on toast.

It had never occurred to her, however, with all her awareness, how quickly spoils could rot. The rats had not even waited for the ship to sink before abandoning it. They had not waited for Hiro to be proven guilty, or even be indicted. All those powerful friends had not waited to hear him formally charged. For that matter, neither had Hiro.

She had gone into shock for a few days after his suicide in November. It was so obvious why he had done it that she couldn't accept the obvious. "Do you know why he did it?" she asked everyone who still admitted knowing him, his doctor, his valet. From his doctor she got no report of a mysterious, fatal disease. From his valet she got the same confused stare she saw in her own mirror. "Do you know why he did it?" she had asked his lawyer, a few weeks after Hiro's death.

"Have you ever been to court?" Ed McShane asked, his smooth face regarding her with sympathetic curiosity.

"No," Melissa answered.

"It's a terrible experience. Your limbs begin to ache from sitting. People look at you with hatred in their eyes. You're being judged by those who don't know you. I went through that with Hiro on a civil case, and he almost died. He sweated going into the courthouse. To him it was a disgrace. In the rooms all around him were heroin peddlers and murderers being tried. He wanted to know what he was doing there, when all it was was an argument over money.

"The Japanese aren't like us, you know. They don't have a lot of courtrooms. They think if something can't be settled over tea, before it gets to court, it's a disgrace. Not a hara-kiri kind of disgrace, but a big one. They call it *jidan jonko*. I saw what happened to him when it was a civil lawsuit. I don't think he could've faced a criminal trial."

"Maybe it wouldn't have gotten to that," Melissa said.

"Maybe not," Ed said. "I'm sorry I can't turn over to you what he left you." He put his papers back in his briefcase. "There's five million dollars in claims against the estate and he's only dead a few weeks. I shudder to think what's going to happen when the rest of his business associates talk to their lawyers."

"Was he guilty?" said Melissa Mae.

"Of what?"

"Of bribing them all."

"I don't know if it was bribery. I know he gave away a lot of money, but I don't want to speculate about it; neither should you. It's over."

"Is it?" she said, and started to cry. "Oh, Hiro, you proud pain in the ass."

"Come," Ed said. "I'll take you home."

He was an imposing man, tall, Ivy Leaguish, dressed in the conservative dark shoddy elegance of his trade, a man who could afford three hundred dollar suits but preferred looking slightly shabby, knowing how prejudiced juries were against those with money. He had been as tender to her as if she were a baby, a solicitous solicitor. He had held her arm and guided her gently down the hall to her apartment, taken the key from her shaking hand, unlocked the door, led her inside, helped her to the bedroom, and jumped on her. She was so stunned, her clothes were half off by the time she recovered herself.

"You dirty son of a bitch," she shouted, flailing. "I'll kill you."

"Now, now, Melissa," he said. "You can relax. You've put up your struggle."

"Fuck you," she said, and kneed him in the groin.

When he could walk, Ed left the apartment. She was so filled with rage she just lay there, trembling. That was who she was now, the abandoned whore of Hiro Takeda.

She could go back to work in New York. In New York she had background, stature. There were firms on Wall Street that would be glad to get her if they didn't read the news.

But in Washington there was no one who would hire her. She had been typed now as strictly a party girl. She lay on her stomach, staring into the mirrored headboard of her bed, one of the flashy additions Hiro had brought into her life. Everything in perfect order for sexual splendor. Except where was he?

She saw him moving toward the bed, tan yellow skin glistening in the soft-lit room. She saw him mounting her from behind, saw him driving against her, in her, saw the strength of his torso, his powerful thighs straining, saw that it was all an illusion.

She went into the bar and started drinking scotch, medicinally, deliberately, until she could no longer stand. She crawled to the sliding doors that led to the balcony, and couldn't figure out how to open them. The catch was too complicated for her.

Somehow, she got to the bathroom. She didn't know why she was there. After a while she remembered she'd wanted to kill herself.

She opened the medicine cabinet, pushed the razor aside. Blood was too ugly, slashing too hideous. She wanted to go pretty, like Ophelia. She took out a bottle of pills and carefully counted out twelve Nembutal. Twelve was a magical dying number, just enough, not too many. Too many made you vomit, especially with liquor inside you. If you vomited you didn't die, except if you were Lupe Velez.

To love a man, to die for him, because he was married in Lupe's case, because he had abandoned her for death in Melissa's, had to be one of the womanly acts of the world, she'd always thought. Manly acts were acts of courage, as men labeled them. Womanly acts as tradition framed them were open declarations of surrender. I can't go on without him, they seemed to say.

So how cruel of the universe to sneer at the womanly act of Lupe Velez, sending her vomiting into the bathroom, because she had over-overdosed. Knocking her reeling toward the toilet, spinning her against it, fracturing her skull.

To die for love, in a pool of vomit, by a toilet, with a fractured skull. Women were supposed to die in bed, neatly, of something vaporous. Especially in a love story. It had broken Melissa's heart for Lupe Velez, and made her sick to think she could go the same way. So she was very careful to count out exactly twelve Nembutal, drunk as she was.

Then she went to bed, to die. Just before she passed out, she remembered how much she had loved Hiro. She hoped all that shit he had believed about an afterlife was really the truth.

She awoke at seven-thirty in the morning, painfully hung over but still alive. She went into the bathroom and saw the twelve Nembutal still on the sink.

She filled a glass of water and took them, six at a time. She did not feel as depressed as she had the night before, but she didn't stop to examine her feelings, she just took the pills. She brushed her teeth, washed the sleep out of her eyes, peed, and went back to bed.

The maid found her at nine o'clock. Melissa later contended she hadn't known it was Wednesday, the maid's day. But naturally there were those around Washington who considered it a token suicide.

Still, her relationship with Hiro had been exorcised by the suicidal act. Now the town could forgive her. She'd really loved him, whatever his corruption. That they could understand. In spite of being black and sassy, she had finally fallen into an appropriately feminine mold, acceptable to society.

After her recovery at Payne Whitney she returned to Washington an exaggerated object of interest, one inspiring both compassion and wishes for the worst at the same time, a common duality among the citizenry. There were countless messages on her service, many from men she'd seen around town but never spoken to. She was a target now. A good name for gossip interest on a party list, an emergency hump for a visiting dignitary.

She trusted no one. In her mind she had been betrayed by every person in town, all pretending to welcome her, all pretending to like him. She saw the world now through jade, tinged with envy and hypocrisy. There was no one alive she believed was sincere, including the only other man besides Larry Cochran to admit to being Hiro's friend. She had a lunch date this January day with him at the Sans Souci.

He was one of the takers of the world. He'd probably dined out on standing up for Hiro, gotten invitations so that people at the smart tables around town could know what had happened with the FBI. Dined out on Hiro dead just as he had done on Hiro alive.

And now he was coming to lunch at her invitation. She'd arrange beforehand to pick up the tab and have it sent to Hiro's attorney. Then the restaurant could sue the estate along with everybody else.

It annoyed her to pull herself wearily out of bed, alive still another morning. Her therapist had said true courage was realizing you were responsible for your own life. She told the psychologist he was as full of shit as everybody else.

Still, she liked him better than the rest of the people in town. She promised him she'd try. She was ready to resume her place in society, such as it was.

¶ The night before Jess rejoined the business world, finally, he had been unable to sleep, so great was his excitement at the prospect of working. He got up several times and went in to look at the faces of his children, round, angelic, smug with sleep and innocence. He resisted the impulse to wake them, to dance with them. He kissed their pouting lips and went back to his own bed.

At six o'clock he showered, taking a long time, turning the water to its hottest, as if it could cleanse away the past. He scrubbed himself till his skin was red, scraped off the shame that had covered him like a garment, tried to tell himself it was gone, that he was fresh, new. But he still remembered the nightmare, remembered the day that Richard Nixon left Washington, no longer President.

On that day a plane had arrived from Alaska. On board was the Deputy Chief of Protocol for the White House returning from his summer vacation, bringing with him three hundred pounds of Icelandic lobster, thirty salmon, and eighteen trout, the special favorites of his President.

When the deputy had left for his vacation, Nixon was under siege but still firmly entrenched. On his return, the shocked protocol deputy learned that the President had resigned. The deputy went directly from his plane to Air Force One, in the process of loading its gloomy cargo, and added to the freight his bounty of fish, because, he said, "I wanted the Chief to have one last good meal."

There were tears in his eyes when he told them that at the White House, after the departure, while the shadows were still on the walls. Jess Betzer had had to leave the room, because he had enough emotionalism, real and induced.

In all the harried months since Watergate had begun to surface, Jess kept a veneer of calm. Every drawer in the press office contained Valium and aspirin, every shelf carried the burgeoning libraries of Nixon material, marked to indicate on which page everybody's name appeared. Somehow Jess had raised himself above the paranoia.

From the beginning he had suspected the extent of Nixon's involvement. Still, he never spoke aloud his doubts, not even to Chris.

But the scene of the speech of resignation in the East Room, marines crowding everyone together to increase the emotionalism, had been too much for him. When the leaving turned to kitsch, with military music and forced tears, Jess allowed himself to see for the first time how terrible the taste really was.

Still he did not wish to dissociate himself from the Nixon Administration. On the contrary. His collection of presidential memorabilia was one of the great joys of his life. But his past began to haunt him, by being all there was. He would spend hours in the darkly paneled den, studying the papers and the photographs, searching the words that the man had spoken for the key to it all.

Jess felt pity for him now, an abstract pity, as though Nixon had been the pawn in a cosmic drama: an object lesson in the folly of ego gone wild. That it had ended with the marine band was grossly fitting.

But as for his own association with that President, Jess did not belittle or disclaim it. The years at the White House had been, until the last, the happiest and most productive of his life. His second child had been born, a son. His wife had published her first successful novel. Together they'd become a golden couple. That there were debts of character one had to pay for times when it was too easy did not surprise him. There was in his philosophy a certain angry sadness, a knowledge that the world had a tendency to even you out.

What he hadn't counted on was the fact that it also deballed you, or at least tried to. For every one who had gladhanded him when he was at the White House, there were two who sneered at him once he was out. Men he had considered friends dodged his calls, avoided him at parties. There had still been invitations, because of Chris. At first he tried to avoid going out. But when he stayed home he was mesmerized by the news. He would watch without thinking, battered by events, coming back to consciousness only when he heard the unemployment statistics.

That it was a woman who had finally helped him was not surprising to him. He had discovered in his years of unemployment that women were more merciful. They understood what pain was, and they saw the pain in Jess.

He was starved for the company of men, but except for a very few of them, no one understood where he was coming from; without a job, he had no standing. He could no longer report on deals pending or made. He had never realized before how much of men's social conversation involved business until he didn't have any to discuss.

But now, mercifully, thanks to the generosity of Abby Cochran, the horror seemed to be over. For four years he'd been sleeping late in the mornings, as if the less day there was to face, the better.

This morning, though, he was out of the house by eight, a beat ahead of the children, kissing everybody goodbye several times, a proud ceremony. He was the head of the family again.

Chris stood watching him drive away, her sense of relief almost as great as her feeling of disquiet. In a curious way she had gotten used to his being around.

¶ "For you," Jess said to Abby, his arms filled with flowers, plucked expensively from the pails of the District's leading florist.

"You shouldn't have," she said. "But I'm so glad you did."

They drove to the museum in Jess's car. On the way Abby filled him in on the pertinent details. "The politics in a museum are the same as where you were," she said. "There was a lot of back scratching to get them to take the exhibition. Now you have to do your part. The public information officer is a woman named Adrienne Harvey. You'll be working with her. She's a little cold, but I know you'll be able to charm her."

"I'll certainly try."

"I'm sorry you won't have a lot of space . . ."

He reached over and touched her hand. "Don't apologize for anything. Ever. I'm so grateful to you I don't know what to do."

"Do a wonderful job. Make this opening the event of the season."

"Yes, ma'am," Jess said. "I intend to do just that."

¶ Adrienne Harvey was waiting for them in her office. Abby had phoned ahead and said she wanted to introduce Adrienne and Jess herself. There had been just the slightest hint of frost on the edge of Adrienne's voice. She knew exactly how important a woman Mrs. Cochran was, how valuable to the museum, how liked by everybody. That the liking did not include Adrienne's was no fault of Abby's. Adrienne had had a very hard life by the standards around her.

She was a beautiful young woman who kept her origins a mystery. Where she had come from were two very nice people who started out poor in the Bronx and ended up rich in the garment district. Adrienne was smart, remarkable, clearly a misplaced gift with which her parents had been rewarded for reasons they didn't understand. For all their gratitude at having her, there was something aloof about the child, alien. They were anxious to move her to the realms of the golden goyim, where maybe she'd be happier, being among those who, like herself, expressed little emotion.

They sent her to Smith where for four years she struggled to imitate the marbled tongue of the svelte young Amazons of Brearley, Miss Porter's, and Westover. It faintly embarrassed her to think about her parents in the presence of Rockefeller daughters, nieces of the Clifton Sangers, children of Biddles, Coffins, and Cabots. But she was ashamed about her shame. She loved her parents. They'd worked hard to get her into this new world. As her Smith friends spoke of past debuts, summers at Martha's Vineyard, dances at the Plaza, being on the shelf, she realized it was more than a different language such people spoke. They came from a different planet, one which they owned.

She was suddenly confronted with the rich lineage of America. She had read about the robber barons, the men who owned the railroads, but she had never thought of them as living people, with flesh and blood heirs. Slender and blonde, their hair hanging like flax, they seemed like princesses in fairy tales, possessors of the dream.

Her hair was jet to their pale radiance. Her nose, though well shaped, was a nose. She had never seen noses like those on the rich: flaring nostrils, tips so chiseled and arrogant they seemed to be snubbing the rest of the face. Abby Cochran had a nose like that: Abby Cochran was clearly from that legendary world and evoked in Adrienne the unease she remembered from those days.

Abby was no more beautiful than she, but her style was all slimness and blonde grace. Adrienne found her own body too fleshy for her taste. Her breasts were too big, especially when she stood beside a golden woman like Abby, who had one of those long sleek bodies that spoke of lineage.

Abby's smile was always so convincing, so friendly. It wasn't possible to feel that friendly toward everyone, Adrienne knew. Still, when Abby and Jess came to her office that crisp January morning, into the space she was so comfortable in, that she was now going to have to share, she had no choice but to respond to Abby's smile.

"Adrienne Harvey, I'd like you to meet Jess Betzer," Abby said.

"How do you do," said Adrienne stiffly, extending her hand and shaking his.

"With a handshake like that you could run for President," Jess said.

"Is that a compliment?" Adrienne said icily.

"I can see you two are going to get along just fine," said Abby. "I'll leave you alone to get better acquainted." She fled the room.

"They've brought in your desk, Mr. Betzer," Adrienne said, pointing to a Lucite and chrome desk in the *L* of the room. "The phone company's coming tomorrow to install a line for you."

"I appreciate your letting me share your office," he said. "Thank you."

"Thank Mr. Hammermill. It was his idea."

"I see," Jess said softly.

"I hope so," said Adrienne. She started to sit down at her desk.

"Are you going to fill me in on the exhibition?" he asked.

"What do you want to know?"

"As much as you're willing to tell me." He smiled at her, leaned toward her desk, rested his hands on the edge of it, so that he wouldn't seem to be looming over her. "I want to do a good job on this show, and I need your help. My background isn't in art."

"Yes, I know," she said, and held a pencil between her two index fingers, rolled it with her thumbs. "It's *politics,* isn't it?" The word was a sneer.

"Hey, listen," Jess said. "Why don't you just say what's bothering you? I can't stand being around people with secrets."

"You really want to know?" she said, her eyes blazing.

"Yes, I do."

"You worked for Nixon. That was a political appointment. This is *art.* Publicity about *art.*"

"Public relations is the same, whatever you're doing it for."

"Is it *really?*" It was one of the finest words in her assumed diction, so entrenched in her speech now she didn't even think about how to say it.

"I know key men at all the papers and the major magazines," said Jess. "They'll be glad to hear from me."

"Do you know Bob Hughes, the art editor at *Time?* Do you know Nancy Rose at *Vogue?* Do you know that *Harper's Bazaar* has a three-month deadline, and if we're going to get a story in there we have to have it ready by the middle of next week?"

"I do now, because you told me." He tried to smile.

"Just as I'm going to have to tell you about *Art News Magazine* and *Oriental Arts* and all the publications that would be interested in this particular show."

"And are you going to die from that?" Jess said, his green eyes narrowing. "Is that going to put you in the ground, that incredible generosity?"

She looked at him evenly. "I just could have handled it myself. I can't understand why they hired a political man when I would have done a good job myself, and I'm going to end up doing it all myself anyway."

"And that's how you feel?"

"That's how I feel."

"Okay," said Jess, and lit a cigarette. "Now I'm going to tell you how I feel."

"Must you smoke?" Adrienne said.

"Yes," said Jess, "I must." He backed away from her, leaned against the wall, and inhaled deeply. "For more than four years," he said, his voice catching on the words, "I have been on the balls of my ass. I can hardly look at my children, they're so mixed up because I'm home all the time. I'm living off my wife. Everybody I knew in this town who could have helped me disappeared when I needed help most."

His tone became surer, anger giving it resilience. "This job is more important to me than anything else in the world except my family. I'm going to lose them, and I know it, if I don't get back on my feet. I want to make this exhibition a smash, I'm going to bust my back to do the job well, and I don't need any flak from some officious bitch. You got it?"

"I got it," she said very softly.

"Good," said Jess. "Then let's have lunch."

¶ To enter the Sans Souci, patrons opened a very heavy door, walked up three steps into a small hallway, and passed a checkroom, where a pleasant Frenchwoman took their coats and greeted them by name if they were regulars, which almost all of them were. At the front of the restaurant mezzanine edged by a wrought iron railing, small tables for two were artfully arranged, giving those who sat at them a visual command of the rest of the room, diminishing possible anxiety at not being at a banquette, the preferred location.

At one of the mezzanine tables, Congressman Ellerbe was lunching with his lawyer. The topic of their conversation, hushed, was whether or not Ellerbe should sue Amelia Gomez for her column the evening before. The implication had been clear that Ellerbe's connection with Hiro Takeda was continuing and corrupt. It disturbed Travis Ellerbe greatly: he had already lost money on two business deals with Hiro, his plan to run for senator had been scuttled because of publicity about their friendship, and now he wasn't even seated at a banquette.

It was a matter of record, acknowledged by a spokesman of Ellerbe's, that Ellerbe had received $5,050 from Hiro as campaign contributions. Two of those contributions, for $1,800 in 1972 and $2,850 in 1974, were publicly disclosed in reports legally required for all congressional candidates. The spokesman pointed out that Ellerbe himself had helped draft the disclosure legislation.

The third contribution had been for $450 in 1970, prior to requirements that campaign contributions be disclosed. But Travis Ellerbe had admitted it anyway.

He had also acknowledged that he had once flown to Haiti to visit Hiro and a few of his friends at Hiro's invitation. But he stoutly maintained he had paid his own airfare, even though he couldn't find the receipt, and that he had picked up the tabs for all his own meals.

There was no doubt in his mind, his lawyer's, or anyone else's in Washington that he was one of the twenty-two congressmen under investigation by the Justice Department. In an unprecedented move, a subpoena had been issued by that organization to the bank where Hiro Takeda had kept his money, to discover the movements of Hiro's cash. It had aroused alarm and controversy on the part of other foreign nationals about the secrecy of their banking records in the United States, and also caused Ellerbe to rush forward with the disclosure of the $450, which had previously been left out of any of his statements.

The fund-raising party at the Jeffersonian which Hiro had thrown for Ellerbe in 1976 had raised, according to Ellerbe's testimony to a House Ethics Committee, $7,400. Amelia Gomez's snide innuendo that the figure was probably untrue had caused Ellerbe's hackles to rise, along with a case of shingles.

"This column libels me," he said, holding the paper out to his lawyer.

"Not exactly," said his lawyer. He preferred the Sans Souci in spring, when they had the soft-shelled crabs. In general, he was not a man who enjoyed eating lunch, especially when he had to pick up the tab which he always did with Ellerbe. It was a pity, he considered sometimes late at night, that the House Ethics Committee didn't investigate congressmen who accepted favors from their lawyers.

"But the whole tone is snide and snotty," said Ellerbe.

"No question."

"Doesn't that show malice?"

"Nothing we could prove in court."

"What about her saying that the party cost more than the seventy-four hundred it raised?"

"Do you know how much it cost?" the lawyer said, eating joylessly.

"No," said Ellerbe.

"I'll bet Amelia Gomez does."

"Shit," said Travis Ellerbe, but not very loud.

In the corner of the mezzanine, two tables down from Congressman Ellerbe, a young couple seemed absorbed in their lunch, which in his case was an omelet and in hers was filet of sole. Every few minutes soft words would pass between them, and they would seem to look at each other and miss, their glances glancing off in opposite directions.

He was at the State Department and she'd just come to HEW. It was her first time at the Sans Souci. He had spent considerable time preparing her for this noon. The secret of top echelon behavior at lunchtime, he instructed her, was to seem to gawk at no one, not even each other.

"It is," he whispered. "I thought so. That's Congressman Ellerbe. The one who's under investigation. Don't look."

"Which one?" she whispered.

"The man in the navy suit with the tie with the whales on it."

"Lean back," she said.

"I can't lean back. The chair's in the way."

"Then tilt," she said. "I can't really see him."

He tilted toward the wall. Then he turned and signalled for the waiter, his arm raised very high behind him so that he could see the rest of the room.

"You see the girl with the hat?" he asked.

"Yes."

"Who is she?"

"I don't know," said the girl. "Why are you asking me? I'm new here."

"Well, she must be someone," he said. "She has a key table."

The woman he referred to was waiting alone at the third table from the steps down in the center of the room. It was not peculiar that the young man didn't recognize her. It was

doubtful that her friends would have known Megan O'Flannagan right away.

She had dressed for the occasion as though she were going
to testify before a committee comprised of southern senators:
down-home lady in a high-necked dress and hat. The brim
drooped over her right eye, which gave her the advantage of
seeming hidden while permitting her left eye to watch the
entrance to the Sans Souci.

She still found it hard to believe that Larry had called her.
Her nervousness was matched only by her sense of wonder,
that miracles could still occur, even in Washington.

Her hat brim gave her a mild feeling of protection, con-
cealment, so she would be free to look at him with longing,
without his actually seeing. But since he had called her it was
obvious that he had been as attracted as she. Her reputation
would be safe, of course, since she was practically incognito.
As for his reputation, she'd urge him to be more cautious, and
their next lunch would take place at a dark little restaurant
where no one knew either of them, somewhere lit by candles,
where the shadows could dance mysteriously across their faces.
And they wouldn't do anything shabby like go to a hotel, especially since he couldn't afford one. She'd have to ask Howard
if they could meet at his place, since there was a possibility
her building was being watched.

She lifted her hat brim slightly to smile across the room at
Melissa Mae August, who did not seem to see her or respond.
Megan considered going over to her, welcoming her back to
the world, but suppressed the impulse. As glad as she was to
see Melissa alive in the world again, she did not want Larry
to come into the restaurant and find her table-hopping.

At a banquette against the right wall of the restaurant, one
hand tucked carelessly over the top of the wood behind her,
the other around the stem of a wine glass, Melissa Mae August
yawned. Her doctor had told her if she had to drink, to limit
herself to wine. She hated wine. It soured her stomach. But she
figured her stomach might as well be the same as the rest of her.

Beside her was Ellis Moody, Jr., the man who'd admitted
being a friend of Hiro's. Ellis had come to lunch with his eyes

very red, and attributed it to having wept in the taxi. "But *Caroline Livingston, Caroline Livingston.*" He said the name like a liturgy. It carried in it cleanliness, sanctity, all the things people didn't usually discuss at lunch. "How could it happen to *her*. She didn't drink!" He clutched the stem of his martini glass and tried to bring it to his mouth, but his hands were shaking. "My God, I'm so upset, can you believe it?"

"I didn't know her," said Melissa Mae.

He leaned halfway down to meet his glass, so he spilled only a few drops. "She was one of the angels of the earth," he said. "Blonde, generous." They were obviously the two best adjectives he could think of, with respect to women. "And she went like *that* from cancer of the liver. And she didn't drink." He took a gulp of his martini.

"You want another one?" said Melissa, a slightly bored edge to her voice.

"I think I'd better," he said. "It's been a terrible shock."

She signalled to the maitre d', passing their table. "Do you think we could get Mr. Moody another martini?"

"Of course. It's a pleasure to have you back with us, Miss August."

"Thank you, Paul," she said, and smiled. The maitre d' moved away.

Ellis Moody turned and looked at Melissa, marked the fine line of her body, thinner it seemed to him, more suited now to the tailored clothes she wore. "You look really great, Melissa Mae," Ellis said. "The best I've seen you."

"Stop lying," said Melissa.

"No, it's the truth. I love that look on you. I never saw you dress like that."

"Hiro didn't like it," she said. "But I guess that's besides the point now."

He looked away and sipped his drink. "The Rogers are giving a party Friday night and there's talk that Liza Minnelli might come in for it. The Chatsworths and I are going down in their limo. You want to join us?"

"No."

"It's too soon, I suppose. I hope you're not offended. I

thought that Hiro would be glad if you started going out."

"He might. I wouldn't." Melissa leaned back.

"I'm really going to miss him, you know," Ellis said, lifting his eyes in acknowledgment as the waiter set another martini in front of him. "What a gentleman. What a partygiver."

"Well, maybe he can throw a little welcoming 'do' for Caroline Livingston," she said.

On the mezzanine, the young man whispered through stiffened lips, in case anyone was reading them. "On the banquette wearing the pink suit, that's Chris White, the novelist."

"I've seen her on television," the girl said, excitement carbonating her voice. She strained to see.

"Don't stare," he said. "People will know you've never been here."

The girl dropped her napkin under the table and bent down as though to redeem it. She lifted a corner of tablecloth next to the railing and peered through the bars at Chris. She came back to a sitting position, smoothing her hair. "Who's that with her?"

She was referring to a stunningly coiffed woman, the white streak that ran the center of her skull combed into large half curls on her forehead like quotation marks. She was dressed with youthful modishness, gypsy stole with fringe casually draped over white peasant blouse tucked into tight slacks that outlined her still remarkable figure.

"That's Sylvia Kranet, the senator's wife."

"I thought she was older," said the girl.

"She is."

The young girl's eyes were radiant, dancing, excitement giving their blueness extra light. In spite of everyone celebrated there, the young man was moved to look at her. He moved his hand across the table, slowly, fitfully. It came to erratic rest on hers.

She looked at him directly. They had kissed goodnight once after a concert, but he'd never taken her hand or made a pass at her. She assumed it was because he, like her, wanted a career in politics and so needed to be available for someone who could help him advance. Neither of them had any connections at all. Except of course he'd been able to get a reservation.

"Would you like some dessert?" the waiter said.

"Just coffee," he said. "You?"

"Just coffee," she echoed. The waiter went away.

"Be sure and linger over it," the young man said.

Next to Chris, Sylvia Kranet was having a third gibson straight up, without the onion. She was always most bored when the Senate was in session and the senator would start expressing opinions, as other men whistled around the house.

"Isn't that your husband?" she asked Chris, noting the man coming down the stairs.

"Yes, it is," said Chris, sitting up straighter, smiling at Jess. She felt slightly annoyed at his having invaded what she had come to regard as her lunch sanctuary. She had forgotten that when they'd first come to Washington it had been his discovery.

The intense feeling of possessiveness about the details of their lives apart came as a surprise to her. She had not realized how competitive she had become.

"Who's that with him?"

"I don't know. Unless it's some new colleague from the museum."

"Colleague," Sylvia said, and sipped. "Is that what they're calling them now?"

Chris smiled. "Why are you always looking for the worst, Sylvia?"

"Because the best is boring. And usually a lie. Aren't you worried?" Sylvia craned her neck slightly, studying the woman with Jess.

"Maybe a little." It was the least she could do for Sylvia, the least she could do for Jess, seeing him happy, handsome in dark suit, back among the working world, to think that an attractive woman could be interested in him. She herself had fifteen cents clutched in her left hand ready to call Scott.

Jess was moving past the banquette, stopping to shake hands with Art Buchwald, leaning over to kiss Melissa Mae. "Ah, and here's someone else I know," he said, coming around their table, bending to kiss Chris's cheek. "This is my wife, Chris, and Sylvia Kranet. I'd like you to meet Adrienne Harvey. She's the public information officer at the Kirkeby."

"I'm happy to meet you," said Adrienne, extending her hand to Chris.

"It's nice to meet you too," Chris said, studying the woman a little more carefully than she'd intended.

"Maybe we can all have coffee together later," said Jess.

To her surprise, Chris watched them during lunch. She wondered how it was possible to be jealous of a man she intended to be unfaithful to.

¶ In the middle of the room, Megan was making a pretense of eating. She watched the flash of Larry's smile, listened to the thoughtfulness of his words. His high, square forehead wrinkled as he talked of sober matters. His bold, straight nose swooped down toward its center, nostrils flared, Jeffersonian. The subjects he introduced were general, impersonal. She wondered when he would bring the conversation around to them.

"Do you believe in reincarnation?" she said finally.

"No," he said. "But anything that the mind can think of is a possibility."

"I think I know who you were," she said. "One of the Founding Fathers."

He smiled at her, an indulgent smile. Then he pressed his lips together and looked away, very hard, at something he couldn't quite see. "You know, once when I was at Justice, I had occasion to go over some Revolutionary documents. And when I ran my finger over the page, I got the most peculiar buzz."

"I think it's the truth," she said excitedly. "It makes strange sense. A man can't possibly grow as much as he needs to in one lifetime. You have to keep coming back till you get it right."

"Don't say it too loud," said Larry. "We're already in enough trouble."

"I think you were Thomas Jefferson," she said.

"I appreciate the compliment," he said. "But I don't think I could have been old Tom. It feels more like Massachusetts."

"Then you *do* believe in it." She resisted an impulse to

seize his hand. A conservative who could accept reincarnation. It was possible to change the nature of the world.

"I wouldn't discuss it with too many people if I were you," he said. "It's a lunatic notion."

"So was democracy once," she said.

He smiled. "I wish Amelia Gomez could be here to share this conversation. It would, as my daughter says, 'blow her away.' "

"Amelia Gomez?" she said.

"We were in her column last night. Not by name. But it was unmistakably us, unless you know a cuter redhead from the last administration. I certainly don't."

"You and I?"

"Someone told her we were together at Meeting and she made it sound ugly."

Megan looked away, pulled the brim of her hat down even further, so that he would not see the hurt and disappointment in her eyes. "And that's why you asked me to lunch?"

"So everyone can see for themselves what the truth is," he said. "And of course because I find you charming."

"Dessert?" the waiter asked, moving a sweets trolley past their table.

"No, thank you," Megan managed to say.

"Coffee?"

She moved her head.

"Two coffees," Larry said to the waiter. "Abby said she might join us for coffee," he told Megan.

She took a deep breath. "Your wife knew we were together?"

"It was her idea," Larry said.

"Excuse me." She was gone from the table before Larry could get to his feet.

¶ Downstairs, in the ladies' room, Chris was dialing Scott's private number. She felt so anxious, so humorless, so pressed, that lunch had been unbearable for her—she hadn't even been able to wait for Jess to leave the restaurant before going to make the call.

She heard the blunt, beloved voice. "Scott?"

"Hello," he said, a world of affection in the greeting, as if her voice were the first good news he'd heard all day.

"Does the Republic still stand?" It was an old byword between them, from the frenzied days of Watergate, when she had called Scott's newsroom for bulletins of truth that she couldn't get from Jess.

"Not only does it stand, it actually looks healthy today," he said. "No blatant errors of judgment."

"What do you suppose went wrong?" she said.

He laughed. "How are you?"

"Desperate."

"Stop it," he said, his voice constricting, as if her openness strangled him. "You're too bright a woman to be foolish."

"I'm afraid not. I can't wait anymore. I have to be with you."

"What about Jess? My God, if I were a young man his age and couldn't get it started again, I don't know what I'd do."

"You're not much older than he is."

"Jess is thirty-eight," said Scott. "I'm forty-nine."

"That's young."

"It feels pretty old to me."

"That's because we haven't been together," said Chris. "I'll show you how young it can feel."

"I'll bet you could," he said, admiration, distant longing, drying his tongue. "But I couldn't do it to Jess."

"You don't have to be so considerate of Jess anymore. He's got a job."

"Good for him!" Scott said. "Doing what?"

The door to the ladies' room flew open, and Megan burst in. "I'll call you later, mother," Chris said, and hung up the phone, curiously relieved by the interruption. If there was one thing she didn't need, it was Scott's judiciousness, his journalistic curiosity even about Jess. It was their affair that should have been the center of his interest, the day, the night, the news.

¶ At the rear of the Sans Souci to the right of the bar was a short flight of stairs, leading to a raised landing with one table on it, at which sat Adrienne and Jess. He was winning her with an easy charm, returned to him suddenly, change of fortune having eased away his heaviness. The terrible tone of importance he had found it necessary to lay on words, as if he sensed their emptiness, had left his voice and he was light again, good company. By the end of lunch, Adrienne was his reluctant ally.

They bumped into Chris at the top of the stairs coming up from the ladies' room. "We were just coming to join you," he said.

"Oh, heavenly!" said Sylvia, when she saw the three of them moving toward her banquette. "A group!" She signalled for the waiter. "We'll have four stingers," she said to him.

"Not for me," said Jess. "I've got to go back to work." There was a glow of pride around the word, an up note in his voice.

"What about you, colleague?" Sylvia said pointedly. "Will you have a brandy?"

"I don't drink," said Adrienne, sitting down in the chair Jess held for her.

"Don't you get lonely in Washington?" asked Sylvia. "Chris, a stinger?"

"No, thank you," Chris said. She wanted to have her wits about her when she called Scott back. Brandy made her mind sluggish, her words come a little too fast, as if they had spun away from her lips before she could think about them. She wanted to be impeccable, as Scott was, about everything she said, so that it could begin to be perfect, finally.

"Then I guess it's just me," said Sylvia Kranet. "I hate to drink alone. A double brandy," she said to the waiter.

Jess turned to Chris. "You're very quiet today."

"I've got a lot on my mind."

"I've heard that about you." He smiled.

"How's it going?" she asked him.

"Well," said Jess, indicating Adrienne. "You see how pleasant the scenery is in my office."

"A little too pleasant if you ask me," said Sylvia Kranet.

"As none of us is with *Women's Wear,* Sylvia," Chris said, "we're not dying to hear your opinion."

"I enjoyed your last book, Mrs. Betzer," said Adrienne.

"Thank you. You're probably one of the few who read it."

"I'm a voracious reader," said Adrienne.

"I could have told you that," said Sylvia, snidely.

The waiter set the coffees and brandy on the table.

"Are you a Washingtonian, Miss Harvey?" Chris asked.

"I'm from Northampton, Massachusetts." Adrienne named the town where Smith was located, as Harvard men, when asked where they had been educated, sometimes said "Cambridge." It was a small affectation, not exactly a lie. Who she was now had been born at Smith.

"Massachusetts," said Sylvia Kranet. "Are you one of my husband's constituents?"

"I didn't vote in the last election," Adrienne said.

"Why, do you know him?"

"We'd better be getting back to the museum." Jess got up and held Adrienne's chair. "I've got a lot to learn about art."

"I have a feeling you'll be a quick study," said Adrienne, taking her purse from the table.

"Fortunately I'll have an expert teaching me," said Jess.

"I wouldn't be at all surprised," said Sylvia. "Christ," she murmured, watching them leave. "What a tight ass she has. Why aren't you more nervous? He's vulnerable, like all the married men in this town. Aren't you scared? Don't you love him?"

"Certainly," said Chris, unconvincingly. "He's a wonderful man."

"His ass isn't bad either," mused Sylvia. "God, you women who are married to great-looking men. What do you see in them?"

¶ On the balcony, the young man and the young girl were holding hands, gazing into each other's eyes. "Well," she said, finally, breathily. "Have we lingered long enough?"

"I guess so." He signalled, dazed, for the waiter.

Abby and Larry were both at the table when Megan got back from the ladies' room. She had pulled herself together, after a fashion. Disappointment came from having expectations, she had learned that in the desert. But she hadn't been wise enough to wait and find out what Larry Cochran wanted; she had assumed he wanted her. The truth had been so crushing she nearly wept.

Abby stretched out her hand. "Megan. How lovely to see you."

"It's lovely to see you, too, Mrs. Cochran," Megan lied.

"Please," said Abby. "The papers practically have us related. Call me Abby. That's such an attractive hat."

"Thank you." Megan sat down, searching the serene blonde countenance across from her for traces of Martha Jefferson, to whom Thomas had been faithful for forty years after her death, till his own. Perhaps that might explain the depth and virtue of the Cochrans' attachment to each other. A previous life with a previous wife.

"What are you working at now, Megan?" Abby asked.

"Nothing. I can't find a job."

"But that's appalling. Someone with your intelligence and experience. Can't you make some calls for her, Larry, see if there's anything in the administration?"

"I can try." He signalled the waiter for a check. "But I can't really hold out much hope. The city's crawling with career unemployed."

The waiter handed him the bill. Larry's fair complexion mottled slightly. "Can you lend me three dollars?" he whispered to Abby.

"I don't know," she said. "How can I be sure you'll pay me back?" She smiled at him and gave him the money.

The restaurant was clearing. There was a moment at lunch at the Sans Souci when the buzz reached a definite pitch, when excitement hung in the air like an anthem, the hum of the world's most public city. A moment later there would come a rush of leaving, and a lull. In the hush that followed, the remaining conversations would seem the more intense.

"That was extremely kind of you," said Megan to Abby. They were alone now at the table, Larry having returned to the office. "Suggesting your husband look for something for me."

"I don't think it was kind. I think it would be good for the administration."

"It wouldn't bother you, after the Amelia Gomez thing, to have me working around Larry?"

"No," said Abby. "Why should it?"

The place was almost deserted now. The waiters had adjourned to the kitchen to eat their lunch, except for one who hovered near Chris's banquette, waiting to be asked for the check.

A gust of wind blew from the entranceway, so powerful that the flaps of the tablecloths on the mezzanine waved like surrender flags in the wind. At the top of the steps, suddenly, framed in fur the same honey color as her hair but not so radiant as the deep amber tan of her skin, stood Gloria Stanley, champagne eyes darting around the room.

"Chris!" she squealed, pointing a beige gloved finger. "How fabulous! I knew I'd find you here!"

Gloria came tripping down the stairs, holding to the railing as though she were still on board ship. Burnished rust leather boots tightly embraced her calves. Earrings and bracelets jangled, her own musical accompaniment.

"I told Akhmed we had to get to Washington in time for lunch. He almost ruptured his airplane." She leaned over to kiss Chris. "And Sylvia." Her voice turned chill. "How nice to see you." She warmed again.

"Oh, I'm so excited to be here, Chrissie. Are you excited I'm here?"

"Surprised would be more the word," said Chris. "I thought you were in the Indian Ocean."

"Well, I was," said Gloria. "But when I called you, we'd just landed in Bombay. I wanted to feel you out about my coming here before I told you I was on my way. I didn't want to wear out my welcome before it was hatched."

"But how did you get here so quickly?" asked Chris.

"Akhmed," said Gloria, as if it were an ancient word that explained everything.

"I'm afraid I don't know who that is."

"But, darling, that's only because you don't read the *National Inquirer*. Akhmed Bakutta. He's got his own Jumbo Jet and he insisted on flying me here. He's always meeting me places." The honey face grew suddenly pained. "My God, I was in the air with him for twenty hours. It could have been a miniseries. The longest battle of my career. Turks are not morally opposed to rape, you know."

"I didn't know that," said Sylvia, fascinated.

"Fortunately Akhmed is a romantic. He keeps thinking I'll marry him if he behaves himself. He's waiting out in the limo with my luggage. I've got to find someplace to stay. I can't go to a hotel. He'll take over my floor, or buy the place. I won't be able to hide from him. Oh God, I'm so disoriented. I must have dessert. Ooo-ooo," she sang to the waiter. "Do you have any sweets?"

"I'd invite you to stay at my house," Sylvia volunteered, "only we're expecting some constituents."

"I'll bet you are," said Gloria.

"Well, I must go," said Sylvia, wrapping her gypsy stole around her shoulders. She leaned over and kissed Chris's cheek. "Thank you for the lunch, dear." She left the table.

"I thought she was a good friend of yours," Chris said.

"Not exactly," said Gloria, looking after her. "She came along on one of my honeymoons."

"*Et voilà*," said the waiter, pushing a sweets trolley to their table.

"Oh, goody," said Gloria, her eyes moving hungrily over the variety of cakes, rising high and chocolated, ringed with meringues and whipped cream, seven-layer cake, chocolate mousse, lemon pie, puddings. "I'll have that," she said, pointing to the profiterole, pastry puffed like a miniature castle bursting with custard, glazed with spun sugar, beacon lit with red and green cherries. "And that." She indicated a petit four.

The pleasure on her face transmitted itself to the waiter's own, as he piled her plate high. "For the beautiful lady," he said.

She hardly waited for the plate to touch the table, seizing a fork, stabbing into the balls of pastry, eating it greedily, closing her eyes, making audible sounds of pleasure. "Oh," she groaned.

"How can you do that to yourself?" Chris asked. "You look so thin and wonderful. How can you eat two desserts?"

"Have you finished my play?" asked Gloria.

"No," said Chris.

"Then you understand why I'm insecure." She picked up a tablespoon and started eating in the European manner, piling it with the spoon onto the fork, hoisting it to her mouth, chewing with gleeful sounds.

"May we barge in?" asked Abby, Megan standing beside her.

"Oh, but Abigail is here too," said Gloria. "Perfect. It's a perfect day."

"Hello, Gloria," said Abby. "You remember Megan O'Flannagan?"

"Hi," said Gloria. "Excuse me for not shaking hands. I'm having an anxiety attack." She gulped some more custard.

"But how marvelous you look, Gloria," Abby said, pulling up a chair for Megan and sitting down. "Where did you get that gorgeous color."

"In the Arabian Sea."

"Was it wonderful?"

"Water is water," said Gloria.

"There's a sheik waiting outside with his own Jumbo Jet. She finds that boring," said Chris.

"No, I don't," said Gloria. "I find it sad." Her voice crumpled slightly, in her throat. "Everyone imagines I'm pursued by everybody, and the truth is nobody's after me but a deranged Turk."

"I know several men who'd be happy to run after you," Megan said.

"Really?" said Gloria, and her face brightened. "Are any of them smart?"

"My closest friend is a psychologist, and he greatly admires you."

"How kind," said Gloria. "Maybe there's hope. I'm so tired of adventures."

"Want to trade?" asked Abby.

"Well, yes, as a matter of fact." Gloria looked at her very straight. "I'd give my caps to be a part of a family. To know what it was like to really *live* in this city. To feel like a person. I'm so sick of hotels and studios and villas and staterooms."

"I'd invite you to stay with us," said Chris. "Really I would. Only we don't have a lot of space, and I can't work with anybody around. . . ."

"Are you seriously looking for someplace to stay?" asked Abby. "Because we have what is laughingly called a guest room. It isn't elegant at all. Just a room with its own little bath."

"Does it have a closet?" asked Gloria.

"A nice-sized closet," said Abby.

"Would you really let me stay with you?" Gloria's eyes were suddenly brimming. She lowered her spoon.

"But my dear," said Abby, touched by the vulnerability in the perfect, heart-shaped face. "We'd be honored to have you."

"You're a saint," said Gloria, and clasped her hand.

It was true, Megan thought. Not only was Abby beautiful and charming but with Megan's luck she was a saint. Not enough to try and find a job for a woman linked with Larry. Now she was going to move Gloria Stanley into her home.

"I have to go," said Megan, standing.

"No, no," said Gloria. "Please. You must have a glass of champagne! This is a celebration! Waiter! Your finest champagne!" She clasped her hands together like a child. "Oh, isn't life the most amazing thing. Holding out its arms so unexpectedly." Tears fell from her extraordinary eyes. She opened her shoulder bag, emblazoned with its pattern of *BULLSHIT,* took out a Kleenex, and blew her nose. "Who would have thought I'd find sanctuary among Republicans."

7

¶ A light rain fell on O Street. If she had been blessed, Megan considered, she might have been in London, where her unrealized passion could play against fog, near someplace called Waterloo Bridge. But as she was blighted, she'd been born in Evansville and was nursing a wounded spirit in Georgetown.

Her feet seemed to have nearly the weight of her heart. She tried to lift them, move them, place them, one at a time, as they'd taught her in the desert, to bring herself back to awareness of bodily movement. But all she could feel was leaden sorrow, heaviness that hung between her and the world.

She raised a hand to her slightly soggy brim, and tilted it upward so she could peer at the sky. Grey, with wisps of black clouds, it loomed above her like melodrama. She couldn't even die on a moor of wasted love and lung congestion, being in civilization, and hearty. If she lay face up on the red bricks of O Street and let it rain in her nose, the worst she would get would probably be a cold.

She dragged her aching psyche toward Howard's house, clung to the iron railing as she walked up the steps. That it was the middle of a workday made no impression on her. Howard had offered his love numberless times, unprofessionally. Megan believed when you loved somebody, you were available all the time.

She pressed the bell, gave her name in response to the mechanical-sounding "Yes?" that piped through the metal box by his door. There was a buzz. The latch was released. She moved inside the yellow-painted entranceway, decorated with encouraging slogans from Jean Cocteau and Abraham Maslow, and opened the double doors into his reception room.

She sat down and started thumbing through the neatly arranged magazines, *Harper's, Psychology Today.* She picked up a stubbed-out cigarette that lay in the ashtray, examined the bright red lipstick that waxed around its filter, like a garish crescent moon.

The door from Howard's inner office opened. He was in a suit, grey, with a faint pinstripe. It made him look businesslike, professional, less vulnerable than he had on Sunday, in his sweatshirt, with his slender fingers manipulating her toes. He bore no resemblance to this weekend self, except for the look of love in his eyes.

His smile was an office smile, efficient, carrying affection, but not too much time to spare. "Hi," he said, closing the door behind him. "To what do I owe the pleasure?"

"I'm having a nervous breakdown," she said, and started to cry.

He moved to her, put his arms around her. "Can you hold yourself together till I finish with this patient?"

"I'm sorry to barge in on you," she wept.

"Don't be," he said. "Don't be sorry for anything." He reached into his pocket, extracting a neatly folded wad of Kleenex, and gave her one.

"You're so good to me," she whimpered.

"You have no idea how good I'd like to be to you." he said softly. "I'll be out in a second." He went back into his office.

Megan could hear muffled words from inside, followed by what sounded like the closing of a door. He was back.

"Come inside," he said. "Please."

"Where's your couch?" she managed, when they were inside.

"The chair's more comfortable." He indicated it. She sank into the deep suede, letting it close around her like arms. She wept.

"Take some deep breaths," he said. "Center yourself."

"I can't," she wailed.

He took a few for her. "You want to tell me what happened?"

"He asked me to lunch. . . ." She gasped between the words, struggled to catch up with her sobs. "I was so excited. I thought he wanted me. But it was all *her* idea. Abby's. There was a nasty item in the paper, and she thought the way to squash it was for us to . . . be TOGETHER." She wailed the word.

"She sounds like a very smart woman."

"I don't need you to praise her," she wept. "The whole world praises her. Everybody's crazy about her, especially him. She's so damned sure of herself she's invited Gloria Stanley to stay with them."

"That *is* secure," said Howard.

"It isn't enough I have to compete with a saint," she wailed. "He's going to be living with Gloria Stanley."

"It seems like a powerful argument for forgetting about him."

"Forget about him?" She looked up from her soggy wad of Kleenex. Tears ran like streams of crystals from her reddened eyes. Swollen with weeping, the bright blue color was still dazzling. The humidity had dampened her hair. It curled into ringlets, little orange dancing lights around her head, peeking out from beneath her hat.

"How can I forget about him?" she said. "He's the finest man in the world."

"You're glorifying him," he said. "You're being irrational."

"Love is irrational," she said. "Except in this case."

"Did you wear that hat to lunch?"

"Why? Don't you like it?"

"You haven't got a hat face," he said. "Why do you persist in loving an unattainable man?"

"I don't know."

"Every woman in the world has fantasies about an unattainable man. It's a way of trying to get Daddy's ultimate approval." His voice softened. He got up from the edge of the desk and moved close to her, kneeling, conciliatory. "The relationship you want but can't have. Why do you want an unattainable man?"

"It's not my fault he's married."

"That's right. Any more than it's your fault you wore that hat."

"What does that mean?" she asked testily.

"You picked it out. What to wear. Who to love. The typical syndrome of the Catholic girl and the priest. Every little girl wants to marry Daddy. But at some point she has to grow up and be a whole woman. Who can have . . ." He reached for her. "A whole man."

"Stop. . . ."

He put his arms around her. "I appreciate the intensity of your feelings." He kissed her temple. "Your feelings are very real to you. But why a fantasy relationship? Why not a man who can really appreciate you?"

"Because I love him," she said weakly.

"Do you? Or isn't it really fear of intimacy?"

She sat up rigid in the chair. "I have no fear of intimacy."

"Good." He kissed her.

"You're breaching your ethic," she said, pushing him away.

"You're not my patient, I love you. There are no ethics in love."

"There would be with Larry," she said.

He leaned back, anger blotching his face with red, as if he had shaved too close. "Why is it that therapists have to be the sensitive ones? Why shouldn't patients have to watch what they say? Someday I'm going to tell my patients what *real* problems are."

"You don't have to get mad," she said. "I appreciate the intensity of your feelings." She looked down at the ashtray by the chair, picked out a cigarette stub, and held it toward the light. It carried the same bleeding color she'd seen in the anteroom. "I wish I still smoked," she sighed.

"Sure you do," said Howard furiously, getting to his feet. "That way you could be sure of taking time off your life that you might otherwise have lived. That way you could really shed the responsibility of being a healthy, loving person."

"Why do you want to hurt me?"

"I'm not trying to hurt you. I'm just dealing in truth. If you can't handle truth, you're welcome to delude yourself. Go on thinking that one day Larry Cochran will turn from his adored wife and children and fall in love with you. Nurse that delusion. That and the idea that you look good in hats."

"You hostile bastard!" she said.

"Hostile? I love you. I even love you in that hat."

She slammed out of the office.

¶ Louise Felder had had a devastating winter. Cruel were the icy winds of the East, which had driven too many folk westward. Crueler still was the mind of man, constantly changing, so that even those who had once voiced contempt for California were moving there. Doc Simon's relocating had made L.A. suddenly acceptable to the theatre crowd. Gore Vidal was making it his "winter quarters," so even the *New York Review of Books* had to admit there was something west of Riverside Drive.

The news of the literary greening of Los Angeles did not bring much joy to Louise's heart. Much as she had loved being a pioneer, moving to Hollywood when it was still Hollywood and contemptible, she had no wish to proselytize and make everyone else want to be there, too. One of her greatest pleasures in the beginning was flying back East, golden skinned, and lunching with her old boss, watching him wither and whiten under her honeyed California success while he tried to speak with enthusiasm of his summer house in Sneadon's Landing. Toying with her celery remoulade, she remembered how hard she had once striven for invitations to the Hamptons, when the promised land seemed to be a weekend at the end of a three-hour schlepp. It was almost enough to make her feel uncompetitive.

Now the very fate that had dubbed her doyenne of a select society had rained on her a merciless melange of trash. Not that she meant to judge people: she couldn't do that and make deals, or read the trades. But with everyone coming to town, her peace, such as it was, was over.

In her youth she had dreamed of giving exceptional parties. Friend of the greats, that was the most she had aspired to be. That she should have become a bigger success than many of those she represented was a shock to her. People fought for invitations to her dinners. Now that everybody wanted to be with her, she had lost her appetite for entertaining. Still, she couldn't stop. It was good for business, and good for the part of her that secretly believed in romance. If the house weren't crowded, she was afraid she might discover how empty it was.

But now that Beverly Hills was filling with last-ditch lemmings, and stranger scandals than Watergate had surfaced, she hated to be home. With her malaise at her adopted soil, she was glad to get the call from Gloria summoning her to Washington. Not that Gloria had the fiscal heft anymore to make Louise go someplace she didn't care to. But she genuinely liked Gloria. And Washington was a cakewalk. The fascination of politics, its veneer of high purpose, cracked to reveal the same people Louise had been dealing with in Hollywood. And she could outmanipulate any man in the crowd.

She sat back in the taxi from Dulles Airport and watched the vestiges of winter parading past her window. It was a pleasure to observe a real season, knowing the cold was at her option. By the time the cab got to Chris's house, Louise felt actually benign.

"I bet you think I've come here to ask about the progress of the play," she said, when a stunned Chris opened the door. Louise moved brusquely past her into the entrance hall, depositing her purse on the small Sheraton table, picking up the letters that lay unopened on a silver tray, shuffling through them. "How are you?"

"Fine," Chris said. "I think." She closed the front door.

"You look healthy," said Louise, reaching for Chris's hands, turning them over, like a manicurist, examining them. "No broken nails?" She moved toward the den. "That was my greatest ambition when I was a secretary: to have someone else do all my typing, so I could have long nails. Where's Jess?"

"He's working."

"What happened?" said Louise, walking through the double doors that led into the study. "Is Nixon running again?"

Chris laughed. "He's handling the opening of a show at the Kirkeby Museum."

"How elegant," said Louise approvingly, taking off her gloves. "That must be a load off your mind."

"I can't tell you how much," said Chris, unconvincingly. "Can I offer you a drink, or something soft. . . ."

"I don't want to interrupt your labors," Louise said, moving toward the desk. "I just couldn't wait to see your sweet face, so I dropped my luggage at the hotel and came straight over."

"How very lucky for me," said Chris. Once, when she was still overtly a puppy, panting with enthusiasm at the world, Chris had been introduced to Ingrid Bergman. It had been one of the few occasions in her life when she was nearly speechless. "It's a thrill to meet you," she had said, finally, bereft of any camouflage of words to help her, genuinely awed. "You're one of the most beautiful women in the world." "How very lucky for me," Ingrid Bergman had answered, in a very bored voice. It turned out to have been a line from *Saratoga Trunk,* but having that piece of trivia at her fingertips had in no way diminished Chris's vast disappointment at the meeting.

"Now that Jess is off your back you must feel truly carefree," Louise said. "Your work must be just zipping along." She riffled casually through the typewriter paper on the desk. "Not that I would dream for a minute of asking to see how it was coming."

She looked at the typewriter. There was clean white paper in it. Louise touched the grey metal surface, turned on the switch. It hummed.

"Well, at least it's still working," she said. "Even though the motor's cold."

"What are you, with the CIA?" Chris asked angrily.

"If I was, I wouldn't have to deal with TALENT!" Louise

circled the desk. "My God, where's your compassion? All you damned writers are always carrying on about how sensitive you are, and here she is, the world's greatest victim, putting herself at your mercy, and you won't even show her what you've done."

"I haven't started it," said Chris.

"Oh, well, then we're all right," Loiuse smiled, and sat on the arm of the sofa. "I was afraid you weren't showing it because it was lousy. There's plenty of time. We don't go into rehearsal for four weeks."

"I don't even know what it's about," said Chris, despairingly.

"You have all afternoon to think." Louise got up again. "I'll meet you at the Madison at eight o'clock. You can tell me the plot over dinner." She moved toward the door.

"You've got to get me out of it," said Chris in a very low voice. "I'm not going to be able to deliver."

"Of course you will," said Louise. "There's no pressure. Nothing is at stake here but three careers." She paused at the threshold and smiled. "I'll see you at eight. Don't bother to see me out. I don't want to diminish your creative flow."

"But the children will be home soon, and . . ."

"The what?" said Louise through frozen lips.

"The children."

"It's not my fault you have children. I only told you to marry Jess, not breed with him."

"I can't work with them around."

"Then have them kidnapped," said Louise.

"If Jess were here he could take them someplace. . . ."

"You've managed to have a career *and* children till now. . . ."

"But Jess was home."

Louise put on her gloves and stared at her friend, studying her for all the happiness that should have been there. "Then get him fired," she said. "That ought to take less influence in this town than getting him a job."

¶ By six-thirty, when Jess hadn't come home, Chris was frantic. People were standing waiting for her to be clever, and her spirit was dry. Her children were fighting with each other, the zipper on her skirt wasn't closing, and the telephone was ringing. It was as if every part of her was being assaulted.

"Hello?" She stood in the kitchen by the breakfast alcove where Billy and Caroline were insulting each other over Top Ramen. "I can't hear," she shouted at them. They fell silent, meditatively caught in the long noodles, slurping.

"Hi, honey." It was Jess.

"Where in hell are you?"

"I must have the wrong number," he said, and hung up. In a moment the phone rang again.

"Hello?"

"Hi, honey," Jess said.

"How are you?" she managed, more quietly.

"That's better," he said. "How was your day?"

"Jess, please. Don't be so on top of everything and friendly. I've got a crisis here. When are you coming home?"

"Soon," he said.

"But I need you *now*. Where are you?"

"I'm at work."

"Still?"

"I don't believe this. After what we've been through? It's my second day at work and you're complaining?"

"I've got to meet Louise."

"Get a sitter," he said quietly. "For God's sake, give me a chance to be my own man."

"Your own?" she said coldly. "Or Adrienne's?"

"I'm not hearing this."

"I saw how she was looking at you at lunch."

"I've gone mad," he said, after a moment. "This isn't you, it's your mother."

"Don't attack my mother. If you have to say something bad about a mother, why don't we talk about your mother?"

There was a click on the line.

She replaced the receiver. She looked over at the children and saw them mesmerized, frightened.

A smile broke on her lips, tenuous, pulling erratically at the flesh of her mouth. It occurred to her that she was about to weep with rage. She remembered the terrors of her own child-hood, fear of abandonment, parental anger. Seeing the wide dark eyes that watched her every movement, she collected her-self and sat down with them. They were quiet.

"If you get a divorce," said Billy, finally, in a voice too deep for six years, "can I live with Daddy?"

"We're not getting a divorce," she said. "People fight."

"I know," he said. "And then they get a divorce."

"I'm never going to get a divorce," said Caroline haughtily.

"You're not even going to get *mar-ried*," said Billy jeeringly, "because that would mean you would have to have babies. And you know what you have to do to get babies." He rolled his eyes.

"I'm going to adopt them," Caroline said. "Twins. Twin *girls*." The word carried the superiority of her breed, the con-tempt she wanted so deeply to express to him, and even more to believe. "I'll buy them at the orphanage and take them home to my mansion."

"If your husband gives you a mansion you'll have to make babies with him," Billy sneered.

"Twins will be enough," she said certainly. "We'll adopt them."

The worst of it was that Chris loved them. It would have been easy to run away to dance on a table top in Paris except that she was happy with her children, she felt responsible for them, a maternal trait that seemed to skip a generation, genet-ically, in her family. Still, the part of her that yearned for high adventure, for the sheik that had never carried her away, for the Greek island she'd never explored, still existed. At moments it compressed itself into longing indistinguishable from sexual desire. But from time to time it showed itself as exactly what it was, a wish for freedom.

Jess slammed into the house a half hour later. "What the hell was that about," he said coming into their bedroom. She put a finger to her lips and signalled him into silence. She closed the door and continued dressing.

"I had them all afternoon," she said. "I'm supposed to be writing a play."

"Get a live-in housekeeper," he said.

"We decided we couldn't really afford one," said Chris.

"Well, let's change our minds." He took off his coat. "I'll be happy to pay for it."

"But Jess, you only have a short-term job." She applied her lipstick, looking at her own reflection so hard she could not even sense him.

He sat down on the ottoman, a sudden sag in the shoulders of his dark grey suit. She had ordered it for him as a Christmas gift from the best custom tailor in town, because she had seen his depression. Women were supposedly the ones who cared about those things.

But he did look wonderful when he dressed, the width of his shoulders giving an impressive hang to any jacket he wore. She could see how appealing he would be to Adrienne.

"You know," he said softly, "all the way home I kept telling myself that it couldn't be true, what I was thinking. That you're angry because I'm working."

"Don't be ridiculous," said Chris.

"I was afraid you had contempt for me because I couldn't get a job. But maybe you really *liked* having me home."

She smiled a little lopsidedly. "Well, you're a very pleasant person," she said.

"Don't give me that crap. I read you like one of your books, lady. I'm finally on my feet, and you're mad. 'Only a short-term job.' What disdain you have."

"I just don't want you to get unrealistic. We can't start spending like crazy when we have limited income."

"I'm going to go over the moon with this art show. It's going to be the most impressive opening anyone's ever seen. . . ." There was light back in his pale green eyes. "If it takes every minute of my life these next few months I'm prepared to give it every moment of my life."

"And what about my play?"

"That's *your* problem," he said. "It's my turn to be a success."

"You're jealous," she said.

"That's right. You've had your moment. Now let me have mine."

Rage inspired her. In the taxi to the Madison the play suddenly flashed before her eyes, in between angry visions of Jess, complacency gone from his face, his jaw stubbornly set. It would be a love story, about her and Scott. Only she would make him very young, and that way Jess would never know. And she could speak to Scott all the erotic words she was longing to speak, demonstrate the wit and affection stored up for him, embrace him with Gloria Stanley's arms in the middle of the Kennedy Center. It was perfect. All she had to do now was write it.

¶ "I love your house," said Gloria Stanley to Abby. "It's so . . ." She paused, poised at the threshold of the Cochran living room, her feet right-angled delicately in flat shoes, like a ballerina about to take flight into the right word. "Real," she said at last.

She was not referring to the worn parts of the rug, which she had not been able to help noticing, but considered part of the authenticity of the Cochrans, representing as they did in her eyes true Americana. Nor did she mean that the stuffing was edging out of certain parts of the sofa, which it was. The best suites in the Dorchester in London had chairs with padding falling out the bottom, and so far as Gloria knew, that was style. When you had been sure of yourself long enough, as England had, it was permissible to go slightly to seed. What really impressed her about the Cochran home was the visual confirmation that people lived there. For a woman who had spent her life on sets, in hotel suites, in passage, it was touching.

She fingered the sterling silver frames of the photos on the piano, a young wedding, Abby and Larry, he in cutaway, she in long satin gown. "I envy you," Gloria sighed. "No matter how much I accomplish in life, I'll never be married once."

¶ Outside the small square basement window, the only natural light that shone in the large L-shaped room, a grey bird sat on a fire hydrant, a chilled harbinger of spring. Once Adrienne Harvey had chosen for herself a commitment to art, and those who could contribute to it, she had lost any interest in nature, not realizing how frequently the two combined. But the bird on the hydrant riveted her, held her more rapt than a Renoir. Because, had she looked the other way, she would have seen Jess.

As emotionless as she prided herself on being, she had a scholar's curiosity about elation. Occasionally someone would pass her with a look of such joy on his face that Adrienne would be tempted to chase after him and ask what he was feeling, where it had come from. If there were an actual radiant pleasure in being alive, it had eluded her. But she knew that happiness was out there somewhere, only a few feet away. She had a suspicion she could almost reach out and touch it if only she knew what direction it was coming from. Lately, that had seemed to be from Jess.

The air of silence she had adopted in college to conceal her accent, and so her origins, had earned her a reputation as mysterious, garnered her chic summer invitations to Marblehead, Massachusetts. She kept the silence now, in the hope that Jess would be affected.

As an undergraduate, she had been successful in Marblehead. The Clifton Sangers had considered her charming, especially Mrs. Sanger, who greatly admired silence, particularly when coupled with beauty. The full almond shape of Adrienne's blue grey eyes gave her the advantage in glancing. Every one of her looks was loaded with meaning. At least it seemed like that to those who spoke a great deal.

These did not include the direct descendents of Clifton Sanger. His own children turned up for a day at a time in Marblehead that summer, stopped in with private planes and helicopters, able only to stay for lunch, and then get back to town. But his nieces and nephews were fairly lively, as was the occasional stepchild who dropped by, stayed a few days, and then disappeared.

There was bright conversation over breakfast. There was a

silver server on the sideboard in the mornings filled with kippers, eggs, sausage, and chicken livers, each under a different lid. Baskets of hot toast wrapped in fine linen at the side. There were silver pots of coffee and steaming cocoa, and creams, two strengths. Breakfast all Adrienne's life had been simple and uniform, an occasion you got over with to serve nutrition. At the Clifton Sangers it was an event, accompanied by the clanging of lids, the ringing of silverware. And talk of regattas, cups. Fairyland.

In her philosophy she had always been vaguely socialistic. She was a selfish girl in the main, as most girls her age were. But her intellect was so far in advance of her spirit that she knew the world would be easier if people weren't hungry. It made more sense if everybody shared. Still, she liked being one of those waiting at seven-thirty in the morning to be next at one of a selection of dishes under silver.

She decided not that she wanted to be rich but that she wanted to be classy. It was a word that, had she spoken it aloud, would have told the Sangers everything about her. But class was what they had, the habit of being elegant. She intended to copy it the best she could.

She began by changing her major to History of Art. The girls who had come to college lacking determination for a particular field seemed to drift there. It included the promise of future Junior Years Abroad, in Italy, France, the places with dreams in their names.

By the time her sophomore year was over, she was genuinely in love with the subject, fascinated by what she was being taught. She imitated the neat little squarish printing of the girls with whom she took classes and became dedicated to study, although she did accept weekend invitations to Princeton.

She belonged to a generation that hadn't quite made up its mind about sex, so neither had she. She had never lived with a man. She had opened herself to a few on Princeton occasions, as she called them, weekends when the rich had had enough of the regatta. Usually these were after what would have been considered courtships, proms at colleges, vacations at the family home. She never gave in easily. Those of inherited wealth did not admire pushovers unless they were Scandinavian maids. Nor did they seem too hungry for sex, except as something to go with beer, like a pretzel.

None of them really excited her, except for their names. They were not as impressive in bed as they were at breakfast. Sex to her became less a source of satisfaction than of self-improvement. She had determined early on what her goals were: to rise very high on the loins of someone with rank. To pass, in the truest sense of the word, to move in a universe peopled by graduates of Harvard there was a certain warm-bloodedness one had to get over. To the Clifton Sangers of the world, passion was something to be avoided more carefully than an audit. She had taken her clue from them and tried to divest herself of all that was giving.

But when Jess was close, something ancient and powerful stirred in her. She wanted to do things for him. She began to listen to the sound of his breathing, to study his voice as he talked on the phone behind her, telling the press to save the night of April 26, their invitations were on the way: the evening was going to be magic.

Magic. She could hear him shifting around, his foot on the chair, his powerful legs straining the material of his suit, so that she could almost see his muscles, if she dared to look at them. Magic. She didn't believe in it, anymore than she believed in passion.

She had never thought much about the bodies of men, except those by Michelangelo. She had noticed very early on in her limited sexual career that reality bore almost no resemblance to *David*. Putting it down to the genius of the artist, rather than the generosity of the Creator, she assumed most men were frail. But she could see how strong Jess was, through his clothes.

The air was heavier with him in the room, smelling of him, man mingled with soap. She'd started coming to work very early in the morning so that she could breathe him in before he got there, essence of Jess, superclean. He looked always as if he'd just stepped out of a shower. In her dreams they showered together, and he soaped her all over, inch by inch, moving the cake slowly around her breasts, in between her legs. She would awaken tense and irritated and not be able to look at him, for fear he would see in her eyes how badly she wanted him.

It was no plan of hers, a married man. Especially one with a successful wife and no real money of his own. She knew all about him. It was a very small town, Washington, D.C., with all the petty interest and gossip of a small town. And no way of keeping anything private, least of all how much you were worth. All anyone had to do was go to the Bureau of Records to see how much you had paid for your home, making curious neighbors as potentially informed as the FBI.

There was no way of hiding economic status, and no way of concealing unemployment. Like the handicapped, the unemployed were noted with a pity that cloaked revulsion, relief that it wasn't the observer so struck down.

America. It raised you to be clever and taught you everything except how to fail. So most of its citizens went through life carrying a small burden of apology for not quite measuring up: to what, they weren't sure.

She watched Jess through lowered lids, out of the sides of her lush, black-lashed eyes, studied him without seeming to be looking, as he told the networks to be sure and plan to attend: it would be the art event of spring, Gloria Stanley would be there. His voice had a prideful tone, as if he had learned to deal with his wife's success and her access to celebrities.

Adrienne would have despised his situation. She could not imagine a man alive who could stand a woman's outdistancing him. She had had a brief flirtation with the women's movement, and read a few issues of *Ms.*, including an article on menstruation in literature, which attributed the argument between Oberon and Titania in *A Midsummer's Night Dream* to Titania having her period, after which Adrienne abandoned being a feminist. But even during the time when she danced with the idea, she'd still regarded women whose careers surpassed their husbands' as unnatural.

So for him to have maintained his spirit during all that difficult time was a triumph of something she hadn't known men had.

Somehow, with all the difficulty of the Nixon years, he had apparently managed to keep the friendship of newsmen. All the major publications interested in art had given space, or promised it. A friend of Jess's at UPI had put it on the wire from Colombo that a hundred thousand Sri Lankans a day visited the temples and shrines that housed the art coming to the Kirkeby. It was clever PR. To admire his work in addition to the man was intolerable.

Worst of all, he brought her daisies and small bouquets. She didn't need any more fragrances throwing her off balance through her nose. Hers was a life of design, not accident. Everyone she knew maneuvered. The higher up they lived, the more subtle were the manipulations. She'd watched a rich friend of good family have her father transfer a huge portfolio of stocks to the brokerage firm of a young man she coveted, trapping him into marriage with the account. It was design of such subtle thread it made politics look gross. Adrienne had observed the machinations of the privileged, and good student that she was, maneuvered herself into exactly the web she wished to be caught up in.

Jess Betzer belonged nowhere in her life. That was why it was so insupportable that he'd become the center of it. She studied the bird on the fire hydrant as if its wings contained the secret of the universe. She had a look of such passionate intensity on her face as he moved nearer her desk, she was sure he would never suspect her feelings, as powerful as they were.

"Now all we need," Jess was saying exuberantly, "are some professors of art to dignify the proceedings." He handed her a piece of paper with notes on it. "Do you like that as a rough of the invitations?"

"Be sure and add that it's under the patronage of the Arts Council of Sri Lanka," she said, studying it with inordinate care. "Otherwise it's perfect." She handed it back to him, without raising her lids.

"Do I get an A?" he asked.

"You get an A." She turned back to look at the bird. It was gone. There was no way she could sit and meditate on a fire hydrant.

"And you get these," he said, pulling a brightly colored nosegay from behind his back.

He looked at her like a schoolboy, an overgrown schoolboy with a barrel chest.

"Why do you do things like this?" she asked.

"I enjoy giving flowers to beautiful women. It makes me feel great simplicity about the difference between the sexes. I understand the division perfectly then."

"And the rest of the time?"

"The rest of the time it puzzles me like it does everyone else." He grinned. "Be gracious and say thank you."

"Thank you," she said. "But I wish you wouldn't do it. It embarrasses me."

"I know," he said. "That increases my pleasure." He was smiling at her.

She lifted her eyes. "Why don't you ever ask me to lunch anymore?"

After a moment he said, "Because it wouldn't end with lunch."

"Would that be so terrible?"

"I love my family too much to mess it up," he said. "And you're much too smart to get involved with a married man."

"No, I'm not," said Adrienne.

They looked at each other so deeply, in that moment it had all happened between them.

There was a knock on the door. "Saved by the knock," Jess said, smiling a little ruefully.

"Come in," said Adrienne.

Dr. Sam stood in the doorway, the natty check on his vest matching the check on his tie. "Is this an inconvenient time?"

"Not at all, Dr. Sam," she answered.

"We have a terrible crisis," he said, his hands slightly out of control, as if the air were full of gnats. "The carpenters are constructing pedestals for the sculptures, everyone's coming, we're six weeks away from the show and everything's in perfect order except I haven't got my three key pieces."

"What do you mean you haven't got them?" asked Adrienne.

"I was afraid something had gone wrong in the cataloguing. But they quite simply haven't been sent. They're new, from the *stupa* they dug up last year." He moved toward her, holding out a sheaf of papers. "We're dealing with the Minister of Education, or some subordinate who wants to foul up our show." Panic ruffled his natural nattiness. His hair seemed to rise in little grey bunches from his head. "Just look. Here's a letter advising us that the paper necessary to release the pieces is lost!" He pointed to the paper with despair.

"Why don't they get another set of papers?" asked Jess.

"It's a typical case of bureaucratic foot dragging," said Dr. Sam. "They don't want to send the pieces. You must speak to their embassy, Mr. Betzer. You understand the machinations of bureaucrats. If we don't get these bronzes, there isn't a show. Sri Lankan art is not exactly a glut on the market."

"Will you take care of it please, Mr. Betzer?" Adrienne asked, crisping formality back into the relationship with the address.

"Of course," he said, just as stiffly businesslike. As if their eyes had never met, their souls had never touched.

¶ The last time Louise had been with a show in Washington, it had been an out-of-town tryout for a musical "in trouble." There had seldom if ever been a production that had not had difficulties on the road, with the possible exception of *West Side Story*. But there had been a particular hysteria about this show. Sixteen writers had been closeted, anonymous, invisible, working on rewrites. None of them had known about the others, nor had the author of the book known any other writer was in town. Everybody had suspected that more than the usual duplicity was going on. The star had been on the verge of a nervous breakdown from having to learn so much new material, none of which suited her. The critics had suggested that the show could use more nudity, so the director had undressed the boys. Two directors had secretly stood by to replace him in the event he attempted suicide, as he had in Philadelphia with the last show.

It had been an intrigue that surpassed politics, somehow more maddening because of its humorlessness. Louise expected senators to be grim. But the producers of shows? They took chloral hydrate at night, to sleep, that winter in Washington. Men who voluntarily gave themselves Mickey Finns should not have been in charge of musical comedy.

They were all crazy, people in the theatre. The sanest of them went beserk, were struck suddenly tasteless, as if by a lightning bolt, when a show wasn't working. She had seen distinguished men of the Broadway community running up and down theatre aisles during previews, disjointed, shrieking, flapping in the darkness like fairies. Not the homosexual kind, the ones that lived in trees.

To come back to the theatre was the least of Louise's ambitions, as she knew it was the least of Chris's. She wondered how she could have been so foolish as to embroil them in that insanity, and knew at once the answer was Gloria Stanley.

Louise had stood with her on a terrace high in the Hollywood Hills, the lights of the city sparkling behind Gloria like a second array of stars. Tears coursed from the champagne eyes. "What's going to become of me?" Gloria had said.

Inside, the partygoers gathered, the glittering names of the community, the fabled faces, starting to jowl slightly and tire around the eyes. The house was awash with Christmas lights. Tubs of sangria with silver ladles, pitchers of Tom and Jerrys, for those who preferred tradition, sat on the tables, in between the canapés. There to celebrate the birth of the Christ child, who was a hit again, thanks to Franco Zeffirelli, were all the major people of the major studios of the major industry, what little of it remained. The rest were the classical hangers-on, the ones who had made Gloria their queen, and vice versa.

And all the while, on the terrace outside, Gloria wept to Louise. "I have no place to go. This town doesn't want me anymore."

"Of course it does," Louise soothed her.

"Then get me a job," said Gloria, words to strike terror into the heart of an agent.

Louise was tired. She didn't have the energy to make those calls anymore, talking people into what they didn't really want. It was strictly a business industry now, and strictly business had no vehicles or patience for Gloria Stanley, much as they loved her parties. Now that Louise had achieved the success for which she had hungered more than love, she liked it better when things were easy. She was getting older.

And so was Gloria Stanley. Not that she was one whit less the ravishing beauty, hair like spun honey whirling around her head, fingered by warm Santa Ana winds, a living monument to the city that had spawned her, its lights glittering below. Her eyes asparkle with tears, a key light seemed to emanate from inside her. Her skin was darkened to amber by the sun, her beige chiffon dress blew softly against her, outlining the high, perfect breasts, the tiny waist, the long, slender thighs.

She was every inch the movie star, the victory of the movies, their emblem, an argument for them. If it was life that imitated art, which Louise suspected was the case, how perfect that Gloria's life should be a better movie than any she'd ever appeared in.

"What's going to become of me?" Gloria said again.

That she could actually speak that line, and to her agent, touched a part of Louise's heart she didn't think she had anymore. When the moment came that Gloria was offered the play at the Kennedy Center, it reaffirmed Louise's occasional belief in Providence. Probably God, too, had been a fan of Gloria's, and wondered what would become of her Himself.

The cab pulled past the rounded sparkle of the Watergate apartments. Louise remembered the first time Chris had driven her past the then-new complex. "There's the Watergate," Chris had said. "And there . . ." pointing to the Kennedy Center, "is the box it came in."

The exterior was exactly that, cold, barren, squarely symmetrical, releasing no warm flood of feeling for the arts housed within. That the building lacked character was, to Louise, beside the point. A theatre was a theatre. Like men, in the dark they were all the same: the only difference was size and smell.

She paid the cabdriver and went inside the building, past the American Film Institute office on the right, the souvenir counters, the information booth, down the wide red-carpeted corridor with the flags of all nations suspended brightly above. On the left in a sheltered arcade the ticket booths were open, doing what seemed to be a vigorous business for that hour of the day. There was no way to tell if the people were buying tickets for the symphony, some other play, or the play starring Gloria. But it was an encouraging sign, buyers in the afternoon.

Sunlight streamed through the ceiling-high windows of the rear lobby, cascading the reflected sparkle of the Potomac across the corridor. Thousands of tiny lights, like mirrors, spun from the sculptured cheeks of the giant head of John F. Kennedy. It was so colossal that for a moment Louise forgot her cynicism. She could understand how people could devote themselves to art, to the nation, make a pledge, make a commitment, not a deal. Naturally she had no intention of ever being that idealistic. But it was comforting to know there were people like that around, for as long as destiny and murderers and critics let them stay.

She walked up the steps at the rear to the Eisenhower theatre. She tried a few doors till she found one open, and started inside.

"I'm sorry, miss," said a security guard. "You're not allowed in here."

"It's all right," she said. "I'm the mother of the bride."

"Excuse me?" he said.

She pointed to the stage. "I'm Gloria Stanley's agent."

On the stage, lit by rehearsal lights, a naked light bulb on a stand burned into the air near Gloria. She was holding a script in her hand, trying not to look at it. The effort was enormous, visible even in the back of the theatre. Louise came down the aisle and found a seat in the darkness, five or six rows behind Chris, who sat stiffly watching the stage.

Onstage, at a table to the left, the director sat, his jaw lightly clenched. Facing Gloria, his back to the director, a wiry young actor danced in place like a show pony. Behind him, the naked slate grey of the rear wall cast on the proceedings the color Louise felt in the atmosphere.

Gloria closed her eyes. "It's not that I don't love my children. . . . It's not that I don't want to be with them. . . . But I'm . . . I'm . . . I'm . . ."

"Why don't you open your eyes and read the goddamned line," the actor said, prancing.

"Stop doing that," Gloria said angrily, indicating his legs. "You make it impossible to concentrate."

"I have to keep myself in shape while you try to learn your lines," the actor said. "We're supposed to do it without the script tomorrow."

He was very dark and slender, with an unruly head of thick black hair, and black eyes, heavily lashed. His features were a little too lush, Louise considered, but there was no doubt she could make him a star, something he desperately wanted to be, as she knew from the night before.

"I'll be ready tomorrow, Dwayne," Gloria said to the director.

"I know you will, honey," he said.

"Then tell him to stop razzing me."

"Stop razzing her, Tony."

"Who's razzing?" he said. "I only want her to do what she has to do. This isn't the movies."

"I'm aware of that," said Gloria, white-faced.

"You have to be prepared to work in the theatre," said Tony. "Nobody's going to cut you so it looks good."

"Make him stop," said Gloria, and started to cry.

"When did you get your degree in psychology?" the director said to Tony, and put his arms around Gloria. "It's all right, honey," he said. "You're going to be fine."

"He treats me like a moron," Gloria wept. "I'm not dumb, you know. I can learn lines. I know how to do all these things, it's just . . ." she sniffled. "I've never had anyone to do them for."

"Audrey Hepburn said that in *Roman Holiday*," Tony said, sneering. "You can't even say something sincere from inside yourself."

The tears stopped; Gloria glared at him. "You're not old enough to have seen *Roman Holiday*."

"You are," he said.

"I will not work with this insufferable boor." Gloria turned and froze Tony with a glance. "Is that sincere enough for you?"

"Now, let's take all this good emotion and put it in the performances," Dwayne said, "and we'll have a big smash hit."

"I'm serious," said Gloria. "I want him out!"

"Okay," said Tony mildly, and went over to the chair, picking up his leather jacket. "You better get somebody else."

Louise smiled. He wasn't only cute, he was smart. A little mean around the edges, but he knew damned well it was a tour de force, and Gloria didn't have the technique he had. There weren't many young men around that dynamic, who could hold up half of a two-character play. More than half. Most of the time it would be his energy that had to sustain Gloria, inexperienced as she was.

Louise moved up in the darkness and sat beside Chris. "It's all going to be all right," she whispered.

"I don't think so," said Chris, biting her lip.

"Come back here," the director said to Tony. "Stop being a damned fool. And stop rattling Gloria."

"You're supposed to be supportive," Gloria said to Tony. "Everyone says you're a very supportive man."

"Who says?" he asked, as though it were a foul accusation.

"My agent," said Gloria.

"Yeah," he said. "Well, she's trying to sign me."

"Louise!" Gloria peered out into the darkness, the script over her eyes like a shade against the rehearsal light. "Louise, are you out there?"

"Right here, Gloria," said Louise, getting to her feet.

"Is that true?"

"Is what true?"

"Are you romancing him on my time? You're supposed to be here protecting *my* interests."

"That's what I'm doing," said Louise. "He's good, and that will help you."

"Must you say that in front of him?" Gloria reddened. "Isn't he arrogant enough already?"

"Relax," said Tony, and put his hands on her neck and started to massage it with his fingers. "Leave the driving to me."

"Get your hands off me," said Gloria.

"Get your hands off her," said Louise. "The punk," she murmured to Chris, sitting down. "After the promises I made him."

"Okay," said the director. "Let's take a fifteen-minute break. Everybody cool down."

In her dressing room, Gloria lay face up on the chaise, a cloth over her eyes. The chaise had been purchased by the theatre specifically for her after she expressed some disappointment on seeing her dressing room for the first time. Although she could grasp the fact that things had changed since Jeanne Eagels, she had still expected a little grandeur. It was enough that she was struggling for reality in her daily life: she couldn't handle it at rehearsals.

"I'm going to bomb," she said weakly.

"No, you're not," said Louise. "You'll be fine."

"He's going to eat me up alive onstage, that little wop."

"Gloria!" Chris said.

"Excuse me," said Gloria, taking the cloth from her eyes, nodding at Chris, and covering up again. "I meant to say dago."

"He'll be very supportive when the audience is there," Louise assured her. "You can't worry about him. You've got to think about you."

"I'm floundering," said Gloria. "I can't say the lines right. Much less remember them."

"Why do you think that is?" asked Chris.

"I don't understand the woman. She is always saying how much she loves this boy, but you don't see that she loves. You don't see why she's willing to risk her beautiful marriage and her terrific children."

"Stop being a critic," said Louise. "Chris has enough trouble with critics who are critics."

"But she's right," said Chris, nervously getting to her feet. "The play isn't going the way it should."

It was a bittersweet comedy of an extramarital affair, with an unsatisfactory ending. Chris suddenly realized it was unsatisfactory because the key scene, the passionate love scene, was empty, flat. How could it be full, when she had never been with Scott?

But if they held each other once, naked, made the love they had felt with such heat over backgammon, she would see it all, know it all, be able to put on paper what they each should say. She had full confidence about that, because she wanted it so badly.

"I've got to make a phone call," she said and left the room.

"Where will I go after this disaster?" Gloria said, almost singing. She trailed her fingers over the edge of the chaise, moved them gracefully along the floor, as though it were water and she, Ophelia. Louise got up and went to the vase of fresh-cut flowers delivered that morning, took two long-stemmed white roses, lay them on Gloria's chest, and crossed Gloria's arms over them. Gloria sat up.

"Laugh if you want to," said Gloria. "But when this play dies I'm finished. I won't go back to Hollywood. And there isn't a man in the world I can trust. Not one I could love." She started to weep, softly, into the larger of the roses. "The best of them betrays you. The kindest is cruel. They're all fakes and users. There isn't a decent one out there."

"You don't really believe that," Louise said.

"I know," lamented Gloria. "I wish I could stop looking."

¶ Chris spoke furtively into the telephone. "But it's important, Scott. I need you. There's more at stake now than just us."

"I don't understand," he said.

"Yes, you do. You're too smart not to understand. I've got to be with you." Her conversations with Scott had always been secret, urgent. But this one, on the wall phone by the fire exit backstage was sotto voce, adding a dimension of operatic intrigue to the love affair. "Too much depends on it now," she said.

"What does that mean. You're being so evasive."

"*I'm* evasive?"

"You've always been so straightforward, so truthful. You open your heart." He said it as though he were speaking of her thighs. "What are you talking about? What's happening? What's at stake?"

"I'll tell you when we're alone together in a hotel room. What time, Scott? Where?"

There was a deep sigh on the other end of the phone. "Forty percent of the marriages in this country end in divorce."

"Don't give me statistics."

"I have respect for marriage," he said. "Respect as great as my love for you." His voice sounded strangulated. "Don't you want to preserve what no one really cares about preserving?"

"I want to be with you."

"But what about Elise? I'm fond of her."

"So am I," said Chris. "She'll never know."

"And what about Jess?"

"He's consumed with the show for the museum. He's all caught up in his career again. So you won't have to worry about kicking him when he's down."

"All right," said Scott. "When can you get away?"

"What?" Chris asked, sure she hadn't heard him.

"I'll make the arrangements," he said. "When can you get away?"

¶ She was so excited she was singing love songs. He was actually making the arrangements, taking the initiative himself. It caused a flow of such adolescent intensity in her that she remembered all the songs that had been popular when she was in high school.

Her children did not like her singing around the house. They were afraid their friends would think she was crazy. It disturbed her only slightly that her children judged by the joyless standards of their society, wanted to quench her spirit, make her behave. It disturbed her slightly more that she listened to them.

So she kept the singing inside while she plotted her assignation. She would tell the director that if anybody called the theatre, to say she was closeted, working on the rewrite. He would delight in the instruction. The word "rewrite" had about it the gloss of industry, salvation, especially out of town.

The play terrified her less now, knowing she would be with Scott. Truth, all the answers, would come in a blinding flash, hot on the wings of inspiration, and his body. The revised ending was only a matter of hours away.

There was about her plan to meet him a radiance, a sunny glow, rather than the dark subterfuge most people considered adultery to be. It no longer occurred to her that she was going to be unfaithful. She had been with Scott so often in her mind, in her warm fantasies, that it was almost as if it were he to whom she belonged, and Jess who was the intruder.

She took a warm soapy douche with her bath that afternoon, cleansing herself of her sexual past so that she could be fresh for Scott, new. Powdered, she put on a quilted robe and went downstairs to sit with the children while they ate dinner. She sat at the table and drank them in with her tea, the beautiful duo she had imagined would bring an end to all her longings. That there were no more gaps of solitariness in her life astounded her. Especially as, in the middle of them all, she still felt lonely.

"Hello, family," Jess said, coming into the kitchen. He had his coat over his arm, as if the day had fulfilled his expectations of spring. In his hand, he held two nosegays, yellow and mustard and white. "For you," he said to Chris, bending to kiss her.

She did not pull away, even though it was her inclination. She was a fiercely faithful woman in her way, and her way right now was Scott. Still, she did not shrink from Jess with her body. She let his eyes study her, without turning to see what he was looking for, and smiled as though she appreciated the attention.

"And for you," he said to Caroline, handing her the second nosegay. Her face opened with such delight it could have been one of the flowers.

"What do I get?" said Billy.

"You get to appreciate that you're different from girls and can give them presents," Jess said, hugging his son.

In the bedroom after dinner, Chris put the tiny bouquet in a water glass. "That was sweet of you, to get one for Caroline too," she said to Jess.

"I enjoy spending money," he said.

"I know," she answered, her back to him. She had no idea why she still felt bound to make him feel guilty about all the time he hadn't contributed to the finances of the house, hadn't been able to. She suspected that guilt about money in men diminished their sex drive, and if she drove that subtle wedge between them he would leave her alone, and she wouldn't have to turn him away. She didn't want to have to turn him away. He was the father of her beautiful children, and she'd loved him once. It wasn't his fault that there was someone finer, more suitable for her, more subtle around the edges, tenderer of touch.

"Surely you don't begrudge a nosegay for your daughter?" he asked.

"Of course not," she said. "I just don't think you should start easy spending. It's only five thousand dollars, Jess. . . ."

"That's *this* job," he said with quiet fury. "The first of many."

"Well, I'd drink to that, too, if I had the champagne," she said. "But should we start having champagne tastes quite so soon?"

"My God," he said. "You do know how to take the joy out of things."

"I don't mean to," she said. "But I get scared, Jess." She sat down on the flowered Louis Fifteenth bench by her dressing table. "I hate to argue about money," she said miserably.

"Maybe we argue about money because we're afraid to argue about what we really want to argue about."

She did not ask him what that was, for fear he might tell her the truth, for fear he had seen all the way inside her to where she didn't want him anymore. She wondered every so often if he knew about Scott. She suspected he did. There had never been an emotion in her life Jess hadn't anticipated the moment before she felt it. He was such a sensitive man she wondered how he'd been able to survive in Washington, and why she didn't love him more.

"I may have to go to Sri Lanka," he said.

"Is that a political announcement?" she asked. "Like when Eisenhower said I will go to Korea?"

"There's some kind of foul-up with the show," he said. "Some important pieces were never sent. I may have to fly there."

"Will the museum pay?" she said.

"Of course," he answered.

"Well, if you have to go, you have to go," she said, wondering when the plane left, wondering if she should help him pack now so that his suitcase would be there by the door waiting, and she wouldn't have to come back at all from the rendezvous. No one to report to, except the children. "You certainly are colorful," she said. "I don't know anybody who's been to Sri Lanka."

"You want to come with me?" he said.

"Just about," she answered. "In the middle of the play."

"Maybe that's what you need," he said. "A little tropical moonlight."

"I've had enough tropical moonlight," she said, unable to believe her own words as she said them. Once she had thought there could never be enough moonlight, tropical or otherwise. Once she had longed so for someone to hold her hand, it had never occurred to her that it would be a struggle for a man to hold her attention.

She got into bed, yawning noisily so that he would know how tired she was, how impossible was her situation, how absolutely sapped she was. "But thanks for the offer," she said, pulling the covers up over her shoulders. "It's the best I've had all day." Rejoicing in the lie.

8

¶ Across the street from the Watergate apartments was a Howard Johnson's hotel, shiny, urban, new, different from the orange-shingled roofs of its New England antecedents, distinguished from every other chain motel less by its decor than its remembered place as the lookout post during the burglary of Democratic National Headquarters. Scott wasn't sure of the wisdom of meeting there, even though it was he who had chosen it for their assignation, dredging up a little more history to counterpoint their romance.

"I know you like these touches," he said on the phone, "so I suppose I'm pandering to you."

"I love the way that sounds," said Chris.

She had reassured him that no one they knew would be likely to be found at a Howard Johnson's. It was practically the safest place in town, and convenient to the Kennedy Center where Chris was watching rehearsals of her play.

Now Chris stood at the window, peering out at the building whose name had become synonymous with political scandal. Political scandal. It all seemed so tame, suddenly, compared to what it would be to taste him, touch him. Who cared anymore what anyone said on March 21, 1973?

She dialed Scott's private number. "I'm in room 225," she said into the phone. "Across from Watergate. I guess you could say it's a room with a déjà vu."

He chuckled delightedly. "What an enchanting creature you are."

"Then how have you managed to stay away from me?"

"It hasn't been easy," he murmured.

"I'm taking my clothes off, and I'm getting into the tub, so I'll be warm and wet and naked when you get here." She hung up the phone and hugged her arms around herself, as if the right person had finally asked her to dance.

She was elated, breathless, like a girl, the little child who still lived inside her, hungering for affection, approval, the exceptional man who would affirm her existence by his love. It had been worth all the delays, she understood that now, all the waiting. Sometimes procrastination was the thief of time, and other times it was very exciting.

¶ In her bedroom in the Foxhall apartments, glories fled, passion gone, eyes closed, Melissa Mae lay on her back and tried to shut from her ears the sound of Ed McShane's unlawyerlike grunting as he drilled into her. Her body was numb; she couldn't even feel him. But her ears were still working, so she could hear him huffing and puffing like a little bad wolf.

She had no wish at all for sex anymore. It was as if Hiro's death had robbed her of all animal energy. But the IRS had seized Hiro's house and club, and there was nothing liquid to work with, Ed complained. He was performing legal services for her gratis; it seemed the least she could do to service him in return. Especially as she couldn't feel it.

Melissa's doorbell rang. "Are you finished?" she asked Ed wearily. He was lying collapsed on top of her, breathing into her neck. He rolled off her for answer. She got out of bed and drew the belt of her white satin robe around her waist, her voluminous breasts like shiny coconuts against the fabric.

"You want me to leave through the back way?" Ed asked.

"The back way is through the kitchen which is through the

living room just like the front way," she said. "What do you
think I'm afraid of, my reputation?" She closed the door to the
bedroom and walked to the foyer. "Who is it?" she said through
the door.

"It's me."

Melissa looked through the peephole. She saw Megan O'Flannagan. "Oh, it's you," she said, opening the door.

"God, I love this place," said Megan, nearly waltzing into
the room. "It's so glamorous. Every time I come here, I feel
like Marilyn Monroe."

"So do I," said Melissa sourly. Her slippers scuffed across
the thick white carpeting as she went behind the white leather
upholstered bar angling out from the smokily mirrored wall.

"I was in the building," Megan explained as she sat down on
a white leather barstool. "I had an interview with a law firm
downstairs."

"You're going to be a lawyer!" Melissa said. "I knew there was
no way to keep you down. How soon will you be done so you
can take my case?"

"I didn't know you had a case."

"I have twenty," said Melissa. "It's all this crap against
Hiro."

"Why doesn't his estate handle it?"

"I am his estate," Melissa said. "You want a drink?" She
picked up a pair of silver ice tongs, opened the ice bucket, and
started putting cubes into a glass.

"It's only eleven o'clock in the morning!" said Megan.

"Not in London," Melissa Mae replied, pouring some scotch.
"When you going to pass the bar?"

"I was having an interview with some old friends of Larry's.
They know a lot of people. He thought maybe they could help
me."

Melissa took a long swallow of her drink.

"I thought you were off whiskey."

"I am," she said. "I'm just drinking this to disinfect myself."
She lit a cigarette.

"Why don't you just take a hammer and hit yourself over the
head?"

"I'd probably miss," said Melissa.

The door to the bedroom opened. Ed came out, carrying his briefcase. He did not look at Megan. "I'll call you."

"Sure," said Melissa.

The door closed behind him.

"Who was that, if I'm not being too curious?" asked Megan.

"Ed McShane."

"Hiro's lawyer? But I thought you couldn't stand him."

"I can't."

"Then what was he doing here?"

"Well, the estate's all tied up, you know. Ed's working on the come." She laughed a grim little laugh and stubbed her cigarette out in the ashtray.

Megan picked it up. It was the same brand she'd seen in Howard's office, glaring the same outrageous shade of red lipstick. "Are you Howard Kummer's patient?"

"Yes," said Melissa, and poured another drink.

"You're certainly a tribute to him," Megan said.

"Megan, honey, I have no need for sarcasm. My day has been too long already. He's crazy about you, you know."

"Howard? Did he tell you?" Megan's face brightened. As annoyed as she was with him, it was pleasurable to think of being talked about in session.

"No. I just know. You should fall in love with him and give up this stupidity with Larry Cochran."

"It isn't stupidity. He has integrity and honesty and strength. . . ."

"Are you addressing me or the convention?" Melissa asked.

"I have no need for sarcasm either."

"How about bed? You have a need for bed? Or you just going to Joan of Arc it through the rest of your life, getting off on voices. Don't you want to *be* with a man?"

"Well, certainly not Howard," Megan said. "There's nothing sexual about Howard. He's too cerebral and thin."

"He's a wonderful lover," said Melissa. "The best. Jam up."

"Really?" Megan tried to say casually, when she was recovered enough to speak.

"Very sensitive to a woman's needs," said Melissa.

¶ When she had been a girl in fact, not just feeling like
one, waiting in a Howard Johnson's motel, Chris had gone to
Bryn Mawr. There she had prided herself on accruing little
pieces of knowledge about the Greeks, whose culture wove in
and out of the traditions of the college, affording hymns to be
sung on auspicious occasions and respect for the mind above
all else.

Bryn Mawr was a fitting parallel for Mount Olympus, with
its admittedly ivory tower attitude, educating women as if the
world would take them seriously. It did not occur to her in
those prefeminist times that the obstacles in her path were sex-
ist ones. She wanted to be a writer, and writers were considered bizarre, regardless of their sex.

She was so eager for attention she'd let what lovers there were
before Jess run roughshod over her body, as they did her spirit.
She was flattered by masculine attention, thinking men did her
a favor by wanting her. Rape to her seemed not so heinous a
crime.

But her love for Scott changed all that. As thoughtful a lover
as Jess had been, concerned about her needs as much as his
own, his touch had begun to seem brusque when she thought of
Scott's, wisping, fleeting, flying across her palm as he handed
her the dice: an angel's kiss. Jess's weight on her breasts had
begun to seem an assault: Scott was lean, tight; he wouldn't
press on her. He would lift her, lighten her body as he had
her brain.

But she'd never been able to bring herself to ask Jess not
to make love to her. So she'd joined her sisters throughout
America in feigning fatigue and illness, welcoming a head cold
as others did a beloved friend. Now it was over finally, the pretense, the aching emptiness. He was knocking on the door. She
could sense him through the wall. She didn't even ask if it was
Scott, she knew it was him, from the way her body was feeling.

She opened the door. And he was inside, and they were in
each other's arms, at each other's mouths. His tongue was
lightly pepperminted, his lips massaged hers. Birds fluttered

inside her mouth with wet wings. A rush of heat enveloped her. Her naked body pressed against the soft material of his jacket. She took it off him and opened his shirt, button by button, until she could press her breasts against his skin. She moved in slow rotation, hardening her nipples on his flesh.

"You sweet, sexy woman," he said, and plunged into her mouth. She had sighed for him so often, now that they were together there was a great bellowing pull of all the sighs inside her, a collection of breaths, a cyclone of longing. A moan escaped her.

"You sweet, sexy woman," he said again, and kissed her neck. His lips trailed clouds of glory down her naked throat, his tongue moved storms into them.

"Take your clothes off," she whispered. "I have to touch you."

His lips were the most insistent she'd felt in her life, but his words excited her more. In all the time with Jess, he had never been lavish with verbal embraces, When they were done making love, he would tell her he loved her, and sometimes just before he came he would cry out she was beautiful. But he'd never called her a sweet, sexy woman.

She lay down on one of the beds and closed her eyes, not watching Scott undress, not wanting him to think she cared about how his body looked. Bodies were transient. You were in them for a while and then you died, and if you were lucky, in between you got to go to a motel. Paradise for her had become simple.

She could feel him kneeling beside the bed, his cool naked skin lightly pressing against her side, as he leaned over her and kissed her breasts, his lips slightly damp on her nipples. "Please," she said, opening her eyes. "Come lie with me."

"Sleep with me, sleep with me," Potiphar's wife had cried to Joseph, giving adultery horned roots in the Pentateuch. Passion was a part of life, illicit longing as old as man's commitment to be faithful. There were biblical precedents in the hunger between them: she felt practically sacred.

He moved up onto the bed and lay beside her, devouring her mouth. She strained against his naked body, and felt the warm, peculiar softness against her thigh. When she and Jess made love, when there was even the suggestion of their making love, he came to her already aroused, his big cock jutting angles in his pants. That Scott was not erect was strangely exciting to her. She could minister, nurture him with her hands, her lips, the deep accumulation of affection that she'd never yet fully expressed, not even with her children, who already moved so independently through the world.

There was something sweetly thrilling about arousing a man. She moved her face down Scott's chest, brushed her cheek back and forth across his nipples, cooled them with her tongue, dipped down into his navel as though it held sweet juices. He had a slightly sour taste: Jess's skin was always baby fresh. It disturbed her to be making the comparison, as if her infidelity were to Scott.

"You're wonderful," Scott said as her head moved across his pelvis, and she traced the bones millimetrically with her tongue. "Oh, my God," he said, clutching the back of her hair, sighing as she had. But when her tongue got to his penis it was still soft.

She ran her lips along it softly, kissed it, warmed it, wet it, nursed it with infinite care, took it in her mouth. It just lay there. Chris sucked the sorrowful instrument. It gave not the slightest tic of movement.

"I'm tired," he said.

"I understand," she said, and tried to. Her head was on his belly. She tried to make eye contact with it, his flaccid pink penis, lying there like an exhausted Cyclops. She thought of Jess, with his big purple-tipped cock dancing at her, daring her not to love him back.

It dawned on her suddenly what intimidation really meant for men: not being able to get it up. No wonder they wandered the world avoiding aggressive women. What an indisputable failure. But rather than Scott's failure, it felt like hers, that it was she who had let them both down, not being able to excite him. It was a terrible statement about her womanhood, she was sure.

To the sexuality that had seemed to be between them there

was now added the inimical feminine element of heartbreak. She was tied to him now by sadness, belonged to him more deeply than if he had swollen inside her. Felt for him a tenderness she'd experienced only for her son, for the six-year-old fear of inadequacy parading as male bravado.

So pathetic did it seem, she began to try and tender to it again, darting her tongue between his balls, rubbing her breasts against them. She barely had to touch Jess with her breasts for him to be ready to enter her. It was ugly of her to think about Jess. For months she had survived in bed by pretending Jess was Scott.

Scott lay her back on the bed and proceeded to duplicate the paths on her body she'd made on his. He worked his way down her belly and stuck his tongue between her legs a little too harshly. It was not as subtle as he'd been in her mouth. She wondered what she was doing in bed with a man with a hard tongue and a soft penis.

"Don't do that," she said.

"Don't you like it?"

"I don't feel like that now." What she felt like was weeping. Cunnilingus without subtlety behind it and passion following it was Latin, clinical, as antiseptic as the word. She got up from the bed and put on the negligee she had brought. "Maybe we should have the champagne," she said.

She moved to the waxed paper bucket, ice chilling the Dom Perignon she'd brought from home. She started to untwist the wire.

"Not a good idea," Scott said. "Not for me, anyway. I'm tired."

"I understand," said Chris.

"Champagne in the middle of the day puts me to sleep."

"Well, we wouldn't want that," said Chris.

"Are you angry with me?"

"Of course not." She ran to him and kissed him, gently stroked his scrotum. Nothing happened.

"Come, let's have the champagne," he said. He opened the bottle, poured some into the champagne glasses she'd brought from home, and handed her a glass.

Drops fell from it. Her hand trembled.

"Are you upset?" he said. "Do you feel guilty?"

"What's there to be guilty about? It was very innocent."

"Yes," said Scott. "I guess it was."

His voice was heavy with regret, apology, just as his eyes were. They did not quite look at her, but focused slightly above her head as if she were the light on a camera. She had never realized how impersonal he was, how uninvolved. What she had always viewed as journalistic detachment now showed itself as lack of blood. She shivered slightly, less for herself than for him.

"What shall we drink to?" he said.

Once, she might have said, "Us." Once, after a childhood of attending museums that showed old movies, seeming to offer warm arms on cold afternoons, she might have gazed into the future looking for Paul Henreid to light two cigarettes. But as it was, she moved to the window, lifted a corner of the blind, and looked at the Watergate apartments across the way. "Let's drink to Washington," she said. "Let's toast the downfall of delusion."

Sometimes it was wonderful being a writer.

¶ On the way to Dulles Airport, Jess thought about his family, remembering Chris's offer to pack for him. He hadn't let her: packing was one of the things he did best, putting the portable things in his life in neat compartments. It helped ease him into a sense of departure, an awareness of how little he really needed. And it gave him moments with his children, his black-eyed, red-lipped children, staring at him with so much love and loss he might have been on his way to the moon.

It seemed to Jess that the fall of the family, if it were indeed going to come, which he suspected on rainy days it would, would be due to people's considering it a concession, a kindness for the children. People seemed to have forgotten it was a benefit to adults, too, a sanctuary in a judgmental world, a place where one could be loved unconditionally, unqualifiedly, not on the basis of accomplishment, but being. It was balm to the soul to be cared for irrationally, instinctively. But Americans were acquisitive, wanting more and more for themselves, and more as a society. No one wanted an average anything, including an average marriage. So marriages, too, were competitive. Unless it was exceptional, the family was too easily sacrificed in America.

Jess loved his family, his marriage. Being home so much after his own descent from active life, he had become aware of Chris's restlessness. It had been almost amusing, ironically entertaining to be in the way. He had seen the looks that passed between her and Scott. He could feel her heart fluttering across the room when she was in Scott's presence, like a little bird's. Her passions were unmistakable to Jess. She was at the level preceding an affair. There was an irresolution about her, a tenuousness, a dissatisfaction, an eagerness to make her whereabouts known to him, so that he could check to find out she was really where she said she was, against the day when she wasn't.

He was fiercely jealous, of course. Being unable to show it for fear of forcing her to the wall, he packed it into the same place as the rest of his anger, where it became indistinguishable from the frustration he felt with the world in general.

Throughout his unemployment, he had somehow held himself together. He had at least avoided liquor: there was no need to give society further reason to despise him. He remembered with wry amusement a picture on the cover of the alumnae bulletin from Bryn Mawr, Chris's college, featuring a smiling young woman in jeans and sneakers, perched halfway up a ragged rock, with two smiling men standing nearby. Beneath them was the quote "We've found strength in an idea that men and women can join hands, work together creatively, respect and love each other, and yet maintain their separate, special identities." An idea as unrealistic as the college itself, Jess considered. In Washington, a city that measured victory by the bills that passed and the people that didn't, to be a man who supported a woman's success was anathema.

That he was on his feet again, on his way to Sri Lanka, was a visa back from an inner circle of hell. To be dead in the world was his definition of purgatory. The emptiness left by his experience with Nixon, the knowledge that what should have led to elation had degraded everyone connected with it, had created in him ambition's opposite: yearning. It was an ingredient he hadn't known was in him, a thirst for beauty, a hunger for peace. A wish that the journeys he took might also include a path.

He boarded his plane at Dulles and settled in for the long flight, eager to get on with life but still anchored in the heaviness of his recent relationship with Chris. In the beginning, the turnabout in their situation had not bothered him. Tasks that others considered menial gave him a curious pleasure. Cooking was a joy for him. He'd sprung from a neighborhood of friendly Italians where men got together and cooked for each other on robust Sunday afternoons, lush sauces for ziti, veal, fettucini, escarole. That he was available to his children after an almost total absence from their lives seemed fitting reparation. Only when he realized there was not enough to keep him busy, that there were holes in his day, with his day leading nowhere except to the same day again, did he begin to understand the silent screams of housewives.

He could still see their faces, glazed, as they pushed their metal baskets up and down the aisles of the supermarkets, little tics of confusion pulling at their mouths. Agoraphobia, fear of the marketplace, Howard told him it was. The same fear started to possess Jess.

He had been hypnotized into indecision by the cereals alone. Dazed by the vast arrays of cans and jars he bought things that no one ever ate. He understood why women ran away, ran mad. If it was the purpose of man to grow in his lifetime, and not just grow old, it had to be the same for women, a spiritual hunger that gnawed at them in between Joy commercials. It was cruel and unusual punishment, being a housewife with no hope of change, surcease. And no one knew it better than a househusband who had never been called one.

¶ "But imagine," Megan said to Howard, as they walked their bicycles on the path that ran alongside the Potomac. Little buds of spring greened by the muddy bank. Wisps of clouds left over from a spring rain trailed along the sky. "She has to go to bed with him to take care of Hiro's legal fees. Have you ever heard anything sadder than that?"

"Only that you're telling me," said Howard.

She looked at him out of the side of her eyes. His lips were fuller than she had noticed before Melissa's pronouncement. His nose was very long and thin, with flaring nostrils, his eyes were heavily lashed. And he had wonderful hands. Big hands but with slender fingers. Now that she studied him carefully, he was a great deal more sensual in appearance than she had previously considered. "Hasn't *she* told you?"

"Why do you ask?"

"Isn't she your patient?"

He didn't answer.

"You won't damage your professional ethics. She already told me. *Everything.*"

"Everything?" he rolled it back at her, with her own emphasis, laughing.

"I know that you're lovers."

"No kidding," he said, and laughed. "Is that what she told you?"

"You don't have to try and fool me," Megan said. "I understand your having an affair with someone else, even though you pretend to be in love with me."

"I am in love with you," Howard said.

"But I'm hung up on someone else, that's it, right? So I forgive your humping Melissa."

He giggled. It was a very silly laugh he had. She found it very annoying. "You probably think you can throw me off with that attitude. I'm very surprised at you, Howard, I have to admit it. I mean, not that you owe me any loyalty, but how could you make love to Melissa?"

"How can you be so possessive about something you don't even want?" asked Howard.

"Don't flatter yourself," she said. "I'm not being possessive."

"Of course you are." He stopped, leaned his bicycle against his thighs, wrapped his scarf tighter around his throat. The air still had a trace of winter chill in it, in spite of the sunshine. Birds chattered in the trees around them, as if reassuring each other they had not come back too soon. "It's making you say ugly things."

"They're the truth," she said icily.

"Don't be silly. The truth is seeing things the way they are and not being disappointed when they don't come out the way you wanted. Because it isn't your expectations that determine how things should be. That's the *truth*."

"How could you make love to Melissa?"

"I didn't."

"Ha!" she said, getting back on her bicycle and pedalling off, wondering to herself why she was so unstrung.

He got on his bicycle and pedalled after her, caught up, rode beside her. "You're afraid of being lonely," he said.

"Everyone's afraid of being lonely." She pedalled very briskly, drawing away from him. To her horror, he did not try to keep up with her, and she was alone.

¶ As the plane descended toward Colombo's airport, a resplendent island it was, just as they had told Jess at the embassy. Sun dazzled the sea, shot mirror light into his eyes. A million daggers of color danced on the horizon.

"What's that over there?" he asked the stewardess, indicating the colors.

"Kites," she said, leaning unnecessarily close to him as she looked out the window. "People on the beach flying their kites. It's a favorite national pastime." She was a round-hipped Eurasian with grey velvet eyes, and she smiled at him as if she had a few favorite pastimes of her own. Her breath was very sweet, lightly cloved. "Do you mind if I sit with you for landing?"

"Not at all," said Jess.

She belted herself in the seat next to him, her very round thighs golden through the sheen of the stockings she wore. He could see nearly to the tops of them. Her mouth was slightly puckered, with a light orange gloss on her lower lip. He'd read an ad that invited him to find love on Singapore Airlines, and he wondered for a moment if he was meant to take it literally.

"Is this your first trip to Sri Lanka?" she asked him.

"Yes."

"You should come sometime by sea. You can smell the spices twenty miles out. They grow everywhere on the island. Cinnamon, nutmeg, mace. It's very romantic."

"I'll have to do that," he said. "One day when I have more time."

"Everybody says that," she pouted. "One day you might have time and there won't be any ships."

The plane bumped gently to earth. "My name is Jenny Chang." She smiled at him, unbuckled her belt, got up, and started down the aisle.

He watched Jenny Chang moving slowly, her derriere a masterpiece, golden, like her thighs, probably firm to the grip. It was the one area in which Chris was deprived: they both lamented her having no ass. He had grim potential as an adulterer, Jess realized. Even when considering a fantastic bottom, he compared it to the one his wife was missing.

The door of the plane opened. The air enveloped his skin, clung damply to his face. He felt suddenly languid. Tropical climates had always made him tired, debilitated. What love of art and God there had to be in such a place, he thought, to have sat in that liquid heat and fashioned intricate Buddhas, forged the bronzes, carved out the giant statuary that made up Singhalese art.

In immigration, a security poster warned: "Caution, do not engage the mouth until the brain is in gear." A handsome, wiry, blue black man in European slacks, a Gucci belt, barefoot, took Jess's suitcase.

"I'm Solomon," he said. "The driver you engaged to meet you at the airport."

"I didn't engage a driver."

"You made a big mistake," said Solomon. "It's lucky you know me."

On the way into town, he braked the car suddenly. "Why are we stopping?" asked Jess.

Solomon ran onto the lawn of the estate, toward a tree, took a knife and cut off a piece of the bark, ran back and put it under Jess's nose. "Cinnamon," he said.

"I can tell."

"Very sexy, spices." He started the car in gear again. "A good smell is very sexy."

"That's true," said Jess.

"You should be in Sri Lanka with a woman."

"My wife is very busy."

"Too many children?"

"Something like that," said Jess.

¶ The girls of Colombo were dark eyed, straight haired, looked at the world half shyly, half audaciously, as though they were peeking over daisies. They were long limbed and full breasted and moved with a sweet serenity, colorful saris cloaking them with exuberant grace. The streets of the city were bustling with early morning tourists up from the waterfront, waiting for the jewelry shops to open, stores offering silks and spices, bargains from what used to be Ceylon. When it had been British, after it was Dutch and Portuguese, civilization had swept it into the present, made it one of the world's leading ports, given it sidewalks and roads, quiet fans in the ceiling, whirring the atmosphere into a fit locale for Somerset Maugham. Having been made a Dominion, and granted independence finally, the country rose from the sea offering treasures like embraces. But its capital was like any other port city in the world, undistinguished except for the tropical setting, the humidity, and the black-eyed girls.

Jess walked among them on his way to the Ministry of Education, with Solomon at his side, bobbing local color and information at him. He felt in no mood for the guide's enthusiasm. He felt exhausted, on edge. He had slept badly his first night, having awakened at three o'clock in the morning and been unable to go back to sleep. When he'd travelled with Nixon he'd formulated his own theory about jet lag. It was, he decided, due to the body's weariness at holding up the plane.

On the beach, below the park, the air was giddy with kites. People were already down on the sand, flying them higher than Jess had ever seen kites being flown: all manner of kites, all colors, shapes, and sizes. Box kites, dragons, griffins, birds. High winds buffeted them, lifted them into loftier regions, where they studded the sky with radiance.

"Hustle bustle," Solomon said, approvingly, as they moved through the streets, built wide to accommodate the already growing flow of traffic. Whole families waited in line outside one of the shops, waiting for it to open, holding empty bottles. Infants dozed in their mothers' arms, ragged children clung to fatherly hands.

"Are they waiting for milk?" Jess asked Solomon.

"Toddy," Solomon said, grinning. "It's a pretty good drink from coconut sap. Takes about an hour to ferment, in a paper bag. Best early in the morning, fresh from the tree. You have a good dinner?"

"I ate in my room," said Jess.

Solomon looked as though he'd been struck. "Why you didn't let me take you to Singhalese place? You can't get a bad meal in this country."

The Minister of Education was unavailable, a pretty young woman in native dress told Jess, cool frost-green sari heightening her burnished beige skin. "He's sorry he can't see you," she said. "There's a council meeting. But it isn't him you want to talk to. It's the head archeologist. He must sign the papers before the pieces can be sent."

On their way to the car Jess and Solomon passed the toddy shop, open now, outside its doors whole families, with empty bottles, sprawled along the sidewalks, drunk. Children dozed in parental laps.

"I told you," Solomon said, grinning. "Pretty good drink."

"It looks like the floor of the Congress after lunch," said Jess.

Seated in the back of Solomon's air-conditioned fifty-six Chevrolet, Jess tried to relax. The business district gave way to bungalows, proliferating palm trees. Above, huge white puffy cumulus clouds were already gathering for the afternoon rain.

The pervading smell was coconut. Natives climbed the trunks of trees, picking coconuts, taking sap from cups hooked into the bark.

They reached the address the girl at the Ministry had given them, as different from the minister's office as were the neighborhoods. No grandeur decked it. All that distinguished the white stucco bungalow from those surrounding it, fronting on dirt, was a totem, still fluttering with ribbons from an exorcism.

"He's gone to Sigiriya," Solomon said to Jess, after conversing in Tamil with the servant. "To check the restoration of the Resplendent Ladies."

"Sigiriya?"

"Famous archeological site in the middle of this beautiful island." Solomon grinned. "You're going to love it there, boss."

¶ Sigiriya loomed like a fist threatening the sky. A half mile high, the rock seemed to serve a warning to the countryside that no matter how peaceful and green things were, there would always be anger. In the fifth century, the ruler Kassapa had established it as his citadel, to escape the vengeance of his half brother for the murder of their father, Solomon said. Once palaces had adorned it, fortresses marked its foundations, flowers and gardens bestrewed its base. Now nothing remained but fragments and ruins. It was like nothing Jess had seen in his life, that cliff, rising so abruptly, insanely, in front of him.

The ride there had lulled him into a state of openness, an acceptance of the fact that no matter how rushed he felt, he wasn't driving the car. He had let himself look out the window and actually see what was passing, enjoying the trip instead of worrying about where he was going, experiencing his life instead of reviewing it. The colors tranquilized him. The green lulled his spirit. The country was dominantly green, plantain and palm trees, wild jungle growth crowding onto the roads, tea plantations rising up on gently rolling hills. Pale butterflies danced in the air, like ectoplasm at a happy seance, emissaries from the world beyond that the news was good.

The clerk at the Holiday Inn had made arrangements for Jess to stay in a government rest house in Sigiriya, but Jess told

Solomon to proceed directly to the archeological site. He started climbing the steps, Solomon preceding him, guiding, gesturing, urging him up the cold grey cliff, unscalable on either side of them. The steps narrowed, led up to a winding metal stairway. "Only a few more steps now, boss," Solomon told him, leaning down, face toward him, from the landing above.

Jess came to a sheltered niche and tried to catch up with his breathing. He could feel his blood pounding in his ears, blotting out some of Solomon's syllables as he pointed to the wall and trumpeted the famous Resplendent Ladies of Sigiriya, a fresco of seventeen golden-skinned women, huge breasted, slender waisted, serving each other food and flowers, adorned with candlelights on their crowns, jewels above naked bosoms, rising from hip-high clouds like oriental angels in a heaven where lust was all right with the Almighty. On their faces were the rapt expressions of those meant for love in a time when such a fate was not considered cruel, when poets dreamed of passion as the world's best purpose, and women its best design.

Jess felt an impression of shadow, as if the place had subtly darkened. Sheltered as it was, the niche was bright with light —the afternoon sun, and reflections of it, glinting on the pink grey granite, beaming from a mirrored wall, polished by a thousand anxious hands into shining tribute. The sense of glare and shadow was so strong, he had difficulty making out the man in the corner, a slender brown-skinned Sri Lankan in traditional native garb, sitting on a campstool, studying a detail of a mural through a magnifying glass.

Jess made his way toward the man. His legs felt unconnected to the rest of his body, his breath seemed separated from his lungs. Heat shot through him on small tense wires. At the height of his career when there was no time, he'd made time to keep himself in shape, jogging daily around the Tidal basin. When the future had seemed to cancel its promised inheritance, he'd stopped taking care of himself. Embarrassed by too much time, he'd discontinued his physical activity, fearful that someone would observe him staying alive during hours when other men were working.

He regretted it now, sweating, hardly able to catch his

breath. "Are you by any chance Dr. Panavita?" Jess asked.

"I am by every chance Dr. Panavita," the man said, sun reflecting from the metal rims of his glasses. Thick lenses magnified his eyes so that they seemed to sit directly atop his thin nose, irises huge, black, like an owl's. "Who are you?"

"Jess Betzer. Kirkeby Museum."

"I'm sorry about the papers," Dr. Panavita said. "Are you all right?"

"I'm fine, just a little winded."

Jess lifted his briefcase onto a ledge and opened it. "I have another set for you to sign."

"At first," said Dr. Panavita, getting up slowly from his camp-stool, "when I looked down and saw a man climbing this rock with a briefcase in his hand, I was afraid I had lived too long in the sun. But now I see you are what they call an enterprising American."

"That's correct," said Jess, handing him the papers.

"These pieces are only recently dug up. We haven't had time to properly evaluate them."

"Is that why you refused to ship them?"

"I lost the papers," said Panavita stubbornly.

"We've remedied that," Jess said, handing him a pen. "I'll need a separate release to carry them with me. There's no time to ship."

"Things that give peace to the spirit should not be used to promote business. These are religious art. They belong here, not in a country where business comes before everything."

"I didn't come here for political discussions," Jess said. "An agreement was made. People are counting on my bringing back these pieces."

Dr. Panavita studied Jess's face as though it were a detail of the mural. "How tiring it must be to be so driven."

Jess tried to laugh. He had learned that when people presented a truth, there was no better way to make them shaky about its veracity than to laugh at them, rather than argue. So he meant to laugh. But it came up a gurgle in his throat, a far-away strangling sound. He reached out to steady himself on the ledge, but it moved away from him.

He plunged into darkness, fell soundlessly screaming. He could see himself coursing headlong, jaws gaping with cries of horror that were mute. He struggled to hear himself, so that someone else could hear him. When he struck the bottom of the pit it was strangely soft. Oblivion embraced him with gentle arms, pressed herbs on his brows, wiped the wetness from it, spooned sweet teas between his lips, kissed him. Set him on a pillar of stillness where he could see, blazing like a shaft of light, the bright radiance of his soul.

When he awakened, he was lying in a room so whitely barren he thought he had died and gone to true damnation. A dark face blurred into view, its features unfuzzing, settling into the sharp, bright-eyed visage of Solomon, hovering over him.

"How did I get here?" Jess asked, remembering where he'd been.

"It wasn't easy," said Solomon. "We carried you down, Dr. Panavita and me."

"Did he sign?"

"What an impossible breed of men you are," Dr. Panavita's voice boomed from the corner. "Is that all you care about, that you finished your business? Doesn't it make any difference to you that you could have died?" He came over to the bed. "How do you feel?"

"Tired." Jess said. "Where am I?"

"The government rest house in Sigiriya."

"Did you sign?"

"I signed," said Dr. Panavita sadly, as though the world had run out of sanctuaries.

"Can I get up?"

"If you feel like it."

"What did the doctor say?"

"You take yourself too seriously," said Panavita. "I suggest you enjoy your life, and your lovely wife."

"My wife?" Jess eased himself from the bed, tested his legs. They belonged to him again.

"She was waiting for you when we brought you here."

"How did she find me?" He sweetened his mouth with water from the pitcher, combed his hair with his fingers. His beard was scarcely more than a stubble, so he hadn't been unconscious that long. But she'd given up days, at least, just for the travel. Right in the middle of her play. Chris had sacrificed for him, made his needs equal to her own, even taking precedence over hers. It was a level of love which he had never thought she could reach.

"The clerk at the Holiday Inn told her where you were," Solomon said.

"She loves you very much," said Dr. Panavita. He smiled, the first time he had done so. "She's waiting in the room across the hall."

Jess nearly ran, shaky as he was. He moved across the tiles and flung open the door opposite. The room was aglow with flowers, vases filled with purple wild flowers and green orchids saluted his eyes, dazzled him back into a world that was heady with color and vibrance, fragrant with flesh. Beautiful flesh lying half-clad in the midst of the bed, like a flower itself, the soft curve of her body broken with the line of a towel, flung across her naked hips, lustrous back to him.

"Hello, my love," said Jess.

She turned. "Hello, my darling," said Adrienne Harvey.

¶ When he lay beside her, naked, when he hadn't entered her yet but had savored her, sampled her mouth like chocolates richer than any ever tasted, when he'd held her in his arms and nourished her breasts into hopeful expectation, dipped into her sweetly flowing well with his tongue, he raised himself to the level of her eyes, where he could see the depth of her longing. "I am a very married man," he whispered. "This is only for now. Whatever happens here is all there is."

"I can live with that," said Adrienne.

"I hope I can," said Jess.

¶ In the evenings, in Sigiriya, elephants roamed the countryside, bleated, roared, sometimes stampeded. Wise natives and even foolish ones stayed indoors after darkness. The moon rose on deserted, lush silence, a countryside surrendered to beasts, gentle beasts but ponderous ones, mentalities as heavy as their steps, confused by their own capacity for destruction. Some Singhalese built fences against them; bamboo fences fifteen feet high, unsecured at the base, leaning against trees, so that when the elephants pushed, the fences would give completely, making the elephants nervous, frightening them away.

"A fitting lesson on how to deal with warlike men," Dr. Panavita said over dinner. "If we could be clever enough to learn. Aggressors expect struggle and resistance. Yield. Be flexible. Confuse brutes instead of fighting them. It would mean an end to war."

Outside, two elephants saluted each other. "A mating call," said Dr. Panavita. "Lust is not reserved for the graceful."

Jess and Adrienne did not take their eyes off each other. They stared across the candles flickering on the carved oak table at which they and Dr. Panavita sat, attended by six half-naked servants, wearing native G-strings, their dark bodies moving quietly about the room, like shadows.

The dining room itself was low ceilinged, austere, like the rest of the building, stucco walled, brightened only by flowers and plants, candles on the table in elaborate bronze holders, wall decorations that were small facsimilies of the huge Buddhas that were everywhere in Sri Lanka, standing, lying, hands folded in meditation, wearing Sanghatis. Except for the table and chairs, the room was empty of furniture, carpetless, so sound, no matter how soft, took on the illusion of echo. The words of Dr. Panavita seemed to come from all around them, as he ate and talked in equal measure, exclaiming his delight with the food, seconding an occasional squeal of pleasure from the servants, who accompanied with vocal appreciation what they served: rich chicken redolent with spices, thickly crunchy with nuts, vegetables fresh from the garden outside. At Dr. Panavita's insistence, the meal also included durian, a fruit two feet high and nearly as wide, with a green orange skin, so strong in smell that few were the noses that could tolerate it, as delicious as was its flavor.

"An addictive taste," he said, biting into its white, pulpy insides. "Exotic. Succulent. It smells, I believe, like your limburger cheese."

Jess and Adrienne ate, observed its taste, each other's mouths, chewing. Dr. Panavita rambled on, of art, and men, and health, and pleasure, seemingly undisturbed by their silence.

"It's good to see you looking so well, Mr. Betzer," Panavita said. "Although you could do with some sun. Time you came out of your room. Three days is rest enough." Jess and Adrienne smiled at each other.

"The *ayurveda* helped you recover quickly," Panavita said, looking at Jess, whose eyes were fixed on Adrienne. As peculiar as Americans were, as difficult to distract from self-interest with discussions of art or philosophy, he had never failed to capture one with talk of their health. "Homoeopathic medicine, I think you would call it in your country—a combination of herbs, diet, and relaxation through meditation and prayer, practiced in this country for thousands of years. You seemed to respond well to it. The human mind is very powerful. A will to survive is the finest healer in the world."

"Except for love," Adrienne said, her words scarcely more than a whisper, her thickly lashed blue eyes shining, radiant, fixed on Jess's lips.

Panavita looked slowly back from first one to the other, chewed the fruit on the end of his knife, and stared at them. "How long did you say you'd been married?"

A servant stood in the doorway, announcing dessert. Outside, the elephants called to each other, blew their longings onto the wind. Six servants danced around the table, the first of them carrying a rum omelet, another besotting it with more rum, a third setting it ablaze with the flames from two tapers. They shrieked with delight, laughed, applauded, as if it were something they saw for the first time and might never see again, a blazing rum omelet, a dish so fine that only heaven could have conceived it, only guests were worthy to feast on it. White teeth shone against blue black skin, fire blazed against the somberness of the room. The fan whirred like a whisper on the ceiling, rippling the air, feeding the flames.

"Have you ever tasted a rum omelet?" Panavita asked Adrienne.

"I've never tasted anything till now," she said.

¶ In their room, Jess and Adrienne sipped orange spice and cinnamon tea, and each other. They explored each other's bodies like the landscape outside the bamboo-shaded window, the soft terrains, hidden passageways, sheltering jungles. She moaned with pleasure.

He did not think of his wife or his beautiful children or the laws of God or man. All he thought was how soft she felt, how pliant, how hungry beneath him, around him, on top of his loins, like a hot little puppy, panting at him for exercise and affection. It was as if he had freed her from a cage.

He drank her mouth, softened it into caring, probing, sweet persistence, making her lips moister, more giving, more seeking, more yielding in tender combat, fluttering the tongue, aiming at the heart, without meaning to capture it.

He made it clear between them how it was going to be. But he did not keep that in mind when he was naked with her.

On the morning of the fourth day, there was a cable for him from Chris, worrying that she hadn't heard from him, wondering when he was coming back. Adrienne watched him open it, read it, her oversized eyes slightly pink around the lids, as if she had slept too heavily or already wept at their parting.

He crumpled it in his hands. She pulled the sheet up to her throat and waited for the words, like a blow.

"Isn't it amazing," he said. "I haven't even thought about her."

"But now we have to go back?" She was on her haunches, her round, graceful breasts pressing against the sheet, her wide golden shoulders arched slightly backward a little too proudly, as if she were defying him to think she was hurt.

"We always had to go back," he said. "But maybe we could steal a few more days."

She grinned like a child, her eyes filled with tears. "Oh, Jess," she said, and started to weep.

"Hey." He ran to the bed and put his arms around her. "I didn't think I was that bad company."

"It's just that I love you so much," she said. "I know I said I could live with just this, but when the cable came I realized what it would be back there, without you."

"Don't think about that," he said, stroking her back as if she were one of his children. "Don't think about anything," he whispered against her lips.

¶ Solomon drove them to Polonnaruwa, where reclined the giant Buddha, carved in grey stone, curls cut from rock crowning his peaceful face, serene in sleep, where stood the huge Buddha, where shimmered reservoirs and shrines from the twelfth century. They drove to the coast, to Trincomalee, rented scuba gear, dove through coral caves and reefs, touched each other beneath the blue green waters. Fish floated by them, stupid eyed, showing no curiosity at the pallid embraces of humans.

They searched through pearl banks, rose to the surface with oysters, one of them yielding a pearl. They lunched on lobsters and crabs and wiped each other's mouths with napkins and kisses. They walked along the beach, collecting shells.

On the last day, both of them knew without speaking it was the last. In the hotel room looking out at the the sea, they inventoried their treasures. She gave him her favorite shell, a pale pink cone that rose like a castle from its own translucence. He held it in his hands, gently, tentatively, as he had held her. Then he put it on the dresser, next to his watch and the airlines schedule, the indisputable reminders of responsibility. He opened the pamphlet and looked at the departure times. She watched his face.

"When we get . . . back," he said in a voice that was too tight in his throat, she could hardly hear him.

"Speak it out," she said. "I'm not afraid to hear it. Are you afraid to say it?"

"Yes."

"You told me how it would be going in. There are no bad surprises coming, are there?"

"When we get back I'm moving my office back to my

house. From here on in it's all follow-ups on the phone. I can do that from my den."

She sat very stiffly, only her thick black eyelashes moving, every few seconds, as though she were being slapped.

"You only said it would end," she whispered. "You didn't say I couldn't be with you."

"I can't be in that room and not want to hold you."

"Oh, Jess," she said and ran to him, threw her arms around him, hugged his face against her chest. "What are we going to do?"

"Exactly what we said we would. End it."

"But we can be in the office. . . ." She was pleading now, negotiating. She hated the tone of her voice, arrogance gone from it, wheedling, like a child's.

"I'm no good at deception," said Jess. "I've had enough of it in my life that I didn't even know about. I can't be around you every day and not want to make love to you."

"You never said you loved me," she said, tears moving down her cheeks.

He did not answer. He stroked her hair.

"I guess you never said it because you don't. Well," she broke away from him and stared up at him, with a terribly twisted smile, as if part of her face wanted to be somewhere else. "Maybe you'll take me to lunch sometime?"

"If I take you to lunch I'll have visions of blazing rum omelets, and having you in bed." She was sobbing openly now, as though her heart would break.

He put his arms around her gently, folded her to himself. "I wouldn't have to stay away from you if I didn't love you."

She lifted her face to be kissed. "Remember me," she whispered.

He moved his lips on her skin, slowly, as if to memorize, to absorb the imprint of her flesh on his mouth. He recorded her lips, her eyes, her breasts, her fingertips, her toes. He tasted her as though she were the spices of Sri Lanka, mingled with the salt of her tears.

9

¶ From the amplitude of the voices, the laughter, the ahs of appreciation, the press preview of the Sri Lankan art at the Kirkeby was a great success. Word had gone out far in advance of the show that Gloria Stanley would be there, so important press had clamored for invitations. Since going into rehearsal Gloria had not been seen in public: her mystery had been restored, along with her magnetic ability to produce malignant rumors. So far they ranged from her having a complete nervous collapse, and gaining fifty pounds, to having cancer and being reduced to a shell.

In fact, in person, she was radiantly the same, only lightly tranquilized at the prospect of facing all those reporters. As sympathetic as the press had always been to Gloria, they liked her better when she was dying. If she appeared too healthy she had the apprehension they would turn on her.

As it was, she had enough potential murderous press to worry about from the critics. She threw up before every run-through. The opening was a week away, and even though the play was better since Chris's rewrite, and the wop was helping

Gloria occasionally, feeding her from his warm animal presence and understanding of the stage, she was still terrified.

Living with the Cochrans had brought a certain quiet to her, in between anxiety attacks. She adored their children, who looked at her with so much affection there were moments she believed herself as wonderful as they did.

She had always been equipped with a ferocious will to survive, which had served her well in Hollywood, and in Washington she had appended it with a will to live. She got up now and exercised in the morning, but not in front of the mirror since she saw her inner arms, jiggling. It was the nature of the body to wrinkle and grow old, and there was no way to escape that, only delay it, unless you died young, which she already felt too old to do.

Her dream of love had now been augmented to include an altruistic and patriotic nature, since she saw how happy Abby was. Life had been hard enough for Gloria when all she had sought was Romeo and Albert Einstein. She moved through the press preview hoping for that thunderbolt that only happened in her movies, the eyes that gripped hers with instant recognition.

There was a cluster of reporters around her, pressing microphones toward her mouth. "Is it true you're thinking of moving here permanently?' one of them asked her.

"I'm thinking of moving everywhere permanently," she said. Behind her was a pedestal, on which danced a female figure striking a classic posture, balanced delicately on her right foot, a goddess forming the Buddhist gesture of turning the Wheel of Law, adorned with armlets, necklaces, bracelets, almost as many as Gloria.

"And what about reports of friction with your co-star in the play?"

"I think they're better than the rumors that I'm marrying him."

"Are you nervous about your stage debut?"

"Of course," she said. "Now may I see the rest of the exhibition?" She smiled at them in a manner so innocent and open that any of them who had asked another question would have felt a cad. They more or less followed her at close distance like the gently worshipful retinue of a female monarch.

The main room of the exhibition was bisected longitudinally by a 120-foot gauze scrim, dyed the same fuschia as the cloth draping the pedestals, stretched from the ceiling to a bronze bar about five feet off the floor, the color of the metal statuary. It was Dr. Sam's design, to help isolate the perceptions of the art.

Jess leaned back against the burlapped wall, hung with glass-encased sculpture and crystal reliquary, and watched the proceedings with undisguised delight. Almost all the important press in Washington were present, either trailing Gloria or interviewing the expert on Indian and Sri Lankan art, a professor from California whom the museum had flown in to add academic distinction to the festivities. It was, according to the buzz around the room, the most impressive preview since the black tie dinner preceding the opening of the Tutankhamen exhibition, when Kissinger was present and the city still had an aura of elitism. In a purportedly populist era it delighted Jess to see that art still attracted the best people in town.

They moved in polite bunches in between the turquoise- and saffron- and fuschia-draped pedestals, reached for hors d'oeuvres with a studied slowness, as if hunger never came to the better classes. "You got quite a turnout," said a railroad executive, champagne in one hand, a miniature pizza in the other. "Celebrities, press, politicos. An admirable job, Jess."

"Thank you, Charley."

"You know, we could use a little snappy PR." He ingested the hors d'oeuvres, chewed, wiped his mouth. "Why don't you give me a call in the morning? Maybe what we need is a lobbyist with a fresh approach." He handed Jess his card.

In the corner, Megan O'Flannagan stood next to Howard, shielding herself with his body so that she could look around him and not seem to be staring at Larry Cochran. She was wearing the gown she had bought for Ford's inauguration, a last optimistic extravagance the day before the election. It had hung in her closet for two and a half years unworn, slightly sparkling with pale pink sequins, a modest number, set into the material distances apart, like the freckles on her skin. "You were good to come with me, Howard," she said. "Especially after the way I've been behaving."

"That's true," he said, and sipped his champagne.

"You don't have to agree with me," she said.

"I do when you say the truth."

"You're a very exasperating man."

"That's why we're so well suited." He leaned over and kissed the tip of her nose.

"You look like you're ready for the prom," she said. "Very handsome in your tuxedo."

"Thank you."

"Aren't you going to tell me I look pretty?"

"I've told you you're beautiful. I love you. I want you to marry me."

"That's hardly cocktail party conversation."

"Very well," said Howard. "I'll say it where it belongs." He took her hand, and started pulling her through the exhibition.

"Where are we going?"

"To bed."

She tried to breathe a sigh of despair, but to her surprise it came out of her throat with slightly erotic tinges to it, pleasure around the edges. He was pulling her past Abby and Larry Cochran, who were so absorbed in each other they didn't even notice she was being dragged from their midst, kidnapped practically. "Congratulations on your exhibition, Mrs. Cochran," she managed as Howard whirled her past them. "It's absolutely magnificent."

"Thank you, Megan," said Abby. "It's nice to see you."

"Goodbye, Larry," Megan said, giving to it the same poignancy she imagined Wendy and Michael and David had when they flew out of the nursery with Peter Pan, calling "Goodbye, mother."

"Goodbye," he said.

"What a lovely girl she is," said Abby, looking after her.

"Clever, too. Maybe I could find something here for her at the museum."

"What a lovely woman you are," said Larry, smiling. "Clever, too."

She moved into the circle of his arm, pressed lightly against him. "Any smart woman would have to admire you. I can't be jealous about how people feel."

"Ciao, hello." A bright-faced pretty young blonde smiled at Larry, waved fingers at him. "Remember me? Alana Perkins. From Meeting."

"Of course," said Larry. "How are you. Alana—my wife, Abby Cochran."

"Hello," said Abby, shaking her hand. "I'm sorry we haven't met before. I'm afraid I've been a little remiss about going to Meeting."

"Good!" said Alana. "So have I. It makes me feel better when someone of obvious virtue is as naughty as I am." She smiled, her slightly overlapping front teeth shining. "Isn't it a fun exhibition?"

"I hope so," said Abby. "I'm so glad you could come."

"So am I," said Alana. "Well, ciao, goodbye."

¶ By the cloakroom, a journalist with long unruly hair in a rumpled tuxedo had cornered Louise Felder. "What I'm going to need is an agent who's sensitive, and a killer," he said. "Every reporter has a great book in him. Of course it helps to have the story of the century. Woodward and Bernstein caught all the luck; their marriages were breaking up, so they had fourteen, fifteen hours a night to kill."

A few feet away from Jess, Chris stood, trying not to study Adrienne Harvey, just as she had tried not to question Jess on his return from Sri Lanka. He had been tanned and glowing, filled with tales of falling ill in Sigiriya, needing to recuperate, doing a little sightseeing, spending some time in the sun. Jess had no patience for sun, no joy in resting in it, no eye for tourist pleasures. That he had been gone ten days and returned with so much quiet about him, so many private spaces in his head, frightened Chris. In all the time she had planned her infidelity, prayed for it, it had never occurred to her that he might find someone else.

He and Adrienne were not avoiding each other exactly. They did not avert their eyes when they came in contact. But he seemed to look at her with a little too tough an edge, as if he were on mental tiptoe, straining toward a businesslike attitude.

That he had moved his office home from the museum astounded Chris. He had waited so long for work, hungered for a job as some men hungered for freedom, that to make his base of operations the place he'd finally escaped made no sense to her. He'd had a phone installed in the den and cleared out the Nixon things, putting them in huge boxes in the cellar, till the time, he said, when posterity, or rats, claimed them. That part of it seemed healthy to her. But he'd been given the aegis of the Kirkeby—it was like a resurrection, an embrace from a separate and dignified world, to work out of the museum. She couldn't understand why he would give that up and come home.

Still she didn't question him about it: she had no right to question him about anything. She had been a fool about Scott, impressed by his unavailability: it had appealed to some leftover need for rejection which was almost as great as her need for approval. She'd confused his detachment with calm. He had always seemed so balanced, so judicious. It had never occurred to her that what he was was cold.

Sex had reared its ugly head but nothing else. She was prepared to be faithful to Jess for the rest of her life, but that wasn't good enough. If Scott had been half the lover Jess was, the foolish infatuation with him probably would have continued. So her emotions were basically that of a child afraid she was missing something. And for her foolishness she had risked her home, and her children.

It frightened her when she stopped to think about it. She was also panicky about Jess. She wondered if he was involved with Adrienne Harvey. She hadn't been at the museum when Chris called several times to find out what was holding up Jess in Sri Lanka.

Adrienne this night showed the last flush of a suntan, a

glow of remembered color on her usually light skin. And she was being too polite to Chris, a little too interested in her. For a distant woman she seemed to have become strangely warm.

"You must be very excited about your play," said Adrienne.

"This is Jess's night," Chris said. "And yours. You've done a phenomenal job, the two of you."

"It's Jess. It's all Jess. He's an incredible man. Without his determination we wouldn't have had the show." Her face shone a little, with more than recollected sun.

"I know exactly how you feel," said Chris. "Without his determination I wouldn't have had two children."

"Excuse me," Jess said, and moved away from them, toward a group of the press.

"You don't have to rub his face in it," Adrienne said, quietly.

"I beg your pardon?" Chris said.

"Jess knows he has two children," said Adrienne, tears welling in her eyes. "Believe me he knows it."

Chris stood very quiet for a moment. "I suppose if I asked you, you'd tell me everything."

"I would," she said softly. "Except that Jess wouldn't like it."

"Excuse me," said Chris, moving away from her, filled with sick uncertainty, glad she was wearing a gown, so that no one could see that her knees were shaking, nearly buckling beneath her. She loved him with all her heart, finally. There had been times in her life when she'd despised being married, envied the freedom of her single friends. Except always, at some point, into their conversations would creep the word "lonely."

"Adrienne!" A tall young man with yellow hair caught the dark woman in the circle of his arms. "You beautiful creature, I haven't seen you since Marblehead!" He took her left hand and turned it over, examining her ring finger. "Still available?"

"I don't ever have to get married," Adrienne said, quietly, but not so quietly the words didn't carry to Chris, burying themselves in her brain like a tomahawk. "I've already had the perfect honeymoon."

In front of a statue of an elephant god sitting crowned, on

hind legs, four humanoid arms waving, one hand holding jewels, another an axe, the curator of the Kirkeby discoursed for a reporter from the *Washingtonian,* Mr. Nadapura beside them. "This is a unique collection," he said. "The first exhibition of Sri Lankan art in America. Singhalese art is too cumbersome to travel. Buddhas sixty feet high, temples, friezes."

"You must come to our country and see it," Mr. Nadapura said pleasantly.

"All of the art that could travel is here tonight." Dr. Sam went on. "If it hadn't been for the digging up of the *stupa* last year, there wouldn't have been enough to make a true collection."

The reporter looked up from her notebook. *"Stupa?"*

"S-T-U-P-A. It's a monument, covered with stone, huge, bell shaped, containing ancient relics. They're all over the island."

"And all of them have art in them?" asked the reporter.

"Of course," Mr. Nadapura said. "It can only be consecrated if it contains a relic."

"My husband says the same thing about me," said an elderly dowager, and laughed a bawdy laugh.

Mr. Nadapura smiled, uncomprehending, and moved away. He felt someone pulling at the sleeve of his silk tunic.

"Ciao, hello, excuse me," said Alana Perkins. "I just happened to overhear you. If there are so many undiscovered treasures in your country, why don't you dig them all up?"

"Too expensive."

"How much would it cost?"

"Oh . . . a hundred thousand dollars."

"That doesn't seem like a lot of money."

"It does in Sri Lanka," Nadapura said.

Alana laughed, her prettily bucked teeth setting her mouth slightly askew. "Isn't it a pity that art depends on economics."

"A terrible pity," said Nadapura.

"But if you're such a poor country, I'm surprised you could afford a woman like Abigail Cochran to set this up for you."

"Well, Mrs. Cochran is a kind and lovely lady," Nadapura said. He pointed to the activity around them, the buzz of approval surrounding the art. "She graciously arranged all this for only ten thousand dollars."

"Really?" said Alana, and extended her hand. "I'm Alana Perkins."

The Singhalese shook it. "Pol Nadapura, of the Sri Lankan Arts Council."

"Lovely to meet you," she said. "Ciao, goodbye."

Alana did not run from the party. She eased her way out with the same smiling sweetness she had crashed it, and went to call Charlotte.

¶ "I am alive at last," Megan thought, her head on Howard's chest, the warmth of his skin softening his spareness, his long-fingered hand tight against the cap of her orange curls. "I am alive at last," she thought, as she had thought when she became a novitiate, joined the White House staff, learned to meditate in the desert, taken est. This was the first time, however, that the euphoric observation had been accompanied by a feeling of total body relaxation. He had given her orgasms in her toes.

That she loved him, that the brain and the humor and the compassion she had always so admired had suddenly coupled with their coupling was, for her, a miracle. Howard was the great love of her life. She had just never noticed because it was so obvious. Everything else had been an infatuation, she saw that now. And felt it. My God, had she felt it.

She raised her lips and kissed him, sweetly. She was still so shaken with physical fulfillment she wanted to rest in it, to savor it for a while.

"You were wonderful."

"Thank you," he said. "So were you."

"So what does this mean?" she said. "Do we decide to fall in love?"

"I'm already there." He turned his body to face hers, his face a few inches from hers on the pillow. "I want to marry you."

She started to cry and turned away from him. He put his

hand on her shoulder. "Don't cry. I know you loved Larry Cochran. I don't care about any other men."

She whirled, angry, her face a remembered subscription to *Ms.* magazine. "For heaven's sake, Howard. This is 1979, men and women don't care about things like that anymore. Of course you don't care what happened before you. And I don't care what happened before me."

"Good," he said.

"Did you sleep with Melissa?" she asked.

"No. Will you marry me?"

She started to sob, turned away from him, covered her face with the sheet.

"Why are you crying?"

"Because I can't get married. I can't. I have terrible secrets, Howard."

He pulled the linen from her face, wiped her eyes with a Kleenex from a box beside the bed. "There's no such thing as a terrible secret," he said. "Let it go, and it won't be terrible anymore. Share it, and lighten the burden."

"And you won't tell anybody? You swear?"

"Never. It's privileged information."

"I'm with the CIA," she wailed.

"Far out," he said. "So am I."

¶ Charlotte Dean was fifty years old, and no one had ever really loved her. Not her mother, not her father, not her husband, not her dearest friend. It was a hideous realization, when more than half her life was over, and the spectrum of those who might tender her affection was certainly not widening.

It was all going, the prettiness, the smoothness of skin. She had never considered herself vain, until she realized she'd have no reason to be. It was one of the peripheral pains in her life that she was aging.

Another peripheral pain was the fact that people had started to bar her from parties. Parties were her way of connecting with life, allowing her to seem interested in other things besides her career. But Abby Cochran had refused to send her an invitation to the preview. In spite of pressure from Charlotte's editor in chief, and promises of extra coverage in the *Courier,* the museum had made it quite clear that Charlotte would not be welcome. So she'd had to send Alana Perkins, who probably didn't appreciate caviar.

Most of the people in the world, Charlotte considered, were peripheral pains in the ass, never caring what damage they inflicted on those who pretended to be hard. She had no choice but to build up callouses against all the peripheral pains, like no one ever loving her. The center pain, the one she never focused on, never dared examine, was that she could love no one.

So she gave her full energy and considerable intelligence to her career, why not. Journalists had become heroes, big business. It had given Charlotte a bit of a turn, to see her own kind so enshrined, especially as she did not seem to be among the revered. At parties where heads usually turned in the direction of politicians, all the neck craning these days was lavished on Cronkite, Chancellor, and Brokaw.

To elevate newsmen to supercelebrity status was something they weren't prepared for. Nor was Charlotte. Still, she was quite ready to be a monumental success, with accompanying dollars. She had already started on her book on Washington, an exposé, naturally, which would sell in the millions, she hoped.

It was a shame about the universe, how limited it was, how short the sight of man's eyes, Charlotte couldn't help thinking. Had she let herself be one of the suckers dealing from compassion, she might have been moved to sorrow that it seemed to be the bad news that really got people going.

But as it was, her heart leapt more than slightly when Alana Perkins called with her report. "Abby Cochran's employed by whom?" Charlotte said into the phone.

"Sri Lanka," said Alana. "They gave her ten thousand dollars to set up the art show."

"Beautiful!" Charlotte said, picking up her pencil. "Who's your source?"

"Pol Nadapura. He's with the Arts Council of Sri Lanka."

Charlotte was so excited she hung up the phone without saying goodbye. Getting up from the bed where she'd thrown herself, furious at not being allowed at the party, fortifying her rage with brandy and chocolates, she was a little unsteady. Lobbying for a foreign government. Influence peddling.

The wife of Larry Cochran. One of the most admired couples in Washington, except by Charlotte of course, who had known all along there was something a little too sanctimonious about them, too holier than anybody, except possibly Anita Bryant. Those were the ones you had to watch, and thank God she had, as Anita would say. What a bonanza. Charlotte could hardly wait to write it.

She knew all the laws about libel, having studied the law in great detail, after her heartbreak with Amelia. She was careful not to make allegations that couldn't be proved, simply stating straight out that Abigail Cochran, wife of one of the President's most trusted advisors was, according to a very high Sri Lankan source, secretly employed by that country. Charlotte wrote briefly about Larry, giving a list of his responsibilities in government, and moved back to Abby, telling all the charities with which she was connected, to which she supposedly "donated" her time. She put the word in quotes, so that the implication would be clear that Abby probably skimmed off the top with the rest of them. It was not illegal of course. Almost everybody who ran a charity evening took ten percent off the top, but that was one of the truths about so-called altruism that most people preferred not to know. Here was Abigail Cochran, a pillar of the community, with columns of clay.

Hardest of all, Charlotte worked on the headline. Usually it was the copy editor who did that, taking the substance of the story, condensing it, sharpening for quick comprehension. But as far as Charlotte was concerned, a headline determined the emotional thrust, and she wanted people as shocked as possible when they read the story. As shocked as she was, with an equivalent feeling of betrayal.

Abby Cochran taking money from a foreign government, one

whose policies differed sharply from those of the United States. Possibly currying favor in the White House. It was the appearance, not the reality that mattered. Had Larry Cochran known? Would anyone believe him if he said he hadn't? How many days, weeks, before he tendered his resignation? The President would be too considerate to fire him, even if Larry hadn't been a close personal friend.

Tomorrow, after the early editions hit the streets, she would begin interviewing Larry's enemies for their opinions. No matter how loved a man was, there were always the envious, Charlotte thought. If everybody liked everybody, there wouldn't be Easter.

¶ When Chris saw the story in the morning paper, she went directly to the phone and dialed Abby. The voice on the other end of the line sounded normal, unalarmed, unhysterical. If she had seen the story, Abby couldn't possibly sound like that. "How are you?" Chris asked.

"Oh, I'm wonderful," Abby said. "Wasn't it a beautiful show?"

"Fantastic," said Chris, wondering if she should tell her, knowing suddenly she couldn't. To break that news would be to seem aligned with the ill-wishers, the Rumpelstiltskins of the world, who clapped their hands in glee at each other's misfortunes.

"Is Larry home yet?"

"He's taken the children to Florida to see my parents," she said. "The angel."

"Why don't you come and have dinner with us? Or maybe I could come over there."

"Is something wrong with you and Jess?"

"No," Chris said, wondering if she should tell Abby the truth, if she could handle the burden of Adrienne Harvey. She decided against it. If she told no one, maybe it wouldn't exist.

"Then if it's all right with you I'm going to beg for a raincheck. I've just been looking forward to putting my feet up."

"Will you call me if you need anything, Abby? I mean anything?"

"Why, of course."

"If I'm not at home, I'll be at the theatre, backstage. I'll call you tomorrow."

The moment Abby hung up the phone, it rang again. "You ought to go live in that country," said a rasping woman's voice. There was a click on the line.

Abby went to the refrigerator, took out some milk, put it in a pot. She had discovered the pettier the task she involved herself in, the easier it was to deal with anger. After all the years in Washington she had still never gotten used to how rancorous people were. Her hand shook slightly as she set the pot on the stove and ignited the flame beneath it, trying to keep her thoughts away from the anonymous caller. It was probably another thing like Amelia Gomez's column, some anonymous slur filled with poison. She wasn't even curious, she told herself.

The phone rang again. She picked it up with a slight edge of impatience to her voice, as if aware in advance that it would be something that would not improve her life. "Hello?"

"Abby? This is Sylvia Kranet."

The doorbell rang.

"Can you hold, please, Sylvia? There's someone at the door."

She had shut the latch as a token protection in Larry's absence. There was still tranquility in the Cochran part of Washington, so some people left their doors unlocked, with no bad results. But with Larry gone she locked it. Still, she didn't ask who it was.

"Melissa," she said, seeing her outside the door. "What a pleasant surprise." It was a surprise. People didn't just drop in on each other in Washington, unless they were beloved friends.

Melissa smiled a rueful smile. She was dressed all in brown, unicolored. "Can I come in?"

"Of course, how rude of me." She indicated the sofa. "Please. Make yourself comfortable. I just have to get rid of someone on the phone." She ran into the kitchen and picked up the receiver. "Sylvia? Will you forgive me? A friend of mine just dropped by. I'll call you tomorrow, all right?"

"I just want you to know neither the senator nor I believe it about you," Sylvia said quickly.

"Believe what?"

"Haven't you seen the *Courier*?"

"No," said Abby softly. "I haven't."

"Well, I hate to be the bearer of bad news," Sylvia said with obvious gusto, "so better get the paper and read it for yourself."

"Thank you," said Abby very softly, and hung up the phone. She reached for her purse and a coat from a hook in the wall and flung it over her shoulders, starting toward the front door.

"Was it something I said?" Melissa asked from the couch.

"Oh, Melissa . . ." Abby turned, consternation jagging her normally composed features. "Forgive me. I forgot you were here. Do you mind coming with me to the shopping center? I have to pick up a *Courier*."

"No, you don't," said Melissa. "You don't need to read that trash."

"What did it say?" Abby asked, white-faced. Something of a terrible guilt stirred in her, a shriek of despair and fear. What was happening?

"A lot of bullshit."

"Please, Melissa, don't be colorful. What did it say?"

"It said you're on the payroll of Sri Lanka."

Abby sank to the couch. She stared at the floor, at the worn part of the rug beneath her feet, the chips on the coffee table. She touched the arm of the sofa, where the material was shredding, and pulled at the cotton inside.

"I wanted to send the children to school. I wanted to recover the couch. Damn it, Melissa, it was just an art show."

"I know. I understand. But you know Charlotte Dean's style."

"Is that why you came?"

"I know how it feels," said Melissa. "You and your husband have always been kind to me."

"What am I going to do?"

"We're going to get drunk," Melissa said.

¶ Abby was not used to alcohol. When she had first arrived in Washington, the mindless habitual consumption of it alarmed her. She saw drunks at nearly every party, every official function: remarkable men, admirable women they had probably been at some point, with bloated noses, broken veins in their cheeks, struggling for words, staggering. She saw beautiful women, the casualties of a system devoted to power, success, turn alcoholic with the pressure of the town.

Nobody saw the real tragedy of America—that it was the women, those who had promised to stand by their men, who gave. They gave their souls, and their minds, and their energy, and sometimes their breasts. It was a very hard battle to be the wife of an important man in politics, and most of the time you lost.

Abby had watched them all and struggled through the difficult years not to be like them. But now she sat, drinking with cold deliberation from a crystal wine glass, in the back booth of the Jeffersonian. It was, except for her and Melissa, deserted, wooden shutters nailed against the occasional vandalism of the neighborhood, electricity shut off. Two candles burned rosily into the darkness, set into an elaborate silver holder, badly tarnished. The flames softly highlighted the faces of the two women, casting too gentle a glow to reveal the scalding slashes of red in Abby's cheeks as she read Charlotte's story in the *Courier* for the fourth time.

Melissa refilled Abby's glass, shaking last drops from the bottle, adding it to the two that were already standing empty to the side of the table. "It doesn't do any good to keep reading it over. It's not going to change."

"She makes me sound like a traitor," Abby said, a little slowly, a little thickly. "Like an influence peddler. Like I sold out my country." She drank some more wine.

"Sue her," Melissa said, and got up from the booth, moving toward a carved wooden loveseat set into the bay of a boarded-up window. "You got a good lawyer."

"But nothing she said is a lie, exactly. It's the way she says it. She even makes my charity work sound dirty, like I did it for money."

"People do," said Melissa. "It's no crime." She pushed a hidden lever, and the boxed bottom of the loveseat opened, revealing a hidden wine rack.

"I never did. I never would. I didn't ask for the money. They offered it to me. All I could think about was keeping up appearances. I didn't want to put any more pressure on him for money."

"I understand," said Melissa.

"There seemed to be such freedom in not being pressed for dollars." She sighed, a kind of tearless cry, as if something were sitting on her heart. "But it wasn't my idea. It never occurred to me I could earn money for what I've always done for nothing."

Melissa took a bottle out and pressed a button, springing the treasure trove closed. "You should have grown up in my neighborhood. You would have known that at twelve." She hugged the wine to her big bosom. "Oh, Hiro, you sweetie pie, you saved us some Chateau Petrus." She looked at Abby as she corkscrewed open the bottle. "One of the *rare* vintages. I didn't see any point in letting the IRS have it." She held the lip of the wine bottle to Abby's glass.

"I've drunk enough," Abby said, her eyelids heavily punctuating the statement.

"Okay," said Melissa, and filled her own glass. Still standing, she set the bottle down, then slowly whirled her arms in the air as if she were testing it for invisible webs. "I love it here. It's like being in a tomb."

"I appreciate your trying to cheer me up," Abby said.

"I can feel Hiro's ghost."

"On second thought, I don't mind if I do." Abby held up her glass.

Melissa poured. "I didn't think Internal Revenue would appreciate fine wine. Or the fact that I kept a key to the club." She giggled and started spinning around the room. "Come, Hiro," she called. "Dance with me." It was a spectral dance she did, moving with an eerie grace, reaching for a phantom lover, holding him, kissing him, weeping.

"Why do you come here?" Abby said.

"The same reason you keep reading that story. I haven't suffered enough." She took a tissue from her purse and wiped her eyes.

"Oh, God." Abby started to cry. "My poor Larry. How could I do this to him?"

"You haven't done anything. Here's Charlotte's number." She scrawled it on a napkin, and handed it to Abby. "Call her and tell her to go fuck herself."

"She made it sound like I was influence peddling at the White House." Abby crumpled the napkin in her hand. "That I was trying for special considerations for Sri Lanka." The words were heavy on her tongue: they caught on her lips and came out as J.J. might have said the name of the country, as if there were a speech impediment in the middle of it. She sobbed once at the sound of herself. She had disgraced the finest man in the world and ruined his future, she was sure of it. She had known from the moment Larry tangled with Charlotte Dean in public that she would try to find ammunition to hurt him, and Abby herself had handed Charlotte the gun. "I've got to go home now." She got to her feet, heavily, her movements a little too deliberate.

When they got to the Cochran house, Melissa helped her out of the car. "You don't have to do that," said Abby. "I'm perfectly capable of walking by myself." She was, but barely.

"You sure you don't want me to come in?" Melissa said. "You all right?"

"I'm just tired," said Abby, standing inside the screen door. Her accent was a little more drawly than usual, as if the wine had warmed her far back into the South. "I thank you for everything, but I have to go to sleep."

"Okay, I'll call you." Melissa went back to the car.

In her bedroom, Abby undressed, letting her clothes fall sloppily to the floor. As she put on her nightgown she turned on the television, an automatic habit, connecting to too many nights of being lonely, because no matter how much he loved her, he loved duty more.

The late news was nearly over. ". . . in the wake of Washington's latest scandal," the newscaster was saying, "a White House source has indicated that Lawrence Cochran may be asked to submit his resignation. Mr. Cochran is Special Advisor to the President, the only Republican to hold a post of such confidence. Sri Lanka, formerly known as Ceylon, is headed by Prime Minister Jayawardene. His policy is known to be anti-American.

"On the national scene, food prices . . ."

Abby turned off the television and started to sob, brokenly. "Oh, my darling," she said. "What have I done to you?" A rush of guilt and anguish overcame her. She wanted to run away and hide, she wanted to disappear, to go to sleep and wake up to find out that none of it had really happened, it was simply a terrible dream because she'd had too much to drink, lived too long in Washington.

She looked in the medicine cabinet, the one she shared with Larry. There was not even aspirin. There were perfumes, nearly empty, not expensive, some old toothbrushes, and sample powders. Nothing that could help her out of the terrible place she was in.

"Gloria," she said aloud, and started toward Gloria's room. Gloria would have tranquilizers and sleeping pills, the basic diet of movie stars. Abby started rehearsing in her mind how she would ask for them. But it wasn't necessary. Gloria wasn't in her room. It was hung, walls, windows, closet doors, bedpoles, and picture hooks, with clothes, as if there had been an explosion of dresses. There were clothes hanging in the shower stall of the bathroom. Nearly as crowded as the place was with garments, was the medicine cabinet and sink and the top of the toilet with makeup and drugs. Pills sparkled from their bottles in rainbow colors, red, yellow, pale green, blue, like candy from a depressed fairyland. "For tension," read one label. "For muscular relaxation." "For sleep," read several. Abby took the Tuinal, four of them.

She stumbled back to her room and lay on her bed, waiting

for the mercy of sleep, the bottle of pills still clutched in her hand. She looked at them and wondered if she had taken enough. She set them on her bed table, closed her eyes, opened them again, sat up, and looked at the bottle. She couldn't remember how many she had taken, or if she had taken them at all. She got a glass of water from the bathroom, set it by the pills, and took five.

There was a picture of her children on the bed table. She picked it up, held it to her breast, and wept. "I am so sorry," she murmured. The heaviness of the pills and the wine combined to enfold her. She wiped the tears from her eyes with the crumpled napkin Melissa had given her, opened it, saw the haughty crest of the Jeffersonian and the number written there. Clumsily, she reached for the phone, pressed the numbers. Drowsiness suctioned her into herself. She could hardly speak when she heard the voice on the other end.

"Hello?" Charlotte rasped a second time. "Who is it?"

"Miss Dean?" The words sounded slurred, stuck together. "Who is this?"

"Abigail Cochran," she said, and started to sob. "Oh, please. . . . Leave him alone. He didn't know about it. I . . . ." She stopped herself from weeping. "Please." It was the only word she could think of. And then, she could think of nothing.

On the other end of the line, Charlotte looked at the phone, held it close to her ear. The woman sounded plastered. But more than plastered, drugged. Charlotte had fears herself of going like Dorothy Kilgallen, so she never combined booze and tranquilizers, but she knew how stupid people sounded when they did. "Mrs. Cochran? Mrs. Cochran, are you all right?" She jiggled the receiver, as if the woman were inside it and that would wake her. She could hear dull, labored breathing, a gargling rasp. She listened for another moment, then hung up the phone.

He would probably come home and find her in time, they always did. There were four children in the house, and they'd probably come in in time to call the rescue squad. It was none of Charlotte's business. Maybe it was all in her imagination anyway, the woman hadn't overdosed at all. She was probably just an alcoholic. So many were.

In any case, it was certainly not Charlotte's job to call an ambulance. The little alcoholic who cried wolf. Probably just a way to try and play on Charlotte's pity, so that she wouldn't continue it to the end, which she had every intention of doing. She went to bed and slept a kind of sleep, picking up the phone from time to time, wondering if the silence she was listening to was Abby Cochran dying.

¶ Tony Asperte had learned to drive in the Bronx, so his style in a car was as aggressive as his presence onstage. Gloria sat huddled as far away from him as possible in the front seat, as he shouted at drivers who were nowhere near him, swerved to avoid oncoming vehicles that were limbs of trees blowing in the spring night. She envied him his Catholicism. It would have been nice to be able to say a rosary, to clutch her beads, to close her eyes and pray her way back to the Cochrans. As it was, she figured if they got killed, the critics wouldn't be mad at her.

He pulled the car to a squealing halt in front of the Cochrans'. "Okay, sweetheart," he said, in fair imitation of Bogart. "This is it. The end of the line."

He reached over, Gloria supposed, to open the door on her side, so that she could get out. Instead, his hand tucked itself around her hip, his lips were inches from her breasts. "I decided that what's wrong with you in the play," he said, "is you're not really feeling the physical attraction between these two people. So for both our good, I've decided to throw you a hump."

Gloria laughed. "How romantic." She pulled his hand away.

"Haven't you had enough romance, baby? Wouldn't you like to get down to the nitty-gritty?"

"As a matter of fact, no. Especially not with you. Although I imagine your nitty would be more gritty than anybody else's." She opened the door.

"Not even for the sake of the play?" he asked, darkly disappointed.

"Not even for the sake of the country," she said.

When she got inside the house, she was laughing to herself. As loath as she would have been to have him touch her, really, it was always nice being wanted. After seventy movies, and several lovers (she had stopped keeping count, and hoped God had), she was still flattered at the attention of men.

She felt girlish, absolutely girlish again, as if she had just come home from the prom she had never attended. There was such a lovely atmosphere at the Cochrans', books everywhere, their bindings breaking from much consultation. Once Gloria had played the lead in a murder mystery that took place at a New England college; the set decorator had visited Dartmouth and given its touches to the dormitory in the film. It was not unlike the Cochrans' home, its furniture used, unpretentious. She felt a swell of love and belonging, as if she were having the college career she had wanted but was too pretty for, a joy that she had come back after lights out still pure, a need to share the audacity of Tony with Abby. She knew that Larry had taken the children to Florida, so she wouldn't be interrupting them. She knocked on the door of their room.

It opened to her touch. From the way Abby was sprawled on the bed, Gloria was afraid immediately. She ran to her, spoke her name, shook her, listened for her breathing. She heard nothing. She picked up the phone, touched the button, freed the line, and dialed the operator for emergency. She tried to be efficient, helpful, the way Abby would have been. She loved Abby Cochran so much she did not even hear that she was screaming.

¶ The ambulance arrived at Sibley Emergency just as Eleanor Wickleham was going off duty. In her youth Eleanor had been one of those pretty nurses who take themselves so seriously nobody else does. Now her cheeks were wrinkled, liver-spotted from drinking herself to sleep after the night shift, as she had every intention of doing this evening. She knew perfectly well what it did to the liver, that she was poisoning herself, but she didn't care anymore. Life was cheap, you learned that at a hospital, including her own. Still, she did linger for an extra moment when the ambulance came in, to see what it was, how bad.

When the ambulance doors opened and Gloria Stanley got out after the stretcher bearers, Eleanor almost had a seizure. She looked again at the victim, with more interest.

"Who is she?" Eleanor asked the attendant.

"Abigail Cochran," he said.

"What was it?"

"Overdose."

"How is she?"

"Looks dead to me."

She could hardly wait to get to a phone. She dialed the number Charlotte Dean had given her to call, no matter what time of night, if anybody interesting came into Sibley.

¶ The emergency room was filled with drug addicts, alcoholics, people with broken legs from auto accidents, knife wounds, the late-night afflictions of an angry city. In a cubicle ten by fourteen feet wide, a young doctor checked Abby Cochran for vital signs. He looked at her pupils, shone the light in them. They were fixed and dilated.

"No respiration, no pulse," he said. He listened for her heartbeat, heard something faint. "Let's give it a try. Call a Code Blue."

Everyone in the area moved into action. The doctor cleared the secretions from Abby's mouth. A laryngoscope was forced into her throat and an endotracheal tube through the scope deep into her trachea, while a nurse tried to start an intravenous feeding in her arm. Artificially they began to maintain her heartbeat, the doctor pressing on her sternum, bearing down hard. Oxygen was forced through the endotracheal tube into her lungs.

"Get the IV going," the doctor said.

"Her veins won't pump up."

"Get it going," he said.

"All right," said the nurse. "I'm in."

"Start sodium bicarb." He stripped Abby's nightgown to connect the leads of the electrocardiogram. It showed a straight flat line.

"She's straightlined," a nurse said.

"Asystole!" the doctor shouted. "Intracardiac epinephrine."

A nurse handed him a long-needled hypodermic. He inserted it below the sternum, pointed it up toward Abby's left shoulder, and drew it back until blood appeared in the syringe. Then he shot the drug into the chamber of her heart.

"Ventricular fibrillations," he said. "Get me the paddles."

They placed saline-soaked pads on her chest and two paddles over them.

"How much energy, doctor?"

"Three hundred watt-seconds. Everybody get back from the table," the doctor said.

The charge sent into her lifted Abby's body off the table. The doctor looked at the monitor. "Push in an amp of bicarb and reset the paddles."

With the second charge, the line on the screen resumed a normal cardiac pattern. The doctor smiled. Once in a while it was really possible to doctor things in the truest sense: to change the way they were.

¶ Before she actually sat down to write, Charlotte called her managing editor to tell him they better get out an early extra, before anyone else picked the story up. She felt the excitement of great finish, squelching any darts of remorse that such a young lovely woman had come to such an end. After all, it had nothing to do with her, Charlotte was convinced. What happened to Abigail Cochran she had brought on herself, what happened to everybody was what they brought on themselves. Charlotte gave no credence to karma: she had no patience for mystical beliefs, debts from a previous life. But there were debts incurred from this one: if you pushed, somewhere in the universe the push would come back at you, she was sure. It was a natural law.

She began the story with the respect due a front-page obituary, saying that Abigail Cochran, prominent Washington socialite and wife of Lawrence Cochran, presidential advisor, had died of an overdose of sleeping pills at Sibley Hospital, an apparent suicide. Exact time of death could be established for the later editions, Charlotte thought, it wasn't the meat of the story. Besides, little accuracies no longer mattered, because Abby Cochran was dead.

That thought set off in Charlotte a wave of creative inspiration, in which she added little fillips, such as Abby's having been depressed in recent weeks and under treatment for chronic alcoholism. That would reflect badly on Larry, implying neglect on his part, although Charlotte charitably intended to say not one word against him in his loss.

From the library she selected the most flattering picture of Abby on file, showing her at the previous season's Symphony Ball, radiantly blonde, slightly imperious of features, warm smile, a woman on top of herself and the world. The bulk of the copy of the story she copied nearly verbatim from her exposé in the previous day's edition, revealing the financial tie with Sri Lanka. And once again, Charlotte listed the charities with which Abby had been involved.

As she read the story over, the shadows did not loom quite dark enough to suit Charlotte. Inspiration struck her. To give it the final fine symmetry that fiction had, that she'd always admired, she added that Abby had been on the payroll of Hiro Takeda.

The dead needed no mercy and had no rights. Not under the laws of libel. Especially when they had never really loved Charlotte.

¶ In the place Abby had gone, there were lights spinning with exquisite precision, interplaying on twisted paths, like streamers being strung on maypoles. And all of them were souls.

She had felt a sudden loss of fear: not clinging to life released her; there was no more doubt in the universe. She felt no pain, no longing to return, even as she watched them working over her body. She left herself there in the emergency room, feeling strangely unrelated to the weary woman on the table, and drifted out to a place of light and shadows, loving energy, lost friends she recognized, and peace. Free, for the first time actually free, she was nobody's mother or wife or child, she was simply herself.

And then she remembered Larry, how very great was the need he never showed. And how heroic was the stance, and how hard it would be to keep it up without her. And she remembered her children, the twins about to be women with no woman to guide them, Laddie bumping into adolescence, J.J. stumbling in his galoshes. She realized that they needed her just as much as she needed herself.

So she came back to the emergency room and let them save her. She felt a little reluctant about it, especially as she realized how much explaining she would have to do. But all regret at her return left her when she saw Larry by her bed, his eyes red rimmed from weeping, their expression searching, hurt, filled with apology.

"Hi," she said. "I missed you."

Tears welled in his eyes.

"Don't you dare do that," she said. "Don't make me more ashamed."

"I'm the one who's ashamed," he said. "All the times I've neglected you, all the things you should have had. . . ."

"Things," she murmured. "They're only things." She reached for his face with strangely blue white hands.

"I've been so selfish," he said, his words barely distinguishable. "I'm going to look for a job."

"Did he ask for your resignation?"

"He specifically asked me not to resign. But it doesn't make sense anymore. We have four children who need educating and a real father. I've been thinking only of myself." He touched his fingers to the pale blue veins in her arm, leaned to kiss the dark bruises where the intravenous needles had been. The sight of them, blotched, blackening on that astonishingly fair, translucent skin made him remember the dreams he had had of a golden woman, a Saxon goddess, sent to earth in a cottage garden, surrounded by roses and children, the realized fantasy he had nearly lost. His grief caught in his throat. "I'm such an ordinary man."

"Oh, my darling," she whispered, and smoothed his hair. "If there's one thing you're not, it's an ordinary man."

When the doctor made him leave, Larry walked through the hospital corridor, mind raging with angry thoughts of his own foolishness. Everything he had aimed for had seemed to be his, a well-ordered life, beautiful children, a fine career. But at what cost. He had never really examined the pressures on Abby. There was no doubt in his mind that the events which had taken place were all his fault. Charlotte's vendetta had been against him: it was Abby who had become the innocent victim. Her small transgression was because of financial need and his neglect, nothing more.

Fond determination welled up in him: he would take self-sacrifice and heap it at her feet like flax spun into gold, making himself and his ambition part of the offering. Moving past the hurt, the ill, the dying, the about to be born, stretched out on the gurneys around him, he saw himself as part of a flawed humanity, some with weakness of flesh, some with sickness of spirit, torpor of will. He felt a terrible compassion for all of them, including himself. There would not be enough he could do in his life to make it up to her.

¶ The faces of the rich do not change after forty. Their lines merely deepen, like assets. It had been years since Larry had seen Clifton Sanger, but the owner of the *Courier* looked exactly the same, hands immaculately manicured, skin tanned from a recent tropical holiday, grey hair fanning slightly around his head, features even, as though they were balanced as well as his accounts. His deep-set brown eyes were lit with confidence, and savvy, something it was hard for Larry to imagine not having when you were worth three hundred million dollars.

Sanger sat behind a great oak desk, from the boardroom of his grandfather's railroad. He stood when Larry came in. "Larry!" He extended his hand. "How the hell are you?"

"I've been better, Mr. Sanger."

They shook hands. "I can understand that," Clifton Sanger said. "Sit down." He indicated a wing chair opposite his desk.

"I didn't realize you were the owner of the *Courier,* sir."

"I wasn't too aware of it myself till my attorneys told me we had a ten million dollar libel suit." He leaned back in his great leather chair and crossed his hands under his chin. "How is Abby?"

"Physically she'll be all right."

"You met in my house," Sanger mused.

"I remember."

"Christ, it all goes by so fast," said Sanger, something like genuine pain on his face. "I'm sorry this had to happen to you." He leaned his head back, studying the ceiling, with its painted frescoes, some in the manner of the *Rape of the Sabines,* some, the rape of the land. "Then again, maybe it's a good thing it did. Maybe you can really understand now about this country you're so fond of. What it does to those it admires." He got up and started striding around the room, his big feet heavy on the carpet that had covered his grandmother's private rail car. "You're a man people envy, Larry. When that happens, there's an impulse to destroy. It's the Aztec syndrome in us. The Aztecs took maidens and warriors and for a year bathed them in luxury, gave them succulent food and flowers, all the pleasures of the senses. And at the end of the year they took them to a hilltop and tore their living hearts out.

"That's what this country does. It makes favorites, loves them, praises them, lavishes gifts on them, and when it raises them high enough, it rips their living hearts out."

"I don't think Charlotte Dean is representative of this country," Larry said.

"I'm afraid she is," said Sanger. "If there weren't an audience for people like Charlotte, she wouldn't get power in the first place. I've fired her. She'll never work on a newspaper again."

"That isn't quite good enough," said Larry. In his suit for defamation, he had named both Charlotte Dean and the *Courier,* asking for five million from each of them. It was his hope not to take it to court. As stacked as the case would be in his favor, he could not imagine submitting Abby to the humiliation of the witness stand.

"What would satisfy you?"

"Justice."

"Maybe we could turn her over to the Aztecs," Sanger said, and made an attempt at a smile.

"How did they choose which maidens and warriors to sacrifice?"

"They volunteered."

"That's insane," said Larry.

"Why?" Sanger opened a cigar box and offered one to Larry, who shook his head. Sanger nipped the tip from one with a cigar cutter and lit it. "Don't Americans volunteer for success?"

"Not always, sir," said Larry. "Some of them inherit it."

"That isn't success," said Sanger, drawing on the smoke. "That's only money." He opened the newspaper on his desk, looked at the headline. "I deplore this, Larry. You must know that. Certainly you're entitled to restitution. But ten million dollars?"

"That story was written with deliberate malice and reckless disregard for the truth. That would hold up as libel for punitive damages in any court in this country."

"Court. You don't want to go to court. It's so time-consuming. So costly."

"What do you suggest as an alternative?" Larry asked.

¶ All her life, Chris had covered her eyes in horror movies, so she never saw the truly frightening parts. She was dealing like that now with Jess. Afraid to study him for signs that he didn't love her anymore, afraid to face his possibly loving somebody else, afraid to look hard into the center of their marriage.

She watched him with the children. There was anguished love for them in his eyes, together with an emotion she hadn't seen there before and couldn't define. It was not quite pain.

More like grief, as if he had already mourned whatever it was that was lost.

She wanted to kiss forgiveness from his lips, cover him with whipped cream, break chocolate-covered strawberries on his cock, and eat him hard. Her remorse about Scott was combined with such morbid eroticism toward Jess, she could hardly keep her hands off him.

But he didn't really want her, she could tell that. They had made very little love since his return from Sri Lanka, and always at her instigation. She was exhausted during the final week before her play opened, so welcomed the rest with the part of her body that didn't long for Jess.

She kept touching him all through the opening night performance. In a patron's box, surrounded by her favorite people, Abby, beautiful again, Larry, Louise Felder, Howard and Megan, Melissa Mae, Chris still felt lonely, because Jess was beside her but not with her. She watched him watching her play, laughing a little too heartily, as if the performance weren't going as well as one might have wished, and neither was life. She put her hand on his leg and tried not to wince when he lifted it and placed it gently on the arm of her chair.

Gloria tried too hard for the next laugh, and the moment died. Chris closed her eyes and willed them both tranquil, Gloria with her terrible need and Chris with her terrible failure.

It was the final scene in the play. As the married woman, Gloria was coming back for a last goodbye to her young lover, having phoned him that it was ending, hearing him weep, scream he would die without her, kill himself. She found him lying sprawled on a mattress in the Greenwich Village loft where they had loved in secret. Seeing him, she began to weep and deliver an impassioned soliloquy on the meaning of love, the foolishness of life thrown away. Tearfully, she leaned over to kiss his dead mouth, only to have him snort and come awake. At that moment, Gloria looked at the audience with a face so open, so amazed, so disappointed, she seemed to be Everywoman, looking for the man who would die for her, only to find one who could fall asleep in the middle of a crisis.

The red velvet curtain came down. "She was good," said Jess, stunned, joining the applause.

"Good, hell," said Larry, getting to his feet. "She was wonderful." He whistled through his fingers, adding his shrill approval to the loud applause of the audience.

"Congratulations," Louise said to Chris, and kissed her cheek. "Is it okay?"

"Okay it is," said Louise. "Next, it's going to be good." The group in the box were all on their feet, applauding Gloria. "Not too much," Louise said to them. "You don't want to confuse her."

"That's true," Howard said. "She's failure oriented."

"Is *she* your patient, too?" asked Megan.

"Paranoid," he suggested, liltingly.

"Married," she corrected him.

¶ In her dressing room, Gloria wept. "What's the matter with you?" asked Louise, standing near the mirrored table, flooded with lights and flowers. There was hardly room for **any of** them, Abby, or Louise, or Chris, moving among the baskets and pots and vases of flowers on the floor.

"I was good," Gloria sobbed.

"Well, of course you were good," said Louise. "What did you expect?"

"I didn't know I was good. I always thought I was a movie star, not an actress."

"Then you haven't been following your private life," said Louise. "Well, sweetheart," she turned to Chris. "It's a hit with fixing."

"What does that mean?" asked Chris.

"You have work to do. You'll have to beef up the first act. I figure six weeks on the road after here before we can take it to New York."

"I can't face that," Chris said.

"Sure you can," said Louise. "It'll take your mind off your marriage."

Chris looked at her, stunned. She hadn't known it showed.

She was being paid back, in full, for her would-have-been adultery. "I don't want to go out of town," she said.

"You are out of town," said Louise.

"I was a hit, I was a hit," sang Gloria, slipping into the satin dressing gown her maid held for her, tying it around her slender-again waist, pirouetting around the room. She bumped into the chaise.

"Just because you were good onstage doesn't mean you can dance," said Louise. "Sit down before you hurt yourself."

Gloria obeyed.

"Oh, Chris, what a talented woman you are. How lucky to be able to express yourself," said Gloria. "Thank you for my lines. Thank you for my chance. Wasn't I good?"

"You were wonderful." Chris kissed her.

"I couldn't have done it without you. Your play is magnificent." She fanned the air beside Chris's cheeks with her lips.

"It's uneven," said Chris. "I have to make it better."

"Oh, please don't be humble," sang Gloria. "Not tonight. If you're humble, I'll have to be humble, and I don't feel like it."

"I have an agent who makes me humble," said Chris.

"Well, thank God I can do it for you," said Louise. "I'm totally ineffective in Beverly Hills."

Outside, in the hallway, next to the dressing room door marked with a radiant star, gold, with the legend beneath, Miss Gloria Stanley, Jess waited with Larry. "Is Abby all right?" he asked. "She looks beautiful, but is she all right?"

"She'll be fine," said Larry.

"I owe her everything, you know. Half of the money she got she gave to me. That and my self-respect, and a second start in life. I'm now a lobbyist for the railroads."

"Good for you!" Larry held out his hand, and hugged him, the formal affection and the informal one both extended at the same moment. "Good for them."

"Thank you. What's going to happen with you?"

"I'm going into private law."

"Good," said Jess. "Maybe that'll help make you more realistic, more practical. You'll see the outstretched hands. Everybody does it. It's a part of life."

"Abby didn't have her hand outstretched," Larry said, angering.

"Hey," said Jess, "I didn't say she did. But Larry, the whole world operates on payoffs. That's how bills get passed and movies get made, and wars get started.

"The closest you've come to reality is Hiro Takeda, and you're such an innocent you still think he was a nice guy. And maybe he was, but he knew the world was founded on graft and bribes."

"How come we never had a conversation like this before?" asked Larry.

"This is the first time you've been out from behind your veil," said Jess.

The door to the dressing room opened. A smiling black face appeared. "You can come in now, gentlemen," the maid said. She was dressed like Hattie McDaniel in the pictures of the forties, with a frilly little cap set toward the front of her hair, a lacy white apron over her uniform. She thought that if she were lucky enough to serve Gloria Stanley, she ought to look like a maid in the movies. That there had been a revolution in her stereotype did not affect her views. Gloria Stanley was shinier than equal rights.

Gloria received them, a queen restored to her accustomed place on the throne, shimmering in casual flame-colored satin pajamas. She hugged both men, while they told her how wonderful she was. "Oh, you darlings," she crooned.

"And congratulations to you," Larry turned to Chris. "It's a lovely play."

They kissed each other's cheeks.

Jess came toward Chris, took her elbows in his hands. "You should be very proud of yourself," he said.

"I wish I could," she answered.

They arranged to meet at the party. Chris and Jess made their way out of the darkened theatre alone.

"Is this how it's going to be now?" Chris asked Jess. "Painful silences?"

There was a full moon illuminating the trees outside the glass wall edging the lobby, willow trees, their roots spreading on the top of the earth, so they weren't really anchored. They stood, obviously foreign, transplanted, like most Washingtonians, like Chris. She was afraid of his silence, almost as much as she feared what his words might say, should he speak them.

"Maybe we shouldn't go to the party," he said, finally.

"We have to go. It's for us."

"It's not for *us*. It's for *you*."

"I can't do any of it without you, Jess." Her voice was muffled.

"You would if you had to."

"Don't make me." She grabbed his hand and held it, stopped him, put her arms around him, and wept against his chest. "Oh, Jess, honey, I'm so sorry."

He patted her hair.

"I was in love with Scott."

"I know."

"I thought I was missing something. I wasn't. Whatever you do to me I deserve."

"I already did it," he whispered. "It's over."

"Do you love her?"

"I came back to you."

"That doesn't answer my question," she said.

"It answers a better one," he said. Jess wiped her face with his handkerchief, gentled it with kisses. Friendly ones, she could not help noting. But then, it was still early. The party hadn't even started.

¶ In the forecourt outside the Kennedy Center, Louise and Gloria waited for their limousine. "Miss Felder!" a voice called out, raucous, ear-splitting. Louise turned and saw Charlotte Dean moving toward them, in a walk too rapid to be called a walk.

"That's what I hate about the theatre," said Louise. "Anyone can come."

"Don't knock the theatre," Gloria said. "My home is the the-a-tre." She was already breaking the word into syllables, giving it the loftiness of one who had spent a lifetime with the Lunts.

"Congratulations," Charlotte said grudgingly to Gloria. "I thought you were superb."

"Don't make me doubt myself by giving me your good opinion," Gloria said.

Charlotte ignored her. "Did you enjoy the play, Miss Felder?"

"How sweet of you to ask," said Louise. "You in trouble, darling?"

The tips of the feathers on Charlotte's hat danced around her tight mouth. "It doesn't matter. I'm not going to waste my time with newspapers anymore. I'm working on a book that's going to blow the lid off this city, whatever lid is left. It'll make a fortune. I have everything about everybody in this town documented. I know where the bodies are buried."

"You probably put them there," said Gloria.

"I want you to be my agent," Charlotte continued to Louise. "It'll make a fortune."

For a moment, in spite of Louise's vow never to make judgments while doing business, it crossed her mind that she might have difficulty selling Charlotte, documents and all, because she was too contaminated. Then she remembered Richard Nixon and wondered if anybody was ever too contaminated to sell. She looked at Charlotte very hard and thought about the money.

"Call Swifty Lazar," she said finally, and got into the limo. She fell against the seat, breathing heavily.

"Louise, you all right?" Gloria asked, getting in beside her.

"I just turned down money," Louise said. "I feel dizzy. Quick!" She put her head between her legs. "Get me a hot fudge sundae."

¶ Opposite the entrance to the Kennedy Center, a great frieze, carved in grey sandstone, glittering with mica, depicts a German sculptor's view of America, riddled with strife, bustling with industry, and loneliness. Like all outside concepts, it is accurate and extreme, missing the laughter, the occasional gift for self-deprecation, that salvages the nation from time to time.

Standing across from it, Larry Cochran wondered if he was as innocent as Jess had accused him of being, or if the whole country perhaps was not innocent, always being surprised when it turned out that people cheated. All the politicians in the world were on the take, all the time; it was part of politics. But Americans were always amazed when it happened at home. It was like finding mom with the milkman.

He put his arm around Abby and helped her into the limousine. "Is this Gloria's car?" she asked.

"It's yours," Larry said. "For the occasion. From me."

She touched the pearl grey velvet upholstery. "You shouldn't have," she said, delightedly.

"Why not," he said, handing her an envelope. "I'm married to a wealthy woman."

She opened it. Inside was a check for two hundred and fifty thousand dollars, made out to her. "Two hundred and fifty thousand dollars! Is it real?"

"It's better than real," he said. "It's from Clifton Sanger. In exchange for your full release of any claims against the *Courier*."

She threw her arms around him, kissed him. "You wonderful lawyer."

"I just might start to enjoy private practice," he said, smiling.

She looked at the check, tested its sound, rattled it near her ear. "I'm going to send the children to college," she said triumphantly. "And take you to Sri Lanka."

"Sounds good to me," he said. "What'll you do with the rest of it?"

"Start a fund to run you for senator," she said, her childlike mouth turning up at the corners, as if she were only joking.

Sometimes, once in a while, there were victories, even tainted ones. Virtue triumphed, the good guys won, the birds were singing in the trees, and there was reason for hope, and that's what made it America.